GREENWICH CONNECTION

Novella and Short Stories

Richard Natale

Better Than Starbucks Publications

Greenwich Connection

Copyright © 2024 by Richard Natale

All rights reserved. This book or any portion thereof may not be reproduced or used in any manner whatsoever without the express written permission of author and the publisher except for the use of brief quotations in a book review or scholarly journal.

First Printing: ISBN 979-8-9886211-1-9

Cover image: Friendship, 1908, Pablo Picasso

Better Than Starbucks Publications
1524 Camino Real, Hobbs, New Mexico 88240 USA
(575) 441-5417

Table of Contents

Novella

In The Fall of Forty-Four   1

Short Stories

Barbara's Poetry Lesson   69
The Seven Forty-Five   80
All And Nothing At All   90
Shrimpy's Opening Night   99
Village Diner: Nighttime   107
Art Ain't Easy   119
Sora and Declan   130
Simon   141
The Lost Brother   152
Carmen and All That Jazz   163
Curious George   174
The (Unlikely) Book of Samuel   186
Opus 66   195
The House on West 4th Street   203
The Man in White   211

IN THE FALL OF FORTY-FOUR

PART ONE

TERRY

It was the fall of 1944, a few months before Hitler dosed Eva Braun with cyanide and shot himself in the mouth. I was stationed in Naples, working in the supply room of the Army hospital. Had plenty of time on my hands (too much time, if you wanna know the God's honest truth). And I was nursing a giant hurt.

So I'd walk. Not to forget so much as to keep from remembering. To keep from fixating on a wish I'd made. An impossible wish.

The wish was Monty. Impossible. But I wished it anyway.

Great walking city, Naples, even with the huge piles of rubble from all the bombing — first by the Allies and then the Germans. Or the starving kids with their bloated stomachs, roaming around grimy-faced and wailing. The older ones would offer to shine your shoes. I'd say no thanks but throw them a few lire anyway. Didn't do much good, since there wasn't much food to be had at any price (us Americans saw to that), except on the black market. Even then, they'd have to shine shoes day and night for a week to put together enough to buy a crummy crust of bread.

Naples. Beauty and decay all thrown together; and people and noise and filth and stench. Life and death around every corner. But even in the middle of all the craziness, the city's natural beauty and the seaside were enough to knock your eyes out. In spite of the bombed-out buildings and the god-awful stink of garbage — the place was a monument to trash — there were still pleasures to be had. Like losing yourself in the maze of ancient streets no wider than alleyways. The actual alleys, called *buchi* (holes), were even tighter, threading up into the hills to the ritzy parts of town, the Vomero and Capodimonte.

You had to hand it to the Neapolitans. They'd been through hell, through disasters natural and man-made. Not just now. For centuries. But giving up just wasn't in their nature. They continued shouting and laughing and fighting and fucking just like they always had. Most of them were nice to us; I mean, what choice did they have but to put on the *bella faccia*? They knew — and you knew — it was all an act. They'd be all buddy-buddy, waving at you when you passed by, big smile, their eyes dancing. But behind the eyes they were thinking, Hey *Americani*, kiss my ass; behind our backs they were calling us *a merda'di cani*, literally dog shit.

I don't blame them for hating our guts. We were not the best-behaved bunch. Treated them like each and every one was a first cousin to Il Duce. So they decided to bide their time until we shipped out. They could afford to wait. Not like they had anyplace else to go. We weren't the first invaders and wouldn't be the last. Neapolitans have been here for thousands of years, starving and conniving and reproducing and singing break-your-heart songs. You didn't need to understand their nutty dialect to burst out crying whenever they started strumming their mandolins: tragic love ballads, nostalgic hymns for some special place or forgotten time. The tunes weren't always gloomy. They sang cheery tarantellas, too. Even when they weren't singing, their voices had music in them, as if any minute they were gonna explode into an opera aria and reduce you to pulp.

Beautiful people. Especially the men.

I have a weakness for men. Hey, we all have weaknesses. That was mine.

But Monty. That was something else. That was love. The kind you hear about but don't really believe exists until it hits square between the eyes. Yeah, that kind of love.

Walking and smoking cigarettes, drinking sweet vermouth, and cup after cup of that pitch-black espresso that wrecks your stomach — that's what I would do when I was off duty. And eat. Though food was rationed, these guys could whip up a feast out of thin air. Close my eyes and I can still smell marinara sauce bubbling on the stove and the toasty odor of wood oven–baked bread or pizza. If there'd been more food available, I probably would have eaten myself to death. Why not? I wanted to die. Can you think of a better way to go?

Sometimes I felt bad complaining on account of how much better I had it than those poor bastards I saw every day at the hospital — pieces missing, brains battered and fried to a crisp, or the buddies I'd lost over the past two years, especially Monty whose face had been blown off on a beach near Salerno — a face that kept looking back at me every morning until I taught myself to shave without a mirror. Never quite got the hang of it, though. Nicks and plenty of 'em, and always a little stubble here and there. But if I smashed one more mirror, I'd lose count of how many years of bad luck I'd racked up. Not that I was superstitious or nothing, mind you. Besides, I figured that sooner or later they'd be sending me back into the thick of it against the Krauts or maybe even the Japs. And this time, I'd make damn sure I didn't come out alive — even if I had to pull the pin on the enemy's grenade myself.

Don't think I had any illusions of dying like a hero or nothing or making the ultimate sacrifice for my comrades in arms. Knowing me, I'd probably go out by stepping on a land mine or being picked off by a sniper. Something dumb and shabby like that. Just prayed that I got killed right off the bat. The last thing I wanted was to be wounded, twisting and howling in my own filth, like some of the GIs in that crumbling pile of rocks we called a hospital.

Oh man, what a chump I was, thinking I had some control over my lousy life. I mean, what could be more dumb and shabby than that?

One of my favorite places to walk in Naples was the Via Caracciolo along the bay, from which you could see Mount Vesuvius and its quiet twin Mount Somma. Picture postcard now, but a few months earlier, it was a different story. In March, not long after I got here, old Vesuvius decided to put on a show for us. And what a show it was. Mother Nature making a patsy of the men who thought themselves so high and mighty because they'd developed some fancy machine guns and tanks and aircraft carriers. Well, let me tell you, that eruption pulverized more of our planes at the airfield in Pompeii than any Luftwaffe air raid. That's right. We got caught with our pants down just like the folks back in 79 AD.

So much for progress.

After a few days of belching and lava flows and the nauseating stink of sulfur everywhere, the smoke came out white and the Neapolitans joked that it meant a new pope had been chosen. Those guys were a hoot.

One day, after my shift was over, I headed down the hill to the bay, moseying along, taking my time, sucking on a fag like I didn't have a care in the world — an attitude I picked up from the locals. Comes in handy when you've been around guys screaming for somebody to take away the pain and then calling you a sonofabitch for still being able to walk on two legs and see out of both eyes.

I could hear a little of Monty in every one of them and in every curse they threw at me. As if I was the one who blew his face off and not some Kraut who didn't even know who the hell he was. But what I did was worse. Or rather, what I didn't do.

A sin of omission is still a sin. Ask any priest. He'll tell you.

I decided to sit for a while out in Mergellina to watch the afternoon sun go from yellow to blood-orange. A bunch of kids and a guy around my age were scavenging for mussels that cling to the rocks near the shore and for this other kind of tiny, single-shell clam that sticks to the surface, the meat acting like a suction cup. A tiny shell, but if you pry it away from the rock just so, you got yourself a nice little antipasto.

The young guy was an old hand at scraping away the little crustaceans and licking off the meat with his thick lips and sticky tongue before tossing the shell back into the drink; probably been doing it since he was a kid himself. When he turned and gave me this big old grin, I didn't breathe for a whole minute. Like I was underwater and if I exhaled, I'd drown. Full face he resembled what one of those cherubs might look like as an adult: ripe, rosy cheeks and gigantic round eyes so brown they were almost black.

Now that I've been around longer and learned a thing or two about art, I'd probably compare him to a ragamuffin in a Caravaggio painting. He had broad shoulders and tanned olive skin and a long, slim torso with two little dots for nipples that God had put there almost as an afterthought. Below the waist though, he was fleshy. Thick legs and butt and a beefy set swinging in his wet khaki shorts, which was the only piece of clothing he had on. Choice. Then he nodded and winked, which woke me out of my daze. I could almost swear that it was a come-on. But then I remembered that Neapolitans were flirts by nature.

I didn't stick around. Wasn't taking any chances at getting beat up by some beauty who lured me into a dark building with the promise of hanky-panky only to punch out my lights and lift my billfold. If I wanted sex with an Italian guy, there were other places to go. Sometimes I hung out in a little dive that was packed with plenty of local guys. The kind who told themselves they were only doing it with GIs to feed their families. Sometimes we paid them off in C-rations we'd snuck out, other times with actual greenbacks. A few times, I exchanged coffee or chocolate for favors. Most of the time we did it in shithole alleys, though one guy laid me in his mother's bed. She was at her daughter's house in a suburb called Portici helping take care of the grandkids. He spoke a little English and, afterward, he told me that he'd closed his eyes and pretended I was a woman. Whatever floats your boat, I told him. He had no idea what that meant, and I didn't take the time to explain.

The bar guys weren't actually hustlers. Most of those were down by the docks. Dangerous types, rickety from starvation with missing teeth and so desperate that, for a few coins, they'd go down on you behind the nearest tree where anybody passing by could see them. They called out to you like nasty beggar children, but I never went near them. Who knows what I would have caught if I had? Sometimes, I took pity and tossed them some spare change or handed off a half-smoked cigarette.

A few days later, on my daily walk by the shore, I saw the grown-up cherub again wearing the same cut-off, clingy shorts. He smiled again but this time he didn't wink, and I moved on. Half a mile down the street, heading toward the marina in Posillipo, I heard the scuffle of footsteps behind me and when I turned around, there he was in a wife beater with a pair of half-demolished leather shoes on his feet.

Ciao, he said. And I said, *Ciao yourself*, back at him. He pointed to his chest and said Enzo, Enzo Chiari. He said it like it was the greatest name in the whole friggin' world. I tapped my sternum with the flat of my palm and said Terry Morse. Pleased to meet you. He wrinkled his brow and sneered, parroted what I'd just told him as if to say, Terry Morse? What kind of dumb-ass name is Terry Morse? A good, old Irish name. That's what kind. Why, you want make something of it? Then his frown turned up again and he cocked his head indicating for me to follow. I was nervous that I was being set up. I was also jonesing for him.

Told you I had a weakness. Got the scars to prove it.

We walked about a mile up into the city, stepping over the giant mounds of debris and around the rancid-smelling trash. Hey, at least the flies weren't going hungry. He behaved as if he was merely taking a *passeggiata*, though every so often he'd look over his shoulder to make sure I was still following. What was his game, I wondered? If I'd had half a brain I would have just cut out. But after, I would have spent the whole night thinking about what could have been.

I'd been doing a lot of that lately.

We came to a small hotel (okay, hotel is being generous) on a narrow dead-end street. I'd heard about the place from my buddies, though I'd never actually been there. For a modest honorarium, the lady at reception let the soldiers spend some time with a *signorina* they'd picked up in one of the nearby hooker alleys.

Oh, so that's it, I thought. I'd never actually laid out cold hard cash for a guy, but I had some change to spare. And I wanted him bad.

How was this gonna work, I wondered? Was he actually going inside with me? Would the old lady give us a room no matter how much money we laid out? I mean, even the amoral have their morals. And another thing. Most Italian men who did it with other guys were very hush-hush. Their stud reputations were on the line, and death by hanging was better than the shame of being called a *finocchio*. Beats me how the Italian word for *fennel* came to mean *fruit*. Then again, *fruit* don't make much sense either.

Since we didn't speak much of the other's language — though over the past few months I'd absorbed some real Italian and a few choice words of the marbles-in-the-mouth Neapolitan lingo — he acted it out for me. I was to go inside, pay the woman for a room and say that when my fiancée arrives, please send her up. He'd take care of the rest. For a moment, I thought he and the dame might be in cahoots. They'd split the commission and I'd be left sitting on some lumpy horsehair mattress with unfinished business on my hands. But I was twenty-two and randy. On the off chance that I might get to spend an hour with Enzo, I decided to toss the dice.

The old woman fingered my lire and nodded at every word I said like she was so tired of the sight of us GIs that she wanted to blow her brains out. The room on the third floor was tiny. The door hit against the side of the iron bed and I had to squeeze myself inside. It had a single window that faced out onto an air shaft. I sat on the edge of the bed and waited. But not for long. I heard somebody whistle and when I stuck my head out the window, there was Enzo below. He mimed a rope climb, though there was no rope, not even a drainpipe.

Don't ask me how he got up there, not to mention how he did it so fast. All I could think was that he was a spider by nature or had suction cups on those beefy but surprisingly delicate hands. The guy had all the makings of a cat burglar, and who knows, maybe that's what he did in his off hours. Pulling himself over the window ledge, he picked me up and twirled me around like I was some five-year-old kid. Then he threw me onto the bed, stripped down and ran those giant eyes over me. Lickety-split, I fell out of my uniform, everything except my shorts.

He raised his hand, giving me the *uno momento* sign. He went over to the basin in the corner and gave himself a quick sponge bath to remove some of the brine and sweat from his body. His johnson was already at attention. He looked down and smiled, rolling his eyebrows at me as if to say, this is your lucky day, Yankee.

Hell, I knew that already.

Even a two-hour scrub down wouldn't have been enough to remove the smell of the sea on him, not that I cared. I enjoy the smell of a man (Monty's odor used to het me up like pure cocaine), though I have my limits. Some of the Italians I'd been with were so rank that I had to send them away. They cussed me out but good.

Enzo threw himself on me and filled my nostrils with his salty scent. He had a tongue that was really thick, as were his juices. Got me so excited I wrapped myself around him like a boa constrictor. I didn't understand much of what he said, but I caught the word *amore*. It was part of a question, as in shall we make *amore*? Hey, I guess he needed to make it sound legit.

The sex was not what I expected. Fierce and affectionate at the same time. Both selfish and attentive. Enzo took as much enjoyment from my attending to his needs as he did from pleasing me. I couldn't remember the last time I'd had such a great orgasm.

Not true. I remember it exactly. Like it was yesterday. It was the last time I was with Monty. We were on leave in north Africa, huddled in the hull of a burned-out tank at the edge of the desert. But that was different, because what led up to it was more than sex, so much more that when we were done, I was almost sorry. I didn't want it to be over. Not ever. I can still tell you every single thing that happened that night. Every word Monty said. And every word I said — and didn't say.

It's the ones I didn't say that hurt the most.

Monty must have said he loved me a dozen times and that does things to a guy. He didn't just *want* me, he wanted *me*.

To my everlasting disgrace, I never quite had the nerve to actually say the words back, even though I felt the same way. What a rat, sending Monty off to be killed without knowing how nuts I was about him. And still am. If

I rub my fingertips together, I can still feel his cheek, and hear the squishy sound his tongue made when he licked the inside of my ear.

At the time I thought different, though. I figured it was better not to kid myself into thinking that life was worth living, since it could end at any second. Besides, telling Monty that I was a goner from the moment he first looked at me with that open, trusting smile, would have given him false hope. And that would have been criminal. Even if we both somehow beat the odds and made it out alive, what then? When the war was over there'd be no place for us. All the old rules would come back into fashion. We'd have to toe the line or pay the price.

In the end, I was totally right to say nothing. And totally wrong.

Still, I wish that the last words he heard from my mouth weren't so dumb. See ya 'round kid, I said like I was friggin' Jimmy Cagney. On the nights when I couldn't sleep for missing him so much, I wondered whether his last thoughts were of crushing fear or the fact that despite my cool attitude, he realized he wasn't going to die unloved.

I kept trying to convince myself that that's what Monty must have been thinking when he passed from this lousy world into a better one. I'm sure he did. He was a smart guy, much smarter than me. Book smart and he had good instincts. That was part of the attraction. To say that most of my fellow GIs were dumber than dirt would be an insult to soil. Being no Einstein myself, I didn't look down on them. Low IQ or not, they were brave sons of bitches, even the cowards. Believe you me, it takes courage to be a coward. Everybody hates you and you don't die once, you die every day — from the shame, from the guilt.

The day my good buddy PFC Ziegler told me how he'd picked up Monty's damaged body and how the force of the explosion had been so powerful that his dog tags were blown 200 yards away, I lost my lunch, which made sense, because it was like my insides were being ripped out.

On occasion, I still experience the dry heaves, and as I stoop over gagging, I can feel his hand across my forehead telling me, Come on, Terry. Don't be so hard on yourself.

Easy for you to say, Monty. You're dead. You're at peace.

After Enzo and I finished, he went out the same way he came in, and I left the hotel whistling some happy radio jingle for toothpaste. Maybe Pepsodent or Ipana? The old lady at the front desk looked at me funny. She must have thought I was one of those guys who gets off on listening to people doing it in the other rooms. Which was kinda easy since the walls were like paper. Let me tell you, those Italian gals put on quite a performance for our boys, carrying on like wild nymphos. Gave our GIs their money's worth, all right. Sent them back to the barracks thinking they was Romeo and Casanova rolled up into one.

Enzo was a bit of a noisemaker himself. He moaned and coaxed and cussed, could not have cared less who was listening or what they thought. Later, he met me around the corner from the hotel and we walked down to Mergellina, almost to the exact spot where I'd first seen him. He left me on a street corner and in sign language said that if he was free, he'd meet me right here at (five fingers) in the afternoon so we could go back to the hotel and beat the tom-tom.

That became our regular drill. Wonder where he went on the nights he didn't show up? Probably had a girl and needed to do some missionary work to prove that he was all man. Hell, I could have told him that, though he probably didn't want to hear it from me.

With Enzo, I finally caught a break. For about an hour or so I was free of pain. Sure, it wore off soon enough, but no matter. When I was with Enzo, I didn't have to think. Good thing, too. Thinking for me was a dark, one-way street leading to no place good.

My only regret was that I hadn't met Enzo sooner, so I could have been a better lover to Monty. He deserved the best.

See what I mean? Thinking really louses you up.

My feelings for Monty were automatic; never got the chance to throw up my usual defenses. He was ink. I was paper.

I'd already been with quite a few guys when I met him in basic training. You'd be surprised how many of us fooled around on base, even more after deployment. We were just kids, horny as can be and always in need of release. Can't tell you how many GIs jerked off in the communal showers, even the Bible Belt types. They'd be whacking away using soap and calling out the names of their wives and girlfriends or Veronica Lake or Betty Grable.

Getting it on with another guy helped ease the clammy feeling that today or tomorrow we'd be dead or hopelessly maimed. I don't believe for a second that most of them were like me. A few, maybe. Monty, definitely.

He and I were alike in a lot of ways. Both New York City boys — me from Queens and he from upper Manhattan. We understood each other. Talked the same language. Though his was much more refined.

Oh, and did I mention he was beautiful? At least to my beholding eyes, he was.

Another thing. Monty was solid gold. Right on his sleeve, that's where he carried his heart. And it was just for me. He told me so. Said he didn't care whether I loved him back, just as long as I was with him for however much time we had left. A good six months as it turned out before we were separated. The best six months of my whole damned life. I'd wake up in the morning and my first thought would be, Oh boy, I get to see Monty today and if I'm lucky we'll find a place to hole up together and kiss. I was happy just kissing him. None of the other guys kissed, because that meant something different than just getting your rocks off.

When we couldn't be off by ourselves, we hung out with the other grunts. We thought we were being discreet, but the way we batted our eyes when we looked at each other was like Morse code. Any idiot who was paying attention could have read the signals.

And yet because I'm such a stubborn Irish Catholic, I refused to put into words exactly how goddamn important he was to me. And that I didn't see kissing as a preliminary but as the whole ball of wax. Once, I came just from kissing him. Nobody had ever had that effect on me. He laughed off my embarrassment, said I shouldn't worry about it, he'd make me come again. And he did. Monty never disappointed.

Monty's voice got caught in my head and I couldn't shake it. They say that nobody's fully gone until the last person who remembered them dies. That's one of the few things that kept me going. Only it wasn't enough. I knew full well that even if we eventually won this stupid, useless war there would be no victory without Monty. If I hadn't been able to keep him safe, what good was I?

On the days I got together with Enzo, I sometimes brought him chocolate and other stuff I'd stolen, including medicine, which I'm sure he sold on the black market. Enzo loved chocolate. Couldn't get enough. Ate it right in front of me, slobbering it all over his lips. Then he'd kiss me and I'd taste it in his saliva and lick it off the corners of his mouth. Then he'd let go a belly laugh, which like everything he did was over-the-top. A lot of it was acting, which for Neapolitans comes easy, like rolling off a log.

When I asked Enzo how come he wasn't in uniform, he told me that just as he was about to be drafted, his only brother was shot down over Anzio and the Italians have this rule about killing off all the male children and ending the family line.

I tell you, the girl who's lucky enough to be Enzo's baby maker is in for a real treat. The guy was a dynamo. He enjoyed shocking me, contorting me, picking me up and propping me against the wall. And I got a kick out of the way he'd parade around the room, proudly showing off, like he was saying Ain't I something? Ain't you happy to look at it, taste it, feel it go off inside you like a giant firecracker? To this day, I believe that Enzo screwed the Irish Catholic right out of me.

The hilarious part of Enzo's operatic lovemaking was that it was part and parcel of his Catholic devoutness. After a marathon session, he'd take me to some half-destroyed chapel, get on his knees at the altar rail and cross himself several times over and mumble a few Ave Marias. This wasn't acting. He was as at home in church as he had been in bed with me an hour earlier.

Then he'd push me into the confessional and kiss me and paw at me. The rascal.

Whenever we were out on the street or having an espresso in the Galleria across from the San Carlo Opera House, Enzo enjoyed being with me. Unlike many of the other Italian boys, he wasn't ashamed to be seen in my company. In his mind, no one would ever believe that he was a *finocchio*, and if they so much as dared to imply it, he'd punch them in the nose and that would be end of that.

Not for a second did I delude myself into believing that Enzo had fallen for me. He was simply one of those guys who had to justify their lust under the cover of genuine affection. His pillow talk was something else. He'd fill my ears with sweet nectar words (*amore* and *cuore*, over and over). Then he'd fall asleep on my shoulder with a baby's innocent smile, the sweat of his curls cooling against my skin. And if I should happen to doze off on his chest, he'd wrap me up in his warmth and for a little while there was no war, only peace.

We continued to get together until about a month before VE day. Then, one day, he didn't show up. Or the next day, or the next. I looked for him on the rocky beaches along Mergellina. Saw a lot of the same kids scavenging, but no Enzo. I even asked a couple of them about him. At the mention of his name, they shook their heads. Nope. Haven't seen him. Never heard of the guy. Yeah, yeah.

Not long before I got my discharge papers, I saw Enzo one last time. He was taking a stroll up Via Roma and looking in the shop windows. He was wearing a suit and tie and walking with a pretty *signorina*, probably his girl. I yelled his name and both of them turned around. He knew who I was. I know he did. Only he pretended he didn't. He gave the girl that famous Italian shrug and flipped his hand in the air, as if to say, What do you want from me? I don't know who that is. All those damn Yanks look alike.

I understood what was happening. Still, it hurt my feelings. I continued watching them as they moved up the street. The girl stopped in front of a linen shop, peering into the window putting her hands against her forehead to block out the sunlight. Enzo turned his head slightly and nodded. And winked. Then in the same motion, he swept his hand under his chin, basically telling me to get lost.

I walked away pleased. I was grateful for all those times he helped rouse me from the dead. I could hardly blame Enzo for wanting to move forward, get married, raise a family. I'm sure he'd tucked away the memories of our get-togethers in a corner where they would gather dust but never be completely gone.

Not for him. Or for me.

The GI bill was a terrific invention. Didn't make up for wiping so many young guys off the map, but for those of us who were spared (if you call permanent scars and trauma being spared), school was a way back. While taking classes in office management at Queens College, I parked cars at a lot on 46th Street in the theater district, trading the disorderly chaos of *la bella Napoli* for the ordered kind of Manhattan.

I continued to live with my folks out in Corona and my mom, Gertie, started bugging me about when I was going to marry a nice girl and settle down. And I said when I get a steady job Ma, that's when, though I had no intention of ever getting married. When I was able to afford it, I was going to get my own place in the city. Plenty of my fellow soldiers, after getting a taste of the forbidden, decided not to go back where they came from and settled in places like New York or San Francisco. I'd already met a few of them wandering the downtown streets late at night and got myself invited back to their cold-water flats. Like me, they were lost. And for a few hours, we got lost together. You know like in that song Mary Martin sang, the one that Chet Baker sang the hell out of later.

In the fall of '48, a Lincoln pulled into the lot and I threw open the driver door and out stepped a guy in a natty gray worsted who looked a lot like Monty. Not as scrawny and he had full head of hair. A guy with ambition, a guy with a future. I could tell. He handed me the keys without even looking at me, then went around to the passenger door for his date — a cute-as-a-button girl in a powder blue dress and a white fur stole. He extended his hand and lifted her out and, only when he shut the door and glanced over the roof, did we make eye contact. And I swear his legs gave out, like he'd slipped on a banana peel. He had to grab hold of the door handle to steady himself and I wanted to say, Hey buddy, what's *your* problem? I'm the one who thinks he's seen a ghost.

The eyes were the same and the gaze so intense that I got spooked, and the keys slipped out of my hand. I bent over to pick them up and when I stood up straight again, he was gone. Holy cow, I thought. Must be one of them war flashbacks that I read about in *Look* magazine a couple of months back. I bet when the guy comes back to get his car, he won't look a bit like Monty, and I'm going to feel like a first-class chump.

Caddy convertible came in a few minutes later, dark green with white-walls. My partner, Bo, was on a break, so I got to park it. Oh boy, I thought as I backed it into a space. I could get used to driving this baby, knowing full well that day would never come. I must have gotten lost in the daydream because when my eyes focused again, standing on the other side of the windshield was Monty's dead ringer.

Terry? Terry Morse? he said.
Identical voice.
But I wasn't about to let this lousy poltergeist mess with my head. You

know me? I said, almost as a challenge.

Monty, he said.

Nice try, buster, I said getting out of the car and slamming the door shut. Monty's dead.

He shook his head. No, he said. Swear to God. It's me.

And that's when I fell to pieces.

I didn't exactly faint — but close. Monty caught me. Put his arms around me and I cried like I'd never cried before in my whole life. Giant sobs until I was drowning in mucus, and it started shooting out my nose. Not a pretty picture, I tell you.

Oh Jesus. I thought you were . . . thought you were . . .

Just then Bo came back from his break and found me with my head on Monty's shoulder. Hey, what are you doing? he said, and I noticed two couples waiting for their cars to be parked.

Bo, I said through my tears, this is my old Army buddy Monty. I thought he was dead.

Hot damn, Bo said, and us hugging no longer seemed peculiar.

One of the women who was waiting pulled a handkerchief from her purse and softly wept into it. She'd probably had the same fantasy about a brother or a boyfriend. She was happy for me, but sad too because she'd seen lightning strike and knew it wasn't going to happen twice.

The ladies' dates were also vets and we quickly exchanged names, ranks, serial numbers. They offered to buy us both drinks. I told them I was working but thanks anyway. Monty said he'd be glad to accept. Said he'd see them inside.

I better get back, Monty said. My girl thinks I'm in the john. See you after.

I must have walked around in circles a hundred times waiting for Monty to finish dinner, thinking, His girl? Oh no. I just found him and now I'm going to lose him again. I don't think I can stand to lose him twice. I'd rather suck on a gas pipe than let that happen.

When he and his date finally came out, I yelled to Bo, I got this one, and he didn't object on account of he saw who it was.

I brought the car up. Monty opened the passenger door and seated the young lady and came around to my side. Wait for me, he whispered, and tried to slip me a fiver, which I flat-out refused.

As he drove off, I thought, Wait for you? Are you kidding? That's all I been doing.

Then I walked around in circles for another hour, trying to figure out what the hell happened, how somebody who got his face blown off on a beach near Salerno could show up in a West Side parking lot in Manhattan four years later all in one piece — and even more beautiful than I remembered. Only now that he wasn't dead, he was probably engaged to that girl, which would kill me.

Around and around I walked, until I got so dizzy I had to put both hands on the hood of a car and try to steady my pulse. Where was he? Was he really coming back? And what was he going to say if he did? Nice knowing you Terry, but I've moved on. You understand, don't you?

Yeah, that's probably it, I thought. And I'd just nod like some dodo. Then after he left, I'd go somewhere and punch a wall until my fists were as red and bloody as chopped meat.

At 2 a.m., the Lincoln finally pulled up and Monty stuck his head out. Do you have any place to be tomorrow? he asked.

I shook my head. The next day was Sunday, and I was supposed to study but otherwise I was free. Hop in, he said, and we took off heading for the West Side Drive to his folk's cabin near Woodstock. Over the next three hours he explained what had happened — a fine mess as it turns out, almost comic if you're one of them grim types. But that's his story not mine.

That night was the first time I ever slept in a man's arms until morning. The first time I told Monty I loved him. Said it every day after that. Until it was my turn to go in '98. Even during the bad times. Even when we were apart. And he never got sick of hearing it.

Fifty years. Not always easy. But boy, what a ride.

MONTY

I should have written Terry from jail after I died. But I didn't.

I wasn't sure whether he had been told of my passing or, if he did hear of it, how it affected him. The togetherness we'd known in those few months had altered me completely and, I surmised, Terry as well. But it might also have been projection. You see, Terry was my first, though he'd had numerous prior experiences. For all I knew, he'd fallen for those men too. He was probably one of those serial lover types. Not that any of it mattered, really. Even if Terry had felt the same way, he thought I was dead. He'd had no choice but to bury me and move on.

If I had written to him, even if I'd used the lyrics to "Farmer in the Dell," my feelings would have bled through. I'd been bitten and Terry had left an indelible mark. The Army censors were dim-witted but not so dumb that they didn't recognize hidden meanings. It was their job to decipher codes. Rather than risk getting us both into trouble, I decided that, if and when I eluded a court-martial, then I'd write and tell him all about what he later referred to as my little Lazarus routine.

Love found me, Montgomery J. Benson, in the most unlikely time and place. A latrine during basic training. Romantic, huh? Terry was on his hands and knees scrubbing away, his punishment for wandering in a part of the camp that was strictly off-limits. The MPs assumed that he'd been out there pulling his pud, when actually he was taking the rap for some guy he'd been fellating who'd slipped away unseen. Terry was the noble type, not that he'd ever admit it. He was a scamp, too, and the combination was irresistible. How could I not fall in love with someone like that? Not to mention those shamrock green eyes and that killer grin. Innocence and devilry in one neat package.

When I first saw Terry crouched over a toilet and he turned toward me, I experienced what the French call a *coup de foudre*, a thunderbolt. I could tell we instantly connected because he didn't look away annoyed like other guys do when you stare at them too long. Instead, his eyes bobbled up and down. If he'd been in a cartoon, they would have bulged right out of his head. Terry was eternally on the lookout for trouble and overjoyed when it found him.

We had our very first kiss the next day in a larder behind the mess hall and I remember thinking that our lips fit together perfectly and that the one pair was incomplete without the other. He was someone special from the start. Which didn't stop me from being a nervous wreck the first time we had sex, since I'd never done it before — with anyone — and I knew he had. He tried to calm me down, saying don't make a big deal out of it, just let it happen. And he was right. I passed with flying colors, at least to hear him tell it.

After several months of purloined meetings, we were separated. I was all but certain that one of us would be killed. I'm glad it turned out to be me. Without my death Terry might never have appreciated that what we had was real. In a way, grief freed him to acknowledge just how deeply he cared. Until he was informed that I'd been erased from this earth, some doubt had lingered, he said. Which is why he hadn't been able to say the words to me. Which had left me to question whether the whole affair had existed only in my foolish brain and to assume that some other fortunate GI had already taken my place. As it happens, there were plenty of GIs after me and a few Italians as well. Terry took them where he found them. And he always found them.

None of the men, however, took my place, he assured me. And even later on, when Terry wandered, I never had any serious competition. I'm not bragging. I'm simply telling the truth. I'm as sure of it as my own name. Though my behavior toward him proved to be far from noble, it did not negate the fact that Terry and I were destined to travel in the same orbit. You can say that I'm idealizing. Or being corny. Or that it was nothing more than a stubborn obsession on our part. But you didn't live it. I did.

Lovesickness had a peculiar effect on me. It made me a better soldier. I was no longer afraid of dying. I actually regarded death as preferable to a lifetime without Terry, the man I was meant to be with. Though, admittedly, that was before I gave much credence to destiny, which came into play when

I ran headlong into it, one night on 46th Street in the fall of 1948. Believed in fate ever since, though sometimes you'd hardly know it from my callous behavior. But I'm getting ahead of myself.

After I was wrenched from my idyll with Terry, I was no longer willing to be crippled by the fear of being a casualty or allow it to cloud my judgment. In battle, I now saw and thought clearly. I became a voice of calm and reason in my company. Can't tell you how many dogfaces I propped up and slapped back from the verge of hysteria during the campaigns in Sicily and Salerno. Later they thanked me. The ones who made it out, anyway.

Though I didn't die — except officially — I came close. What transpired on that southern Italian hillside was bizarre to the extreme and could only have happened in war where surrealism was the norm.

Eugene Kohberger, Dominic Forchetta, and I got separated from the others as we climbed up from the beach in Salerno, pushing the Germans farther inland, where we would have them isolated. Since they still controlled the mountain road, we had to climb up via the scree, which was slippery from the previous night's rainfall. We would check each stretch of road from behind a fragrant cedar. If the coast was clear, we'd scurry across and continue our climb.

The three of us were so busy pulling each other up the hill that it took a while to notice that we'd gotten separated from our unit. Forchetta wanted to wait for them but Kohberger, an intimidating sonofabitch if there ever was one, insisted we proceed. He was one of the few among us who had yet to be disabused of the notion that we'd been drafted with the express purpose of becoming heroes. He browbeat us into following him and we did, if only to keep him from calling us pussies, faggots, and sissy boys. Since I was all of the above, I didn't much mind. But Forchetta was having enough of a hard time at it was, forever being ribbed about his Guinea heritage or working as a covert spy. Neither slur had the slightest merit; he was as red-blooded a Yank as I ever had the honor to serve alongside.

Another quarter mile up the hill, we caught enemy fire and flattened against the cold, slippery rocks as, all around us, hell broke loose. Some of our unit was below and to the right, while others had climbed up to a clearing just to the northwest. They were the ones taking and returning fire. We would have been shooting too if we'd had a clear target.

Kohberger insisted we go one way or the other and hook up with the unit. We were about to do so when German bodies started raining down from above. One of them just missed colliding with Forchetta and dragging him downhill. One of the last things I remember from that infamous day was Dominic saying, it would be just my luck to be offed by a falling Kraut.

The German boys already over the top, poor bastards, were scared senseless and you could actually hear them baying like lost dogs. They were trapped plain and simple, and they were either all going down or the white flag was coming out — and I'm reasonably certain that whatever heartless prick was in command had forbidden them to surrender.

Then, in the middle of a sunny afternoon, the lights went out.

Three desperate Germans rifle-butted us, stripped us down to our shorts and donned our uniforms and dog tags. All around, their fellow *soldats* were being slaughtered, so they must have decided that it would be better to look like a member of the winning team until they could slip away. The reason they didn't shoot us, I suppose, was that it would have brought attention to them and, besides, stripping a corpse is not easy, not to mention having to don a blood-and-guts-soaked uniform.

The laugh, as they say, was on them. Not long after they joined the U.S. Armed Forces, all three were blown to smithereens by their comrades, who mistook them for Yanks.

Kohberger got his wish. He never woke up and died a hero, but only because the soldier who conked him got carried away. By the time Forchetta and I came to, late that night, the skirmish had moved inland. So here we were, wandering around in the dark in our skivvies, with pounding headaches. It had turned cold, and our feet got cut up pretty bad. We were both glad to be alive but neither of us said a word out of respect for Kohberger. It wouldn't have been right to gloat.

Next morning, just after sunrise, down by the beach, we ran into a different unit who pegged us for deserters. By the time they'd bothered to confirm our identities, we'd been reclassified as casualties.

Once the Army says you're dead, you're dead. Since they had no idea what to do with us, not to mention having bigger fish to fry, we were tossed in the cooler. Eventually we were identified by our superiors, but until the mix-up was officially resolved, and that was not until months later, we remained incarcerated. In the midst of a war, the red tape can get very tangled indeed.

Being dead probably saved my life. The clink was a harsh place to be, but a lot safer than anywhere I'd been in the months that preceded it.

When I was finally freed, only a few days after Mussolini's body was put on display like a stuck pig, I couldn't bring myself to contact Terry. I didn't know if he was still alive, and if he wasn't, I didn't want to know. I was going home and figured that what we'd had was a wartime thing — especially in Terry's mind. After all, just because Terry was bent like me didn't mean he was bent in my direction. I'd just have to be content with those few months, those precious, life-changing months. I was convinced that eventually I'd stop crying whenever I thought about Terry and try to make a go of the life I had.

In the meantime, my grieving parents held a funeral and buried a faceless German boy in a grave marked with my birth date and his end date. And here's where the whole incident turned into an Abbott and Costello routine. Who's on first and who's buried in Monty Benson's tomb? When I wrote to assure my folks that I was alive, they didn't believe me. They thought some psycho was playing a cruel joke. When I showed up at their doorstep, they were happy to see me, but uncertain about what to do with all their grief. So, they started yelling at me, as if I'd pulled the ultimate schoolboy prank.

Now that they had their son back, they were stuck with another problem. What to do with the conniving little bastard buried in my plot. They couldn't very well mail him back COD: Dear Germans, this was sent to us by mistake. Respectfully, Theodore and Louise Benson. Since they had no idea who he was, they decided to take pity. They let him rest in peace and replaced the headstone with a simple cross. Mother said she hoped some German family would have been as charitable if it had been her son.

After getting my degree at Princeton, I went to work in sales at DuPont and met Bernadette at a social held at our Presbyterian church on the Upper West Side. She was a lovely girl, well-read and a bit on the shy side like me, but just spirited enough not to be a total bore. We enjoyed each other's company, though she seemed no more in love with me than I was with her. You see, she was older, twenty-six, and her options were beginning to dwindle.

I was prepared to marry Bernadette. She would have been the ideal wife for someone like me, since I was reasonably certain that she was looking for security and harbored few romantic notions. I had planned to propose after Thanksgiving dinner at her parents' home. I was still looking for an engagement ring when the earth opened up under my feet and I looked across the roof of my Lincoln and saw my future.

If we'd wed, I probably would have been true to Bernadette, even at the cost of being false to myself. A few days after reconnecting with Terry, I asked Bernadette to tea at the Plaza and broke it off. There was someone else I said, someone I'd been in love with since long before we started dating.

Bernadette was a smart woman. She probably figured it out and was grateful for being spared. She eventually married and had five kids. Perhaps she was more of a romantic than I had assumed and just needed the right man to bring it out in her.

Not that Terry and I committed to each other fully. Even after being in each other's arms and holding on for dear life in that big, lumpy bed in my folks' cabin in Woodstock, I fought the notion of happily ever after. After an extended honeymoon period, the trouble began. Most of it initiated by yours truly. After every lapse, I would crawl back to Terry and beg for mercy.

Even my death hadn't quelled the demons. And we both paid a hefty price for that.

PART TWO

TERRY

That genius, the one who said true love can be a tough slog sure did know his onions. We were over the moon about each other, me and Monty. All I had to do was look at him and something goofy like, Ain't *we* the two luckiest sons o' bitches you ever laid eyes on? Would pop out of my mouth. Then he'd laugh like a kid having his funny bone tickled. His laugh. I could write books about it. Good thing we never stopped being nuts about each other, otherwise the whole thing might have gone south. More than once, we came really close to blowing the one good shot we had at being genuinely happy, the thing that most people only dream about, that some say is just a figment of the imagination. Or a derangement. Well, if so, call me deranged.

For all that, the God's honest truth is that two people who can't stand to be apart for a minute can really drive each other crazy. And by crazy, I mean standing-on-the-roof with your-toes-hanging-over-the-edge crazy. Hey, maybe that's why they call it head over heels. 'Cause the other person can turn you totally upside down. And instead of being glad, since the world looks a helluva lot better from that angle, you constantly try to turn yourself right side up again. Why do you suppose that is? I've asked a ton of people and never got a single satisfactory answer.

I mean, if some other guy had treated Monty the way I did sometimes, he would've been totally justified in walking out and never looking back. And if anybody but Monty had pulled some of the lame stunts he did, swear on my mother, I would have punched his lights out. And worse. It's almost as if we resented needing each other so much that we had to think of ways to mess it up. Me and him, we called it quits more than once, but for some reason, it never took. Even on the nights when I was thinking that I never wanted to see Monty's lousy puss again, I'd tell him I loved him before I fell asleep. Hand to God. If you're trying to figure out why, don't bother. Ain't worth the trouble. The fact is, even on the worst days, I knew that life without Monty wasn't worth jack. And knowing that eats your insides like a tapeworm.

Mind you, this is me explaining the whole thing while looking in the rear-view mirror. At the time, we both had airtight alibis for every lousy trick we pulled on one another. And given the world we lived in, they sounded like perfectly good reasons. I mean, if everybody and his uncle is saying you're a mental case, what choice do you have but to think, well, they can't all be wrong. Even the people who understood just how great me and Monty were together and would have given their right arms to be in our shoes, would say things behind our backs like, Sorry, it just ain't normal what they feel for each other. But don't get me wrong. I'm not laying all the blame on them. No, Siree Bob. There was plenty of blame to go around. Starting with yours truly. If they gave out medals for being a dumb cluck, I'd have a chest full. My closest competition of course, would be Monty, who gave as good as he got.

I'll be the first to admit that sometimes I behaved like a first-class bonehead. Nobody could get my Irish up like Monty. Made me act all spiteful. And proud. What is it with men and their pride? Between us, me and Monty had more than enough for ten average guys. Maybe at the first sign of trouble it would have been better for us to climb into a boxing ring and just duke it out. If we'd seen each other bleeding on the outside, we might have stopped torturing each other sooner. It's the wounds you can't see that fester and grow, 'cause they ain't got a chance of getting out into the open air and healing. Some of those scars, I carried my whole life. A few, Monty gave me. The rest, I gave myself.

That we made it through was a kind of miracle. But hey, on that score, the Pope could have declared me and Monty saints. Because, according to Holy Mother the Church, you only need two miracles to become a saint. Heck, we had that with a couple to spare. The first miracle was that we found each other in that exploding nightmare of a war. The second was that we survived, even though technically one of us died. The third miracle was spitting in destiny's eye and finding each other again. And there's one more, and this is the big one: After we threw it all in the lake, we passed our hands over the muddy water and turned it into wine. Good wine. Vintage. Cost us plenty. Worth every nickel.

I still get a rush thinking about that night in the parking lot on West 46th when I looked over that car and saw him standing there and thought I'd finally snapped. When what I'd really done was call Monty back to life. And he did the same for me. Before we found each other again, we'd been just putting one foot in front of the other, living, but kind of dead inside. Only after we got together again did it dawn on us that the war really was over and we were no longer living on borrowed time. Now we owned time. We were rich with it. Filthy rich. And we spent it like it was going out of style.

Sound romantic? You bet your sweet ass it was. During those first few years, there were days when I'd catch myself looking at him and thinking, Wow, is this really happening? Then, I'd have to touch his hand to make sure that he was actually there, flesh and blood. Didn't matter if anyone was looking. Not to me. Not to him. At least not at the beginning.

Of course, it helped that our timing was perfect. We reconnected at the very moment when New York was just about the best damned place on the planet to be. Manhattan was a firecracker in those days. A Roman candle and a cherry bomb rolled up into one. All lit up. Bright lights everywhere. Neon. Flashing. Twenty-four hours a day. Not just on Broadway. And there was music. And commotion. Everywhere you went. Vendors hawking. Taxis honking. Tires screeching. Crazies preaching. The streets, the subways, the buses jammed, everybody seizing the day like they'd been locked up in solitary and just got out on parole, the wind in their faces for the first time in years.

Collisions were inevitable. But in those days, if somebody bumped into you on the street, instead of getting all bent out of shape and yelling, Watch where you're going, bud, you'd say, Hey there, fella. How you doin'? Swell day ain't it? Sometimes, if we wasn't in a big hurry, we'd stop and tip our hats and chat each other up. Can't tell you how many times me and Monty found ourselves standing in the middle of 57th Street chewing the fat with perfect strangers. Where you from? Where you headed? What are your plans? Not just for tonight but for tomorrow and next year. And wasn't it just aces that we was all here right now smack dab in the center of the world at this moment? Then, maybe we'd invite them to join us at a hot new spot on Swing Street or some Italian dive on Mott Street with a lasagna that brought tears to our eyes. Or, if they had other plans, we'd shake hands and wish each other all the best and go on our way whistling "Some Enchanted Evening," and thanking our lucky stars. Funny thing about surviving, it makes you greedy. The need to cram as much living as you can into every day. Like living a double life. Your own and that of some unlucky son of a gun who never made it back.

Monty and I would start the night with dinner at Lindy's and then head over to the Vanguard or Café Society to moon over Sarah Vaughan. Or we'd hop a train uptown to watch the Copa girls do a rumba or hear Mildred Bailey sing and do impressions at the Blue Angel. Later on, we'd hoof it over to 52nd Street and check out the 3 Deuces or the Downbeat or the Famous Door. Other nights we'd give our regards. Catch a show like *Kiss Me Kate. Gentlemen Prefer Blondes. The King and I. Death of a Salesman. Come Back Little Sheba. Streetcar.* When we applauded, it was never less than full out, heart and soul. Equal parts joy and gratitude.

One moment I remember like it was yesterday. We were on line for the Christmas show at Radio City Music Hall. For hours. In the freezing cold. All bundled up, huddled together trying to crack open the chestnuts we bought from the street vendor without taking off our gloves. Cracking up like a couple of school kids until we were rolling on the ground.

Good times.

Boy oh boy, did me and Monty look snazzy when we went out on the town. We was something else, I tell you. Topcoats. Herringbone or camel hair. Hair slicked back with Brilliantine and maybe a fedora dipped to one side. Wing tips shined and buffed, like they taught us in the Army. White shirt with French cuffs. Since he was born with gold fillings in his mouth, Monty had a closet full of custom suits, the best fabrics, the finest cuts. He insisted I take some. (Lucky me, we wore the same size.) And not hand-me-downs mind you, but the ones he thought looked best on me. He had a feel for that kind of stuff. And he was usually right. They fit like I had them made special for me.

Monty's the one who turned me on to jazz. And I'm not talking swing. None of that moldy fig stuff for him. Strictly hard core. Bebop. Cool. Cigarette smoke and reefer. You know: Hawkins, Blakey, Parker, Gillespie, Coltrane, Miles. Monty lived for jazz. Couldn't get enough. Mainlined it like smack. And like those cats, he was easygoing. Confident. Not a hair out of place. (At least on the outside, he was.) If we ran into some of the swells he grew up with or guys from his work with their wives or lady friends, he'd introduce me around as his old Army buddy and tell them how I'd saved his life. What'd you say that for? I'd ask him later. And he'd say, Of course you saved my life, because without you it wouldn't be much of a life. Hard to get sore with a guy who says things like that to you.

Nobody blinked an eye that we was on the prowl together with no ladies as window dressing. Or that I stayed over at his place a few nights a week. At least not in those years. (That would change. And definitely not for the better.) Even after old Fiorello LaG (and O'Dwyer after him) started yanking liquor licenses from anybody who served drinks to guys on the lookout for other guys, nobody thought that about us. We didn't fit the mold. We was just a couple of good-time Charlies out on the town. After the war, everyone was just too relieved that the world hadn't come to an end and bent on enjoying every minute 'cause, who knows, tomorrow it might all go up in a mushroom cloud.

Even my mother, Gertie, the original nosy parker, didn't give me lip. Normally, if some guy gave me a gift, she'd be looking for the catch. And what did you promise him in return? she'd ask. Maybe help him unload some merchandise off the back of a truck? But when she saw me in the new threads that I told her my old Army buddy, Monty, gave me, she just said, Gee, sounds like a nice fella. All right, if I'm being totally honest here, I might have let it slip that Monty's folks was high society. Bless her Blarney heart, Mammy was a nose-against-the-window-pane type. The way she looked at it, if you got close enough to money, some of the green might rub off on you.

Even on workdays, we'd stay out to three, four, five in the morning, then pour ourselves into a cab. Back at his place, he'd turn into a polecat, ripping and tearing at me. All Monty had to do was breathe in my ear and I was off to the races. After, he'd load me up with sweet nothings, the kind of stuff that can go to a guy's head if he's not careful. Make him think he's a better person than he knows himself to be.

After a couple of hours' sleep, Monty went to the office and I headed off to school. To this day, I don't know how we didn't die of exhaustion. In the summer, on the weekends, while his folks were off on a cruise to Europe, we'd hole up in their place upstate. Or we'd take the train out to Rockaway or Jones Beach, talking nonstop the whole way about who knows what, then coming back home at night, fried to a crisp, poking each other awake so we didn't miss our stop.

Though we never talked about it, somewhere in the back of our minds we knew it couldn't last. And, of course, it didn't.

The excitement died down in stages. Not so much that we noticed the wheels starting to wobble. We were too busy living the high life. As time passed and the war became the last thing anybody wanted to remember, much less talk about, we'd still go out but sometimes on "dates" Monty had arranged for us. The higher up he went at DuPont, the more "dates" we went on. The fifties were rolling in and life was returning to "normal."

Normal. That was the word on everyone's lips.

What they say about guys is true. They never ask for directions. Otherwise, me and Monty might not have ended up on the road to hell. The one that's paved with good intentions. But how was we to know? It's not like anybody ever printed out a road map for how two guys cockeyed in love could make a go of it. We'd never heard tell of anyone in the same situation. Turns out they existed, but I'm getting ahead of myself.

The trouble started when Monty decided to do me a good turn. After I got my degree from City and started looking for a job, he put in a good word at DuPont where he worked and was going places fast. Monty was nothing if not ambitious and he had the folks at DuPont thinking he walked on water. I don't blame them. Anybody who met Monty became his friend after the first five minutes. He was smart. Good looking. Acted like he had it all figured out. Which only goes to show how looks can be deceiving.

Monty was chummy with Katie Dunbar, the top lady in personnel. I could tell she was sweet on him from the way she talked about Monty almost nonstop during my job interview. She made hiring me sound like a done deal. Which it turned out to be. Heck, she'd have put in a word for Jack the Ripper if he was recommended by Monty. Naturally, he'd pushed the brave boys returning from the war angle and how the country owed us. If so, there were more deserving guys than me.

Take my new boss, Mike Carlton, who was the office manager for the entire third floor. Upstanding, straight-arrow and unbelievably screwed up, even by the standards of most shell-shocked vets. Mike was one of those guys who made it back but never got the war out of his system. Walking down the street with no chance of being picked off just didn't cut it for them. They needed to be close to death to feel alive. Mike couldn't stop talking about the Krauts and the Nips, and now the Commies. I wasn't his second-in-command for more than six months before he decided to reenlist and get himself shipped off to Korea. Never heard from him again. Wonder if he made it out?

A few days after I started my new job, I ran into Monty in the lobby and he walked past me like I wasn't there. Since he was with a couple of suits, I figured he was distracted, so I gave him a pass. Turns out the snub was no accident. The next night, over drinks at the King Cole bar, he told me there was something I needed to understand. Him getting me a job was one thing, but being chummy at the office was another. He was a junior executive and I was an assistant office manager. Kind of like in the Army with officers and enlisted men. Now I may not be as smart or educated or well brought up as Monty, but I can tell when a salesman is trying to pawn off silver plate for sterling. You think you're better than me, I said. To which he said, if anything it's the opposite. You're way out of my league. He was smart to flatter me. After that, I only heard what I wanted to hear, which should ring a bell with anybody who's ever been there.

Next thing I know, Monty's off on golf outings with his work buddies or his boss. Or jammed up with business dinners and get-togethers after work, usually on the arm of one of the secretaries or his biggest fan Katie Dunbar. Hey, he said, I have to show my appreciation for her taking a chance on you. His exact words. Like I was some charity case. Let it go, Terry, I told myself. Monty's the one with the thin skin, not you.

Not long after, he suggested we "double date" with his posh friend Barbara Treadwell and her pal Adrian. Good eggs, both of them, and real characters in their own way. I liked Barbara because she wasn't snooty like some of Monty's other Park Avenue buddies. She didn't look down her nose at nobody. And Adrian, well, we didn't hit it off at first. But once I got past the gabardine suits and the tough-guy routine, she was okay. Me and her weren't much on dancing. I got two left feet and Adrian made me look like Fred Astaire. That left Barbara and Monty free to trip the light fantastic the whole night. I get that Monty and Barbara had a lot in common. They'd grown up together with butter on both sides of their bread. What galled me was that Monty and her danced cheek to cheek like she was his lady or something. Adrian was kind of ticked off about it, too. But hell, if I was hooked on Monty, she was over the moon about Barbara.

So far, no serious damage. A little argument here and there. Quickly forgotten. Mainly because when we were alone, behind closed doors, Monty acted like nobody else existed. Couldn't do enough for me. Out on the street though, things changed. Where we always used to be shoulder to shoulder, now he walked a few steps ahead. Or behind. Enough that it was noticeable. If I mentioned it, he'd deny it or claim that he was distracted. Then one day, we ran into a higher-up from DuPont and he got completely rattled. Told the guy he was in a rush. Headed to the Y to shoot hoops with his buddy (pointing to me). Total lie. Monty never shot a hoop in his life. When I asked him why he'd said that he just shined me on. But I could tell that something was up because he started shifting from one leg to the other like some guy who needs to pee real bad and can't find a men's room.

When he got his big promotion, that's when things really shifted into high gear. I'm not laying the blame totally on him. This was both our doing. He acted. I reacted. Two bulls. Same china shop. Congratulations, Mister Vice President, I said. We should go out and celebrate. Absolutely, he said, but not tonight. The fellas from work were throwing a party for him and the other new VPs. I would find it boring, which is why he asked Katie Dunbar. Tomorrow night, he said, I already made reservations for us at the Copa. With Barbara and Adrian. Won't that be fun? Not even Brando could've sold that line. I got my nose totally out of joint and told him I was busy. Tomorrow night and the next night too. But maybe sometime soon. I headed out the door, got on the F train and bit my lip so hard I had to get stitches. I figured that if I made myself scarce for a few days he'd come his senses. I know what you're thinking. Immature. But it worked. Temporarily.

The promotion meant Monty was on the road more often. Not just a night here and there. A week at a time. That's why they're paying me the big bucks, he would say. He always came back hungry for me, but for the first time, I could measure the distance between us. I mean, I'd never expected the excitement to last forever. I figured we'd get used to each other. Even take each other for granted. It's human nature. But this was something else. I could tell he wanted to get something off his chest but didn't have the nerve to say it out loud.

To soften the blow of being separated he'd ask me to do him a favor and stay in the apartment while he was away. Keep an eye on things. Collect his mail. Sure, I said, no sweat. I was coming home one night and ran into the new night doorman, Philippe. I introduced myself and he said, Oh, you must be the gentleman Mr. Benson hired to stay in his apartment. I mentioned it to Monty when he got back and he screwed up his face like Philippe had gotten the wrong idea. By then though, things were already a little hinky. I couldn't put my finger on it, but I wasn't imagining things. I don't have that good an imagination.

On top of that, Gertie was on my case about what she called living high on the hog with my city friends. Time for me to settle down, she said, like Annie Walsh and Jeannie Doyle, whose sons, also vets, had recently done what she referred to as the decent thing — getting married and giving them grandkids. Every time she brought it up, she'd look at her watch like she was timing me. She warned me that sooner or later my fancy Dans were going to cut me loose and I'd be left holding my dick in my hands. (For someone who went to Mass every day, Gertie had some mouth on her.) Always led to an argument. Voices raised. Doors slammed. Dishes broken.

Another thing that got under Ma's skin was me staying over at Monty's most nights and only showing up to pack a change of clothes and, sometimes, stay for Sunday dinner. Who is this Mr. High and Mighty Army buddy, who takes up so much of your time? How come you never bring him around? You ashamed of us? It wasn't that I was ashamed of Gertie and my Da or my sister Felicia. They were good people and Monty would have recognized that. I didn't invite him because unlike me, he wasn't wise to Gertie's tricks. Once she started in with the questions, one after another, rapid-fire like a machine gun, eventually Monty would crack and confess to killing the Lindbergh baby and tell her where Judge Crater was buried.

With things at home on the downslide, I had an idea. One night, as we were getting all cuddly, I mentioned to Monty that we should become roommates. After all, I watched the place for him when he was away and spent most of my nights there when he was in town. Why not make it official? I was more than happy to split the rent and groceries. He didn't have to worry what people would think. Plenty of single guys roomed together to cut down on expenses. Nothing suspicious about it. Besides, the place had two bedrooms. We could fix up the guest room to look like I slept there.

Monty acted like I'd just asked him to go out and shoot the president. Turned me down flat and wouldn't even say why.

Instead of having it out with him, I threw on my clothes and took a powder. Headed straight to the Village in search of company. The one thing guaranteed to make me feel better. After the war, before Monty pulled his Lazarus routine, I used to hang out there sometimes. Got a bead on where I could find other lonely guys like me. I didn't need to go to a bar and risk getting arrested if the place got raided. There were plenty of streets to walk up and down until I caught somebody's eye. Then we'd duck into an alley or if the guy lived in the neighborhood, head over to his apartment. Or if he was from Jersey, the back seat of his car.

Now, years later, nothing had changed. Different guys. Same drill. Not that the streets were all that safe, what with the vice cops setting traps and rounding up the usual suspects whenever they got bored. Thing is, New York's finest were a lazy bunch. Mostly on the lookout for an easy collar, which meant the obvious types, what they called the flamers. Or the guys who stunk of desperation and guilt. Who just wanted to scratch the itch, didn't matter with who. It's like they were begging to be arrested just so they'd have another reason to feel lousy about themselves.

Still, it paid to be on your toes. Lucky thing for me, fighting in the war had sharpened my senses. I was pretty good at flushing out the boys in blue. A lot of them were Micks just like me and we spoke the same language.

Whenever one of them started chatting me up, I could smell vice on him like it was cheap cologne. I didn't let on right away that I was on to him, but after a little friendly give and take, I'd politely excuse myself with a sure-fire exit line like, Nice meeting you, fella, gotta go home and beat the wife. The looks on the guy's face was priceless. All those years, the only thing I ever got nabbed for was loitering. Paid a fine, went home. No big deal.

Back when I was still in school, when I was in the mood, I'd go down to the Village early before heading off to work parking cars. Rode the subway down to 14th or Sheridan Square. During rush hour. You'd be surprised what a cinch it was to score in a crowded car. All you had to do was be awake. Look around. Catch an eye. Look away. Look back again. Get off at the same stop. Stand at the bottom of the stairs and if the guy looked over his shoulder, you were in. If that didn't work, you could head to the supermarket and hang out for a bit or grab a slice at a pizza parlor or a quick bite at a diner or café. If I was in a big hurry, I'd zero in on the flamers. I don't hold no truck with guys who put them down. Anybody's got enough moxie to walk around with a target on his back was okay in my book. For the most part, I liked them because they weren't as hung up as some of your average Joe types. And most of 'em were funny, full of energy and eager to please. Sure, sometimes they could be high maintenance but hey, gotta take the good with the bad.

Another thing. Some of the Village guys hung out in groups. For lunch. For dinner. You could always tell by the way they'd lean into each other. A lot of whispering too. And laughing. I'd grab a table nearby and at some point say, Would you gentleman mind watching my coat while I hit the john? I'd look at them a beat too long to get the message across. By the time I returned, they'd usually decided who was getting first dibs and invite me to join them. It was through these kinds of meetings that I started getting invited to house parties. Which were mostly stag with some pretty window dressing in case the cops got called on account of noise. If you behaved yourself, didn't get too drunk or cause a scene, you got invited to other house parties.

Now, as things with Monty got rocky, I started visiting my old haunts again. For the fun and for the attention I wasn't getting from him anymore. Like when he was away or out on the town with some lady. I tried to convince myself that I wasn't doing it to get back at him, but who's kidding who? Anyways, one night, while I was holding up a wall on West Street sucking on a Lucky Strike, who should I happen to spy with my little eye but the doorman, Philippe, heading straight for the piers. Guess it was his night off. It had occurred to me that a couple of times he looked at me funny, especially when I got back to Monty's place real late. But I brushed it off, figuring he was just being uppity. Did I mention he was a pretty decent-looking fella, wiry, with dark eyes and a beak of a nose? I thought of following him to the piers but changed my mind. I didn't need Philippe knowing my business. Or

Monty's.

Got back to the apartment around two in the morning and was surprised to find Monty, who'd just gotten in a few steps ahead of me. The business trip was cut short, he said. He asked where I'd been and I told him it was none of his damned business. If he could come and go as he pleased, so could I, thank you very much. I noticed he was wearing a tux. Said he'd been to a dinner party. Alone? No, he said, with Katie Dunbar. She wanted to introduce me to her parents. What for, I asked, not sure I wanted to hear the answer. We've been talking engagement, he said.

That's all I needed to hear. Couldn't get out of there fast enough. Hopped a cab and whooshed down to West Street. My anger must have given me X-ray vision. It took me exactly two minutes to locate Philippe. I dragged him to the back of the pier, put a hand over his mouth and got on with it. He didn't seem to mind the roughhousing. But even if he had, I was determined to take it out on somebody that night.

Later, I walked all the way back uptown, feeling better and more miserable than I had in years. When I walked in, Monty was sitting on the bed bawling his eyes out. Cry me a river, I said, and crashed on the couch.

MONTY

The heart has its reasons, as does the gut. Life is a balancing act between the two. Heed one to the exclusion of the other and you're guaranteed to go astray. At least, that's what I was raised to believe. The results speak for themselves.

I wish I had a better defense for my frequently atrocious behavior other than to say that it sprang from fear. Fear of disappointing my family. Fear of public disgrace. Fear of failure. Fear of being less than. Fear of always trying to do the right thing only to have it turn out all wrong.

Somewhere, buried under the rubble of all this anxiety was a deep yearning, and Terry was its personification. On that unseasonably warm night when I pulled into Barbetta's parking lot my life was split asunder. Until then, I'd mapped out my future, carefully, precisely. Career. Marriage. Family. Social Standing. Season tickets to the Metropolitan Opera, the wifey and I seated beside my parents. Dinner for four afterwards at 21. But the sight of Terry standing there wearing a waist-length brown zippered jacket, those eyes of emerald, and the permanently tousled sandy hair, chucked my best-laid plans into the dustbin. All that pent-up desire leaped to the surface overriding, temporarily at least, my trepidation. For a time, I allowed myself to wallow in the joys of companionship and intimacy. Then the hissing fear returned, more virulent than before, its fangs sharpened by cowardice and circumstance.

In those heady initial years, exhilaration lifted us above the crowds and gravity was suspended. We recognized that, separately, we were frail, defenseless against the buffeting winds of life. Together, we felt invulnerable. For as long as we didn't question that shaky premise, we were content in our Fabergé egg universe.

They say you had to be there to appreciate my conundrum. Anyone in similar straits who survived the fifties and most of the sixties will understand my knee-jerk reactions. How I sought to compensate for my inner turmoil by diligently endeavoring to be the good son, the model employee, the debonair suitor. Turned out, I could fake it with the best of them. Even managed to squeeze in sub rosa interludes with Terry. Just enough to keep a nervous breakdown at bay.

It would help to know a bit about my origins. I, Montgomery Jerrold Benson, was born the son of Theodore and Louise (née Montgomery) Benson. My father had a seat on the stock exchange. My mother's name was writ large in the Blue Book. My older brother, Teddy, died at the age of three of the Spanish influenza. Two years later, I was conceived. The consolation child, in whom they placed all the hopes they had originally invested in their firstborn. Made a huge difference in my upbringing. I might have been cut some slack if I'd been the spare and not the heir.

I was expected to be bright. I was expected to be popular. I was expected to excel at sports, at business, at society. I proved to be a better-than-average student, sharp enough to require only minimal intervention on my father's behalf to gain acceptance to his alma mater. I became popular mainly through observation, learning to mimic the finer qualities of my family's enviable connections, businessmen and politicians who were adept at back-slapping and inveigling.

I picked my sports carefully. Tennis, due to my lithe frame and strong shoulders. Also track, another sport requiring no physical contact which, for reasons that only later came to light, made me skittish. My upbringing, my advanced degree, my practiced charm, were sufficient enticement for the campus DuPont recruiter. The connections I'd made through my father and at school paved my way into society. From prep school on I was referred to as Good Old Monty, a moniker I greeted with a broad smile to conceal an inner cringe.

Terry. Now there was the rub. The piece of my puzzled life that had been missing. In Terry, I'd found someone as exquisitely in touch with his emotions as I was estranged. I had book smarts, breeding, standing, but none of his warmth, his kindness, his attentiveness and well-deep empathy. Whereas I denied and was cowed by my inclinations, his response was to indulge them — almost to excess. A middle finger to the world's disapproval. I don't mean to imply that he was ostentatious. He felt no need to announce himself. He was simply take-it-or-leave-it Terry. Like him (and many, many did) or hate him, it made little difference.

I couldn't help but admire and be seduced by his intrepidness. I'd never met someone so open, so tactile, so giving. So at harmony with himself. And so effortlessly amusing. A Gaelic rapscallion with a uniquely wry take on life.

The war brought us together and broke us apart. After I returned stateside, I tricked myself into believing that the separation had been for the best. That no good could come of the feelings he'd tapped into and they needed to be suppressed. I wouldn't be the first man to will himself into sublimation. My father's cohorts had skeletons aplenty. The ones that were spoken of, even joked about, were usually of the wink-wink variety — chorus girls and such. The darker secrets, alcohol, morphine, underworld ties, Ponzi-like business schemes, were spoken of with pity or outrage. My particular aberration, however, was rarely alluded to and if anyone tried, the others would clear their throats and change the subject. Mute it out of existence.

After the war, I'd all but convinced myself that, after a suitable period of mourning, Terry had found someone else and opened his large, giving heart to him. But somewhere in the recesses, I indulged in a fantasy. Of running into Terry (which proves that there are no accidents) and the both of us collapsing into one another's arms. When it indeed happened, I was so elated that I put some of my future plans on hold to spend every spare moment in his company. The thrill of his presence and the absence of any judgment (except from my parents, who accused me of being a vagabond) enabled me to savor every delicious moment.

Terry and I spent that idyll in a town where there was never enough time to do or see everything. We danced through the days and nights to the rhythm of a dizzying percussive beat, expending all our energy, eating too much, drinking too much, going out too much and, sometimes, having to be pried apart with a crowbar.

And no one seemed to care what we did, where we went, how we behaved. Not at that particular moment in time, anyway. The societal change was gradual enough to be unnoticeable. Until it wasn't. A sudden wild pendulum swing and the air reeked of disapprobation. And not just for the likes of me and Terry. During the war, the workplace had expanded to include women. Now they were being forcibly eased back to the hearth. White picket fences were back in fashion. Parenthood was encouraged, even demanded. Conformity was the byword.

I'd gotten so used to our untrammeled existence that, initially, I pretended to ignore the shift or made some minor accommodations to it. I helped him land a job at DuPont, though, in retrospect, I should have used my family connections to secure him a position elsewhere. At a safe distance. Not that what later transpired wouldn't have happened anyway, but it might have bought me time and perspective. Now, suddenly, the differences between us, which hadn't mattered a whit to me, announced themselves. I was the executive on the fast track; Terry was the low-level manager with a marginal future upside. My smug peers enjoyed ridiculing their underlings' lack of polish and breeding. Had fun at their expense.

Something else they joked about were the boys who loitered on 53rd and 3rd and the ladies on 53rd and Lex, speculating on which of the unattached men in the office frequented the former and who the latter. I worried, probably with good cause, about which category I'd been assigned and how it might be weaponized against me.

Thus, I became particularly sensitive to signals — raised eyebrows, sudden silences, subtle insinuations, questions about my extracurricular activities. I was not about to lie, at least not at first. Hanging out with old friends or seeing my folks, I'd say when asked about my weekend or vacation plans. To throw them off the scent, I'd discreetly (but conspicuously) flirt with one of the girls in the secretarial pool. Or ask one of them out to lunch.

Even in anything-goes Manhattan, a crusade had been undertaken to combat "public indecency," i.e., men who didn't ascribe to the Andy Hardy ethos. On the national level, the reaction was even more radical, led by the estimable Senator McCarthy with an able assist from J. Edgar Hoover. The Red Scare was coupled with what came to be labeled the "lavender scare," a purge of homosexuals from government and public life, and the renewed enforcement of sodomy laws. Not for the first time, America was hearkening back to the imaginary halcyon days when morality was a straight line, and any deviation was regarded as a mortal threat.

This meant my association with Terry was no longer invisible and could be held up to scrutiny. The first person to question our friendship was my division supervisor, Ed Reston, who, like me, was a jazz aficionado. We'd run into him and the missus at clubs and though the groups we sat with were mixed, Terry was always among them. Naturally, we'd ask Ed and his wife to join us and by the third or fourth drink, I'd catch him staring at me and then over at Terry. And back again. His nose would wrinkle, triggering my built-in paranoia sensors. At work the following day, Ed and I would chat about Gillespie or Miles or some newcomer we'd seen perform the previous evening. And it was good to see your friend Terry again, Ed would say. Nice guy. The same phrase every time.

Yes, I let Ed rankle me, allowed myself to be discomfited by a man who would die of acute alcohol poisoning just short of his forty-fifth birthday.

Still, I resisted the idea of giving up Terry. Not jeopardizing our relationship while moving forward with my career became a second full-time job. Maintaining proper distance at the office was relatively easy. Terry didn't like it but seemed to understand my reasoning. His reaction to my spending more time socializing with higher-ups and coworkers — dinners, golf outings, get-togethers with their families, often with a date in tow —

was a bit thornier and gave rise to misunderstandings and arguments. Nothing major, not initially.

Then Terry decided to test my loyalty, though he probably didn't see it that way. When he proposed that we live together, I refused. Or more accurately, I panicked. It was one thing for a buddy from Queens to stay over a couple of times a week after a night at Roseland or to apartment sit when I was away, but another for us to officially cohabit. Two names on the mailbox.

This is not to excuse my subsequent betrayal. Indefensible is indefensible is indefensible. It's merely to present a context. You'd think that after enduring the terrors of battle, my courage would have been tempered. But I let the anxiety gnaw at my armor and, abetted by ambition, peer pressure, and the need for parental approval, I began to wean myself from Terry. In increments.

Once I crossed the threshold of thirty, I redoubled my efforts to continue my climb, which demanded I buckle down. Make compromises. Some of them easier than others. I could no longer act the young lothario without jeopardizing future advancement. Being consigned to the category of "confirmed bachelor," would be pitiable at best, suspect at worst.

Freezing the blood in my veins, I began to court my coworker Katie Dunbar, in an effort to cement my social standing. Our parents approved. Claimed we made a lovely couple. I think Katie understood who I was and was willing to look the other way, in return for the perks and security of matrimony, as women often did in those days. Our conjugal fumbling confirmed that neither she nor I were compatible for anything more than the rote requirements of procreation.

The polite word to describe a man like me was "cad." I didn't see myself as craven but then roués rarely do. They're too blinded by their egos. It's not that I didn't have the means to buy my freedom. I could have given it all up and taken refuge in bohemia as my good friend Barbara had for her beloved Adrian. But I foolishly believed I could thread the needle. Have a wife and family and Terry on the side. The thought of separating from him was intolerable. But even as I clung stubbornly to the one true thing in my life, I consciously undermined our relationship.

Philippe the doorman, whose inklings about Terry (and by association, myself) had been confirmed one dark night in an abandoned pier on the Hudson, played a role in this as well. Initially, I didn't tell Terry about the threats. The payoffs. We were estranged at the time. Once we reconciled, I confessed it all even though I was worried that Terry might do something rash and exacerbate the problem.

My timing, however, couldn't have been better. It just so happens that Philippe had been arrested in a Village bar raid two nights earlier. Terry had been out on the prowl and seen him being carted away by the police. When

Philippe returned to work, Terry cornered him. Told him if he didn't cease and desist, not only would he knock his block off, he would rat him out to the building's management, an upstanding uptown firm that would frown on his lowdown downtown behavior.

Though Terry had come to my rescue, this reconciliation, like all the others, proved to be fleeting. Through the torturous years that followed, Terry and I devised a hundred ways to sabotage one another. Eventually, one or both of us would beg forgiveness and the cycle would begin anew. Despite the emotional carnage, however, and all the hurtful things that were said, the words "I don't love you anymore" were never uttered.

The one lie we could never tell.

PART THREE

TERRY

One day, this guy in my office, Lenny Weiner, turned me on to a sweet deal in the Village. The building was on West 10th, and Mr. Carstairs, the landlord, showed me a cozy studio on the second floor for next to nothing and a nice-size one-bedroom on the third floor for even less than that. The catch? The place looked like Dresden after the Allies were done with it. Carstairs asked if I was handy with a hammer and a screwdriver, and I said I was. Back home, I took care of the basic repair work, since the old man had trouble with anything more complicated than opening a can of Schlitz. He offered to let me live there rent-free if I was willing to put in the work to make the place presentable. How I did it was my business. He agreed to front me some drywall and window frames he had left over from one of his other buildings and offered to put in a good word for me with his wholesaler for the other supplies. Gave me two years to finish the job and then, if he was satisfied, we'd discuss a fair price going forward. Or if I wanted, he'd cut me the same deal on another one of his apartments that needed fixing up.

I doubt that I'd have agreed to the deal if Monty and me weren't on the outs at the time. But since we were going at it hammer and tongs, I figured all that busy work would be a good distraction while I waited for him to come to his senses. Eventually, I got a helping hand from a few buddies I made in the neighborhood. Guys I'd hooked up with along the way. In return, I'd go over to their place if they needed help splashing some paint on the walls or changing a fuse. And maybe spend the night.

As soon as I signed the lease, I hightailed it back to Queens and broke the news to Gertie. But she wasn't having it. Other than feet first, she said, the only way I was leaving her house was with a ring on my finger. Oh yeah,

I said, try and stop me. And another thing, Ma. You can stop holding your breath. I ain't getting married. Not now. Not never. Mammy was no genius, but she could put two and two together. And I mean, really, who was kidding who? Mothers always know. They just tune out the truth sometimes because it's easier that way. The day I picked up the last of my things, she said she was going to Mass every day and praying for me. I said thanks, Ma, you do that. A little praying never hurt nobody.

Gertie's not the only one who flipped out about the move. Monty told me that I'd lost my mind. Swore he'd never set foot in that rat trap, to which I said, Fine, and by the way, go fuck yourself. I used those exact words. I didn't mean it, of course. But I think it scared him a little, made him afraid that if he kept pushing me, I might break it off for keeps. Sure enough, after not talking for a few months, one day he showed up on my floor at DuPont, shoved me into a men's room stall and kissed me the same way he did on that first night after we reconnected. Helluva risk to take in the middle of the afternoon with so many people milling around. But in that moment, he didn't seem to care. I knew that soon enough he'd go back to being scared, but I took my victories as they came.

Don't get me wrong. I'm not saying Monty had nothing to be afraid of. If he wanted a future at the company, he had to play by the rules. And not scaring the horses was one of them. For me, not so much. An office manager just wasn't all that important. You're like part of the furniture. If they need something from you, fine. If they don't, it's like you're not even there. Since nobody was after my job, they felt no need to knife me in the back or spread dirt about me. Which is not to say that if my name showed up in the papers after a bar raid or a public men's room, I wouldn't be shown the door. But I made sure nothing like that ever happened and, for the most part, minded my own business. If I talked with the guys in the office, it was usually about the Dodgers or, sometimes, about the new place I was redoing, which kind of impressed them. Most of those guys wouldn't know an Allen wrench from a monkey wrench. They'd even ask me for repair tips so they could show off for the wife.

Though I took a lot of grief from my folks and it didn't do my relationship with Monty any good neither, moving to the Village was the best decision of my life. I mean, other than falling for Monty. That's still number one by far.

The Village back then was a place where you either belonged or you got out of there pronto. I belonged. From the get-go. And that's a terrific feeling for somebody who was always a little out of step for most of his life.

No place like it on this God's green earth, I'll tell you. The Village was low-rise with lots of light. A few buildings on the tall side, but if you were looking for skyscrapers you had to go north or south. The Village is different from the rest of the city, most of which is on a grid. As I used to tell midtown tourists who stopped to ask me for directions, it's almost impossible to get lost in Manhattan. You got your numbered streets going from south to north, crossed with avenues, east to west. With a few exceptions, that was pretty much it.

Except for the Village, which is a crazy quilt. There's a West 4th Street, but no West 5th. To find West 11th Street you gotta go up West 4th three blocks past West 10th. Bleecker Street runs east-west and suddenly changes its mind and goes north-south. Got that? Nah, didn't think so. See what happened was, back in the old days, when the city decided to go on a grid, the folks in the Village said, Thanks but no thanks, though eventually they threw the city a bone. They let 7th Avenue cut through the heart of the Village, but on a diagonal. Off-center like most of the people who live there.

Another great thing, you can cover the Village on foot in a single afternoon. Best place to walk if you just want to be left alone. Or if you're looking to meet a stranger. Lots of trees and pocket parks. And gated private streets and alleys. And diners and coffeehouses where you can hang out all day and shoot the breeze. And more kooks per square inch than anyplace else in the whole goddamned world. Artists and derelicts and square pegs. My kind of people. Interesting and funny. And sad. And smart. And annoying. And weird. And a few, downright scary. There were some posh people too. You know, the artsy-fartsy types. But also a lot of everyday Joes. And for flavor, a few goombahs.

Some of the Village folks were waiting on their big break, barely scraping by, bussing tables during the day and sometimes working the streets at night. Some were crooked as sin. Some were Holy Rollers. Somehow, we all got along.

Even the noises in the Village were different. Mind you, if you don't like noise, you got no business living in Manhattan in the first place. The Village had all kinds of noises starting with the rumble of the subway under your feet. Taxis always honking. Tires always screeching to a halt to load and unload. Blasts of music from cars racing past. Up 6th. Down 7th. Across Greenwich to 8th. Along Bleecker to Broadway. Or the noise from one of them new TVs everybody was buying. The laugh track from Uncle Miltie's "Texaco Star Theater" or that annoying "Call for Phillip Morris" ad. But the best noises came from the people. Old ladies on the front stoop yakking in Italian or Yiddish. Moms screaming at their kids in mile a minute Spanish. Housewives singing along to Doris Day on the radio while they ironed their husband's shirts. Guys and gals breaking up in the middle of the street and wishing each other dead, then kissing and making up and getting all sloppy. Trumpet players blasting out their windows and piano players tinkling out the same scales a hundred times in a row, for hours on end, until you want to go over there and smash their instruments to pieces. And don't even get me started on the ones who fancied themselves opera singers or Broadway crooners, when most of them just sounded like cats in heat.

Softer sounds too. One of my favorites was that of guys scraping their heels on the sidewalks, trailing other guys for blocks, coming to a dead halt in front of a shop and pretending to look in the window until one of them whispers a dirty come-on into the other one's ear.

Late at night, when I couldn't sleep I'd walk down West 12th toward the river, and the Village could get quiet as a heartbeat. Just a breeze whistling through the tree leaves. So many trees in the Village. Along the streets. In the little parks, here and there, popping up out of the concrete. Some had leaves the size of a grown man's hand. And in the winter, when the trees got naked, they'd get all fancied up with shiny icicles.

Dogs. Lots of dogs. Some of my friends said I should get a dog to keep me company and because you never know who I'd strike up a conversation with when I was out walking him. Lots of cats, too, on account of rats hate cats, which saved you time and money cleaning out the traps every morning. At any given time, I had three cats living with me. I didn't invite them over or nothing. They just showed up on my windowsill and decided to hang out for a while. Came and went as they pleased, out the window, down the fire escape. Sometimes they came back, sometimes they didn't. Sometimes they brought a friend.

My life would have been a lot different if Monty had let me move into his place uptown, but probably not half as much fun. Where he lived, the most you got out of a neighbor was a tip of the hat or, from the ladies, a tight smile, like you was about to grab their handbags. Down by me, people were more friendly. Total strangers would come up and hand you a flyer and say, You gotta come see me tonight, I'm reading my poetry, singing my folk songs, performing my play, showing my paintings, opening a restaurant, saving souls, or throwing a big party and everybody's invited. Bring your own booze.

In the Village, at least back then, famous people and nobodies were mostly treated the same. Flashing a fiver didn't get you special treatment like it did at the Stork Club or 21. Downtown people gave you a better table or let you cut in line because they thought you were a good egg. Or because you had a kind face. Or because you had style. A lot of people in the Village had style and I don't mean the stuff you saw in the *Harper's Bazaar*. Guys in berets and turtlenecks and blue jeans cuffed at the ankle. Ladies in men's overcoats and white dress shirts with the tails hanging out. The snooty types said they looked like bums. Which was rich, because soon everybody was copying them. Even in the *Harper's Bazaar*.

Monty, when he deigned to come down to the Village, always had a blast. That is, if he wasn't too busy looking over his shoulder thinking he was going to get mugged. By the by, he wasn't totally off base there, especially since he looked like the kind of guy who had a gold money clip in his pants pocket and a Bulova from Tiffany on his wrist. Which he did.

Once, I convinced him to go with me to a rent party on Hudson, in a room full of people — mostly guys, some of whom I knew personally — he'd never met before, Monty let his hair down. Put his arm around me and looked into my eyes in a way that slayed me. Sure, he was a little tipsy by then. But still.

Even when we were on good terms though, which was less and less, he refused to set foot in my apartment. As if those fancy doorman buildings uptown didn't have cockroaches and mice too. And me being such a stubborn Mick, I wouldn't go to his place neither. Like a couple of schnooks, we usually ended up renting a hotel room. Looking back, I guess it was kind of a cheap thrill. Me and him acting like strangers with no history, no gripes. Just two guys getting together for a little R and R.

Every once in a while, when he got to the end of his rope from pretending to be something he wasn't, Monty would beg me to go with him on vacation. Someplace far away. Cuba. Puerto Rico. Miami Beach. And he'd keep at it until I caved. Which he knew I would eventually since I'm a total pushover when it comes to Monty. He even got me to go along with his cockamamie demands, which included arriving at different times and getting separate rooms like we were outlaws hiding out after a heist, which in a way we were in those days. Without those breaks, when it was just Terry and Monty, two dopes carrying the same torch, I don't think we would have made it through. The worst part was that after being together for a week at a time without a care in the world, we felt so much worse when the vacation ended, and we had to go our separate ways with the sound of all the swell things we'd said to each other still ringing in our ears. Almost like we'd dreamed the whole thing up. Like it had never happened.

I met a lot of interesting people living in the Village. People I never forgot for as long as I lived. They all had stories and not a single one of them was boring. I heard some wild, crazy stuff. Things you couldn't make up — though a few turned out to be first-class liars. Didn't take much to get them to spill their guts either. At least not with me. Maybe 'cause I got what Monty calls an open face. But I think it had more to do with the fact that I was interested in people, and I liked to listen. You learn a lot when you listen. What makes people laugh. What makes them cry. How they manage to make it from one day to the next without jumping out a window. A couple of them did that too.

The lost souls were the easiest to peg. I met plenty of those. A few became friends for life. More often though, they were just ships passing in the night. Most were grateful that you heard them out and didn't judge them.

Others got embarrassed or freaked out because they'd told you too much. If anybody got wise, I could lose my job, they'd say. My wife. My kids. Calm down, I'd tell them. I don't know where you work. I don't know your wife or your kids. I don't even know if you told me your real name. Anyway, I wouldn't say nothing if I did. Not all of them believed me. One or two panicked and even got violent. But for the most part they were relieved to get the stuff that was eating at them off their chest.

The best thing about the Village was the live-and-let-live attitude. The only people who seemed weird were the normal types, the ones who felt pressured to toe the line. Who thought there was a right way to be and a wrong way. I was never like that. I was always fascinated by what made different people tick. Take for instance these two Caspar Milquetoast types I got chummy with by the names of Lester and Kyle. Quiet, shy, but sweet. You'd never know it to look at 'em but, on weekends, they walked the streets dressed like ladies. Not drag queens, mind you. Ordinary dames. The kind you would never even notice, which was part of their shtick. They could be the old ladies next to you in the Laundromat or two holier-than-you types sitting in the front pew in church. For the longest time, I didn't make the connection. And when I finally did, I just shrugged it off. I mean, what did I care? They weren't hurting nobody. Like I said, live and let live.

One of the strangest people I ever met in the Village or anyplace else for that matter, was this little pipsqueak everybody called Shrimpy. To this day I don't know his real name. Shrimpy was a genuine oddball, and that's just the way he liked it. He was thin as a rail, and whoever dressed him needed to get their eyes checked. But he was funny and whip smart. Could crack you up one minute and leave you with your mouth hanging open the next. Never met anybody like him before. Or since.

We met under not the best of circumstances. I was headed down Greenwich late one night looking for trouble when I saw this little guy in a porkpie hat walking a couple of blocks ahead, tooling along, not a care in the world. Then out of nowhere, this car full of joy riders pulled up and started hooting at him, calling him all kinds of names. A couple of them jumped out of the car and fists began to fly. Not that it was any of my business, but it didn't seem right what they were doing. I happened to be standing next to a trash can and I grabbed an empty beer bottle, cracked it and charged right at them. Slashed one guy's arm. Before you know it, they were headed back to whatever shithole they'd crawled out of.

The little guy was smashed up pretty bad. I lifted him and wrapped my arm around his waist. What's your name, I asked, and he said, They call me Shrimpy on account of . . . and he coughed up a little blood. Would you be so kind as to take me home? I live over on Varick. It isn't far. I would be most appreciative. Here this guy's just gotten the stuffing knocked out of him and he's being polite and all. Even cracked a few jokes. Said that usually he only let guys he was in love with rough him up. At the time, I thought he was kidding. When we got to his front stoop, he kind of fainted, so I fished out his keys, carried him upstairs, and fell asleep in a chair next to his bed. Next morning, he thanked me for taking care of him, told me I was a real peach. He said stuff like that. You're a real peach. Or a humdinger. I asked him if he was okay and he said, Oh yeah, sure. Don't worry about me. Then he said, Golly gee, those are the greenest peepers I've ever seen. Tell me handsome, you got anyone special? And don't worry. I ain't fishin'. You're not my type.

I tilted my head to the side a little and blew out some steam. He took my meaning. Said, Oh boy, you got it bad, don't you? I asked, How could you tell? Written all over your face in invisible ink, he said, but when the light hits you a certain way, it's there as plain as day. I was halfway down the steps when he called out to me. By the way, I work at Circle in the Square. Give me a date that works for you and I'll set aside two tickets. The least I can do for my Sir Galahad.

The tickets were for some Tennessee Williams play and the first person I thought to invite was Monty, even though we'd had a big fight over the weekend. I called him and, surprise, surprise, he said yes. He enjoyed the show. I fell asleep. As we were coming out of the theater, I ran smack dab into a buddy of mine named Donald. A decent guy I got together with from time to time. We didn't say much more than hello but after, Monty made a federal case out of it; cussed me up and down and hopped into the nearest cab.

A few days later, I was sitting on a bench in the park on Bleecker with a cup of cold coffee and a bucket of the blues. And who comes skipping along, all bright and cheery-eyed, but Shrimpy. Said, Geez Terry, what happened? You look like death warmed over. If you wanna talk about it, I'm all ears. So I told him my sob story. And he said, I know you don't think so right now Terry, but you're one lucky guy. I seen you two together the other night at the theater. And let me tell you something, he's worth the trouble.

That Shrimpy, so smart and such a dummy.

Another good friend I made over the years was just as kooky but in a completely different way. Dee Andrea Monet. Bigger than life and twice as brassy. For sure somebody you never want to mess with. Not if you value life and limb. Back in the days when she was trolling the streets for rent money, we'd smoke cigarettes and shoot the breeze on the corner of West Street near the river while she waited for some paying customer to come along and take her for a ride. I remember asking if she was afraid of getting into cars with these guys, especially when they found out her little secret. I mean, not for nothing Dee, I said, but some of them look like real hardasses. She just looked me square in the eye and said, Are you kidding? My little secret is why they go with me in the first place. And really, do I look like I can't handle some bridge-and-tunnel halfwit?

She had me there. Dee Andrea was a big, strapping broad, six-two in heels, linebacker shoulders. Played football in high school, she told me. Basketball too. On weekends sometimes, she'd throw on a pair of sneakers and jeans and we'd shoot hoops in the park over on 6th Avenue. She had a mean hook. A couple years after we met, Dee Andrea disappeared for a while after some cauliflower nose who ran a couple of Village bars took a shine to her and set her up real nice. I figured she was happy to get off the streets. Boy, was I off base.

One day, I ran into her at a diner on Hudson and she looked up at me all nervous. I'm not here, she said. You never saw me. Got it? Yeah, yeah, all right, calm down, I said. What? You in trouble with John Law? No, she said. It's the boyfriend. Crazy jealous. Wants to keep me cooped up all the time. Won't let me hang out with my girlfriends. It's driving me nuts. If he knew I was out now and talking to you, he'd hunt you down like a dog. For all that, she was hooked on the guy. Hey, it takes all kinds.

Maybe the closest friend I made in all those years was Adrian. I still get choked up sometimes when I think about her. We first met when Monty set us up on a double date with her friend Barbara. As if people were going to be fooled that we were dating them. Maybe Monty and Barbara, on account of they looked the part. Her with the Rita Hayworth hair, all skinny and sophisticated. But me and Adrian? Butch don't even begin to describe her.

Tell the truth, I didn't much care for Adrian at first, and that's on me. It was the tough-guy routine. I don't know why it bothered me, but it just did. Then again, she didn't like me much neither. But since we were thrown together all the time, eventually we got to talking. Turned out we had a lot in common. She grew up in a cold-water flat in Germantown, not so different from my upbringing in Queens. Her people were Polish and every bit as Catholic as mine. They kicked her out for not wearing dresses, which was fine with her, she said. She got a job as a barback at a dyke dive in the Village, cut her hair, started wearing suits and changed her name from Greta to Adrian because it could be a guy's name or a girl's name. I don't know why, but after she told me about her life, I started to like her. I mean, it took balls to do what she did, and how could you not admire somebody like that? She turned out to be the kind of friend that, if you got into a street fight, you'd want at your back.

Some nights, when I was out of sorts and in no mood for noodling, I'd head over to University Place for a drink at The Bag, one of the bars Adrian worked at over the years. If business was slow, we'd chat. She'd tell me a dirty joke. I don't know where she got them, but honest to God, some of them made me go all red in the face. She got a real kick out of that. From time to time, Barbara would drop by too. She may have looked like a movie star but she never acted like one. Kind and sweet. I can't tell you how many nights she and Adrian held my hand and told me everything between me and Monty was going to be all right. Eventually.

The other ladies didn't seem to mind me hanging out there. Only one or two of them ever gave me lip. But I didn't take it to heart. They were just showing off. Trying to impress a lady. The way guys do sometimes.

The places where Adrian worked got raided every now and then, and I just happened to get caught up in one. Which is rich, because I avoided gay bars for just that reason. The cops wanted to haul me in and I said What for? The last time I looked there was no law against a guy going to a bar and trying to pick up a dame. That got 'em all confused. But they decided to arrest me anyways. As I'm being escorted to the paddy wagon, I decided to give it one last shot. I said, hope you know what you're doing, fellas. I mean what are you going to tell the judge when he asks why you pinched me? I'll drop my drawers if I have to, and don't think I won't. Everybody knows that cops hate getting egg on their face, so they told me to beat it and if they ever saw my ugly puss again, they'd lock me up in Sing Sing and throw away the key. Yeah, yeah. Big talk.

Later, I headed to the station house and posted bail for Adrian. We went out for a nightcap together and had a good laugh. When Barbara heard the story, she thought it was a hoot. Monty, not so much.

There are some friendships that change your life in ways you'd never expect in a million years. Joanie and me was never really all that close. I liked her all right, even though she was a real user. Joanie was more than a little messed up, which appealed to the part of me that wants to fix everything that's wrong with people. Though we was about the same age, I thought of Joanie as a kid sister and became kind of protective of her. Didn't do her much good, not in the long run. But I got something out of the deal that I wouldn't trade for all the tea in China.

We met one day when I headed over to this gigantic bookstore called the Strand to find a finance book for one of the big cheeses at my new job for a bank on Wall Street. After a major blowup with Monty, I quit my job at DuPont. Couldn't stomach being in the same building with him anymore. Katie Dunbar, who was also on the outs with Monty, heard about it and called me. Said I should come back and she'd square things with my bosses. Said I was a good worker and they didn't want to lose me. No soap. I was leaving for personal reasons, I told her, and left it at that. Not that she needed a road map. She said, in that case, she was sorry and to prove it, offered to put in a call to a friend in personnel who worked at Chase downtown. Long story short, two weeks later I was working on Williams Street. Better job. Better pay. Sent Katie the biggest bunch of roses you ever seen.

My new boss, Fred Dodge, was having trouble finding this particular book about finance and, since I can polish apples with the best of them, I volunteered to help. Rang up all the bookstores in town but came up empty-handed. One of the last guys I talked to suggested I give the Strand a try, so I decided to pop over there one day after work.

This nice-looking lady at the help desk, Joanie, said the book wasn't listed in their regular finance section and my only hope was the remainders section downstairs at the back, which was all dusty and dark. You could barely see your hand in front of your face. Joanie grabbed a flashlight and handed me one and said we should divvy up the stacks or I'd be there all night. Sure enough, after about an hour, she pulled out not one, but two copies, and I could have kissed her. On the way to the register, we got to talking and, turned out, we lived a block apart. This happened just before Christmas, and it was already dark out. Real sweet like she asked if I wouldn't mind waiting a half hour until she clocked out and walking her home. My pleasure, I said. One good turn deserves another.

Joanie was pretty in that girl-next-door way, which was deceiving since she was anything but the girl next door. I could tell right off the bat she was a little off her tree. On the way home, she started feeling me out and, real quick, added up the score. Didn't bother her none. Just the opposite. At the time I wasn't quite sure why. Found out soon enough. She asked me up for a drink and since I had nothing better to do, I went. The place was a pigsty. Not that I'm Mr. Spick-and-Span, mind you, but let's just say Gertie would have had a conniption if she walked into that apartment; then slapped Joanie upside the head and forced her down on her hands and knees with a scrub brush and a bucket of soapy water.

A few minutes after we walked in, there was a knock at the door. It was an old German lady from across the hall, who handed over a five-year-old and complained that he'd been a real handful. Joanie reached in her purse and gave the lady a couple of extra bucks. That shut her trap quick. This is my son, Titus, she said. The kid was funny looking but kinda cute the way little kids can be sometimes. And you could tell right off the bat that he was trouble.

Not that you'd know it to look at him, but Joanie said he was a half-breed. A weird thing to say right in front of your own kid. But as I soon learned, Joanie had a real knack for saying the wrong thing. Turns out that, a few years back, she'd lived with this black jazz musician for a while and got herself knocked up. Not long after, the guy booked a gig in Europe and decided to stay there.

Joanie fancied herself a writer, only she didn't do much writing. She was too busy being chummy with writers and artists and parking her shoes under their beds. She was scattered and drank a little too much, partied a little too hard. But at the start, I found her good company. And, as it turns out, I was just the kind of guy she was looking to have on her arm when she went out. Somebody who didn't keep tabs on her and didn't mind if she went off with somebody else. She'd take me to parties and art gallery openings and poetry readings. Introduced me to her arty friends and her beatnik pals. Guys who looked at things as either hip or square. Who called you daddy-o and enjoyed getting zonked.

Personally, I thought they were all trying a little too hard. Particularly the guys who wanted you to know that just because they were artistic didn't mean they were fairies. Their politics might be more to the left than the Commies, but when it came to sex, they wanted to make sure you knew that they slept with chicks and only chicks. And if you still didn't get the message, they threw around words like pansies, fruits, and fairies like it was confetti.

Makes you wonder. What's that thing they say about people who protest too much? Take this artist friend of Joanie's by the name of Rivers. Always hitting on the ladies but one night invited me over to his studio to show me his artwork. And a few other things. But the next time I saw him, it was like he didn't know me. Didn't get my nose out of joint. Wasn't the first time something like that had happened. Wouldn't be the last.

One of Joanie's friends who definitely swung in my direction was this nasty piece of work called O'Hara. Being Irish myself, Blarney boys just don't do it for me. It's too much like getting off on yourself and if that's what I'm in the mood for, I got Mother Machree and her four sisters, thank you very much. Told him so. In a nice way. Didn't stop him from making a real pest of himself. Especially when he was hitting the sauce, which he was pretty much most of the time. Caused a scene one night when he caught me and one of his poet friends getting cozy-like in the men's room at the Cedar Bar. Forgot the poet's name. Not sure I ever asked.

Another reason Joanie wanted me as a friend was that she was always on the lookout for people to pawn her kid off on. Joanie wasn't a bad mom, not really, it's just that Titus crimped her style. I wasn't crazy about the idea of babysitting the brat, at least not at the start. Had no idea what to do with him except maybe feed him hot dogs and beans and park him in front of the TV. But the kid began to grow on me and soon I found myself taking him to the Central Park Zoo, teaching him how to swim in the pool at the Y, ice-skating at Rockefeller Center. I liked holding his little hand in the subway or picking him up in my arms and carrying him up the steps. Sometimes, when Joanie stayed out all night, he'd fall asleep on the couch and I'd wake up and find him curled up at the foot of my bed like a house cat.

Soon not a week went by that I didn't come home from work and find him parked on my front stoop. Joanie had forgotten to feed him or to pick him up from school or she'd gone out for cigarettes in the middle of the day and hadn't come back. What was I gonna do? Leave him out there all alone?

Sure, he got on my nerves. The kid was wired. Just like his mother. But underneath it all, I could see that he was lonely. Takes one to know one, right? He'd look up at me with these big cow eyes and, I mean, c'mon. You'd have to be made of stone. Me and Titus soon became good buddies. And I gotta tell the truth. It felt good to be somebody he could count on. Life is funny that way. I'd never wanted to be a father or even a stepfather, but that's more or less what happened.

MONTY

I was frequently at a loss to understand the persistence of my attraction to Terry. It had to be a character flaw, I reasoned. A failure of will. A weakness that I had nurtured and was allowing to derail me from achieving my goals. Never mind the fact that the only times I experienced the slightest serenity was when I was in Terry's company. Or that the mere sound of his voice lifted me into the ether.

There was always a price to pay whenever I gave in to Terry. Every truce was almost immediately followed by a tortured bout of anger and self-recrimination. Terry once joked that I would have made a good Catholic. He even considered asking his parish priest where he might buy me a hair shirt. He offered to pick a branch of thorns to tie around my waist.

One thing was clear, however. My devotion to Terry would continue to be a barrier to my career advancement. At times it seemed like I was deliberately trying to sabotage myself. And unless I reversed course and burnished my image as the man in the gray flannel suit, only perdition awaited me. According to Terry, I looked and acted the part. Only he didn't mean it as a compliment. While I was no Gregory Peck, who played the eponymous Tom Rath in the film adaptation, I had most of the other qualifications. Intelligent. From good stock. Well-connected. Admired by my peers. And still young enough that the sowing of wild oats was not only sanctioned but applauded. Especially by my already married colleagues who sought to live vicariously through my purported exploits. Nights on the town at the Latin Quarter or the Copa or the Stork Club. Whenever they attempted to goad me for details and I demurred, they pretended to respect my discretion. Good old Monty. Wink-wink.

In continuing to perpetrate this fraud, the women I chose to drape across my arm were largely a variation on a theme, at least the ones with whom I got serious. Socially well-placed (to please the folks). Prepped from an early age to assume the responsibilities of a good corporate wife and mother. A helpmate in propagating the family name, guarding the hearth, and willing to turn a blind eye to any indiscretions.

The engagement to Katie Dunbar was short-lived. She was ready, willing, and able to become Mrs. Montgomery J. Benson. Her folks approved as did mine. My father, the most taciturn of men, went so far as to say that if I didn't marry Katie, he'd divorce his wife of thirty-five years and marry her himself. I tried to set a date. Several times. I was nervous that Katie would slip through my fingers. But she kept stalling. Initially, I thought it was because of our barely competent conjugal fumblings though, in those days, for many women, that was hardly a deal breaker. Social standing and financial solvency usually took precedence over romance and passion.

In Katie's case, however, it proved to be a consideration, she confessed to me years later. She had been prepared to dismiss my lack of ardor, she told me, and even tolerate my taste for men, which she surmised the moment Terry stepped into her office. But she had the good fortune to be rescued from this fate by a recently divorced man on a white horse. Why settle for a rising young star like Monty Benson when she could have Dan Talbot, a debonair senior executive? Dan had even stronger social bona fides and, as she later related, an inimitable bedside manner.

Katie dumped me over dinner at La Côte Basque. Gently, but firmly. I was a good sport about it. And, truth be told, felt somewhat liberated. I even attended her wedding a few months later, which afforded me the opportunity to slather my rival with congratulations. The better man won, I said, shaking his hand and patting his back. For all the good it did me. Dan jumped ship not long after, landing an even more exalted position at Monsanto. Katie and I remained friends and still saw each other for lunch over the next couple of years until she graciously retired to Greenwich and bore Dan three children. In the mid-sixties, he was shot (but not killed) by an aggrieved husband. A suburban scandal torn from a John Cheever short story. Katie filed for divorce, took the kids and most of his money, and decamped to Palm Beach where she hitched her caboose to an elderly titan of industry and amused herself with a succession of golf and tennis pros. We often got together when she came to town. Once she offered to share her latest side man, a dashing, switch-hitting baseball scout. I respectfully declined.

When news got around that Katie had thrown me over, my immediate superior, Allard Middleton, became curiously solicitous. And even a bit empathetic. Turns out, he'd developed an attraction to Katie and had been keeping an eye on her the entire time we were dating, ready to pounce at the first sign of discord. Unfortunately, Dan beat him to the punch. Middleton called me into his office and offered his condolences. Can't win 'em all, Monty my boy, he said, eyes lowered in manly sympathy. For appearances' sake, I pretended to be devastated, and he pretended to feel sorry for me. Told me to take a week off. Go somewhere warm and forget about Katie. Handed me the key to his winter place in Montego Bay. I dutifully kissed his ring and rescheduled all my meetings.

Since my wounds weren't going to lick themselves, I decided to invite Terry along. By now he was living on his own in the black hole of Calcutta on West 10th and working downtown at Chase, having decided that even the off chance of running into me in the lobby was too much to bear. It sent me into a rage, which conveniently masked my relief that he was no longer on the premises, and I didn't have to worry about succumbing to my emotions and dragging him into the men's room on his floor for a make out session. An action completely out of character for me unless, of course, I was in anywhere near Terry's orbit. The pull he had on me was as frightening as it was thrilling.

It had been several months since we'd spoken, and he wasn't exactly elated to hear from me. But given that his resistance was no stronger than mine, he eventually snapped up the free plane ticket I dangled before him. For the next seven days, we enjoyed a celebratory reconciliation in a gated Jamaican villa. The private community's residents and their guests had access to the beach at a nearby hotel, which happened to be closed due to a strike. Since it was also off-season, Terry and I were able to frolic about like naked heathens in paradise.

Back on terra firma, however, I left Terry in the lurch and resumed my ignoble quest for the Good Housekeeping Seal of Approval. On occasion, usually when I was on the road, I would feel strangled by my solitude and seek refuge in anonymity. Men not unlike myself, troubled, solitary, most of them married. They could be found sitting alone at a hotel bar waiting for the alcohol or pills to numb their brains and allow them permission to satisfy their cravings. While Terry thrived on such casual encounters, even found them stimulating, they brought me little pleasure.

I successfully courted several women over the next few years. The one I came closest to marrying was Victoria Harrow, the daughter of one of my mother's closest friends, Bettina Cooper Harrow. The only reason I didn't marry her was because of her brother. And no, it's not what you think.

I was already past the point of marrying late and headed straight for confirmed bachelor territory. The kind of men their friends and colleagues snickered at behind their backs. They were regarded as either deficient or morally questionable because they refused or were simply incapable of stepping up and performing their social obligations: to take a wife and procreate. As they aged, unattached men were no longer glamorous or enviable, but odd men out, regarded with distaste and mild embarrassment.

On the career front, I had gone as far as possible as a solo act. It was time to put away childish things and get hitched. As a married man, I would cut a wider swath. I could drink and cavort to my heart's content, provided that, at the end of the day, I returned home and slept in a conjugal bed.

It was either play the game or be shut out of the clubhouse.

Since I didn't seem to be holding up my end, my mother sprang into action and presented me with a fait accompli. To her credit, Victoria was an ideal choice. She resembled the actress Tuesday Weld down to the purry velveteen voice. She'd recently graduated from Bennington, ran in the right circles, and was not averse to marrying an almost middle-aged man who was already on solid footing. Though her interest in marriage was, if possible, even vaguer than mine, the alternative was worse. Her friends were rapidly pairing up, usually with moneyed schmoes closer to their age. When she looked at me, which was not that often, since she was quite shy, I saw admiration in her eyes. But more than that, I saw relief. The choice had been made for her and she didn't have to worry her pretty little towheaded head about it any longer. She would have a husband and security. In turn, she would provide him with one or, at most, two children, preferably a boy and a girl. Each attended to by an au pair. She would function as hostess to the other corporate wives and flatter, but not flirt with, their husbands. She would summer at the Cape and winter in the Caribbean. She would insist on separate bedrooms and make herself available for occasional visits, provided she received advance notice before she took her sleeping pill. What hubby did the rest of the time was his affair, so long it never reached her ears or, more importantly, the ears of her friends and family.

Such arrangements were quite common, especially in my circle. Men and women rarely married for love. (At least not the first marriage.) Or even compatibility. They married because they fit together. Had a common background, education, street address. Sometimes, as in the case of my parents, things worked out. My folks respected one another. Were companionable. She deferred to his judgment, rarely asked questions. She had her own life, was active in her philanthropic pursuits and had her own walker. An Austrian count, who was always available for dinner or as a proxy theater date. My father may have had other women, or perhaps the occasional prostitute, but his main outside interest was bridge. He played competitively. For high stakes. Usually lost.

For all her diffidence, Victoria Harrow kissed like a dream (she had practiced with her college chums, she confessed), which had the peculiar advantage of arousing me. Though she was not prepared to fulfill her marital obligations until after the ceremony, she occasionally lent a hand when the issue arose.

Victoria was the eldest of three children who had arrived in two-year intervals. Her twenty-year-old sister, Luisa, was afflicted with what at the time was called Mongoloidism and resided on the shores of Lake Saranac in one of the Harrow's country homes, under the care of Bettina's twin spinster cousins. The family rarely uttered Luisa's name and visited her exactly once a year.

Theodore (Teddy) Harrow was the baby of the family. He bore a striking resemblance to Victoria and, like her, was taciturn and a bit of a hothouse flower. Brother and sister were devoted to one another, unhealthily so, although not in an incestuous way. They could frequently be found in corners whispering.

Shortly after our engagement, I attended Teddy's eighteenth birthday party. When we were introduced, he looked at me the same way Victoria did, which I found unsettling. Victoria sometimes asked him along on our dates, probably to keep make-out/hand-action opportunities to a minimum. I did most of the talking, and they would stare up at me, all smiles and approving nods. Every so often though, I'd catch them in a conspiratorial side glance, a gesture that would probably fill an entire page in their diaries. Yes, they kept diaries. Read them to one another. No secrets between them, they said.

Well, maybe one. At two a.m. one morning, my phone rang. It was Teddy. He was calling from a police station in midtown. He apologized for waking me but said he didn't know who else to call. He didn't want to upset Victoria and would rather rot in a holding cell than reach out to his parents. Teddy had been arrested in the raid of a subway restroom. The image of Teddy on his knees amidst the dirt and stench of a public toilet seemed entirely at odds with his delicate nature, but there you are. I bailed him out and later called in a favor from an old schoolmate who worked in city government to have Teddy's record expunged. I've no idea if he shared the incident with Victoria, but I'm certain his parents never caught wise. Or perhaps they were in denial. Which is pretty much the same thing.

The arrest changed him, perhaps deranged him. I extended myself in every way possible, inviting him out for weekend jaunts. A movie. A museum. A bike ride in the park. I had no ulterior motive. Legally he might be an adult, with the attendant yearnings. Otherwise, he was a frail, sad boy with few friends and fewer social graces. I wish I'd been able to console him, but that would have required a healthier outlook on my own desires.

In the fall, he set off for Penn, his father's alma mater. In mid-November, he tried to commit suicide by hanging himself from the rafters in a barn a few miles from the school. The farmer's son cut him down, which I found suspicious, though I never shared my thoughts with anyone except Terry and that was years later. The following spring, he almost drowned and this time I'm almost certain it was because he'd been rejected (or humiliated) by one of his peers.

I expected the Harrows to be crushed by their son's behavior, but they were too busy keeping their upper lips stiff. I suggested to Victoria that they get him professional help, but, like my parents, the Harrows didn't believe in psychiatry. In his second year, Teddy dropped out of school and sank into a deep depression. The only person he spoke to was Victoria, who rarely left his side.

A few months on, Bettina invited me to tea. She told me that Teddy was in a sanitarium. A nervous breakdown. Once he was released, she said, he would be relocated to the family compound at Lake Saranac in a cottage adjacent to his sister, Luisa. Victoria would be joining him as a full-time companion. Under the circumstances, she said, I was free of my betrothal obligations. I offered to wait for Victoria, but she said it would not be necessary. Family first, you see, she told me.

I never saw Victoria (or Teddy) again but did run into the Harrows from time to time. They continued to socialize and dutifully occupy their season seats at the Met and the Philharmonic. They made a sizable donation to the new Lincoln Center complex in Teddy's name. Even in midsummer, whenever I passed by his name, I got the chills.

The moment Bettina cast me off (liberated me?), I went racing back to Terry. I rang his doorbell early one evening. He looked out the window and saw me and just shook his head. I could hardly blame him. Instead of ringing me up, he said he would be right down. When he opened the door, he looked as if I'd just gotten him out of bed. Which I probably had. I don't know why that surprised me. Maybe because, whenever we were apart, I preferred to imagine that Terry lived in a state of suspended animation. Quite the contrary, he was busy carving out a life of his own. Making scads of friends and helping to raise this odd boy, Titus, for whom he'd developed a kind of paternal-fraternal affection. I'd spent some time with them during our thaw-outs, and I quite enjoyed watching them bicker like a real father and son. Titus's reaction to me was complex, even a bit unsettling. When we first met, he seemed to admire me and was always asking to take my photo. Flattering ones at that. But then, after I'd been absent from Terry's life for a while or we'd had one of our frequent blowouts, he began to regard me with disdain. He once asked me why I insisted on behaving like such a shit. I told him I wished I had a good answer for that.

Out of the mouths of babes.

Now's not a good time, Terry said, stone-faced when he came to the door. No hello. No good to see you. But I suppose I had it coming. I told him I missed him and was prepared to grovel even more than usual. Said I'd booked us a night at the Plaza. I don't think so, he told me. Nonetheless, I said I'd wait for him there in case he changed his mind, and he shut the door.

Since our twisted little tango requires more than one participant, several hours later Terry phoned from the Plaza lobby. When he entered the room, I scooped him up in my arms. Being the great empath that he is, Terry indulged my tale of woe and expressed sympathy for people he'd never even met. When I was finished, we stood there in the middle of the floor for what seemed like an eternity just inhaling each other.

I slept soundly that night. No need for sedation for the first time in months. Over breakfast the following morning, Terry said that he'd been anticipating my eventual return. In the interim, he'd come to an important decision. He wanted me out of his life for good. It killed him, he said, because he still loved me and always would, but the cord had to be severed. Once and for all. Before we suffocated each other. I thought my heart would burst through my chest, but my pleading did not sway him. My tears had no salutary effect.

PART FOUR

TERRY

I had to end it with Monty. I just had to. The only way to keep from losing my mind was to kill him off again. To pretend that he was dead and not alive and well just a few miles north. Don't get me wrong. I think being in love is aces. But not this way. The only way to love Monty without hating him was to bury him. A tough decision. And it cost me. Cost me big time.

I'm not saying that what I done was directly responsible for what happened not long after. But it wasn't no coincidence either. One day, after work, I was standing on the subway platform on Chambers Street waiting for the 7th Avenue Express. It was a nice spring day and normally when the weather was good, I walked home. A good way to shake off the workday, clear my head. Usually, I took Church Street/6th Avenue and then cut across Bleecker to my place. On the way, maybe pick up a loaf of Italian bread at Zito's. Fresh out of the oven. Smelled so good that I'd wolf down half of it before I walked in the front door.

That day though, I was feeling off my stride, like I was coming down with something. So I decided to hop the subway, which stopped only a couple of blocks from my place. Then once I got home, I'd pop a couple of Bayer aspirins, get into bed, and sleep it off. It was rush hour. The station was packed, and you know how it can be. When you need the train to come it never does. Felt like forever. The air was heavy, and I remember I was having trouble breathing. Then I don't know what happened. I must have passed out 'cause the next thing I knew, I was in a hospital bed hooked up to a machine thinking, No, this can't be right. I must be having a bad dream.

But it was no dream. The doctor told me I'd had an episode — fancy way of saying I had a heart attack without actually using those words. He said I didn't seem to be in any danger but all the same, he wanted to do some tests, so he was keeping me for a couple of days. I told him, go ahead doc, knock yourself out. But I'm pretty sure I know what's wrong. Oh? He said, his eyes half closed, upper lip curled. As if to say, I did all those years of med school and you're going to tell me what's wrong with you? No disrespect, doc, I said, but my old man's been having these kinds of palpitations since he was a teenager. Anyway, he ran the tests and it turns out I was right. Same thing as my da, an irregular heartbeat. The doctor wrote me a scrip. Said as long as I took the pills, I'd live to a ripe, old age. I said, Heck doc, I feel ninety right now. He laughed and told me not to worry. With the medication and some rest, I'd be back on my feet real soon.

No sooner did the doctor leave the room than who comes traipsing in but Titus holding this enormous bunch of flowers. He was about fourteen then, and already on his way to becoming a real looker. Strange, because as a kid none of the pieces seemed to fit together, what with the permanent tan, the frizzy blond hair, the big lips, and small nose. Then, just around the time he started high school, it all changed. He shot up and his looks came together. People started to notice to the point that they followed him around and told him what a beauty he was. Not that it turned his head. As far as Titus was concerned, he was still that funny-looking kid nobody had time for.

As soon as he walked into the hospital room, I could tell something was up. He was hiding behind the flowers to keep me from getting a good look at him. Uh-oh, I thought. Hope he hasn't gotten into any mischief. Not that he had a habit of getting in trouble. At least not yet. Real casual I asked him, How are things at home? Didn't answer the question. Just looked up at the ceiling, which I took as a bad sign.

Then he said something that really took me off guard. You're not going to die on me, are you? Nah, I said. Healthy as a horse. With a slight ticker problem. Nothing that pills can't handle. Why do you ask?

As I'm saying this I'm thinking, Oh geez, what's Joanie been up to now? Lately, she'd been hitting the bottle extra heavy and, as if that wasn't bad enough, started doing drugs. The hard stuff. Which made her mean and nasty in a way she wasn't before. All her writer/artist friends had dumped her, and I would have too if it hadn't been for Titus, who needed a place to crash whenever she got high and started wailing on him. By now, he was sleeping at my place three, four times a week. I was feeding him, helping him with his homework. (Yeah, me the genius.) It crimped my social life, but what was I gonna do?

To make things worse, the kid's father was back in the picture and making a nuisance of himself. Trying to be the dad he never was. Threatening to take Titus away from his mother. Can't say I blamed him. But he didn't get that Titus was all Joanie had left and she was never going to cut him loose. Another thing that made the dad sore was that, a couple years back, Titus told Joanie he liked boys. As if me and her didn't already know that. Even when he was just a kid, before he knew which end was up, you got the sense. Nothing obvious, but still. Then, the first time he met Monty I caught him staring with his mouth open. The way some guys look at Anita Ekberg. He'd find any excuse to sit on Monty's lap which was a hoot, since Monty was not exactly what you'd call the paternal, or even the big brother, type. The look of shock on Monty's face when Titus excitedly wrapped his arms around Monty's neck was priceless. Then Monty's eyes would travel over to me as if to say, Do something. Relax, I said. The kid's just a little sweet on you. He'll get over it. Like I was one to talk.

The kid's father decided to blame me for how his son was, like I was some kind of Army recruiter. Joanie told him he had one hell of a nerve criticizing me or her for how the kid turned out. For her part, she was tickled pink, because now she didn't have to worry about some girl taking her precious son away. Typical Joanie. Always looking out for number one.

I'm not saying she didn't love Titus, just that sometimes she had a funny way of showing it. Take for instance when the kid was about seven or eight and one of her painter friends gave Joanie a copy of this photo book, *The Americans*, by a guy named Robert Frank. Titus wore out the pages, studying the book cover-to-cover like it was the Bible. He begged his mother to buy him a camera and, to shut him up, that Christmas she gave him a Polaroid. The minute he got his hands on it, he hit the streets and took pictures of everything in sight. Joanie was glad. Not because he had a hobby, but because it got him out of her hair. The next year, for his birthday, I bought him a used Nikon I'd picked up in a pawn shop for next to nothing. He spent every nickel of his allowance on film and developing materials. Turned out, the kid had an eye. And it wasn't just me who thought so. Monty encouraged him too. Said he had a natural talent and he should maybe think about studying photography someday. But Joanie wasn't having it. Told the kid his pictures stunk and that he should concentrate on getting his grades up instead of wasting his time and her money. Eventually, she ragged on him so much, he gave it up, which was a damned shame.

Okay, I told Titus, now get those flowers out of your face and tell me what's wrong. His mouth got all tight and he wouldn't look me in the eye. What, you afraid you're going to give me another heart episode? I mean, how bad could it be? Still couldn't get him to spill. His eyes just started filling up. Little by little, he told me what happened. Halfway through I felt a little tightness, and it took all my strength to pretend otherwise.

The news was much worse than I could have imagined. A few days back, his father dropped by and, when he saw all the empty liquor bottles said, That's it, Joanie. I'm taking you to court for custody. As you can imagine, that went over like a lead balloon. Anyway, they started arguing. Push came to shove. Only this time, the shove happened at the top of the stairs. The father lost his balance and ended up with a broken neck at the bottom. The police showed up. They found the body and the drugs and now Joanie was in the Women's House of Detention right next door to the Jefferson Market. Screaming her head off because she needed a fix.

I thought my heart was going to explode, but I sucked it up. The last thing the kid needed was me losing it. You need my help? I asked him. Anything. Titus told me not to worry. It was being handled. What do you mean, handled? Uncle Jimmy's on it, he said. Jimmy wasn't really his uncle. He was this big-shot writer friend of Joanie's. We'd gone out drinking with him a few times when he lived over on Horatio Street. A real good egg. One of the few people who was like me and didn't care if the whole world knew it. Which took balls. His situation was tough enough because he was black. And blacks don't like our kind anymore than anybody else. The guy had moxie, gotta give him that.

I guess he felt responsible for the kid in some way on account of he'd introduced Joanie to Titus's dad. They'd grown up together in Harlem and hung out in Europe, where Jimmy lived for a while, which is kind of funny when you think about how the father carried on about Titus liking boys.

Titus said Jimmy had given him some money and asked him if he had someplace safe to stay. He needed to lay low for a while in case social services came looking for him. I gave him the key to my place but only on one condition: He had to stay inside until I was released. Then I'd talk to Jimmy myself and we'd figure out what to do next. He wasn't happy about being cooped up, but he also knew he had no choice. Poor kid. That Joanie really screwed the pooch this time.

Jimmy hooked Joanie up with a big-shot lawyer friend of his. Once she finished detox, the lawyer talked her into copping a plea: involuntary manslaughter, drug possession, and intent to sell drugs. I didn't know Joanie had been dealing to pay for her habit, though when I found out, it made perfect sense. Classic Joanie, she didn't make it easy on the lawyer. Only agreed to take the rap if she got the temporary guardianship arrangement she wanted.

That temporary guardian would be her ex-boyfriend, she said. Titus already lived with him part-time. Three guesses as to who this ex-boyfriend was. That's right. Yours truly. Of course, I knew why she said I was her ex. Wouldn't have worked otherwise. Not that she asked my permission or that I volunteered. But what kind of selfish bastard would have refused? Nobody else wanted Titus. Not Joanie's family in Wisconsin (because he was half black) or his dad's mother who already had one foot in the grave. And I was damned if I was going to watch him get shipped off to some home, where God knows what would happen to him. At least with me, he had a place to sleep, three squares, and would be able to finish high school and maybe, if he improved his grades, get into City College. Also, with me, nobody would get down on him for being who he was.

Most of the time, me and Titus got along fine. Except when he didn't get his way. Which I guess made him no different than any other teenager. Hey, at his age, I caused my folks more than their share of grief. But I mostly let his crabbing roll off my back. The kid was already messed up enough as it was without me making a federal case out of every little thing.

Being a permanent babysitter and the aftereffects of my little heart problem put even more of a crimp in my social life. I still got together for "dinner" with a couple of my regulars. And sometimes, on a weekend trip to the market, I managed to score myself a quickie. Not as many in the old days, but that was okay too. No gripes.

The only thing missing in my life was Monty. And no pill was ever going to make that an easy swallow.

Years later, younger guys would ask me if I'd been at Stonewall. Like it was Woodstock for queers, even though there was nothing peace or love about it. I told 'em, Yeah, I was there. And they was all impressed, like I was some big hero. Which I don't think they would have thought if they knew the real story.

On the first night of the troubles, as soon as I heard about the commotion, I jumped into my clothes and hightailed it down to Sheridan Square. I had this sinking feeling that Titus was there and if I didn't act quick, I'd wind up having to bail him out of the clink. For the past few months, he'd been carrying on with this longhair hippie-dippy named Winston, who put all these ideas in his head. I'm not saying that Winston was wrong about standing up for himself. But for all his smarts, Titus could be naive about certain things. It was all part of what made him such a sweetheart and why I could never stay mad at him for long.

The minute I hit Sheridan Square, I saw rocks and bottles flying, punches thrown, police whacking heads. And who do I see yelling up at this big bruiser of a cop? That's right. All five-feet-eight inches and 120 pounds of him. Somehow, I managed to wedge my way through the crowd and dragged him out by the collar, kicking and screaming the whole way. Cussed me but good. I didn't care. My job was to keep him safe. If he didn't like it, well that was just too damned bad. You know your life has taken a strange turn the day you find yourself saying things like, My house, my rules. Sends chills up your spine.

Next night, he told me he was going to bed and snuck down the fire escape. Nice try, buster. I followed him and hauled him back home. Boy, was he sore. Even took a swing at me. I pinned him against a wall and scared him but good. I said, You know Titus, sometimes you act just like your mother. That shut him up but good.

By then, Titus and Joanie were seriously on the outs. Since she got sent up to Bedford Hills, every couple of weeks, me and him would pay her a visit. I wish I could say that being off drugs made her less of a pain in the ass. I wasn't surprised that she'd have a hard time of it. Locked up with riff-raff and not being able to do and say as she pleased. But what really got under my skin was that she took it out on Titus, who, after all that had happened, still cared about her.

On the ride up, I'd try to prep him. Don't let her get a rise out of you, I'd say. And, for the most part, he didn't. Thing is, if she couldn't mess with him, she'd start in on me. Accusing me of things like diddling her son and saying that she'd been out of her mind making me his guardian. I'd just sit there and let her mouth off. But Titus started yelling. Told her she'd crossed the line. You can sound off on me all you like, he said, but I won't let you talk that way to Terry, you fucking drug whore. To which she said . . .

Long story short, the guards had to pull them apart.

After that, he refused to visit her. Not for love or money. Joanie, being who she was, started writing him letters. Pages and pages of batshit crazy stuff. Which I read after he threw them in the garbage unopened. He was through with her, he told me. And I should respect that. Just like he respected me for sticking to my guns about a certain somebody whose name he wasn't even allowed to mention.

On the second night of the riots, after we got home, we both felt kinda bad about how we'd behaved. We hugged and made up, and pretty soon life went back to normal. We even bonded big time when we watched the moon landing together. Him with his head on my shoulder, weeping because he couldn't believe he was seeing what he was seeing. And I was crying too, thinking how great it was to be able to share this moment with Titus. And even though I wished Monty was with us, it was some consolation.

Speaking of Woodstock, I didn't have to wait long before Titus pulled another one of his dumb stunts. He informed me that he and Winston were gonna hitchhike to some concert upstate for the weekend. And I said, I don't think so, buddy. I should have been suspicious when he didn't put up an argument. By the time Friday rolled around, I'd completely forgotten about the concert which, I guess, is what he was counting on. When I got home, he wasn't there and I figured he was staying over at Winston's. Wouldn't be the first time. Besides, he'd be eighteen on his next birthday and, legally, I wouldn't be able to put salt on his tail anymore.

The next morning, when he still hadn't materialized, I realized what a total dope I'd been. I tried not to worry too much. After all, he was with Winston and maybe other guys too. Safety in numbers, right? Then, Sunday afternoon, the phone rang. Collect call. From a phone booth upstate. It was Titus screaming about what a shithead Winston was and how he'd ditched him for another guy and he hadn't eaten in two days and had no money to get home.

Where are you? I asked. Sit tight, I'm coming to get you.

Since I didn't drive and didn't even have a license, I racked my brain thinking who might have transportation. The only person who came to mind was my friend Donald who'd just moved to Brooklyn. We'd known each other for a few years by then. We had a lot in common, both of us suffering from the same problem. Being in love with a guy who loved us back, but for some reason kept cutting out on us.

I took the subway and met him at the 96th Street station in Brooklyn. We drove up in his new boyfriend's delivery van and by the time we reached Titus, it was after midnight. Kid was such a wreck, I didn't have the heart to ream him out. Just gave him a whack on the head and a provolone sandwich. He was asleep on my shoulder before we hit the thruway.

By the end of the sixties, between my heart problem, being a full-time dad and shutting the door on Monty for good, my life was all upside down. Then 1970 rolled in and things started to right themselves up again. Titus was about to start his first semester at City. He didn't really want to go, but since the alternative was getting his ass shot off in Vietnam, he took it on the chin. Titus was smart if not book smart. More the artistic type, and lately he'd tried his hand at writing, painting, even a little acting. Couldn't get him to go back to photography, though. It became such a sore spot that I stopped bringing it up.

In February of that year, a new person came into our life. Remember how I told you my friend Donald was in love with this guy who did him dirt? Well, the guy's name was George. Married fella. With kids. George pulled more crap on Donald than Monty could ever dream of, including pulling up stakes and moving down South. Donald went to pieces for a while. Then along came a new guy who made him forget all about George. Which only goes to show, life can turn around on a dime.

Anyhow, it was February and freezing cold. I was hanging out with two of Donald's former next-door neighbors, Kyle and Lester, the two Midwestern guys I told you about who liked to play secret dress-up on weekends. Titus was one of the first people who noticed them. Even took pictures when he thought they weren't looking. Really good pictures too.

That morning, I'd run into them at Balducci's and they asked me over for coffee. And gossip, though they were too shy to admit it. They were curious to hear about Donald and his new fella. We talked about George too, and what a schnook he'd been, and they told me how they used to hear them fighting through the walls. After which, they'd kiss and make up, which they could also hear through the walls. As I was putting on my coat to leave, I happened to look out the window. I said, Holy Toledo! Speak of the devil. Standing across the street looking up at Donald's window was none other than George himself. In the flesh. I'd only met him once, the time he found me in bed with Donald and gave me a shiner. So, just to make sure, I asked Kyle and Lester to take a look. Yup, they said, that's him. Handsome son of a bitch. What's he doing? I asked. Oh, that was his routine, they said. He'd stand outside looking up at Donald's window waiting for him to notice and wave him inside. What, he never heard of a doorbell?

It was freezing out there and even though I hated to be the bearer of bad news, I could hardly let the poor bastard catch his death. So I walked up to him and said, You know, George, he doesn't live there anymore. And he said, How do you know my name? And how do you know who I'm waiting for? Oh, I know your name, all right. And you're waiting on Donald. Am I right or am I right? How could you possibly know that? he said. And I explained that we'd met before the night he punched my lights out when he caught me making nice with Donald.

He pretended he had no idea what I was talking about, but I knew he did. Something happened to Donald? he asked. Damned right something happened, I said. Donald found somebody else. Somebody's who's good to him. And if you try to mess it up, this time I'll punch *your* lights out.

George dropped back like he'd just taken a bullet to the chest and I apologized for acting like a smart ass. Come on, I said. Let's go to my place. I'll fix you a drink and we'll talk about it. I picked up one of his suitcases and he followed behind me, like somebody with lead in his shoes.

George was nothing like Monty, except they were both the type who hold in their feelings and let it eat them up alive. We talked for hours. He told me how he'd had finally gotten up the nerve to leave his wife and kids for Donald and now he'd missed his chance. I felt so sorry for him that I even offered to put in a call to Donald and tell him he was back in town. But he said no. He'd put Donald through enough. He didn't want to upset him anymore. Besides, he was the one who'd fucked up and he was the one who'd have to pay the piper.

I told him, If it makes you feel any better, I'm pretty much in the same boat as you. I kicked out somebody I was crazy about, and for all I know he's gotten married and settled down in the years since we last spoke. George asked, Do you think he's forgotten about you? Oh no. Doesn't work that way, I said. Monty hasn't forgotten about me any more than Donald forgot about him.

Poor George. He was so pitiful. What are you going to do now? I asked him. I don't know, he said. I don't know. He looked so lost that I offered to let him stay the night. He'd have to share my bed, I told him, but not in that way. He said Yeah, that would be nice. I don't really want to be alone tonight. He said it in such a way that I thought he might do something stupid. He'd hardly be the first guy I knew to swallow a handful of pills when things with a beau went south.

George turned out to be a pretty stand-up guy. Even Titus eventually thought so, though the selfish little prick resented having him around at first. One night turned into a few days and then, a few weeks. He kept talking about finding his own place as soon as he got a new job. But even after he signed on with this big deal architecture firm, he didn't look for a place of his own. He was miserable and, seeing that I was miserable too and for pretty much the same reason, we made good company. Somehow, we worked it out, the three of us. He and Titus became friends in a way that me and Titus never could. Titus saw me more like a parent. But George was like a favorite uncle.

That June, I let Titus drag me to something called a Pride March. The first one ever. He asked George too, but we both knew that wasn't going to happen. George was the original Mr. Uptight. Made Monty look loosey-goosey. Truth be told, I really didn't want to go. But Titus was all excited. I worried that the cops might show up. Or bashers. New York was already on the downslide. Not as bad as it became, but not like the good old days when you didn't have to worry about getting mugged — or worse — if you walked down the wrong block.

Of course, Titus accused me of being overprotective again. And I said, Yeah, yeah. Just shut up and get dressed. When he came out, I said, That's what you're wearing? You're not leaving much to the imagination. He accused me of being an old fart. I laughed and gave him a little whack across the head and off we went.

I don't know what I was expecting. Starting out in the Village, there were maybe a few dozen people, maybe a hundred tops. But, as we made our way uptown, people started coming out of the woodwork. From every nook and cranny in the tristate area. And maybe beyond. By the time we reached Central Park, there were thousands of us. Flamers and straight arrows. Dykes and femmes. Enough people to fill every bar in town ten times over. Some of them hooting and hollering and carrying on, others more serious. War protestors. Civil rights marchers. I recognized some of the faces in the crowd from my past — a couple even from my present. A few said hello. Others ignored me. Takes all kinds.

At some point along the route, Titus took my hand. Something he hadn't done since he was a kid. Felt kind of funny because I didn't want people getting the wrong idea. At around 35th Street we ran into this woman with a sign that said "I Love My Gay Son" and Titus screamed out, I love my gay daddy. What the hell did you say that for? And he said, Chill out. What, are you afraid they'll think you're a chicken hawk? And then he explained to me what a chicken hawk was, and I said, Yeah, exactly. But I wasn't mad, not really. Actually, I felt kinda flattered that he thought of me like his dad. Meant I'd done something right in my life.

In the park, we talked to a lot of different people, all shapes and sizes, old and young, wackos and straight arrows. Like some gigantic crazy quilt in which for some odd reason, the pieces all seem to fit. I gotta say that, a few times, I got a lump in my throat. Never thought I'd live to see anything like this. I'd always assumed things were going to stay the same forever. Shows you how much I know.

A few times I said to Titus, Are you sure you don't want to go off and hang out with guys more your own age? No, he says. I have plenty of time for that. Today is for me and you. Then he gave me this big hug and I lost my cool. Do you have to be such a weepy, old queen? he said. It's embarrassing. Which made me laugh.

At around five-thirty, Titus said we needed to get back. He had plans for the evening and, anyway, he was getting hungry. As we were coming out of the park, I saw this guy across the street leaning against a corner lamppost. He looked kind of familiar, I thought. But then, I said, Nah. You need to get your eyes checked, Terry.

Just at that moment, Titus screamed, Monty! and ran across the street and almost got run over by a taxi.

MONTY

After an eighteen-month dead-end engagement to Victoria Harrow, my parents were suitably chastened. Thereafter, my mother made no further attempts to prod me down the aisle. Not only had her best-laid plan backfired — she now had a more serious concern.

After Terry closed the door on me, I fell into a dark pit. I started showing up at church Sunday mornings looking disheveled, as if I hadn't slept in days. Which I usually hadn't. Over dinner, if my parents asked me a question, I would either reply in monosyllables or break off my response mid-sentence and stare into space. At work, I was late for appointments and once completely forgot about a morning business flight to Denver until I was awoken from a dead sleep by my secretary in the middle of the afternoon.

My parents assumed that I was grieving the dissolution of my engagement to Victoria, though I was actually relieved. I felt bad for Victoria. And her brother. But I also felt liberated from my commitment. And the pretense. My search for respectability had finally reached a dead end. Unfortunately, so had my relationship with Terry, whom I'd finally pushed over the limit. Since we'd had plenty of arguments before, initially I thought that eventually he'd cave. All I had to do was wait and, when he resurfaced, eat another helping of humble pie. I gave him a few weeks to stew before picking up the phone. When he answered, he calmly told me never to call again and hung up. Said the same thing the next time I phoned. And the next. After that, at the sound of my voice or even my breathing, he replaced the receiver in its cradle. This time I'd lost him for good, I feared. And that's when I really came unglued.

Again, Mother decided to come to my rescue. You should see someone, she said. By someone, she didn't mean a therapist. At least, not your typical licensed practitioner. No, Mother had a better idea. A radical one, as it turned out.

Dr. Mila Ostrov (aka Princess Ostrov), was a Russian noble émigré and an accredited hypnotherapist. For the past several years, she had treated several of Mother's society friends, apparently with startling results. I could see why hypnotherapy would appeal to her. She believed that most problems — alcoholism, gambling, unmentionable sexual kinks — were issues of mind over matter. That with the help of suggestion and reinforcement, they could be overcome. A pick-yourself-up-by-the-bootstraps cure — at sixty dollars an hour.

Hypnotherapy was one of those fads the rich pick up and eventually discard. That Dr. Ostrov was descended from nobility was definitely a point in her favor, and mother reeled off a list of her well-heeled patients, several of them close family friends. Without asking, she booked me an appointment, which I only learned about the day of from my secretary. Normally, I would have put up a stink. But I was in such disarray that I simply didn't have the energy to resist. Better to humor Mother as I had with Victoria Harrow. Then I could tell her what a charlatan her doctor/princess had turned out to be.

I ended up seeing Dr. Ostrov twice a week for the next three years. I ended our sessions after my friend Barbara steered me to a proper therapist. Only then did I grasp that what I'd gotten from Dr. Ostrov wasn't actual therapy so much as an objective ear. With her encouragement, I finally began to untangle my knotted life.

Being under hypnosis was different from what I expected. Not at all like those performers who convince people to quack like ducks or hop around on one knee. The experience was akin to sitting across a room and watching someone else be interrogated. Dr. Ostrov enabled me to establish distance from myself. She was the first person to whom I admitted being homosexual. I had never even uttered the word before. And certainly not in reference to myself. Yet this closely guarded secret emerged rather effortlessly while I was under. And remarkably, afterward, I felt not the slightest embarrassment or remorse.

For me, the word *homosexual* was significant. I wasn't a pansy. A fairy. A fruit. All terms that diminished and abased my affectional feelings. It was a characteristic. An immutable one at that. Like being six feet tall. It had taken me years, decades even, to arrive at this conclusion. Any desire to be otherwise was as futile as wanting to be shorter or taller. I was six feet tall. I was homosexual.

The first question Dr. Ostrov asked when I returned to full consciousness was if my homosexuality was something I wanted to change. If so, she could refer me to a therapist who specialized in altering sexual orientation. (She called it sexual preference, but still.) I surprised myself again when I said no. For one good reason. Because if I wasn't homosexual, I couldn't love Terry. I might not be six feet tall for the rest of my life, but my feelings for Terry would never diminish. Of that much, I was certain.

And another first. I didn't feel bad or strange about it. Or guilty. Or ashamed. It was a hard, cold fact.

Dr. Ostrov said she respected my decision. I can't tell you what an affirmation hearing the words *I respect your decision* had on me. Then she asked if there was anything else she could do for me. I thought for a moment and said, Yes, there is. You can help me adjust to the reality that I've lost Terry for good. I don't want to stop loving him because that would be impossible. And even if it were possible, I wouldn't want to. I just want to be able to love him and at the same time accept that we can't be together. I just want it to stop hurting so damn much.

Dr. Ostrov said, Fine, that's what we'll work on then. To this day, I'm thankful she was so non-judgmental, especially since at the time, homosexuality was still officially classified as a mental aberration. While Dr. Ostrov never encouraged my orientation, neither did she condemn it. Her sole aim, she said, was to help me cope with the anxiety of having alienated Terry and the attendant anxiety I felt for having instigated it. While my feelings for Terry would never go away, she could help me build a moat around them. Which would enable me to get back to being Good Old Monty.

The key to achieving my objective was convincing myself that Terry was also in the process of trying to move on with his life. Only later would I discover that, far from putting me out of his mind, Terry kept tabs on me. He sometimes left work early, headed uptown and positioned himself under a doorway in view of my office building waiting for me to emerge. To catch a glimpse of me, to see that I was okay.

I too spied on him, but in a more proactive way. Every so often, I would "accidentally" run into Titus as he was leaving school. I don't think he was fooled for a minute, but he seemed to take perverse enjoyment in our chance meetings. When we first met, Titus said, he had idealized me. Probably not me personally but rather the kind of man he thought I represented. Successful. Well-bred. Well-heeled. He later confessed that I had been the first man who aroused him — involuntarily, of course. A few years back, when the three of us drove down to Miami together, and I emerged from the swimming pool soaking wet, he felt a stirring, he said, and for the first time was able to connect it to his inner self.

His attraction had curdled because of the way I had treated Terry, of whom he was fiercely protective, and initially he had blamed Terry for alienating me. Whenever I invited him for a bite over at the Pink Tea Cup or the Cedar, he would start off by saying that any questions about Terry were strictly off-limits. To which I agreed, if he promised not to tell Terry that he'd seen me. It was a game. But a harmless one, I reasoned.

My motivation, however, was not so innocent. I was hoping to ingratiate myself with Titus, rekindle his admiration. Then, perhaps, I could enlist him to chip away at Terry's resolve. I never asked him to do so outright. Mostly, I just let him ramble on about his life, and in the process indirectly glean some insight into Terry's. He told me about his father's death, his mother's conviction. About Terry being made his guardian. He also talked about school, the latest guy he was mooning over, and a spate of other predictable teen crises. I pretended to hang on his every word. Which is not to say that I was indifferent or that he was boring. He was far too neurotic and high-strung to be dull. And magnetic. And beautiful in his unique way. Scarred by an erratic and lonely childhood, he was coping as best he could and I admired his pluck. He was a mess, but young enough that he might right himself in the end.

Titus referred to himself as *gay*, a term that had recently come into fashion. Homosexuality, he said, was too clinical. *Gay* sounded more like a real, living, breathing, sexually active young man. Which he already was and had been since age thirteen, he confessed.

Taking a cue from Dr. Ostrov, I asked him how he felt about that. The same way he felt about everything in his life, he said. Conflicted. Uncertain about whether it was a bad thing or a good thing. At the same time, he had no desire to change. Lucky Titus for having come to that conclusion decades before I had.

I never did ask him directly about Terry, but during our little tête-à-tétes he dribbled out some information. I'm not sure whether he did it to soothe or irritate me. Perhaps a little of both, given that he was a bit of an imp. In the midst of one of his many tales of the trials and tribulations of the hormonally addled teenager, he casually (?) mentioned Terry's heart episode. Probably just to watch me fall off my chair. Then, he quickly added, Oh don't worry. Terry's okay. He's on medication. As if that would palliate my fears.

Terry. Heart episode. I didn't sleep for several nights.

I made it a point to give Titus my home and office number and told him to call anytime, for any reason. Which I later regretted. Thereafter, he would call and bend my ear anytime he felt the need. Fortunately, by then I had grown quite fond of him. And, just as important, he kept me tethered to Terry.

During one of our conversations, Titus told me how he'd gotten into a snit about Terry dragging him away from the Stonewall riots, which I'd read about, as had half of New York, apparently. The first time an incident of that nature made the headlines. Can you believe those powder puffs attacking the police? my colleagues remarked. The nerve. Though the comments were predictably disparaging, I noticed that the tone had shifted. Perhaps a begrudging respect for them having come out of the shadows, shaken off their shame, and fought back?

Like the moon landing. One small step.

The timing of Stonewall was critical. By the late sixties, the hangover from the McCarthy era had pretty much passed and anti-government resistance was in vogue. And not just because of the Vietnam War and the continuing battle for civil rights. It was a reaction to decades of enforced normalcy. Of white picket fences and idealized nuclear families. Assumptions about once verboten behavior were being challenged. Upended, even.

Not long after, Titus phoned me with a new complaint. Some Gloomy

Gus named George was squatting with them and getting on his nerves. Didn't take a genius to figure out that if Titus was sleeping on the couch, the only other place this George fellow could rest his weary bones was beside Terry. Though it killed me, I didn't ask about the interloper. Instead, I allowed my imagination to run wild, and assumed that Terry had redirected his affecttions. A conclusion that ate at me. Literally. Until my family physician informed me that I was courting an ulcer. Fine, I thought. Terry with a heart problem. Me with an ulcer.

What happened next was yet another quirk of fate. On the day of the Pride parade, which naturally I did not attend, I was curious enough about the throngs invading Central Park that I decided to take a stroll along the park's periphery. At a safe distance, of course. Outside of Terry and a few of his friends, I didn't know any homosexuals. And only a handful of lesbians. To see them all out in such force, strutting along the streets in various states of undress, as if they had a perfect right to be there, was what they call an eye-opener. I won't lie. But I was as conflicted by the open cavorting as by the realization that the parade was actually passing me by.

I clutched my gurgling stomach and swallowed a pill and leaned against a post waiting for the discomfort to subside. Ah well, I thought. Better to have loved and lost and all that kind of malarkey. A Terry word, *malarkey*. Terry, who was now sharing his bed (and his life?) with this mysterious George.

Out of nowhere, I heard my name being called. Over and over. Then the sound of tires screeching. And before I knew it, Titus, clad in nothing but a cape and pair of Speedos, had jumped into my arms and curled himself around me. My shock gave way to a case of the giggles, which caught in my throat when Terry's shadow fell over me.

The moment wasn't lost on Titus, who uncoiled and stepped to the side. For what seemed like an eternity, Terry and I stared at one another, neither of us having a clue about what to say, what to do.

It was so good to see him. And so painful.

We probably would have stood there forever if Titus hadn't said, Oh for pity's sake you two.

And there, on the corner of Central Park South and 58th Street, with hundreds of people milling past, in broad daylight, I kissed Terry. And he kissed me back.

Epilogue

In order to move forward, Terry and Monty decided they needed to go back to the very beginning and recreate the exhilaration of that life-altering night in the parking lot during the fall of 1948. A return to that halcyon period when they lived only for each other and tuned out all the static around them. Before that was possible, however, they had to set aside all the hurt and guilt, and rejection of the intervening years. That they loved each other to distraction and had since the first moment was indisputable, but so too was the damage they'd inflicted and the pangs of withdrawal from their prolonged separation. Without an agreed-upon case of amnesia, true reconciliation was unlikely. Since they were well into middle age by now this might be their last shot, the paralyzing prospect of losing one another again proved sufficient motivation.

As part of his atonement, Monty sought to assure Terry that he was back for good. "It's not just talk, this time," he vowed. "I'm done hiding. No more lurking in the shadows, waiting outside your office to see if you're okay. I want to be by your side from now on, to start and end every day with you. The whole from this day forward, in sickness and in health, 'til death do us part."

He deliberately omitted the words richer or poorer since his newfound bravado had as much to do with his years of therapy as with a more welcoming social climate and a recent windfall — he was the sole heir of his late father's estate. Financially independent and relieved from the burden of legacy, he was now free to proceed unencumbered. He abandoned his career and went into business for himself, severing ties with anyone who disapproved of his decisions, including several longtime friends and family members. He did it for one reason and one reason only, he told Terry. So that, finally, they might share their lives openly and completely.

The forcefulness of his argument silenced Terry's initial qualms that, for all his good intentions, Monty would again cut and run. He understood that part of the reason for Monty's reversal was due to his having what Terry called 'fuck you money.' But it was more than that. That daring kiss outside Central Park had been completely out of character for Monty, who'd always been assertive in his career, but circumspect in his personal life.

As further proof of his sincerity, Monty purchased an apartment in the Village and added Terry's name to the deed. Though Terry had established roots in the neighborhood, Monty disliked the Village and considered its inhabitants to be 'kooks and weirdos,'" (including most of Terry's nearest and dearest friends). "But since I'm crazy about one of those kooks," he said, "if that's where he wants to be that's where I want to be too."

Though their intentions were honorable, they wondered whether it was enough. Might it already too late for them to forge a meaningful relationship? With few same-sex role models, they were forced to navigate the path ahead blindly, which made it all the more surprising how easily they were able to shed their ingrained bachelor habits. Or how the more time they spent together, the less they wanted to be apart. During the workweek, they chatted on the telephone several times a day, often for no other reason than to hear each other's voices. They shared breakfast each morning and slept in late on the weekend. In the evenings, whether they stayed home or went to the theater, or the movies made no difference as long as they were together. For two such strong-willed people, they couldn't understand why they hardly quarreled, and that the occasional spats were so mundane — like whether they should call a plumber or fix a leaky sink themselves; or if the new armchair in the living room should be placed near the window to afford them a view, or farther back so that the sun wouldn't fade the fabric.

Sometimes, a skeptical inner voice would whisper that what they had was too good to last and they would have to stifle it. Given the depth of their affection, forgiveness had not been too big a challenge. Forgetting, on the other hand, had been a bit more daunting. The land of regret and what-ifs was littered with mines and sidestepping them required conscious resolve. Determined to make up for all the lost years during which fear and stubborn pride had kept them apart, to their credit, they succeeded in reconstituting those early, heady days — only this time filtered through the prism of hindsight.

For the next dozen years, their lives together were fulfilling and crammed with indelible memories: annual trips to Europe, Asia, and Australia, hideaway summer weekends in Montauk, Vermont ski vacations in winter. Occasionally, Terry would catch Monty, head-tilted, idly staring at him and, reading his mind, would grin as if to say "Yeah, I know. We sure are a couple of lucky sons-of-bitches." Like he had in the old days.

Though they preferred one another's company, they were hardly hermits. Now that they no longer faced the danger of arrest, after an evening out, they sometimes dropped by one of the local gay bars for a nightcap, or for a chin wag with some of Terry's 'kooks and weirdos' friends. Monty's attitude toward them gradually shifted and, eventually, he formed personal ties with several of Terry's unorthodox comrades. A few would become valued confidants in later years, providing the kind of moral support he never received from disapproving kith and kin.

Given their distinctive appearance, Terry and Monty frequently caught the eye of passersby but, fortunately, were never harassed like younger couples who flaunted their attachment in public. Aside from the demonstration of affection outside Central Park, caution was too deeply ingrained in men of their generation for anything more overt than a fraternal hug or brush on the cheek when they separated — though they admitted to twinges of envy when younger men embraced or walked down the street hand-in-hand.

Nonetheless, anyone who paid attention could tell that they were a couple, despite (or perhaps because of) their marked differences. Terry, a dyed-in-the-denim bohemian, favored jeans, pea coats, and work boots. For several years, taking a cue from John Lennon, he protested the Vietnam War by refusing to cut his hair, then chose to keep it long even after peace was declared. Monty's look was more traditional and cultivated: a carefully maintained salt-and-pepper mane, Brooks Brothers three-piece suits, and cashmere topcoats – and in summer, polo or button-down Oxford shirts and khakis. Though Monty wistfully recalled their early days together when they both went out on the town nattily dressed in bespoke suits and ties, he understood that it no longer reflected Terry's persona. His one peeve was the unkempt mane, which Terry sometimes pulled back into a loose ponytail. After some gentle prodding, Monty convinced him to twist his locks into a braid that eventually reached the middle of his back. The coif gave him a gravitas, a certain ineffable nobility.

The noteworthy mismatch between the two men was eye-catching, and their emotional attachment was subtly conveyed through body language: the similarity in their gait as they strode confidently shoulder-to-shoulder; and the way they leaned into one another to share confidences.

Monty and Terry were transitioning contentedly into their senior years when their ordered life was brutally disrupted. Monty compared those days to being in the middle of a peaceful dream and having it suddenly morph into a nightmare. Around them, men in their prime were being felled by a wasting disease, and expiring suddenly from unexplained cancers, pneumonia, and other rare opportunistic infections. Initially they panicked since the origin of the illness or how it was transmitted was unknown, and like other men their age, they already had some concerns about their health.

When it was discovered that the malady was primarily targeting gay men and/or intravenous drug users, years of growing public tolerance came to an abrupt halt, and a new era of condemnation and marginalization began. Since he'd never given a whit what other people thought of his behavior, Terry was saddened but not especially troubled by the shift in public sentiment, though he was appalled by the neglect and mistreatment of the afflictted, which spurred him to action.

Terry's decision to put himself in danger drove a wedge between them. Terry tried to reason with Monty, but it was no use. "I get why you're scared. But I just can't sit back and do nothing for these poor guys who've been abandoned and are dying alone. I hope you understand that." But Monty did not. The AIDS epidemic, which largely targeted gay men, at least in the U.S., had reawakened Monty's demons. He was again swamped with feelings of self-loathing, guilt, and shame. Abashed and fearful for his life, Monty moved out of their apartment into one of his nearby rental properties and sank into a deep depression.

Terry let him go but he did not despair. The past few years had been the happiest of their lives, and their bond was now indissoluble. He was confident that, eventually, Monty would come around.

His faith in Monty was well-placed. He did relent but only after a near disaster eclipsed his fear and self-hatred. Titus, whom they regarded as a surrogate son, and whose progress from aimless young hellion to a respected photographer they'd witnessed up close, was stricken with pneumonia and actually died for a few minutes before being resuscitated.

The moment he learned of Titus's condition Monty rushed to the hospital where he found Terry asleep in a chair at his bedside. Gently, he roused him. "Go home and get some rest. I'll take the next shift," he said. Monty returned the following night, and the next, and the next until Titus recovered. He didn't sit passively by the entire time, either. If his physician was inattentive or a nurse refused to bring Titus a bedpan or take steps to relieve his pain, he would read them the riot act. "You're a regular Shirley MacLaine," a weakened, yet still acerbic Titus teased, referring to the protective matriarch in the recent film *Terms of Endearment*.

Shortly before Titus was released from the hospital, Monty asked Terry if he could move in again. "You don't need my permission. It's your place too," he said, outwardly aloof, but quietly elated. "Come back any time you want."

"Is that your way of saying you forgive me?" Monty said.

"There's nothing to forgive," Terry announced. "You are who you are, and I am who I am. We shouldn't fit together, but we do. Without each other, we make no sense."

Thereafter, they resumed their normal lives — or at least what had become the new normal — and save for the occasional kerfuffle, their contentment carried them through until the end.

"We're like a couple of old shoes, all broken in and comfy but slowly falling apart," Monty would sigh.

"Who you calling an old shoe?" Terry would reply in mock outrage.

What were perhaps the final and most fitting observations about their convoluted romance were spoken not by Monty and Terry, but by Titus who, miraculously, would outlive them both. On Pride Weekend in 1995, he threw them a surprise twenty-fifth anniversary party. The commemoration date seemed arbitrary but was also curiously fitting. While they'd been in love since the meeting as soldiers during the war, they'd only been a committed couple since that kiss after the Pride parade in 1970 — for which Titus boastfully (and endlessly) took credit.

As the celebration's master of ceremonies, Titus addressed the audience from a raised podium in front of a large screen displaying photographs he'd taken of Terry and Marty over the years.

The first shot flashed behind him: Terry, in his mid-thirties. Puckishly handsome and casually dressed, engaged in friendly conversation with someone out of frame. "This is the first picture I ever took of Terry with a camera he gave me for my birthday. To my eight-year-old mind, Terry was a combination of a cool dad and a protective older brother. I don't know why he agreed to babysit and, eventually, raise me. I was a total brat and all I ever did was give him grief. But I wouldn't be standing here today if he hadn't been there to guide me, even if it didn't keep me from making several birdbrained mistakes along the way. I'm grateful that he was always there to help pick up the pieces."

A photo of Monty, taken around the same period. In a swimsuit, a beach jacket, and Ray-Bans. As distractingly attractive as he is elusive. "Monty was my first crush. I mean, look at him. At the time, I had no idea that he and Terry were lovers. Or even that I was gay. All I knew was that I couldn't take my eyes off Monty and I'd use any excuse to take his picture. Then later, I'd moon over them like a lovesick schoolboy. I resented Terry, every time Monty disappeared from our lives. Dumb kid that I was, I blamed him for scaring Monty off."

A photo of the famous kiss from the 1970 Pride Festival. "What you see was all my doing. Yes, ladies and gents, Terry and Monty have yours truly to thank for getting them back together, and I've never let them forget it though I might not have bothered had I known what a frumpy old married couple they'd become. I mean, what part of the word 'gay' is still not clear?"

A wide shot with Monty and Terry on opposite ends of the frame, surrounded by beefy, shirtless young men. They are staring directly into each other's eyes. "Case in point. One night, I dragged them to a dance club, and instead of appreciating all the gorgeous bodies swimming around them, they spent the night cruising one another. Eww. Seriously, guys?"

A party in Monty and Terry's apartment. The two of them are huddled in a corner chatting intently. "When I took this photo, I remember thinking 'What is it with them? They're together day and night. What more could they possibly have to say to one another? It's the kind of thing only someone who's never truly been in love would think."

The final photo of Terry and Monty, of recent vintage, taken from two rows behind them during a concert at Carnegie Hall. "This tells you everything you need to know about Monty and Terry. Monty's dozed off with his head perched on Terry's shoulder and Terry is leaning his head on Monty's. They're like Siamese twins. I'm not sure how, but somehow their relationship has managed to survive a world war, decades of oppression, and a plague. And here they are tonight, still going strong, and to paraphrase a line from the poet W.E. Henley, 'bloodied but unbowed.'"

Titus's speech was followed by a toast. As the gathered rose to their feet and held up their glasses, he said, "To Terry and Monty," and a tear rolled down his cheek. "On your silver anniversary or golden, whichever you prefer." The guests echoed "To Terry and Monty" and sipped from their flutes.

Terry and Monty clinked glasses, stared at one another, and sighed, grinning broadly. In the moment, words were unnecessary. They did not need gold, silver, or any other precious metal to commemorate the occasion. Their relationship was far more tensile and enduring, like tempered steel.

BARBARA'S POETRY LESSON

As her dress was being fitted, Barbara Clay Treadwell stood on a pedestal in front of a three-way mirror. All that tucking and pinning, pinning and tucking; the only way to pass the time was to let her mind wander.

In the mirror to her left, she envisioned Robert Clyde, a poet and a good one at that. In a rhyme once, he'd likened her laugh to a spray of freesias. He was easily the handsomest of the men who'd courted her, but they'd parted ways because Barbara could not envision a life in academia, residing in damp campus housing and baking pies and entertaining professors' wives. Also, Robert had a fondness for the bottle — as poets often do.

Luther Forrester, to her right, was an industrial scion, and would have been the pragmatic choice if only she'd been willing to overlook his appetite for waitresses and barmaids. Goodness knows how his current wife, Esther, endured his brazen public flirtations.

Full front was the life Barbara had chosen. Malcolm Treadwell. A distinguished attorney, Malcolm exuded sobriety, which more than compensated for his other shortcomings. He could be a bit gruff and stuffy, particularly in his clumsy attempts at being amorous. Fortunately he didn't bother her much, hardly at all since JoAnn was born, and he transferred most of his affection to his daughter.

Still she had to admit that when they were out together, at the opera or the symphony, they made a handsome couple. Among their circle, the consensus was that Malcolm must possess some hidden virtues to have attracted a woman like Barbara which, to her, was a source of pride. Even at thirty-two, she still cut a handsome figure, tall, with beautifully proportioned breasts. Her vermillion mane was legendary and when she tossed it, she could actually see men's hearts palpitate against their rib cages.

"All finished, madam," the seamstress said, rousing her from the reverie. Barbara lingered a moment on the platform to congratulate herself, though she seemed unable to summon up even a half-convincing smile.

Barbara Treadwell ate lunch alone every day at Schrafft's on 13th Street. At the same table, near the uptown facing window, unless it was unavailable, and then she took her meal at the counter. Chilled peach salad with lettuce, cottage cheese, and black coffee or, on really cold days, eggs scrambled in butter. Once a week, she indulged in dessert, the crushed strawberry sundae.

On the one day she ordered dessert, Barbara would take a brisk walk, usually down to Washington Square Park and around its perimeter. Nothing too strenuous, but enough to burn away those extra calories and maintain her waistline.

The sky was overcast and the air thick as she strolled toward the park along lower 5th Avenue. She left her spring coat unbuttoned to let some air circulate. As she passed under the arch, she had the sensation of measured footsteps behind her. The park was sparsely occupied, a sprinkling of idle college students from NYU and ladies pushing baby carriages. She always crossed to the southern perimeter with a sense of trepidation since some of the streets jutting off the park were a bit sketchy. But given that she was within earshot of several pedestrians, she wasn't overly concerned. As she reached the park's northern end, however, her discomfort turned to pique and she decided to confront the cad dogging her steps. One sharp glare should be enough to convey her displeasure, she reasoned. Any decent gentleman would tip his hat and retreat.

She turned quickly, the edges of her coat flaring, and caught him unawares. A thick, square-cut man, no taller than she, with a blunt, greased-back hairdo topped with a fedora. Somewhat youthful in appearance with a smooth complexion, though of indeterminate age. Then, from the pronounced ridge under the stranger's taupe gabardine suit jacket, it dawned on Barbara that her stalker was not a man at all. "Can I help you?" she said pointedly, attempting to be gracious and no-nonsense at the same time.

"I wasn't sure you'd noticed me," the woman said, breaking into a grin. "Whenever I eat lunch at Schrafft's, I can't take my eyes off you, and today I decided to follow you."

Barbara was shaken by the woman's audacity. She was not unfamiliar with the neighborhood's inverts. She saw them sometimes at the bank or the post office, usually the effeminate male variety, but a few blunt-cut women as well.

"Well, it's very rude," she said. Her tone wasn't especially harsh, more like a mother chastising a quarrelsome child.

"I guess I should say I'm sorry, but I'm not," the woman replied. "I never imagined you'd actually talk to me."

The stranger's candid manner disconcerted her, and the only thing she could think to do was pull her purse close to her body.

"Oh, I'm not looking to rob you or ask for a handout," the woman said, indicating her tailored suit and the polished brown Oxfords on her feet. "I was just wondering if I might pay you a compliment."

"A compliment?" Barbara said as if the word was alien to her.

"You have a beautifully clear voice and the way the light plays off your hair is delightful," the woman said, through half-closed vulpine eyes.

Instead of taking the compliment, Barbara merely clutched her purse tighter.

"Don't worry. I'm harmless," she said. "Well, maybe not completely harmless," she added with a wry chuckle.

"And what is that supposed to mean?" Barbara said, arching her back.

"Oh, I'm just a kidder," she said, flashing her palms and taking a step back. "I meant no disrespect."

"Well, then," Barbara said, uncertain as to why she continued to engage this odd person and not hail the nearest policeman. She wasn't the type to strike up conversations with passersby, much less with someone so importunate.

"By the way, my name is Adrian," the woman said, extending a rather short and stubby hand.

Adrian, Barbara thought. Could be male or female, and in this case clearly a bit of both.

"Barbara Treadwell," she said officiously, extending her gloved fingers as she would to a bank manager. Adrian held on to her hand and before letting go said, "Now that we've met, would you mind if I walked alongside you? I promise not to be a bother. We don't even have to speak."

"Well, I don't know," Barbara replied. The woman's request was polite enough, though if she'd been a man, Barbara would have most certainly refused. "I suppose that would be all right. But I'm not going to be out long. I live nearby."

"Oh, I know where you live," she said, which seemed to alarm Barbara.

"Don't misunderstand me. I found out by accident. One afternoon as I was leaving Schrafft's and just about to turn west on 10th Street, I saw the doorman nod as you entered your building."

Satisfied with the answer, Barbara turned and resumed her stroll. Adrian took two long strides until they were abreast. She strode with a deliberate pace, shifting her weight heavily from one foot to the other.

"So, I gather that you are . . ." Barbara began only to find herself in a verbal cul-de-sac.

"One of those?" Adrian said, completing the sentence. "Yeah."

"And how do you suppose that came about?" Barbara said, discomfited and now completely out of her depth.

"Just lucky I guess," Adrian said, beaming.

Barbara lost her composure and tittered, covering her mouth to conceal her amusement. What a cheeky woman, she thought.

"It's good to see you smile. In all the time I've been watching you, the only time I've seen you do that is when the busboy brings you a glass of water. And that's more of a polite grin."

Barbara acknowledged that she was not a terribly demonstrative person. She was cut from Protestant granite and even Malcolm, hardly the most effusive of men, referred to her parents as "starchy."

"Well, you certainly are a peculiar fellow," Barbara said, then gasped at her error.

"It's okay. I don't mind being called a fellow. Otherwise, why would I dress this way? Just don't call me a gentleman."

"And why is that?" she said, another involuntary laugh escaping her.

"Because I have a reputation to uphold. Which is not to say that I don't know how to treat a lady."

"My, my," Barbara said, shaking off the remark. "I'm not quite sure I approve of the drift of this conversation."

"I told you. We don't have to talk. It's a pleasure just walking beside you," Adrian said.

They continued for half a block in silence, which Barbara found no less unnerving. "Now, tell me, uh, Adrian, are you employed or do you have a . . ."

"Husband to support me? I don't think so. Yeah, I work. Six days a week. As a bartender."

Barbara's eyes bounced in surprise. "You tend bar?" she said.

"Yeah. In an out-of-the-way place. The clientele is mostly gals."

"Oh, I see," Barbara said. "Women such as yourself."

"And some women like you as well."

"Oh, come now," Barbara said sternly. "I hardly think that likely."

"You'd be surprised. See, women like me don't go for other women like me," Adrian explained. "Two bulls don't make a right."

Barbara shook her head, confused. "But if the woman isn't like you then how can you know . . ." She stopped short and flushed with embarrassment. This conversation, while intriguing, was getting completely out of hand. Noticing a bench up ahead, she walked over and sat down.

Adrian sat beside her but maintained a respectful separation. "You just know from the way they look at you. Like they trust you but aren't completely sure they trust themselves," she said.

"I'm not sure I understand," Barbara said, looking up and catching herself staring into Adrian's eyes, which were aquamarine and offset her rather pug-like features, a wide nose and a fist for a chin.

"That kind of attraction has its own rules. It's a gut reaction." Adrian said slapping her wide, firm stomach.

"From the gut, then," Barbara repeated as if it were an alien concept.

"Uh-huh. Like when your husband looks at you in that way and you feel like you're being tickled from the inside," Adrian said with a wink.

Malcolm had certainly never cast his eyes on her in that manner. When he was interested, he merely knocked at her bedroom door and, unless she objected, slipped under the covers. But, a few times, when she was dating Robert Clyde, he had eyed her with something more than aesthetic appreciation. If she'd been a modern girl, she might have fallen into his arms.

Now she would never know that feeling of wild abandonment and the thought saddened her.

"I bet men write you poems," Adrian said.

"Remarkable," Barbara said. "I was just thinking about a man who wrote me poems all the time. Lovely poems. A few were even printed."

"I wish I could write you poems," Adrian said. "I'm not much good at putting pen to paper. But I make up for it in other ways."

"I am a married woman, Adrian," Barbara said, breathing through her nose, "and right now if you were a man, I would slap you."

"Be my guest," Adrian said, offering up her cheek. "You can even take off your glove."

Outraged, Barbara raised her hand but did not follow through. "I'm going home now. Please don't follow me." She jumped up and quickly crossed the street, buttoning her coat as she headed uptown.

Adrian sighed and watched her go.

The Schrafft's menu no longer appealed to Barbara, she decided, and began scouting for a new lunch spot within walking distance of the apartment. She liked to be home when JoAnn came in from school. Felt it was her duty as a mother to ensure that her child did not return to an empty house.

For a time, she settled on Patricia Murphy's but found it a little too white-gloved even for her taste. She shifted to the Cedar, but quickly tired of the largely male clientele, artist and writer types puffed up with their own self-importance. A noisy lot and often raucous, especially with some drink in them.

The more eclectic choices in the neighborhood, she discovered, were either subpar or seedy. Her wanderings eventually drew her west to Stewart's Cafeteria on Sheridan Square with its inexpensive basic fare. She preferred eating upstairs where it was brighter.

Most of the regular clients were also male, workers and idlers. The workers were on their lunch hour and in a hurry, and the idlers seemed to be interested only in one another. But a few took notice and, on occasion, would pass by the table and compliment her outfits, her accessories and, of course, her luxuriant mane. They referred to her as "classy" and "uptown" and once even "dynamite."

The more forward men politely asked if they might join her, and depending on her mood, she accepted. They weren't exactly masher types. They seemed more interested in where she bought her outfits and chatting about current fashion trends. When she mentioned that she owned genuine Diors and Chanels and even a Charles James, they clucked with admiration.

Some of the men enjoyed discussing opera and ballet and theater. Malcolm never wanted to discuss the performances they attended, probably because he was usually fast asleep by the middle of the first act. But these men seemed eager to hear her opinions, and even when they disagreed with her assessment were never dismissive.

One of the most peculiar and strangely endearing fellows was a little man named Shrimpy, or at least that's what everyone called him. The first time Barbara saw him, he was sitting across from her, fidgeting and gaping at her. No longer able to keep his peace, he blurted, "Golly you're beautiful. In my next lifetime, I want to come back as you."

Shrimpy was a self-described klutz. He walked into doors and tripped down stairs and perpetually sported a bruise or a bandaged wound. Though not as entertaining or witty as some of the others, he proved to be quite intelligent. He worked in the box office at Circle in the Square on Bleecker Street and made the most insightful observations about theater, his love of which seemed genuine and uncompromised by current fads.

Often, as she hurried back home in time to be there for JoAnn, she found herself laughing at conversations she'd overheard or an anecdote one of the men had shared. She tried repeating them to Malcolm or to friends at dinner parties, but from the stares and disapproving snorts she elicited, realized that she had no talent as a raconteur.

The afternoon was blustery and she regretted not taking her lunch somewhere closer to home. Halfway to Stewart's she was caught in a downpour. The umbrella sailed out of her hands and was swept away in an updraft. Soaked and shivering, she decided to wait out the storm under a doorway. A half hour later with the tempest still raging, she was reduced to tears, guessing that pneumonia or at the very least bronchitis was in the offing.

"Barbara," the voice in front of her boomed. At first, she didn't recognize the figure in the long, dark trench under a midnight-blue umbrella. Then she remembered the blue-green eyes she'd thought of every so often since they met. She uttered a pitiable titter as if to say, "Here I am, an orphan of the storm."

"You're drenched. Come. Let's get you inside and get something warm in you," Adrian said. They huddled together and Barbara scampered down the street as daintily as a geisha, sidestepping puddles and laughing at her foolishness.

"We could stop in Stewart's if that's okay with you," Adrian said.

"Why not? I eat there almost every day," Barbara replied.

"You do? I've never seen you," Adrian asked.

"I sit upstairs," Barbara clarified.

"And watch all the boys flirt with one another?"

"Do they now? I knew something of the sort was afoot," she replied coyly.

"I would expect you to say something like that," Adrian said. Barbara looked at her intently. She was shaking and her fists were clenched from the cold.

"I have a better idea. I live around the corner. I have tea and homemade soup and towels and a red-hot radiator to dry your things."

Barbara shook her head from side to side. "No, I have to be back at the apartment. JoAnn, my daughter, will be home from school in a half hour."

"You'll catch your death," Adrian castigated. "Is there no one else?"

"I suppose I could ask Mrs. Wagner downstairs to mind her for a bit. Her daughter Mimi and JoAnn both go to Spence and ride the bus downtown together. Do you have a telephone?"

"Yes, in the hallway," Adrian said.

As they huddled under the umbrella, Barbara realized she had never met anyone with a telephone in the hallway.

"I warn you, it's not much," Adrian said on the third-floor landing as she unlocked the door.

The single room was ample-size and pleasantly appointed. The Pullman kitchen with yellow-and-green wooden cabinets was fronted by a chrome and Formica table. Under the far window stood a large bathtub and, on the opposite wall, a bed with a metal headboard that doubled as seating and was scattered with brocade cushions.

Prints and primitive art pieces hung on the walls alongside Dodgers and Giants banners. Some knickknacks were strewn on rickety end tables, which were clearly secondhand as was the lumpy horsehair armchair draped with an afghan and the footstool covered in embroidered damask.

The room was brought together by an oversize and decidedly faded Persian with an ineradicable dark stain on one end. It had likely been tossed by its original owner and somewhat rehabilitated.

"This is lovely," Barbara said as she dried her hair. She thought the room quite masculine but with warm, feminine overtones, quite like its current inhabitant.

"You don't have to say that," Adrian replied.

"But I mean it. You have very good taste."

"Thank you. Now if I only had the money to go with it," Adrian said, as she walked to the bathroom and pointed inside. "There's a robe hanging on the back of the door. Hand me your wet clothes and I'll put them on the radiator. Unlike most landlords, mine is not stingy with the heat."

Barbara felt more naked under the men's silk dressing gown than if she'd been wearing nothing at all. She tiptoed out of the bathroom and sat in the armchair, propping her bare feet on the footstool. Adrian brought her tea. "Sip this while I heat up the soup. Mushroom barley. Made it myself this morning. Old Polish family recipe."

"I never pictured you as a cook," Barbara said as she took a sip of tea.

"I told you I wasn't a poet, but I make up for it in other ways. That's one of them."

"I take it then that your people are Polish?" she inquired.

Adrian nodded, stirring the soup with a wooden spoon. "Second generation. Grew up in Yorkville. Six of us in a three-room apartment. This is kind of a step up for me."

"I was raised on the Upper East Side myself."

"But not the same Upper East Side," Adrian corrected her. "I'm guessing Park or 5th."

Barbara pursed her lips and expelled an "*Mmm*," and tried to change the subject. "Whatever the size, it must be nice having the place all to yourself."

"A room of one's own," Adrian said, ladling some piping hot soup into a green Bauer ware bowl.

"Beg pardon?" Barbara said.

"A room of one's own," she repeated. "Virginia Woolf?"

"I'm not familiar with it," Barbara said. "Not much of a reader."

"How do you pass the time when you're alone?" Adrian asked.

"Listen to the radio. The classical station. Sometimes the hit parade," Barbara remarked.

"And dance by yourself around the living room?"

Barbara's eyes bobbled. "How did you know that?"

"It's something I imagine a girl like you might do on a quiet afternoon. Would you prefer eating your soup at the table or should I bring it over there?" Adrian asked.

"It's so comfy here, do you mind?" Barbara asked.

"Whatever madam prefers," Adrian said, bowing at the waist.

Then Barbara suddenly jumped up. "Oh dear. I completely forgot to call Mrs. Wilson." She reached for her bag and fished a nickel from her change purse.

"Be right back," she said, disappearing out the door and leaving it ajar. The phone was only two steps down the hall and Adrian caught a word here and there. Halfway through the conversation, Barbara's voice darkened and she sounded flustered. When she returned, she was clearly upset.

"Something wrong?" Adrian asked as she arranged the soup and a plate of crackers on a tray.

"That terrible woman," Barbara said, tossing herself back into the chair.

"What did she say?"

"I explained what had happened and she implied that I was at an assignation. Of all the nerve," she said, trying to maintain her composure.

"I'm sorry," Adrian said.

"And to make it worse, I chipped a nail dialing. I just had a manicure yesterday, and it's such a lovely shade of pink."

"Let me see," Adrian said, forgetting all about the soup and walking over to Barbara who held out her left hand. The index fingernail was partially scratched.

Adrian sighed, sat down on the footstool and began to gently kiss Barbara's fingertips.

No one, not even Robert Clyde had ever attempted such a gallant gesture. Adrian ran her lips along each finger and they finally came to rest in the palm of Barbara's hand, which she kissed repeatedly. Her other hand fell onto Barbara's knee.

Barbara should have resisted but found herself unable to do so. The hand worked its way gently but steadily up her thigh, coming to rest on the now-moist patch between her legs.

Adrian pushed away the folds of the dressing gown, and Barbara discovered an entirely different kind of poetry.

Unlike the other important life decisions she'd made — which man to marry and when to start a family — Barbara's feelings for Adrian had not been a choice. She was ineluctably drawn to this odd woman and however much she debated her loss of control, the attraction persisted and grew. The only time choice entered into the equation was in deciding how to incorporate those feelings into her life while still meeting her familial obligations.

In the mornings, after her husband left for work and she got JoAnn off to school, Barbara took a long, hot soak, dried and brushed her hair and dressed quickly. She arrived at Adrian's apartment around eleven and let herself in with the key under the mat. Adrian, who didn't leave the bar until four a.m. and rarely got to bed before six, was usually asleep but gradually woke up to the smell of coffee and bacon and eggs or griddle cakes. While she ate breakfast, Barbara put on the silk dressing gown.

She was usually gone by two, two-thirty at the latest and home in time to greet JoAnn with milk and cookies she had picked up at Balducci's en route. Those few weekday hours with Adrian soon proved to be insufficient and on evenings when her social calendar was clear, she waited for her husband and daughter to turn in before dressing and quietly letting herself out of the apartment. She headed over to 8th Avenue to The Coast, where Adrian tended bar. Adrian insisted that she sit at the stool closest to the cash register and the rear exit door, so she could make a quick getaway in case of a police raid.

Barbara was content to nurse a martini all evening and watch Adrian work. She was never bored and if she talked with anyone it was usually the other "hens," as Adrian called them. The chats usually centered on fashion or a casual exchange of makeup tips.

None of the other hens were as striking as Barbara, but the bulls knew well enough to keep their distance save for the occasional discreet compliment, usually about her hair.

At about two, Adrian called her a cab, and with a kiss on the cheek, Barbara departed.

Barbara sensed that although Malcom never addressed the issue directly, he was aware of her absences. "I believe he thinks I've taken a lover," she told Adrian. "And he's being quite a good sport about it."

"A male lover," Adrian said.

"Well, yes," Barbara admitted, smiling as she secured the ties of her dressing gown. "I mean, is it all that different?"

"And you call me cheeky," Adrian replied, amused. "What about him? Think he has a lady on the side?"

"I hope so, though I would be surprised. When he used to come to my room, it was mostly out of a sense of duty."

"Duty is important to your kind," Adrian noted.

"Please," Barbara implored. "I've given up so much for you. I feel that I owe them. You don't mind that I put them first, Malcolm and JoAnn, do you?"

Adrian shook her head. "I know you're mine," she said confidently.

Barbara had never confirmed it in so many words, but her affection for Adrian was apparent from the Morse code of her moans, from her helpless tremors and the way her unpinned hair floated across the bed pillow like waves on the sea.

Adrian did admit to moments of jealousy, however. On her night off, if Barbara was free, they double dated with one of her old friends, Monty, and his boyfriend Terry. They'd head east to the Cinderella Club to hear Monk or to the Vanguard when Anita O'Day or Miles was on the bill. An attractive woman in the company of three men (well, at least two men) was perfectly acceptable.

It was when they went out dancing, though, that Adrian got uneasy since Barbara spent most of the evening talking or gliding across the floor with Monty while she and Terry watched.

The other patrons assumed that Barbara and Monty were a couple. As it happens, they had grown up just a few blocks from one another, belonged to the same church and had several friends in common. On the dance floor, they seemed to be made for each other, moving with confidence and even intimacy. Terry didn't seem to mind. He was too busy eyeing or flirting with other men in the club, a habit to which Monty tried to turn a blind eye. Adrian was not as accommodating and for the next two or three days she was flinty and petulant.

"You're being ridiculous," Barbara complained. "You're acting just like a man, a foolish man. Monty's nothing but a friend."

"Then why do you look into his eyes and dance so close together?"

"When I look at him, I see you. When he looks at me, he sees Terry. But even if we were allowed to dance with the person who brought us, the two of you would stay glued to your seats. You won't even dance with me when we're alone."

"I told you, I've got two left feet" Adrian griped.

"Then I'll pretend to have two right feet, and we'll fit together perfectly," Barbara said moving over to the hi-fi. She folded through the albums and placed one on the turntable. "Come on. A slow dance. You don't even have to move your feet. Just sway. I'll show you how."

She moved the needle to the middle of the record, Nat King Cole's rendition of "Blame It on My Youth."

Adrian just sat there, arms resolutely folded across her chest. "If you don't get up this instant, I'm getting dressed and going home," Barbara said, an idle threat to be sure.

Groaning and grimacing, Adrian rose and stood motionless in the middle of the floor. Barbara took her left palm and placed it against hers. She pressed her body against Adrian's and began to move back and forth dreamily.

The sensation of Barbara's breasts rubbing against her shirt and the movement of her pelvis along the fabric of Adrian's trousers sent unexpected jolts through her body. Emboldened, Barbara lodged her right thigh insistently between Adrian's legs. The more excited she became, the more purposefully Barbara moved.

"Didn't I tell you that dancing would be fun?" Barbara cooed in her ear and then placed her lips against Adrian's.

Adrian's breathing became increasingly shallow. The sensations heightened and multiplied until she emitted an involuntary guttural noise and her body rattled in a manner she had never imagined possible.

Barbara gasped, as surprised as Adrian at what had just occurred. But instead of sapping Adrian's strength, it energized her. She pushed Barbara back toward the bed and began to pull at the ties of the dressing gown.

"Careful," Barbara said with a titter, "it's silk. You'll tear it."

THE SEVEN FORTY-FIVE

At first, Donald saw the man intermittently, noting him through half-open eyes as he walked past. He was a smart dresser, the same gabardine suit in two shades of taupe during the warmer months, one lighter, one darker. In fall and winter, he switched to twill, navy and midnight blue. The ensembles were more tailored, less baggy than the current fashion, and with a lower waist. The man must be European, Donald surmised. They tended to be dandies, "show-offy," as his wife, Helga, might say. "Isn't he full of himself?" she would snort at some indeterminate foreigner combing back the sides of his brilliantined hair in public or chewing on a toothpick from the side of his mouth and grinning as if he had figured out the secret of existence.

Except for the clothes though, he did not get a good fix on the man. Donald usually had to run from the bus to make the 7:45 ferry, heart pounding and sweaty, or he'd be late for work. He was a problem sleeper, the insomnia exacerbated by his wife's "little talks."

"We need to have a little talk," Helga would say. Nothing little followed, and she did all the talking. Donald would nod dumbly throughout the monologue after which he promised to "think about it." To which she would rejoinder, "Don't just think about it. Do it."

From their very first date, when she disparaged the service at Nino's restaurant in Port Richmond, Helga seemed to have a permanent burr under her skin. A shame, since she was otherwise sweet and certainly pretty. Donald fell for her cherry lips, which required no more than a dab of lipstick; that's how naturally plumped and ripe they were. And she was lithe, with a wonderful bosom, ample without being ostentatious, highlighted by ice cream–color angora sweaters. Her best feature was the Jayne Mansfield dirty-blond hair, curly and loose. No beehive or Jackie Kennedy flip for her. He admired the way she tossed it when she spoke. To his mind, it epitomized femininity.

Putting up with her petty dissatisfactions was the price he paid for having a wife that other men appreciated — and how! "You dog, Donald," his coworkers said when he announced his engagement. "How the hell did you land a doll like Helga Guilfoyle?"

"I have my charms," he replied with a wink; just enough to imply without being vulgar. Not much truth to his boast, however. During their courtship, the furthest he got was some under-the-sweater action; and once, she gave him a peek. Donald was different from the other unattached men at the Miami Club where they first met, she claimed. "They always get too close when they talk. You keep a respectful distance even when we're dancing. That's what I like about you."

Gliding across the floor with Helga was exciting. All eyes in the club were focused on them. But he never lost control and she appreciated that. The occasional hand job was his reward, either in the front seat of his DeSoto or under a newspaper while they were watching a movie at the Victory Theater. She complained about that too: "You take too long."

When they'd been dating for six months, Helga's mother, Berta, gave him an ultimatum. Either he proposed or moved on. Their neighbor, John Capodano, who owned a chain of dry cleaners, was waiting in the wings and eager to give her "plenty of grandchildren."

His grandmother loaned him the money for the ring, and he worked at his cousin Pete's tire store on weekends to pay her back and save up for the honeymoon. Niagara Falls. Someone's idea of romantic. Helga found it damp and hair-frizzing.

At weekly Sunday dinners, Berta reminded him that he needed "to get busy." Two years and Helga was not yet with child. "I'm trying," he explained. He stepped up on the appropriate days if he wasn't too tired and Helga was "in the mood."

"Leave it be, Ma," she said through a haze of cigarette smoke. "If it's going to happen, it's going to happen. I'm in no rush to lose my figure. Hell, I'm only twenty-two."

Donald was a year older, but if he didn't get a good night's sleep soon, he'd look fifty before long.

Then he saw the man more regularly. The same ferry in the morning and, sometimes, even the 4:45 coming home. Once or twice, Donald could have sworn he was loitering in the ferry terminal waiting for him to arrive. Always brushed past with his attaché, the *Times* under one arm, and raced to the front of the boat; never so much as a sidelong glance. Still, he managed to fill in the details: Not a foreigner at all; more than likely of Scots-Irish stock. Strong jaw. Manly stance from behind. Feet planted wide apart. He didn't need to brace himself when the ferry bumped against the pylons as it docked. Probably played football in college. Had the shoulders for it. And the heft. Fordham was his guess.

At night, in mid toss and turn, he found himself wondering where the man had his suits made. They might even be off the rack and then tailored. Went to an awful lot of trouble, that's for sure. Donald made it a point to scope out the right hand for a wedding band. Sure enough. Wide, gold, etched. Probably had a wife out of a TV ad — perfectly coiffed, pearls and an apron, two kids and another on the way. Definitely a man with purpose. He fervently hoped that in a few more years, when he was more seasoned, someone would make a similar observation about him. He'd like that.

Perhaps the first step would be sitting at the front on the ferry to get a jump on the exiting crowd. When he did so, Donald discovered that the extra five minutes he gained from his proximity to the exit doors made a difference. No more over-the-glasses glares from his supervisor.

Also, the man was now in his line of sight for the entire twenty-minute ride, usually positioned diagonally across, features obscured by the *Times*, folded neatly, one-column wide. How did he get it to do that without making a mess? He read with full concentration, only looking up if someone knocked over the attaché by accident. Then, without remark, he righted it and went back to his newspaper.

For their anniversary, Donald took Helga to the Copa. Xavier Cugat. They danced and drank; one too many and, later, he was unable to perform. "That's okay," Helga said in a tone that clearly indicated the opposite. "Take two aspirins and drink plenty of water or you're going to have a bitch of a headache in the morning."

He did as he was told and was up half the night peeing. Add to the mix the two cups of coffee he drank that morning to get his motor running and Donald barely made the 7:45. He immediately headed downstairs to the men's room. Just in the nick of time too.

A sigh of relief as the trail began, matched almost exactly by that of the man less than two feet away, the one with the *Times* under his arm. Donald looked away and then back and down. The man took no notice of his inquisitiveness as he tapped off several times.

Reaching for a paper towel after he rinsed his hands, the *Times* cascaded from under the man's armpit and splayed on the ground. Donald picked it up. The man nodded a curt thanks and with one or two flips, the paper fell back into place. "Impressive," Donald observed.

"All in the wrist," the man quipped as he departed.

Donald stood there half-open-mouthed, the way he did when his favorite team scored.

"You look as beat as I feel," the man said, depositing himself heavily next to Donald on the 4:45 back to Staten Island.

"Tough day," Donald replied as the fine gabardine briefly grazed his thigh.

"George, by the way," he said, extending his hand. The palm was clammy belying the man's composed exterior.

"Donald, pleased to meet you," he replied, rubbing the sweat off on his trousers.

"So what do you do, Donald?" George asked. Hardly a leading question, so why did it sound insinuating?

"Branch management, lower Broadway," Donald replied, trying to make his starter job sound more impressive. "You?"

"Architect, commercial mostly, though I have a little side business remodeling Victorians up in St. George," he said, raising his chin as if they were standing at the bottom of the hill looking up.

"George of St. George," Donald said, a lame attempt at a joke that seemed to bolster Helga's assessment that he lacked a sense of humor.

"I'm no saint, believe me," George said, rolling his eyes. Then he opened his briefcase and took out some papers and was silent for the rest of the trip.

When he got up, Donald followed him outside. "They should have a bar on these boats, especially for the ride back," George said as they stood shoulder to shoulder. "I could go for a stiff one right about now. You?"

"It would certainly take the edge off," Donald said. "But I have to ride out to Grasmere. Wife's waiting on dinner."

"Just one," George suggested, though he did not insist. "There's a bar just a few steps from the bus stop, right across from the library."

George had the salesman gene, a rah-rah attitude softened by a glib tongue. Donald had attended New Dorp High with any number of these "There's no problem I can't solve." jock types. He appeared unflappable, except for the noticeable jitter in his hands, which made the ice cubes in his whiskey clink against the side of the glass.

"I tell you, I fix up these Victorians," he said, "but I'd never live in one. They're dark, and the rooms are small. Not for me. Got myself a nice modern ranch on Todt Hill, double lot. How about yourself?"

"We're renting for now. New development out by Willowbrook. Nothing special," he said, suddenly remembering his wife and glancing at his watch. "I should be on my way in a few . . ." He stopped short, recalling that Helga and her mother had bingo tonight at St. John's Lutheran. She'd left "something on the stove" for him. When he relayed this to George, he said, "Excellent. How about you and I grab a bite then? Let me call the missus and tell her I'll be late."

"She probably cooked for you," Donald said.

"Karen? Cook? That'll be the day," George laughed. "Kidding of course. She makes a mean mac-cheese. Just follows the instructions on the box. Foolproof. Be right back."

Donald had few friends and was flattered that such a self-possessed man wanted to have dinner with him. The guy's energy was a kick. Made his pulse race.

When he returned, George tossed some bills onto the bar. When Donald offered to contribute, he said "Next time," which pleased him. He was already looking forward to a next time and made a note to ask for George's work number before the end of the meal.

"Hey, want to take a scoot up around the corner and have a look at my handiwork, see what you think?" George asked. The request sounded clumsy, a well-thought out invitation that had become muddled on its way from brain to tongue.

"Okay," Donald said, somewhat hesitant.

"Careful now," George said as he tripped gingerly over the debris in the front hallway of the empty house and started climbing the stairs. He looked briefly over his shoulder, indicating that Donald should follow.

He flicked on the light in one of the bedrooms, which was papered in a drab olive damask. "See what I mean? Dark, even with the lights on," he asserted.

"Sure is," Donald said, standing just inside the door.

As he reached over Donald's shoulder to flick the off switch, George thrust his body forward and groped him in the darkness. The helpless terror he felt was contradicted by his physical response. He allowed George to gyrate his body and offered himself up without the slightest struggle, almost as if it had been agreed upon beforehand.

Hitching up his trousers afterwards, he heard George's footsteps descending to the first floor and out the door, which slammed shut. Alone and shaken, he relived the intrusion and the discomfort and elation that ensued. A terrible thought crossed his mind, and he was unable to dislodge it as he lumbered back down the hill.

On the bus, trembling and afraid, he fell into a dark torpor that resembled sleep, but only to the casual observer, and missed his stop. Had to walk a mile back home, and he passed out the moment his head hit the pillow.

This swoon-like sleep became his refuge, kept him from dwelling on his unsettling conjecture. He awoke no more rested than when he'd been plagued by insomnia, but at least his senses were too dulled to summon up any discomfiting emotions. He no longer searched for George on the morning ride, during which he napped until the boat slammed against the pylons. Then he would start as if George were looming over his shoulder, a brutal reminder of his acquiescence.

At home, he was absent, filtering out Helga's nattering, and begging off his husbandly duties. When word got back to Berta, his mother-in-law upbraided him for his lassitude. Donald offered no rebuttal. He occupied himself counting the minutes until he returned home and got into bed.

He was awoken abruptly from his trance-like state by the appearance of a two-toned Buick Skylark across the street from his home. A man was sitting behind the wheel looking down into himself.

Donald threw on a jacket, walked to the curb and got into his DeSoto. The Skylark followed him up a dirt road to the local nature preserve. He got out of the car and walked a half mile into the woods. He could hear the leaves crackling behind him, crushed by the weight of heavy footsteps.

He stopped suddenly and waited but not for long. He was shoved to the ground. George fell on top of him, and he was consumed. When he awoke on the damp earth the following morning, his clothes in disarray, he brushed himself off and trekked back to his car. He waited up the street until Helga left for her weekly hairdresser appointment. Entering the house, he climbed the stairs and emptied out his closet and dresser drawers, tossing as much as he could carry into two cardboard suitcases. He got back into the car and drove off.

Growing up in rural West Virginia, Donald had little involvement with anyone outside his immediate family. When his parents divorced, he was sent to live with his maternal grandmother on Staten Island. And while the locals kept pretty much to themselves, life in an outer borough had still been a major adjustment for a fifteen-year-old. Now he was living in the heart of Manhattan and inexplicably, was entranced by the chaos. His favorite pastime was sitting in the second story window of his apartment on Perry Street and lulling his senses with the cacophony of street noises and passersby, day and night without cease.

The first time he glanced out the window and saw George standing on the sidewalk, he retreated into the apartment to deal with the dread and the excitement. George was bound to find him eventually if he bothered to look hard enough. When he peered out again, George was still there, staring blankly into the near distance; his exhaustion at having tried to stay away, and failing, was tangible. When he called to him, George turned and looked up, a scowl of defeat creasing his face. He climbed the stairs to the apartment, and Donald helped him out of his suit and carefully hung it in the closet.

Donald couldn't determine exactly when he started believing that George was in love with him; a conclusion based on more than conjecture. George had almost said the words a few times when they were in the throes, and he'd demonstrated it in the moments of heartfelt affection that began to seep through the necessary roughness Donald demanded. He worried that any attempt to address those feelings might cause a seismic rupture — and not only in George. It would force Donald to confront his own complex yearnings. Instead he chose to categorize his desires for George as some twisted need. Otherwise he might come permanently unglued whenever he fell asleep on his chest until George slipped out from under him and headed back to his real life.

They didn't talk much at first because it didn't seem to fit into their agreed-upon ritual. But soon, they began to exchange safe information about themselves. One topic George enjoyed discussing was his children, DeeDee and Jonathan. It immediately pepped him up and he became the confident man Donald had first seen strutting to the front of the Staten Island ferry each morning. He took a certain satisfaction in listening to George enthuse over the incidentals of the children's daily lives, mundane activities only a dedicated parent can fully appreciate.

Any talk of the missus however, was off-limits. If George could not be faithful to Karen physically, he had carved out a chunk only the two of them shared. And Donald respected that boundary, depended upon it almost.

During their breaks, the days and sometimes weeks during which George beat back his dependency, Donald found temporary asylum in others' arms. Since he still refused to classify himself as aberrant, he didn't actively pursue other men. He stumbled upon them — on a springtime stroll or while shopping at a local market. The men would look, then quickly look away, then look back again. Donald viewed these non-flirtation flirtations as quasi-comical and marveled that whiplash wasn't more common.

Ostensibly, these men were better acclimated to their wayward lives, though generally they were no less morose and self-recriminating. While Donald was willing to endure George's dourness because — well, just because — he had little stomach for their self-pitying behavior. He was having enough trouble coping without subjecting himself to echoes of his inner voice.

From among these disconsolate souls, Donald managed to befriend one or two men. Reynaldo was his age and masked all his insecurities behind a macho facade. Sexually he was fierce and boasted that he could satisfy women as well as men if he so chose. Women were simply more trouble, he claimed, and he already had one bastard in the Bronx.

Terry was older, a veteran, and by his own admission, permanently restless. He had a marshmallow center, though, particularly when he discussed his friend Monty with the kind of spirited enthusiasm and deep affection George demonstrated for his children. Donald did not object to being Terry's last-chance saloon after a fruitless evening on the prowl or even to being his sloppy second. The vacancy created by George's self-imposed exiles necessitated such compromises.

Stopgap measures, however, were not enough to obviate the sticky patches of loneliness and longing that no intermittent visitor could allay. As much as he endeavored to adjust to these sullen interludes, he often fell short. In moments of claustrophobic distress, his main solace was the babble of the noisy stream outside his window. And if that was still not enough, he would head out and become part of the flow.

He thought to offer George a key, which he refused. Rather than argue, Donald dropped it into George's jacket pocket. Whenever he came home and found him sitting in a straight-back kitchen chair looking completely undone, Donald would quietly undress and wait for him patiently in the tiny bedroom. Then he'd hear a dish break or the chair being overturned and George's shadow would descend on him.

His friend Terry rang the doorbell at two a.m. one night after another wanderlust evening. Donald sleepily went downstairs to let him in. While they were at it in the bedroom, they heard the lock turn. Suspecting a burglar, Terry rolled off him and searched for a weapon. George was already on him by the time his hand found the metal teapot on the kitchen stove. Terry was thrown to the floor, his nose cracking under George's hammy fist. He might have done more serious damage if Donald hadn't yanked him away.

"Get out!" George screamed, and Terry gathered his clothes, limped off and dressed in the stairwell.

"I'm sorry, Terry, I'm so sorry," Donald called after him.

Pointing a finger at him accusingly, George cried, "Who was that? What was he doing here? Don't you know you're mine?"

Donald stared at him and quietly shook his head. Of course he was George's but hearing it out loud forced him into denial. He'd promised himself that he would never complain, no matter how long George made him wait before returning; he always welcomed George as the prodigal, determined not to act the part of the abandoned wife, even if George now insisted on behaving like a possessive husband. Later, after he'd gone, Donald would lock himself in the bathroom and expel his bile. But not in front of George; never in front of George. If he did, he would lose him for sure.

"What do you mean no?" George pleaded.

"You have your life, George, and I have mine," he said calmly. "You're always welcome. But if you continue to react this way, I'm changing the locks."

Donald could hardly believe what he was saying. While he might be inured to George's impotent tirades, however, he saw no reason for anyone else to be subjected to them.

"Do you think changing the locks would keep me out?"

"Then I'll move," Donald said with a flint of defiance.

"I'll find you, I always do," he countered.

"Then I'll move again. Someplace far away."

"I don't understand what you want from me."

A list? Is that what George wanted, a list? How much time did he have?

Instead, he merely said, "Come to bed."

"Not until you clean yourself and change the sheets," George scowled.

"It's the only set I have. I'll take a shower and throw a coverlet over the couch."

His sangfroid only served to rile George further. "Why do you let me treat you like a whore?"

"I like being your whore," he said and, again, was shocked by his own words. But why should he be shocked? That seed had been planted the first time he noticed George's impeccable suits: "A tailor on Delancey fits them for me. Guy's a genius" he had once explained.

"Don't you hate yourself for that?"

"A little."

"Well I hate you. Every day I pray that I'll open the paper and read your obituary."

Donald wanted to laugh. How much more proof did he need that George loved him, loved him so hopelessly that he wished him dead? "That's one way out of this," he said. "As long as you don't die. I couldn't bear that."

Donald wrapped his arms around George's waist. "Don't. You smell like . . ." George complained, but didn't push him away.

"I know," Donald said, squeezing him tighter. "I know."

They kissed, and he could almost feel the anger and hurt drain from George's body.

Rechanneled, those emotions proved potent and Donald was transported — another glorious moment to store in the vault and reflect upon during George's unendurable absences.

Half a loaf, half a loaf, half a loaf onward.

Later, Donald gazed at the ceiling so he wouldn't have to watch George get dressed. Affecting a cheery lilt, he said, "So what are you and the kids up to this weekend?"

"They're away. Karen's folks have a summer place in the Poconos."

"Then feel free to stop by again," he said. "I'll plan to be alone."

"I had considered sleeping over but . . ."

"You can't sleep with your whore," Donald said, finishing the sentence for him.

"You're not my whore. I've never thought of you that way. Never. That's how come it made me so crazy to see you with . . . Why do we have to talk about this? If I sleep here, next thing you'll want is for me to . . ."

"No. I won't. I would never jeopardize what you have. You are who are you to me because they're so special to you."

"Stop doing that to yourself," George cried. "You are, you are, you are." He choked and repeatedly tapped his chest with the flat of his palm. Donald reveled in the swallowed words.

"Ask me to stay," he beseeched. "Please. I want to do this for you."

"Stay the night, George, would you? But only this one time, hear? I don't want you to make a habit of it."

ALL AND NOTHING AT ALL

Miss Dee Andrea Monet smoothed the nylon stocking against her firm left calf, which still bore several almost-imperceptible welts from her childhood. She pulled it up to her thigh and secured it to a black-lace garter belt. Her boyfriend, Mario, claimed he hadn't noticed the marks until she pointed them out. Wasn't that just like a man? Mario had deemed her "gams" perfect and, even after all these years, got as excited watching Dee Andrea don her stockings as he did when he rolled them off her, which he did slowly, savoring each and every moment. Unlike most men, Mario was never in a great hurry. A point in his favor.

Apart from her "gams" though, there were several things about Dee Andrea that he deemed less than perfect, she reasoned as she perused her extensive shoe collection for just the right heel — one high enough to flatter the calf and still maintain the balance between lady and slut. Mario was a stickler about that. He enjoyed arousing other men's envy and ardor but not enough to embolden them to flirt with her. The ones who dared were punished and so was she for attracting undue attention.

"You said you wanted me to look good," she would argue after he lost his temper and lashed out.

"Yeah, but not *that* good," he would reply.

Men and their contradictions.

Back when she was a boy, her father Sonny Prejean, a surly Acadian Métis, regularly beat her about the legs with a switch. Didn't need much of a reason; and it wasn't because his son, Jon, was fey, though he most certainly was that. To Sonny's reasoning, a good "switching," was a preemptive measure, a preview of worse to come should Jon even consider stepping out of line. Afterward, the boy's native Chinese mother, who subsisted on a regular diet of love smacks, would attend to his wounds with her secret Mandarin herbal salve that had been passed down through several generations. Little Jon deplored his mother's simpering and couldn't help but agree with his father's assessment that she was a weak and pitiful woman.

At age seventeen, in his farewell appearance as Jon, the six-foot transitioning youngster returned home and pummeled his father to within an inch of death with a tire iron. Pressing five one-hundred-dollar bills into his mother's palm, which he'd earned hustling on the streets of Ottawa, he counseled her: "Do not call a doctor or take him to a hospital. Do nothing, which should be easy for you. If he bleeds to death, it's God's will. If he recovers and starts hitting you again, you're on your own."

Dee Andrea, who had been gestating for some time, was birthed soon after that, a vivacious, brazen woman who sprang full-blown from Jon's spindly rib. She had her father's tawny skin and her mother's almond eyes, and her company was in demand both north of the border and in New York, where she eventually migrated.

Whenever Dee Andrea chafed at Mario's restrictive demands, she blamed it on Jon Prejean, whose ghost occasionally resurfaced. A sissy boy, as inadequate as his pitiful mother. It was Jon's spirit who had fallen for Mario, as beholden to his passive cruelty as he once had been to his father's direct aggression. And while Mario never gave her the slightest reason to doubt his devotion, Dee Andrea believed him when he said, "If you ever try to leave me, I'll kill you and no one will ever find the body."

The potential for a violent death had been an occupational hazard. But the idea that she would not be laid out publicly, her beauty at least partially restored, was untenable. Being properly mourned was her due. The only fitting ending. To distinguish Dee Andrea's life from that of her parents and their ill-conceived son, Jon.

Early on, Mario realized he would never be free of Dee Andrea. And he cursed her for it. She would be his ruination. Though he never could remember his dreams, he was all but certain that Dee Andrea had appeared in them long before they met. How else could he explain the rush and immediate sense of recognition he felt when he first spied her from a recess at the back of his father's bar on West Street.

Never one to act rashly, Mario bided his time, anonymously observing Dee Andrea for several months before making a move. He had to be absolutely certain that his attraction was bona fide. Despite his tough-guy swagger, he was terrified of crossing that line. Once he did, there would be no going back.

Dee Andrea came into the bar most nights at around eleven and often connected with someone shortly thereafter. How could she not? She was a knockout. A regal bearing, a steel backbone leavened by a fluid tongue and an engaging demeanor that hit a guy right where he lived. She stood out among the other demireps milling about; girls bearing a permanent let's-get-this-over-with scowl. Not real ladies, and certainly not men, they drifted in a kind of identity limbo. Not Dee Andrea. She was all woman with enough masculine energy to render her irresistible.

When Mario could no longer abide one more mook escorting her from the premises, he came out of hiding. Donning his best suit, a double-breasted charcoal pinstripe with a black shirt and white tie, he sidled up to the bar and offered to buy her a drink. His unnerving coolness, which had cowed many a man, crumpled. He was quaking and spoke in a winded staccato. Dee Andrea, no stranger to men with quirks, sought to put him at ease. "Where have you been all my life, stranger?" she said in a breathless tone, flicking her coiffed mane, her mile-long mink eyelashes batting playfully.

A come-on as clichéd as it was effective. But originality was not required and even confusing to a man so clearly flustered. Her display of interest enabled Mario to regain his confidence, his dominance. "Funny, that's exactly what I been thinking about you," he replied. "What do you say we get to know each other?"

"I'm not sure I can run that risk," she said, demurely lowering her eyes. "My spies tell me that you're one of the owners of this particular establishment. If I disappoint you, I might no longer be welcome here. Girl's gotta make a living, you know."

"Not anymore she don't," he assured her. "From now on you're off the clock. A doll like you should be sitting around all day eating chocolates and painting her toenails."

Now it was Dee Andrea's turn to be unnerved. "It's a generous offer," she said, "but just so we're clear. I'm not the kind of woman who enjoys being owned."

Mario was undaunted. "I could tell right off the bat that you was a girl with spunk. Don't you worry about nothing. I'll tie you up. But I'll never tie you down," he affirmed.

Whether Mario believed what he was saying — and his subsequent behavior would belie the glib bravado — he would have made any concession to have Dee Andrea. And the way he saw it, she wasn't the one taking the risk. She could always go back to the streets. But once Mario crossed desire's threshold, the door would shut tightly behind him. No reentry.

Mario had been with a few women, largely as an obligatory exercise, a way to defray suspicion and bond with the other men in his circle. But he'd never courted this kind of woman. Still, he didn't hesitate. He sensed that Dee Andrea had more than enough experience for both of them. She would know what to do. What to say. How to fulfill his every unspoken wish.

"Just leave it to me, baby," she cooed, as she tugged at his tie in the front seat of his Lincoln Continental.

He did and never looked back, though it cost him.

"The thing about Kyle and Lester," Dee Andrea said, speaking into her reflection as she wiped the cold cream from her eyelids, "is that they're inspirational. As a couple, they're like two hands of a clock. Without one another, time is meaningless."

She poked her head through a crack in the door. "Do you understand what I'm trying to say? Are you even listening?"

"Yeah. They go good together. Got it," Mario said, lifting his hooded eyes from the ledger.

Dee Andrea shook her head. Why did she even bother? Because . . . because it would be lovely to have a real conversation with a man who, just a few minutes earlier, had slathered her with adoration. Was a little postcoital chitchat too much to ask?

A cool splash of water and a quick towel-dab and she was done with her ablutions. "What I was trying to say is that finding love is rare enough, but maintaining, my dear, maintaining is the real sticky wicket. I know of precious few couples who've not made terrible accommodations to stay together."

"Why do I get the feeling that you're talking about us?" he said, accusingly. "I'm curious. Exactly what accommodations have you made because, myself, I think you're sitting pretty."

Dee Andrea tossed back her head and silently laughed. Mario didn't get it and he never would. He was different from other men, yet persisted in mimicking their behavior, treating her as an object of delectation and then neglecting her the rest of the time.

"I'm not complaining," Dee Andrea said sharply. "And if you think I am, you clearly don't know what complaining is. I was merely pointing out that, even among happy couples, Kyle and Lester are unique. What they have is pure. They breathe the same air, passing oxygen back and forth."

"You breathe in oxygen, you breathe out carbon dioxide," Mario mumbled. "They'd asphyxiate each other."

"Are you sure?" Dee Andrea asked as she removed her wig and wrapped her head with the geometric-patterned silk Pucci scarf Mario had given her as a gesture of atonement after their last blow-up.

"Basic science. Go to the library sometime and look it up," he snorted.

"I consider them an exception to nature's rules," Dee Andrea said, walking toward the bed. "I wish you could meet them. Then you'd understand what I'm saying."

"Babe. You know that's not possible," Mario said. "You got your friends, I got mine. Now get over here and let me sniff you. It makes me nuts."

"Sniff me? Why do you have to be so . . . so inelegant," she said, bristling.

"Would you have me any other way?" he snickered, and quickly got down to business.

Probably not, she thought, but would it kill him to say something romantic once in a while? Dee Andrea eventually submitted to him because . . .

well, a woman in mink-lined handcuffs doesn't have much wiggle room.

And truly, she owed Mario a great deal. Without Mario, she'd be living in a hovel, turning tricks to pay her rent until the day her luck finally ran out. Whatever his other faults, he was no cheapskate. She was well compensated for the hours and days when they were apart. And she had to admit that she harbored a certain affection for his gruff manner and guarded vulnerability. While not much in the looks department, he had a certain style and could be charming, particularly when he craved her. He aimed to please, and often succeeded.

Yet, she continued to be nagged by the bargain she'd struck. Love should not be pragmatic, she reasoned. It should be a lightning bolt and if that ideal proved unsustainable, especially for the likes of her, at the very least it should be ennobling.

If Mario didn't regard his attraction to Dee Andrea as aberrant, he was in the minority. She was, for all intents and purposes, female, certainly more of a woman than some of the stevedores his friends had married. But she was not presentable to family and friends and never would be. She was his dirty little secret. His dirty little open secret.

Giving himself to Dee Andrea had not been as painful an adjustment as coming to terms with the consequences. If only Dee Andrea knew how much he'd given up. Because of her, his once bright future had been constrained. He would never enter the inner circle and forever be the object of suspicion and veiled ridicule in his family and among his business associates.

Because of her, he'd become dispensable.

Mario's father regarded his fascination with Dee Andrea as a personal affront. Initially, his mother had sought to breach the estrangement. To quell his father's anger, she suggested he find a suitable girl to marry. As long as he maintained a facade of propriety and produced grandchildren, what he did on the side was his own business. She recognized that her son, like most men, was plagued by furtive yearnings and that shaming him would only fan the flames.

While he refused to comply with his mother's wishes, Mario respectfully kept Dee Andrea out of sight, holing her up in a solitary apartment near the West Side Highway a few blocks north of the Battery Tunnel. And when they ventured out, except for a few Village holes in the wall, they traveled to Long Island or central Jersey where they were unlikely to run into a familiar soul.

Regardless, Mario remained a blemish on the family, and how long they would tolerate the affront was anyone's guess. As long as his mother was alive, he'd probably be safe. After that, he faced an untimely and violent end. But he planned to keep on living until then.

And to his mind, Dee Andrea was life. If he could only get her to stop griping. You'd think that after all he'd done for her, she would stay put instead of wandering the streets "like a tramp" with her girlfriends whenever he was away on business. Even if she didn't follow through on their offers (and he'd find out soon enough if she did), the idea of other men paying her compliments enraged him. When he confronted her about it, she complained that he kept her "like a caged animal in the zoo," and started to pack her bags. Which she knew would send him into a panic. The one time he raised a hand to her, she grabbed his forearm and held tight. "If you strike me again, you'd better be prepared to finish the job," she warned, "because it's the only chance you'll ever get."

Mario backed down and wept tears of hair-pulling frustration. Seeking to appease her, he offered to set her up in some kind of business at an unused space he owned on the second floor of a building on 17th Street just off 5th. "But Dee, honey, do something classy. And give it a French name," he said.

Toujours Coiffures opened with a built-in clientele. Dee Andrea's coterie was in constant need of hairpieces and appliances and accessories. What they didn't need was sass, condescension and sometimes threats from store personnel. Dee Andrea understood them. She respected their varied preferences, their differing means of expression. She provided service without judgment.

Eventually, the shop branched out to a theater clientele. That the business catered mainly to "women" pleased Mario. An added bonus was that, as the business expanded and she became more and more involved, Dee Andrea found less time to grouse about his absences. When he was around, she now showered him with appreciation in a way that exalted him, endowed him with a sense of invincibility.

The truce didn't last, however. A sip of independence left her thirsty for more. She became more involved in the Village community, and when she was arrested (not once, but twice) outside a bar during some well-publicized protests in Sheridan Square, Mario suffered the humiliation of having to negotiate with his friends at the local precinct for her release. It would certainly get back to the family and there'd be blowback. He was sure about that. How severe the punishment, however, was difficult to assess.

"You should have seen the way those assholes looked at me," he told her as they left the police station and got into his Lincoln Continental. "Why did you do it, Dee? Make me look like a fool? Why don't you just cut off my balls and be done with it?"

"Would you please shut up," Dee Andrea snapped, tired and disheveled from a night in the tank. "You knew who I was from the start."

"Yeah, you were a whore."

"I'm still a whore," she growled. "An exclusive whore."

"Don't talk that way. You know how much I care about you, baby.

Don't make me feel bad."

"What about me? I gave you everything you wanted. I made a home for you, let you come and go as you pleased. I started a successful business."

"With my money," he reminded her.

"And I paid you back, and now I make enough to buy my own clothes and keep up the house. I do my part. Still, you show me no respect."

Mario began pounding on the steering wheel. "Respect? You think I've had any respect since we got together? My father and I don't speak. The business, which was supposed to pass to me, is going to my younger brother, Joe, who treats me like dirt. All because of you."

"Why didn't you tell me things were that bad?" Dee Andrea said. "You never talk to me."

"You never talk to me. You never talk to me," he said, mimicking Dee Andrea in a pitch higher than her own. Then he began to laugh. "Listen to us. You know what we sound like? Like some old married couple. I don't tell you things because I want to protect you. That's my job. To protect you."

"You big lug," she said, depositing a kiss on his cheek. It was a term of affection she'd picked up from a George Raft movie from the Thirties. And it fit Mario to a T.

Their circular arguments ended in temporary reconciliations. Mario would allow himself to be coddled and mollified. For despite his protestations, whenever Dee Andrea was in his arms, the world went away. For both of them.

As he slept beside her, Dee Andrea sometimes contemplated suffocating Mario with a pillow. Then she would remember that poor woman, Joanie, the one she fitted for a wig after her hair started falling out from doing too many drugs. Joanie accidentally pushed her old man down a flight of stairs because he was trying to take her kid away. She lost him anyway, to prison.

"Sometimes I wish I'd never met Mario," she once confided to Adoree, one of her regular customers, "that I'd gone home one night with the wrong guy and it was all over."

"Honey, some girls would give their left titty to have what you got," Adoree admonished her. "You been watching too many romances on the 'Million Dollar Movie.'"

Maybe Adoree was right, Dee Andrea thought as she rolled Mario over to stop him from snoring. They were two lost souls who'd been lucky enough to find one another. Not so different from Kyle and Lester, if far from ideal.

A pounding on the front door. Mario, who slept with the thickness of a cement block, barely rustled. Dee Andrea wrapped herself in a negligee.

"Can I help you?" she said to the goon standing in the hallway.

"Yeah," he said, looking her up and down with contempt. "I'm looking for Mario. Joe sent me."

"His brother?" she said, her suspicions triggered. "What does he want at this hour?"

"That's his business. Not yours. Stop asking questions and go wake him up."

"And your name?" she said, moving toward the bedroom.

"Tell him it's Tony B. And leave the door open, if you don't mind."

In the bedroom, Dee Andrea stood over Mario and in an audible voice said, "Darling, your friend Tony B. is here. You need to get up."

Mario didn't stir. It would take a good shove to get a rise out of him.

"He'll be with you in a moment. He's getting dressed," she said, returning. "In the meantime, I should get his coat. It's chilly out there."

Opening the closet, she reached inside and deliberately upset some boxes on the top shelf.

Curious about the commotion, Tony B. placed a hand on his shoulder holster and came up behind Dee Andrea to investigate. She pivoted quickly and, before he could react, whacked him across the head with a baseball bat. Two additional blows and he stopped moving. Permanently.

"Mario," she said, poking him in the ribs. "Wake up, honey. Something's happened."

He sat up and with a huge yawn said, "Huh? What's going on?"

Dee Andrea reached into a lower dresser drawer for some old clothes. "I need you to help me get rid of a body."

They barely spoke during the entire three-hour ride to the Catskills where they buried Tony B. in a remote area wrapped in a blood-soaked Persian. She'd bought it from the first money she'd made at the shop. "I'm really going to miss that rug," she sighed, as she patted down the earth with her feet.

Mario promised to take her shopping for a new rug. "I know just the one. I saw it in a window on Delancey Street," she said, as they changed into clean clothes and burned the old ones. The morning air was just above freezing. She warmed her gelid hands over the impromptu campfire and inspected her fingernails. She wondered if her manicurist would be able to fit her in without an appointment.

As they coursed down the thruway back to the city, Mario glanced at her with bewildered affection. "What made you do it?"

"I was afraid he was going to kill you," she said, calmly glancing out the window at the rising sun. "If you're going to die, I don't want it to be because of me."

"Thanks. I owe you," Mario said.

"Don't thank me," she said. "Thank Jon Prejean. He's one tough little fairy."

"And who is this Jon?" Mario asked.

"Oh, just somebody I used to know."

Mario pondered what she'd said and came to a moment of clarity. "You didn't do it just because you were afraid of losing your meal ticket, did you?"

"That might have been true at one time. Now I have my own business. Even if your family refuses to renew my lease, my clients would follow me somewhere else. I can take care of myself."

"No argument there," he said with a twinkle.

"I did it because I like having you around. But you have to talk to me more. I had no idea the situation was so serious."

"I was trying to spare you. I didn't think you could handle it. Shows you how much I know."

"Do you think your brother will try again?"

"No. I'll call my mother. Tell her what happened. She'll give Joe an earful."

"She sounds like a fierce woman."

"I like my women strong, or couldn't you tell?"

"Wish I could meet her."

"In some other lifetime maybe," he said with finality. "Though for the record, I'm sure she'd approve."

"That's sweet of you to say, Mario," she said, leaning over to caress the side of his face. "I guess I don't have it so bad after all. We may not be Kyle and Lester but . . ."

"Them again?" Mario growled.

"Let me finish," she said. "We may not be them, but we're not as bad as all that. I'll try my best not to complain so much."

"Somehow, I don't see that lasting," he chuckled.

"Probably not," she conceded.

"So why have you kept this Jon fellow from me?"

"I don't want to discuss him," she said sharply.

"Shoe's on the other foot, huh?"

Dee Andrea glared at him, then immediately softened. "I guess we are like an old married couple. We fight. We make up. We fight. We make up."

Mario nodded and shrugged. "Yeah. Sometimes I think we fight just as an excuse to make up," he said, rolling his eyes lasciviously.

"A one-track mind," she scowled.

As they crossed the Tappan Zee Bridge, he said. "How about I take you to City Island for breakfast? Then maybe for a boat ride."

"That sounds lovely," she said. "I'm famished. Think I'll go off my diet and order bacon and eggs. Sunny side up."

SHRIMPY'S OPENING NIGHT

Around midnight, Barbara got into bed and cracked open Mary McCarthy's juicy best seller *The Group*, about an octet of Vassar alumna. The unintentionally hilarious lesbian character read less like fiction than science fiction. She highlighted a couple of ripe, purple passages to share with Adrian.

Normally, Barbara tried to stay up until Adrian returned home from the bar, right after closing, but at a little after one, she drifted off and almost immediately fell into a dream about Shrimpy. He was seated at the foot of the bed, his gangly frame leaning against the painted wrought-iron bedpost. His face was heavily bruised with dried blood caked around his ears.

When she gasped, Shrimpy uttered a mischievous laugh. "I know what you're going to say. I should go to the hospital." He dismissed the suggestion with a swipe of the hand. "But I just can't be bothered."

Barbara lay back onto the pillow and forced a stiff-lipped smile, which Shrimpy had once astutely identified as "the polite-society version of a sneer."

"So I hear that in my absence, *Fiddler on the Roof* opened and is the season's hot ticket," he said. "And here I would have bet good money that, after that rat-fink bastard Jerry Robbins blabbed to HUAC, Zero Mostel would murder him during rehearsals and make it look like an accident." He shook his head dismissively. "Boy, and they say *politics* makes strange bedfellows."

Barbara was about to ask where he'd been and when he planned on returning, when Shrimpy announced, "Gotta go. Have a hot date. Don't want to keep the man waiting." And with a feeble flick of the wrist, he trickled away.

In the morning, as she prepared breakfast, she considered mentioning the dream. Adrian was a born fatalist and Barbara could almost predict her reaction. "Bobby, honey, when are you going to let this go?" she'd say. "Nothing's going to change what is."

"Sleep well?" Adrian asked, glancing down at an unappealing bowl of oatmeal: doctor's orders. She was putting a strain on her heart and needed to lose a few, especially around the middle. She had bucked and moaned and evaded until Barbara took control of her diet. Adrian knew better than to balk. She might be able to beat Barbara mano a mano. In any other arena, she was woefully outgunned.

"Yes, I slept very well, thank you," she replied, and Adrian could tell she was lying. Barbara cracked open *The Group* and read the passage soberly as if it were serious literature. By the time she'd finished, Adrian's sides were aching. "Well, I never," Adrian said. "And apparently neither has Mary McCarthy," Barbara replied.

Adrian always took a nap before work, and Barbara sometimes crawled in beside her. But this afternoon she was restless. She paced the length of the studio apartment, her thoughts fixated on Shrimpy. She recalled that he'd once remarked, "You left a 5th Avenue six for this two-by-four? Boy, love must be grand."

The last time she'd seen Shrimpy was right after Labor Day in 1963. He was nursing an espresso at Café Figaro and thumbing through dog-eared copies of *Playbill*. He emitted a gasp as she approached. "My dear, Jackie Kennedy has nothing on you. Where did you get those peachy sunglasses? Let me guess, Nina Ricci?" he said before launching into one of his rambling monologues, this one a lamentation of the past Broadway season.

In a deliberately irritating guttural voice, he offered up a wicked imitation of Anne Bancroft in *Mother Courage*, dubbing her "over-actress of the year." Yet he had kind words for the otherwise excoriated *The Milk Train Doesn't Stop Here Anymore* with the "glorious" (eyes rolled heavenward) Hermione Baddeley as Flora Goforth. The play still needed work, he opined, possibly even radical surgery.

"It's too hothouse, even for Tom. Poor baby," he said of Tennessee Williams, with whom he'd once shared a cigarette in a back alley during the revival of *Summer and Smoke* at Circle in the Square, where Shrimpy tended the box office. "Ever since Frank (Frank Merlo, Williams's lover) died, he's come all undone. I don't think all the king's horses and all the king's men have enough glue to repair the damage."

When Barbara's eye traveled to the nasty gash on the side of his forehead, Shrimpy offered a transparent excuse: He'd slipped getting out of the tub. After so many similarly lamentable explanations, it was hardly worth reproving him.

Though Barbara was inordinately fond of him because of his eccentricities and not in spite of them — more often than not, Shrimpy was the object of curiosity and disdain. He was deemed odd even by Greenwich Village standards. Hooted at, chased, sometimes spat upon. Not that he gave "a fig," he claimed. He had come to New York to fulfill a dream. What that was exactly, he'd never articulated. Since he had no particular talent, Barbara reasoned, perhaps it was to live an art-adjacent life. If so, he had succeeded.

She was one of the few people who knew his actual name, Ezekiel Jackson. He'd moved east in 1946 on the unique notion that there was something in the New York water that would transform him into a swan. Descended from several generations of Oklahoma homely, he was concerned that if he remained in Enid much past his twenty-first birthday, his teeth would fall out one by one, like petals off a dying bloom. Happened to every member of his family and only a handful bothered to pursue dentures.

In every magazine photograph or movie of Manhattan he'd seen as a boy, the citizenry was, if not uniformly attractive, then unique looking. He was willing to settle for unique. And certainly, he was that, if never in a way that elicited general approbation. Shrimpy (the sobriquet evolved from the locals constantly calling him "the shrimp") was pockmarked and pale and always wore the same long-sleeve striped pullover, dark-brown cotton-drill slacks, dirty, white Keds and a honey-colored porkpie hat with a yellowing theater-ticket stub tucked inside the silk red-and-gold-paisley band — a souvenir of his first Broadway show, a revival of Shaw's *Pygmalion* starring Gertrude Lawrence as Eliza and Raymond Massey as Henry Higgins.

"At almost fifty, Shaw complained that Gertie was a little long in the tooth to play Eliza," he said, eyebrows wriggling. "Fortunately, the stage is more forgiving than the movies. There are no close-ups. Truthfully, I didn't mind her so much. It was Massey who got under my skin. Henry Higgins filtered through Boris Karloff. Not an effete bone in his body. And Henry Higgins is nothing if not effete." When Barbara started laughing, he joined in. "I'm a stitch, ain't I?" he remarked.

For Shrimpy, any reaction — from horror to ridicule — was preferable to no reaction.

Regardless of the temperature, Shrimpy perspired and his hands were eternally clammy. His curious gait was the result of flat feet, which he cursed for keeping him out of the war. He'd enlisted the day after Pearl Harbor but "they wouldn't even let me be a driver," he lamented. Neither, it seems, would the New York taxi union after he failed the qualifying test by plowing a yellow-and-black checker into a fence on 10th Avenue. Not that he required a moving vehicle to inflict damage. He lasted only three days in his first job as a dishwasher at the Waldorf.

"The Waldorf," he exclaimed, "I worked at the Waldorf. Can you imagine?" he said as if he'd held some exalted managerial position. "They even let me keep pieces of the dishes I broke. I still have 'em up in my closet somewhere. I'll show 'em to you sometime, if you like."

The McBurney YMCA in Chelsea was Shrimpy's first residence in Manhattan. He became fascinated by the furtive goings-on in the hallways and finally got up the nerve to join in. Through trial and error, mostly error, he happened on a specific type: "Brutes," he called them. "If they ain't brutes, I ain't interested."

Hulking hirsute men with scars and tattoos and broken noses were his siren call and once, late one night on her way home from Adrian's bar, Barbara had seen him in the company of some "Bluto" — as he referred to them. He pursued riffraff, he remarked, as determinedly as they rebuffed him. On the rare occasion when his advances were welcomed, the men abused him and the two events became inextricably entwined. A romantic encounter absent a physical reminder, was somehow incomplete, less than satisfying. "But it's all in fun," he would say coyly. "Nobody really gets hurt."

Shrimpy made no effort to conceal either his masochistic tendencies or his sexual predilection like many of Barbara's other gay friends, male and female. "Three-Dollar Bill. That's what they call me," he joshed. "What, me worry? As long as they don't call me late for dinner."

Dissembling about his injuries arose less from shame than Shrimpy's distorted code of gentlemanly conduct. "I'm not the type who kisses and tells," he said. While gratified by his friends' concern, he urged them not to make too much of his injuries. "You don't never gotta worry about me," he would say, slipping into Sooner twang. "I roll with the punches. I may be shrimpy, but I'm as tough as they come."

His singular passion, however, was the theater. When he spoke about plays and musicals, he turned uncommonly eloquent and insightful. Whether over lunch at Stewart's Cafeteria or afternoon tea at Barbara's following a "me and the blue-haired ladies" Wednesday matinee, Shrimpy's observations and critiques were thoughtful and usually dead-on. He had a cast-iron memory that enabled him to recall every nuance of a stage drama months or years after the fact, transporting the listener into the audience beside him. For Shrimpy, live performance was a spiritual journey. He approached it with the reverence of ritual and had only contempt for playwrights, directors or actors who befouled the holy temple.

Like any true theater aficionado, he was not above gossip, liberally collecting and dispensing anecdotes and arcana. Among the early plays he saw upon decamping to Manhattan was another Shaw revival, *Candida* starring Katharine Cornell and, in the juvenile role of Eugene Marchbanks, Marlon Brando.

"Heck, I didn't need *Streetcar* to see that Marlon was a star. It was there from the moment he walked on stage and held his own against Kit Cornell, and let me tell you, that ain't hay. My problem with the casting was that no one in her right mind would go back to her husband if she could have Brando. Gotta say, though, I don't understand what Marlon saw in that roommate of his, Wally Cox. But I'm hardly one to talk," he confided. "I've given my heart to some pretty strange characters. And they handed it back to me — in pieces. Ah well, blood under the bridge. Blood under the bridge."

Then he looked up and smiled at Barbara in that winsome way that made her sigh.

Shrimpy strewed celebrity names like breadcrumbs and, though Barbara was an avid theatergoer herself, she could hardly keep up. "I'm here to tell you, Quintero had to wrench a performance out of Robards, who was more interested in rushing over to Louis' Tavern during his break than in nailing O'Neill's rhythms," he said of the legendary Circle in the Square production of *The Iceman Cometh*. Or "Miss Geraldine Sue Page is really Tom reincarnated as a woman, didn't you know?" he said after witnessing her indelible performance as Alma in the revival of Williams's *Summer and Smoke*.

Or "normally a ruffian like that Kerouac person would be right up my alley. But after hearing him drunkenly slobber his way through a poetry reading last night, I can't imagine why Ginsberg hangs out with that anti-Semitic mama's boy. Makes you wish he'd stayed *On the Road*. Have you ever tried to read that scribble?" Barbara had, without much success. "It's like Truman Capote said, 'That's not writing. That's typing.'"

Adrian accused Barbara of indulging Shrimpy because she fancied herself an upper-crust Emma Goldman. "Give me your tired, your poor, your misshapen. Nothing more than aristocratic guilt."

"If that's the worst thing you can say about me after all these years," Barbara countered, "I'd say we're getting on pretty well."

Once Shrimpy slipped her comp tickets and, with a wink, confided, "By the by, you won't be the only redhead in your aisle." The seats turned out to be adjacent to Bob Fosse and Gwen Verdon, and she was flattered when the incorrigible choreographer flirted with her during intermission, in full view of his wife — until Adrian stared him down.

"Isn't that Bob a caution?" Shrimpy cackled when Barbara reported back. "How I envy you. If I had your looks and savoir faire, I could have been a great courtesan, like Audrey Hepburn in Anita Loos's play *Gigi*. Ah, but you gave it all up for the love of a bull dyke. How can the theater compete with that kind of drama?"

"The theater is only interested in our kind of drama if we're tortured and suicidal," Barbara reminded him.

In the middle of the produce aisle at Balducci's, a young man, who introduced himself as Donald, approached her. "You're a friend of Shrimpy's, aren't you?" he said. "Have you heard from him lately?"

She admitted that she had not. It had been at least two weeks since they last spoke. He'd phoned from work to tell her about *Luther*, John Osborne's drama starring newcomer Albert Finney, for whom he predicted "great things." Shrimpy said he admired Osborne's play more than he actually liked it: "The man's gotten a little too pleased with the sound of his own dialogue."

Shrimpy had championed the playwright's earlier efforts because it forced British actors to be less declamatory and more natural, similar to what the Actor's Studio attempted with the Method. "It's still performance, and it's still heightened," he said. "But already the line between the stage and the audience is beginning to blur. That's the future, Barbara. You mark my words."

"He hasn't shown up for work in several days. I went by his apartment on Varick with my next-door neighbors, Kyle and Lester," Donald said. "The super hasn't seen him, and his mailbox is full to overflow. I'm worried, given Shrimpy's . . . well, you know."

"Have you checked the hospitals? The jails?" Barbara asked. The possibility that Shrimpy had come to serious harm made her queasy. "With the World's Fair coming up, the police have been on another one of their so-called 'clean-up crusades.'"

Adrian's bar had been raided the prior week. An under-counter cash distribution made the problem go away.

Donald said he had checked, but to no avail. "Well, then he should be reported as a missing person," Barbara said.

"We thought of that. But it should come from next of kin," Donald said.

"All his family lives in Oklahoma. I don't think he's in contact with them. Perhaps his employer?"

"I tried to see the guy who runs Circle in the Square, a Mr. Mann," Donald said. "All I got was the runaround from his secretary."

"Well that simply won't do," Barbara said. Turning on her heel, she set aside her groceries, marched out the glass door and headed for Bleecker Street. Donald trailed behind her. "Look out everyone. Woman on a mission," Adrian would announce whenever Barbara got riled up about some injustice or impropriety. A self-righteous streak was one of the things she liked most about Barbara, who had been so tentative and squelched when they'd first met, more than a decade earlier.

Mann's assistant tried to put them off again. But Barbara was adamant, and the impresario finally agreed to meet with her and Donald. Calmly, but forcefully, she persuaded him to file a missing person's report and, if need be, request an investigation into Shrimpy's disappearance. Barbara said she would do her part, as well. She still had connections in city government through her husband from whom she was separated, though they remained on cordial terms and occasionally socialized.

"I knew I was right to come to you," Donald said, after the police report was filed.

"I'm glad you did," she said. "Lovely meeting you, though I wish it had been under better circumstances."

On the way home, Barbara was unable to shake the image of Shrimpy, cold and battered and beyond repair. She forced her mind back to happier recollections. In the early spring of 1960, she'd gone to the Circle box office and waited while Shrimpy advised an elderly couple who were on a theater tour of New York. He penciled out a list of must-sees. "Go to the Alvin Theatre and ask for Sonny," he instructed. "Have him give you the best seats available for *Once Upon a Mattress*. Tell him I sent you. If he gives you any sass, call me immediately."

The couple trotted off, grateful and beaming. "Well, if it isn't Miss Barbara, the only woman I know who wears white gloves to eat lunch at the Automat."

"Shrimpy, how are you?" she said, trying to overlook the discoloration under his left eye.

"Been better. Been worse," he said. "Oh this? Life ain't no bowl of cherries, I tell you. But like the song says, we gotta live and laugh at it all. What can I do you for, dearie?"

"I know this is short notice, but I was wondering if you could get someone to cover for you on Tuesday night. I have two tickets to the premiere of that new Gore Vidal show *The Best Man*, and I was wondering if you'd be my date."

"Me and you at a Broadway premiere?" he said, shaking his head. "I couldn't. I just couldn't. Why, I don't even own a tuxedo."

"I'll rent you one," Barbara said, retrieving a business card from her purse. "Go see my friend Philip and tell him to charge it to my account."

"But you mingle with all the swells. No, impossible. Get that dreamy pal of yours, Monty, to go with you. Why are you asking me, anyway?" he said. As he always did whenever he was a bit on edge, his brow broke into a full sweat.

"Because I'm going to want to talk about the play with someone afterward, and I can't wait until you get around to seeing it. Please," she implored.

"Oh Barbara," he giggled. "How can I say no to a Brahmin?"

At the time, Barbara was still living in the 5th Avenue apartment with her husband. They had agreed not to officially separate until their daughter, JoAnn, went off to Bryn Mawr. The doorman announced Shrimpy; Barbara waited in the hallway until he emerged from the elevator. He was pulling at the constraints of his stiff-collared dress shirt and wearing his porkpie hat, with the theater stub sticking out.

"Shrimpy, dear, you're not seriously going to wear that hat with a tuxedo?" she said.

"But it's my good luck hat," he whined. "I never go anywhere without it."

Without asking, she removed it from his head. "I'm leaving it here on the entry table. You'll get it back when you take me home." Glancing at the remnants of the bruise and the unruly mess atop his head, she summoned him forward. "Before we leave, I'm going to run a brush through your hair. And maybe a dab of foundation under that eye."

"I told you not to ask me. I'm going to embarrass you," he said, with the pitiable scowl of a schoolchild.

"Pish-posh," she said dismissively. "Otherwise, you look quite handsome this evening."

"Handsome? Naw. You're having me on!" he said, biting his lip with barely concealed mirth.

"I'm serious. Philip did an excellent job of putting you together. I must send him a thank-you note. Now let's get to it. By the time I'm through, Leonard Lyons will want to run your picture in his column."

"My picture on the society pages? Now wouldn't that be something?" he sighed.

At the theater, Shrimpy acted the perfect gentleman, opening doors, attentive, deferential. He wiggled with excitement in his seat, oohing and aahing at the opening night array of celebrities, but offering up no more than a restrained "How do you do?" when Barbara introduced him during intermission. Afterward, in their booth at Sardi's, he dissected the play scene by scene and she recalled that his observations beat the hell out of anything Brooks Atkinson wrote the following morning in the *Times*.

At her apartment door, weary, but still on a high, he thanked her for an unforgettable time. "Being introduced to Gore Vidal in the flesh was nothing compared to being your date," he gushed. "I'm having this *Playbill* bronzed."

Then he grabbed his lucky hat and got into the elevator. Placing it against his chest, he bowed at the waist like a courtier just as the elevator doors closed.

VILLAGE DINER: NIGHTTIME

Late June, 1969

Outside Village Cigars, Phil rests his wide back against the green wrought-iron rampart over the downtown IRT exit, a safe distance from the melee across the way. He chain-smokes Marlboros, lighting each new cigarette with the stub of the old one.

The previous night's eruption was splashed all over the morning paper, and it caught Phil's attention. He isn't quite sure what to make of the protesters — a grab bag of shapes, sizes, colors, and indeterminate identities in heated confrontation with the boys in blue. Not that he blames them, but it's hard to see what good can come of a bunch of nancies and bulls blowing their stacks.

Then he reconsiders. Aw, let 'em have their fun. After all, they couldn't be much worse off than they were before.

Besides, New York summers are prime time for public venting; relentlessly sunny, humid days and sweltering nights when it's too hot to sit still, too hot to think. The simmering blood begins to bubble, atomizing reason and logic, emboldening even the most docile toward defiance, hurtling themselves at truncheoned patrolmen, smashing windows, overturning fetid trash bins.

A swishy young Latino in cutoffs and navel-exposing tank top prances by, oblivious to the shouting and shoving opposite. He holds a powder-blue transistor radio to his ear. A tinny sounding ditty, "Georgy Girl," spills from its innards into the breezeless air. On any other night he might very well be a target, harassed and shoved and poked with a nightstick or beaten up by some drunken bashers who'd driven into town from the suburbs to do some damage. Tonight, he's free to strut as he pleases, maybe catch a shy man's eye and duck into an alley for some mouth-on action. For pay. Or maybe just for play.

A thirtysomething man staggers out of the crowd, dazed and clearly the worse for alcohol. Phil knows from drunks. He's even broken them down into categories. There's the mean drunk, all vitriol and rage; the happy drunk, kissy and capricious; and the I'm-not-bothering-anybody-so-just-leave-me-the-fuck-alone drunk. But this guy, whose features are shaded under a drooping shock of chestnut hair, is unreadable. As he attempts to propel himself forward, he trips and falls off the curb into the gutter as cars and taxis cascade down 7th Avenue, weaving and honking, hitting potholes and swerving.

Phil races across the street. "You okay, buddy?" he says, hoisting the man to his feet and staring into bottomless eyes, deep and confused and wounded. The man recoils as if Phil's fingers were tipped with ice. He rushes off and when Phil trails him, wary that he might tumble into danger again, the man turns and yells, "Go away. I'm not here. You didn't see me."

Stunned for a moment by the man's ingratitude, it suddenly hits Phil. He should have guessed from the pressed khakis, the white button-down short-sleeve shirt, and Top-Siders, no socks. The guy's probably a moneyed type, a lawyer, a doctor, a banker — ripe picking for the vice cops. They regularly threaten to haul his kind in on a morals charge, and when the guy panics, seeing his life detonate, he is only too eager to pay any price to settle. The cops split the hush money with the mobsters who run the bars and tip them off. Poor bastard. Phil almost feels sorry for him. He's probably never done anything wrong in his life, except be born that way.

Born that way, like a curse, right? I mean, who would choose that kind of miserable, always looking-over-your-shoulder existence? How does anyone make peace with that? How do you live with yourself? He asks himself these questions out of curiosity, nothing else. A guy can be curious, can't he?

Retreating back to his safe vantage point in front of Village Cigars, Phil continues to monitor the goings-on for another half hour. Maybe what they're doing is a good thing; it is a free country, after all. Or should be. If it was only free for everyday Joe types, the jails would be full to overflowing, he laughs.

Then he darts around the corner to retrieve his Harley and hightails it back to Brooklyn. It's already past one. He's on early morning detail this week. He'll be lucky to get five hours' sleep.

A Week later. Two a.m.

An evening rain shower has failed to cool the city down. The temperature gauge is stuck at ninety degrees and the streets are an outdoor steam bath. Phil is sitting alone in an all-night diner just north of the Holland Tunnel at the outer edge of the Village sucking on his Marlboro and nursing a black coffee, lukewarm and bitter, staring down into his wavy reflection. The waitress, bored out of her gourd, is wiping the dried crud off ketchup bottles and refilling salt and pepper shakers.

The last paying customers left twenty minutes ago — an obvious hood and his deep-throated lady in tight Capri pants. They bickered and cooed,

cooed and bickered for the better part of an hour, but Phil sensed a deep connection between them. An underlying affection beneath the hostile rhetoric. A hood and a tranny? Takes all kinds, he reasons.

Tomorrow (well, technically today) is Phil's day off and he's been riding around for hours in circles — the hot wind in his face. The diner's air conditioner, perched over the entrance and raging at full blast, keeps him from wanting to rip off his skin. The heat outside. The fever in his head.

The door opens with a metallic scraping sound and Phil recognizes the man who enters from his college-boy pleated khakis, short-sleeve button-down and hair carelessly tossed over his eyes. Drunk again. Blotto. Barely has the strength to hold open the spring-loaded metal and glass door, which almost beams him in the head as he just manages to slip through. When he attempts to park his bottom on the counter stool, it comically spins, round and round, and he goes flying. The waitress glances down at his crumpled body and shakes her head in bemusement.

"You okay there, Donald?" she asks but makes no effort to help him, and it's up to Phil to play Good Samaritan again. He lifts the guy's dead weight and deposits him onto the orange-vinyl upholstered banquette in the booth opposite him.

Donald lowers his head onto the cool Formica table separating them and heaves a sigh. Without lifting his head, he says, "Thanks."

Phil nods, lights another cigarette and expels three perfect smoke rings. "Hey, doll, bring this guy a coffee," he calls to the waitress. "And you can top off mine while you're at it."

The waitress places a steaming mug in front of Donald with one hand and refills Phil's with the other, then walks away, dragging her rubber-soled lace-ups along the freckled linoleum. She grabs a pack of Kools from the counter and plops down in a far corner booth and turns her attention to the dark, empty streets outside, exhaling smoke and fogging the glass.

With a blind hand, Donald gropes for the mug and slowly resurfaces, brushing back his hair. "Here's mud in your eye," he says and Phil is once again riveted by his hazy, dark brown orbs.

"You want to talk about it?" Phil asks.

"What? You think I need a reason to get snockered?" Donald leans in for a closer look at Phil and it seems to jog his memory. Then he dismisses it, as if his mind is playing tricks on him. "You wouldn't be interested in my problems." He lifts the cup to his mouth and blows on the hot liquid, carefully taking another sip.

"Why not?" Phil says, blowing smoke skyward. "I got nothing but time, and there's nobody else to talk to."

"Look, mister, I should tell you right off the bat that I'm what they call a 'Village type.' And I don't mean a beatnik. *Capisce?*"

"Got it," Phil replies.

"And you still want to hear my troubles?"

"Only if you want to tell me." Phil shrugs. "Or we can talk about the Mets. You follow baseball? No, probably not."

"There you're wrong," Donald says, the words sloshing out of his mouth. "Bet you fifty Seaver wins the Cy Young this year."

"You're on," Phil says, amused. "Next thing you're going to tell me is that the Mets will take the series, when everybody knows it's going to be the Cubs this time."

"Don't be too sure," Donald challenges him. "The stars are out of whack this year. The Mets are starting to play like a real team, and Judy Garland dropped dead last week."

"Is that why you're so upset, because some old actress croaked?"

Donald slams down the mug, spilling some of its contents onto the table. Clumsily, he pries some napkins from the tightly packed metal dispenser and inefficiently mops up the liquid, mumbling. "She wasn't old. She wasn't even fifty. I saw the Carnegie Hall concert, you know."

"I didn't know she played Carnegie Hall," Phil says. "Reminds me of the old joke . . ."

Donald interrupts him. "How do you get to Carnegie Hall? Practice," he says. "Ba-dum-bum."

A smile cracks across Phil's face. Donald gasps. "Hey, I know you. From the other night. You were one of the cops, the ones who were beating on us. Up the street, in Sheridan Square."

Phil is rattled. "No, wasn't me. Think again." He should just tell him, he figures. But for some reason, he wants Donald to remember on his own.

"I could swear you were the pig who came tearing after me when I . . ." Donald says.

"When you what? You weren't making trouble, were you?" Phil asks.

"No," Donald protests. "Just lost my head for a minute."

"Lost your head?" Phil says, skeptically. "Meaning?"

"Never you mind," Donald says and motions the waitress for a refill. "Hey, Peg, fill me up again, would you, hon?"

Peg launches to her feet and reaches for the glass pot. As she refills their mugs, Phil pulls out his wallet and hands her two bills.

"And I don't need you paying for me either," Donald snorts.

"Relax. It's just coffee. Not like I treated you to a steak dinner," Phil says. "So, what were you doing that the cop came after you? I won't tell nobody," he adds, flashing "Scout's honor" fingers.

"I threw a bottle at him," Donald lets slip.

"Not a smart move," Phil replies, but in a good-natured way. "What were you thinking getting mixed up with all them crazies?"

"They're not crazy. Mad, that's all. Pissed off. And they have every right to be. But I wasn't part of it, not really. Happened by accident. I'd been sitting alone in my apartment drinking all night and the heat got to me. I had to get out. You know that feeling?"

"Yeah, I do," Phil says. There's a sadness to his admission, and Donald seems to pick up on it.

"I figured you might," Donald says. "I was taking a walk when I heard this commotion and when I got to the square, there must've been, I don't know, a few dozen people there yelling at the cops and throwing stuff. I couldn't figure out what was going on, and then I saw this big bruiser who for no reason, no reason at all, punched one of my neighbors, Lester, in the stomach. Lester, who probably couldn't make a fist if he tried."

"Must have had some reason," Phil insists.

"When was the last time a cop needed an excuse to beat us up?" Donald asks snidely. "Poor Lester. His friend Kyle had to scrape him off the ground and cart him away. But what really set me off was this other cop, the one who looks just like you," he says, jabbing his index finger accusingly at Phil. "He started laughing like it was some big joke."

"Wasn't me. I would never . . ." Phil protests.

But Donald is too wound up to listen. "Made me so angry and I don't even remember where I got it, but I had this bottle in my hand and I threw it at him. Usually I can't hit the right side of a bus, but I beamed him." Donald illustrates by smacking his temple with the flat of his right palm.

"And I'm guessing that didn't go over too well."

Donald's face widens. The grin of a child who's just received his first catcher's mitt. Open. Endearing. "You could say that. Anyway, he comes charging at me, pushing everybody out of the way. And I'm standing there, frozen, thinking 'Oh boy. Now I'm in for it.' Then out of nowhere, this gal I know, Dee Andrea, she jumps on the cop's shoulders and starts riding him like a bronco. The bruiser smacks her across the back with his nightstick, and people go nuts and start to pile on him, like giant ants. In the confusion, I made my getaway. Boy that Miss D, she is one tough lady."

"And then what happened?" Phil says, prompting Donald, hoping to be recognized, though he's not quite sure why.

"I fell down and picked myself up and ran all the way home. I was scared shitless."

"You got up all by yourself? Nobody helped you? You sure?"

"I don't think so . . . but . . ." Donald's voice trails off and he narrows his eyes, looking at Phil as if grasping for an elusive thought.

"I guess it's not important," Phil says, disappointed. "So that's your trouble? That's why you drink?"

Donald shakes his head. "That not the half of it. But the rest is kind of private."

"I may be off base here," Phil says, "and you tell me if I am, but I'm thinking you got love troubles."

"Pretty smart for a cop," Donald says.

Phil bristles and his mouth distorts. "Who says I'm a cop?"

"Well, you look like one, whether you are or not."

"That supposed to be an insult?" Phil says.

"Not necessarily," he says, clicking his tongue. "You know what they say about a man in uniform . . . ."

"Hey, now. Behave yourself," Phil says in mock-admonishment.

"Or what? You gonna take me in?" Donald snaps, and Phil realizes he's being deliberately goaded.

"Never you mind," Phil says. "The love troubles. What happened?"

Donald sighs and motions to Peg again. "I'm going to need another cup of coffee for that. My treat this time." He pulls stray bills from his pocket. Placing both hands on the table he pushes himself to his feet. "But first I gotta take a whiz."

"Need help?" Phil asks, then abruptly adds, "I mean, getting to the little boy's room."

Donald takes a few steps and as he opens the restroom door, looks back at Phil and chuckles, "Little boy's room?"

Phil lights another Marlboro and sucks on it noisily, losing himself in the smoke. Through the haze he hears Donald say, "I don't mean to sound like your mother, but those things will kill you."

"Well, too bad. You sound exactly like my mother. Tell you what. You stop drinking, and I'll stop smoking," Phil says, taking another suck.

"I'm not an alcoholic, if that's what you're thinking," Donald says, collapsing into the booth and laying his head against the window. "I don't drink all the time. Only when I'm in my blues period."

"Gee, I feel for you guys. Must be a sad life," Phil says, prompting a ripple of anger in Donald.

"Funny, but I don't remember asking for your pity. What happened to me can happen to anyone who falls for the wrong person. But just to be clear. George cared for me. He really did. He cared so much that, a few months ago, he had his company transfer him to Atlanta. Uprooted the wife and kids. Said otherwise, he didn't have the strength to stay away from me. That's how much he cared."

The explanation seems to knock the wind out of Donald who places his right forearm across his face to shade him from the diner's unforgiving fluorescence.

Phil is rattled by the nakedness of Donald's remarks. No euphemisms, no subterfuges and not the slightest embarrassment. Fumbling for the proper response, he says, "Don't be too hard on the guy. After all, a man's gotta look after his family."

After stifling a sob Donald says, "I don't feel so good. I don't want to talk anymore. It's too bright in here. It hurts my eyes."

Phil grabs Donald's left wrist solicitously. "Sorry, buddy. Didn't mean to . . . I mean, what do I know about anything? I've never been . . ."

"Too bad. I'm not saying it was perfect. In fact, it was nowhere near perfect. But when it was good . . ." Donald dabs a napkin across his eyes.

"Maybe we should change the subject," Phil suggests.

Donald nods weakly. "So, you're not a cop? Then how come you have a white crash helmet?" he says, pointing to the fiberglass dome on the seat beside Phil. "Or is your name Frank Mills? You live in Brooklyn somewhere?"

Phil is confused. "I don't know who this Mills fellow is. But I do live in Brooklyn now that you mention it."

"So what are you doing in the Village at this hour?"

"Felt like taking a ride, that's all," Phil says, and even he doesn't sound convinced by what he's just said.

"There are plenty of all-night diners in Brooklyn. You didn't need to come all the way to Manhattan," Donald says.

"I just like to get on the bike and let it take me." He tries to sound nonchalant, but from the way he angrily stubs out the cigarette butt like he's trying to smash it through the glass ashtray, Donald seems to have struck a nerve.

"Nice try," Donald says, leaning in. "I've lived here for several years, and I can pick a night prowler out of a crowd."

"Night prowler?" Phil asks. "What are you talking about? I didn't come here looking for nothing like that, if that's what you're saying."

"Nothing like what?" Donald challenges.

"That's not my style," Phil sneers, "if you take my meaning."

"Because you're not interested, or because you're afraid?"

"Afraid?"

"I get it now," Donald says. "I would have seen it sooner, if I wasn't three sheets."

"Seen what? No. You just got a overactive imagination."

Donald nods and slowly lifts himself out of the booth. "Yeah, well . . . thanks for the coffee. And the conversation. You take care now."

Donald swivels, takes a few steps and wobbles and Phil jumps up and grabs him by the shoulders to steady him. "How about I give you a ride home on my bike?"

"It's only a few blocks," Donald says, pulling away. "I can manage."

"Mind if I walk with you then? I'd feel better knowing you got to your door safe."

"For someone who's not a cop, you sure talk like one."

Phil inhales and holds his breath and Donald sets his jaw. "So that's how it was going to go down? Sloppy drunk makes a pass and you flash your badge and cuff him?"

"No. Nothing like that," Phil says, angrily. "That's not how vice works anyway."

"So, you are a cop," Donald says.

"Yeah I am. But I'm not vice and to be clear, my precinct is in Flatbush. I had nothing to do with the other night."

"And why should I believe you?"

"'Cause I swear on my mother, that's why. Come on. Let's go."

"Or what?"

"I just want to get you home safe, okay? You don't have to worry. I'm off duty. No badge. No gun. Aw, never mind."

Phil walks past Donald and out the door and onto the sidewalk. He immediately lights another cigarette. Donald waddles up behind him. "Okay. I'll let you walk me home. On one condition. That we talk about you."

"Sure thing," says Phil. "I got nothing to hide."

"Well, that would make you an exception."

Phil takes Donald's elbow and they walk abreast. "Boy, you are one tough nut."

"I kind of have to be," Donald says and a few steps on, he adds, "I'm not. Not really. You just give me the jitters. That's all."

"I don't mean to," Phil says softly, and they stare at each other long enough for him to become uncomfortable. "Which way we headed?"

Donald points straight ahead and to the right, and they wander up the street and around the corner. "So, do you have a girl?" Donald asks. "What am I saying? A guy like you always has a girl."

"Yeah. Melissa. We been going together five years. We're kind of engaged."

"Kind of engaged? Or engaged?" Donald says, tapping his ring finger.

"No ring yet. I can't set a date right now on account of my mom's not doing so well with her hip, and she's got nobody else to help her with the store. We own an Italian deli in Bensonhurst. And between that and being a cop . . . Well, that's my story."

"Is it?" Donald inquires as they climb the steps to the front stoop. He hands Phil a key ring. "If you wouldn't mind. I'm still seeing double."

"Does that mean you see two of me?" Phil teases as he takes the keys.

"Yeah. Double your pleasure, double your fun," he says, humming the words to the Doublemint gum jingle.

"Oh, a comedian," Phil says, his face flushing.

"There you go sounding like a cop again," Donald says, as Phil ushers him into the vestibule and undoes the inside door lock. "Is there a police manual with suggested phrases?"

"That's quite enough of that," Phil says.

"Yes, sir," Donald teases him. "Bet you look spiffy in a uniform."

"You have to come to Brooklyn to find out."

Donald grabs hold of the bannisters and Phil follows him up the steps to the third-floor landing. "So a nice Italian boy from Brooklyn, who loves his mama," Donald says mockingly. At his door, Phil undoes the top and bottom locks, pushes the door open and hands the keys back to Donald. "Thanks, uh . . ."

"Phil, the name's Phil."

"Thanks, Officer Phil. You're a real gentleman." Donald says before lurching forward and kissing him. Shocked at first, Phil gives himself over to the kiss and wraps his arms around Donald. They do an awkward dance inside. Donald kicks the door shut with his foot and Phil presses against him. Sensing his urgency, Donald undoes his belt and drops to his knees. Phil can feel Donald looking up at him as he throws back his head and moans. A few minutes later, with one last heave, he is done.

Donald rises and walks to the kitchen sink. He runs his mouth under the tap. Phil does up his trousers and, still reeling, falls onto a chair. He rests his elbows on his knees and his head falls heavily into his hands as if he's losing consciousness.

"You can leave now if you like. I won't be offended," Donald says, rifling through a drawer.

Without looking up, Phil says, "Just give me a minute to pull myself together, okay?"

Donald nods and pours him a glass of water. He offers it to Phil, who thanks him and takes a sip.

"You're not going to get funny on me now, are you? Or try to beat me up?" Donald asks, glancing over at a knife on the kitchen counter. "'Cause cop or no cop, I will defend myself."

"No. You don't have to worry about anything like that. I just need to sit for a bit."

"Stay as long as you please. If you'll excuse me, I'm going get ready for bed," Donald says, walking toward the small bedroom. From inside he says, "Hangover and all, I will get my ass to the office by eight."

"I won't stay long, I promise," Phil calls to him, though he is feeling overcome by numbness, his body drained of all resistance.

"I'm not chasing you away. Not that you'd want to, but I can't ask you to stay over. I'm not ready for that. I'm still grieving and . . ."

"Somebody die?" Phil asks.

"George. The guy I told you about," Donald says, appearing in the doorway bare-chested, in the process of donning a striped pajama top. "At least what we had. It died. Suddenly, if not totally unexpectedly."

Phil is moved and unnerved by the words, and his eyes dance over Donald's bare chest. He admires the way Donald confronts even the most lamentable aspects of his life directly and without apology. "I never heard anybody describe a break-up in that way," he says. "Is that really what it feels like?"

"Uh-huh. When you're in love with somebody and they're in love with you," Donald tells him. "And for some reason you can't be together. Yeah, that's what it feels like."

"That's terrible."

"If something happened to your girl . . ."

"Melissa," Phil reminds him.

"Melissa. If something happened to her, wouldn't you . . .? You do love this Melissa?"

Phil reaches for a cigarette and, as he is lighting it says, "I'm very fond of her."

"Fond. I see."

"She's a wonderful person. Comes from a good family," Phil says, the words matter-of-factly flowing out with the smoke.

"And, I'm assuming, the kind of girl who doesn't do things like . . ." Donald jerks his head to the middle of the room as if he was still on his knees in front of Phil.

"No. She's a good girl," Phil confirms.

"I'm sure she is," Donald says with only a dab of sarcasm.

"She'll make an excellent wife."

"Oh, Phil. I guess nobody will ever accuse you of being a diehard romantic," Donald says. This time the sarcasm is molasses thick.

"What? I am going to marry her. Someday. For sure." Though Phil tries to sound definitive, his assertion rings hollow.

"And this stuff? You plan on giving that up then?"

The accusation lifts Phil from the chair. "You think I'm . . . Just 'cause I let you . . .? No."

But Donald doesn't back down. "You kissed me. That's something else."

Again, Donald's directness forces him into a corner. "Never kissed anyone before," he admits. "Except for Melissa."

"So the other times there was no kissing?"

Phil turns his head and blows the smoke away from Donald as if he was doing it out of consideration. But he's just stalling.

"Well?" Donald presses.

Phil shakes his head violently. "No kissing. Just cash money," he says.

"I see," says Donald. "And I was to be had for a cup of coffee."

"Wait. It's not the same. I like you. You're a nice guy."

"You kissed me because I'm nice? C'mon Phil."

Phil feels queasy. Too many cigarettes. Too much coffee. The heat. His mind and mouth refuse to coordinate. "I wish I could explain. I just felt like it. You were in such a bad way and . . ."

"And you thought that kissing me and letting me blow you would make me feel better?" Donald walks right up to him and, feeling threatened, Phil steps back.

"Aw, geez. Don't make it sound like that," he says, with a look of distaste.

"I apologize," Donald says, softening. "And it did make me feel better. The kiss, I mean. You have a lot of potential in that department."

"I should let you get some sleep," Phil says, turning away, embarrassed. He extends a hand and Donald grasps it tightly and jerks him forward until they are mouth on mouth. A wide-open kiss, this time. An exploration, until Phil breaks it, panting as if he was halfway through a marathon.

"Goodnight, Phil," Donald says as if the kiss was some kind of twisted vindication. "Thanks for walking me home. And . . . the coffee . . . and the . . . I appreciate it. A lot."

Instead of bolting for the door, Phil stands there trying to catch his breath and looking for a place to put out his cigarette. Donald reaches for it and tosses the butt into the sink.

"Hey, maybe you and me can catch a movie sometime?" Phil asks, tentatively.

Donald squints. "Are you asking me out on a date?"

"No. I mean like buddies," Phil says.

"Kissing buddies?" Donald taunts.

"Stop it. So a movie? How about Saturday night? You should give me your number."

Donald appears hesitant, disbelieving. "I guess so, sure," he says before scribbling it onto a notepad and handing Phil a slip of paper. He jams the slip of paper into his shirt pocket, grabs his helmet and without a goodbye, rushes out the door in a great hurry.

On the ride home, Phil pretends to forget what just happened. Pretending to forget is his specialty. But this time, the erasure doesn't take. His mind floods with images of Donald throughout the evening, from the sad drunk to the slightly sober tease to the desire-filled kisser and the sensation of Donald's heart beating rapidly against his chest.

But what strikes him most is the way Donald saw him — so clearly. Even through his alcoholic scrim. Like he had an instinct about Phil. That he was a cop. That he had a girl he was stringing along. That he'd been kidding himself by paying for it.

For as messed up as he was, Donald was a no bullshit guy. How often do you meet someone like that? Certainly not in his line of work.

Sitting on his bed, Phil examines the piece of paper in his hand. He considers tearing it up, but instead places it on the nightstand and turns off the light.

Saturday evening

On Saturday evening, he is standing in a Village phone booth smoking, inhaling, exhaling, inhaling, exhaling, trying to tamp down his anxiety. Not about the decision to call Donald. He's already talked himself into it. Found a way to refute every single reason why he shouldn't.

But what if Donald doesn't answer? What if he's changed his mind? What if he doesn't want to hang out with a cop? And what if . . .? And what if . . .?

The coins click and jingle to the bottom. His fingers go round in a circle. Donald picks up on the second ring.

"Hey, it's Phil," he says and takes two long drags while waiting for an answer.

"Phil?" Donald asks.

"From the other night? Remember?"

"Yeah. Of course. It's just . . . I didn't really expect to hear from you again."

So honest. Where does he get the balls?

"Why not?" Phil says. "I said we'd get together Saturday. We made a date."

"A date?" Donald asks, reminding Phil that he'd gone out of his way to call it anything but. Two buddies catching a movie is what he'd said.

"You're not canceling, are you?" he says. And when Donald again pauses for too long, blurts, "'Cause I kinda been looking forward to this all week."

Phil breaks into a sweat at hearing the words, even if he'd blurted the truth only out of nervousness.

"No. We're still on," Donald says. "Come by. Or I'll meet you somewhere. Where are you anyway?"

"In a phone booth on Christopher."

"Uh, wait. You remember the address?"

"Yeah. I'll be there in five."

Phil hangs up and walks a few steps before breaking into a run.

ART AIN'T EASY

Titus was awoken early Sunday afternoon by the clanging of metal trash cans. Three high-spirited youngsters were tearing up 10th Street overturning every receptacle in their path. His roommate, George, roused from reading the *Times*, headed over to the window. "Hooligans," he said dismissively, viewing the scattered debris. "And in broad daylight too. This city is going to the dogs."

"What time is it?" Titus said, sitting up on the sofa, rubbing his itchy eyes and scratching at his BVDs.

"Two thirty," George said, turning on the stereo. "Va, Pensiero," streamed softly into the room, and George hummed along with the chorus. He pointed to three taped cartons stacked in the narrow corridor leading to the bedroom. "Those came for you yesterday. One of your mom's friends was storing them and she ran out of space. It would be nice if you could sort through them and just keep what's essential. There's still some room in the basement storage bin."

"I'll get to it at some point," Titus said.

"Today would be a good time," George said, bluntly.

"But I'm in the middle of inventory at the bookstore," Titus argued.

"Before that then," George replied with finality as he settled back into his armchair and picked up *The Sunday Magazine*.

Titus got to his feet and folded the blanket and bed linens. "Do you need to use the bathroom?" he asked. "I'm about to take a shower."

"No, go ahead," George said without looking up. "Oh, and I bought fresh orange juice this morning. There's still some left in the fridge. Help yourself."

"Thanks," Titus said, shedding his briefs as he headed to the kitchen and scooped the container off the shelf. After sniffing inside a moldy Chinese food container, he tossed it and tried to recall the last time he'd ingested solid food.

Sitting on the can and sipping juice through the spout, he waited for the water to heat up. The boiler had allegedly been fixed but remained temperamental. George, who complained about everything, hadn't remarked, but then he only showered at his private men's club in midtown most days. On occasion, a fellow member followed him home. For (ahem) drinks. The rest of the time, George sat in the living room, absently listening to classical music and quietly beating up on himself. Regret was one of the few things they had in common.

Titus hadn't arrived home until nine that morning. Fortunately, George was already out, so he wasn't subjected to one of his veiled scowls. The previous evening, he'd gone dancing at that new private club The Tenth Floor. At around four, he was retrieving his jacket from the coatroom when two German tourists, Aryan paragons, approached him and cooed "*Schön*" — and asked if he might be interested in a three-way.

"Only three?" he joshed. The humor didn't translate, and Titus waited while one of the Germans went off and returned with a striking young man with idealized African features in tow. "*Ist gut*?" he asked Titus, as if he'd selected the man from a sample shelf and would be more than happy to return him and choose another.

"*Ist gut*," Titus said, and he spent the next few hours at the Chelsea Hotel ingesting coke and performing variations on a theme with three other instruments.

As he toweled off, Titus prepared for the onerous task of sifting through his mother's cartons. The last time he'd seen her was shortly before Christmas when Terry and Monty — with George's encouragement — had literally dragged him to visit her at Bedford Hills. The correctional facility was hosting a holiday gathering for inmates and their families. It was the first time he'd seen his mother, Joanie, in several years. She had recently discovered religion, repudiated her former bohemian life and displayed zero tolerance for what she referred to as Titus's "chosen lifestyle." This from a woman who'd been a certified fag hag long before he was born.

When they parted, she wished him well, hoping that by his next visit he had accepted the Lord into his life. Titus resolved that there would be no next time.

For his mother, life was a straight line, a one-dimensional highway. Foresight or hindsight were unnecessary distractions. Her nonconformity was what Titus had loved about Joanie, perhaps the only thing. When he was a boy, she would vanish for days at a time and he would be forced to throw himself on the mercy of a neighbor or friend, usually Terry. Upon her return, out of guilt, she would dote on him to the point of suffocation, which was equally unsettling.

The first box was crammed with memorabilia from the years after his mother abandoned her privileged life and Christian name (Sigrid) in Milwaukee and emigrated to Manhattan with ambitions of becoming an "important" writer. Among the contents were signed first editions from several prominent authors, which Titus calculated might be worth something, particularly the ones by writers who were now deceased. At the bottom of the heap, he found Joanie's flimsy output: a self-published poetry collection; a few yellowing newspaper clippings; articles she'd written for *The Village Voice* about the Beats and, later, about the incipient feminist movement, including an interview with Betty Friedan, with whom she'd claimed a spiritual kinship.

Shortly before she was convicted, Joanie woefully admitted to being merely an "author by association." She'd been too busy running around with writers and artists to actually sit down and create. After taking up residence in the Village around the corner from Patchin Place, where the likes of E. E. Cummings and Djuna Barnes resided, she'd ingratiated herself with them as well as other Village scribes like Mailer and Auden. She frequented arty haunts like the White Horse, the Cedar Bar and later, the Lion's Head and protested alongside Ginsberg and Berrigan, who argued that poetry readings were art, not entertainment, and that cafés and other venues shouldn't be required to have a license to present them.

While not conventionally pretty, she was pert and spirited and, most importantly, available. She engaged in a series of brief flings with the poetic and the prosaic. Musicians and painters in addition to writers. One of her steadier liaisons was with Barnett Holt, a bass player to whom she'd been introduced by James Baldwin over drinks at Café Society. She became pregnant shortly before Barnett embarked on a European tour with Sarah Vaughan and subsequently settled in Amsterdam.

When the administrators of her Aunt Eunice's trust fund uncovered a morality loophole for miscegenation, Joanie lost her one source of steady income and took a job at the Strand Bookstore, where her young son became a fixture among the dusty bookshelves. Titus would later parlay that association into a part-time position.

Titus was fair enough to pass, except to other blacks. He inherited his mother's strawberry blond hair and his father's tight curl, Joanie's small, freckled features and Barnett's high, solid rump and wide feet. Until he was twelve, the mixture proved clumsy and unappealing. Then, overnight, it all cohered and Titus was regularly stalked through the Village streets.

The less he encouraged men, the more captivated they became. Titus marveled at all the fuss they put into the chase, and he was not above utilizing his looks to string them along — a tactic he'd osmosed from his mother. A free meal, some pocket change, all for the proximity of youth. The only actual sex he had was with a few older school chums.

The second box contained cards and trinkets Titus had received from his father over the years — at Christmas or for his birthday. Titus didn't actually meet Barnett until he was ten, when he returned to the U.S., and entered into a pitched battle with Joanie over their son's welfare. He'd always wanted a father, just not Barnett, who found fault in almost every aspect of his upbringing and personality. The boy seemed headed down the same path as his mother, he chided, undisciplined and unorthodox. It didn't help that Joanie was using by then, and her hair was falling out.

Despite having been an absentee father and a black man, Barnett might have prevailed in the custody court, had he not broken his neck during a scuffle with Joanie at the top of the stairs. Titus had gone from having one barely functional parent, to two bitterly feuding ones, to being an orphan. In return for a guilty plea, Joanie persuaded the court to grant temporary custody to Terry Morse. Titus lived in his 10th Street apartment for several years until Terry moved in with his boyfriend Monty. He was replaced by "lonesome" George to whom Terry bequeathed the rent-controlled apartment on the condition that Titus be allowed to remain for as long as he chose.

Following some initial testiness, they'd settled into a tenuous coexistence, united in being out of sync; Titus because he was raised outside the borders of convention, George because he was hemmed in by them.

Shortly after they became roommates, Titus convinced George to let him style his hair. He'd learned how to cut hair from an erstwhile boyfriend, a professional beautician. It had served him in good stead, earning him more money than his bachelor's degree from City. He hadn't been much of a student and had only matriculated to avoid the draft. George, who was not-so-secretly vain, thanked him "for making me look ten years younger." Now if you'd only act that way, Titus wanted to say, but for the sake of harmony, held his peace.

With a full-time job at a midtown salon and a part-time gig at the Strand, Titus now earned enough to afford his own place, or at least one with a less morose roommate. But whether out of inertia or a growing respect for one another, neither he nor George discussed any changes in their arrangement. Despite his moodiness, Titus admired George's solid work ethic and air of gravitas. He didn't stop to wonder whether the attraction might be libidinal. Not that it would do any good since George had yet to move past Donald, the man he'd abandoned and who, in turn, had abandoned him.

Titus was unprepared for the contents of the last carton: photo equipment and several large manila envelopes containing his output. He had been sure Joanie had sold the cameras and lenses to buy drugs and destroyed the photos, which she'd declared amateurish and undisciplined. "Not all of us are naturally creative," she'd informed him, an opinion seconded by her then-beau Harold, a Soho art dealer. Titus's already fragile, young ego had sagged under her appraisal, and he'd largely abandoned his passion soon after.

Carefully, he opened the first envelope, which contained dozens of fading Polaroids. The photos were appropriately fidgety and jangly, taken by a restless boy who had recently discovered an outlet for his energy and curiosity. Left on his own much of the time, when he wasn't in school, Titus had roamed the Village streets taking pictures, while waiting for his mother to return home. If she failed to show up by dinnertime, he usually headed over to Terry's for shared take-out. If Terry went out for the evening, he'd let Titus stay and watch TV. Joanie considered television the devil's portal.

The Polaroid had given shape to his wanderings, enabled him to capture impressions, even distort them to his liking. Given the cost of each new packet of film, he was selective in his subjects and how he framed them. At the start, he concentrated on stationary objects since they couldn't move and blur the shot. With life teeming all around him however, *nature mort* did not suffice for long.

After Terry bought him a used Nikon from a pawn shop, he began to focus on human subjects. Not posed photos. Found moments, which abounded in his unorthodox surroundings. For instance, Titus noticed that every Saturday morning two elderly ladies toddled down 7th Avenue to the Laundromat to do their weekly wash, dragging their wire shopping car behind them, their Scuffies scratching at the pavement. Something about them caught his eye. He noticed that they never spoke. To each other or anyone else, communicating solely by glance and gesture.

Like many of the neighborhood's other idiosyncratic residents ("If you're out-of-place, the Village is the place for you," Terry had once wryly observed), the women's weekly ritual fascinated Titus, especially after it slowly dawned on him that they weren't women at all. Or old. Then and there, he decided they would be his first live models.

Initially, he kept his distance, using a zoom lens to focus on singular details like the cascade of safety pins along the bodices of their floral-print housecoats, the flesh-colored hose rolled down around their ankles, the worn-out slippers. And facial gestures. Their wearily intent expressions as they dutifully folded their laundry. The way they communicated with a mere flash of the eyes. He was never certain whether the women were aware of his presence, though they sometimes seemed to offer up a flattering profile just as he was about to snap the shutter.

Initially, Joanie supported his new hobby offering helpful criticism. "These are like first drafts. You don't want anyone to see them until your work is more polished," she'd advised. "But keep at it. Who knows? You might get good at it someday." Titus saw through the tepid encouragement. For the cost of a packet of film, he was occupied and out of her hair.

Titus might have grown bored with photography had it not been for people like Shrimpy, one of the few adults who paid him any mind. Titus was amused by Shrimpy's mile-a-minute patter, his singular appearance, his signature porkpie hat and flat-footed gait. One Saturday afternoon, as he was sitting on the front stoop of his building, he noticed Shrimpy in the distance. He had come to a dead halt in front of the washerwomen and was applauding them as they navigated their laundry cart around him and continued on their route. "Flawless," he proclaimed. "Brava."

"Hey, Shrimpy," Titus said, running up to him. "Do you know those ladies?"

"Why everyone knows them my dear, though no one is really sure who they are. I guess like all true great artistes, the air of mystery heightens their appeal."

"Why do you call them artistes?" Titus said, befuddled.

"Because they are," Shrimpy insisted. "They're bringing theater back to the masses where it belongs."

"Theater? What are they performing? All they do is laundry. They don't even speak," Titus said.

"Life. They're performing life," Shrimpy affirmed. "Everyday life. In pantomime. That's the beauty of it. And the art. They create characters by living them. Words are superfluous. Speaking would break the fourth wall."

"Oh," Titus said, though he was completely at sea. "Well, I took some pictures of them. Want to see?"

"Absolutely," Shrimpy said.

Titus was flattered, but he hesitated. "I don't know. My mom said I shouldn't show anyone my pictures until I've gotten better at it."

"I respect that," Shrimpy said. "As I said to that wonderful young composer Steve Sondheim when he came by the theater box office recently, 'Art ain't easy,' to which he said, 'May I quote you on that?'" He let out a high-pitched giggle. "That Steve. What a card. But you hang onto those pictures, hear? They'll be worth money someday. So tell me. Have you photographed all their characters?"

"They have other characters?"

"Oh yeah. A whole slew of them, didn't you know? Mostly women, but sometimes guys too. Some are regulars, others are one-time only. You never know what they're going to come up with next. Keep your eyes open. You'll see."

"I will. I promise," Titus said, his mind already abuzz with possibility. "Thanks, Shrimpy. Hey, do you mind if I take your picture?" he added, retrieving the Polaroid from his backpack.

"What do you want to do that for?"

"I have pictures of all my friends," Titus said. "A whole wall in my bedroom."

"Well in that case, I'd be honored," Shrimpy said, striking a bizarre pose as preposterous as it was endearing.

Titus got off two shots, one head-on, the other a profile. "I'll show them to you if you promise not to tell my mom."

"Who me? Uh-uh. My lips are zipped," he said, running an index finger across his mouth.

Shrimpy studied the photos and remarked, "These are swell. You got a great eye, kid. And good instinct. I'm never wrong about these things. Well, gotta run. I'm late for work as usual. Come by the theater some time, and I'll sneak you into a dress rehearsal."

Intrigued and stimulated by the conversation, Titus began his search for the washerwomen's other characters, trailing them back home to Perry Street and waiting around. For hours. For days. His patience eventually paid off. One Sunday morning, they emerged in their churchgoing best to attend services at First Presbyterian on 5th Avenue and 12th Street; on another occasion, they emerged as twentysomething ballet students, duck-waddling, bun-headed girls in leotards and Capezio slippers on their way to a City Ballet matinee.

Perhaps their most memorable (and controversial) transformation — a one-time only event — occurred shortly before Titus gave up photography for good. Aptly, the occasion centered on Shrimpy, who a year or so after Titus photographed him, vanished. After Terry's friend Barbara reported him missing, he showed her the two Polaroids, which proved to be the only photographic record of Shrimpy. Barbara took them to the police where they sat in a file drawer. A few months later, there was a break.

During a police pursuit through a decaying and notorious cruising pier on the Hudson, a perp narrowly escaped falling through a gaping hole in the floor and being swallowed by the roiling waters below. As the panicked man clung to a jutting beam overhead, his hand fell on a honey-colored porkpie hat that was caught on a rusty nail. The hat was in his possession when he was taken into custody. Something about it clicked with one of the desk sergeants, who pulled out Titus's photos and made a positive match.

A memorial was planned with a procession down West 12th Street to the Hudson, adjacent to the pier where the hat was found. Titus raced ahead of the mourners snapping photos.

When the group crossed Bleecker Street, they were joined by two mourners whom Titus immediately recognized. The women wore matching outfits: exact duplicates of Jackie Kennedy's ensemble at JFK's funeral — a knee length, two-piece black wool suit with a floral inlaid design over the bosom and a shoulder-length opaque veil topped by a mushroom cap–shaped hat.

Though some mourners were outraged, Titus understood that no mockery was intended. This was a sincere homage to Shrimpy, one of the few people who had openly applauded their efforts and would have been the first to marvel at their cultural appropriation for the sake of art. "All this for me?" he would have said. "Gee. You guys are swell."

Titus was poring over the Jackie shots when he sensed George peering over his shoulder. Almost reflexively, he clasped them to his chest. "Just some pictures I took once," he said.

"Mind if I have a look?" George asked.

Hesitant, he handed George the photos. "They're not very good," he said. "Just put them back in the box when you're done. I have to get dressed for work. I'll tidy up later. Promise."

When Titus returned at around midnight, George was still sitting on the living room floor, the envelopes of photos splayed around him, Mahler's Fifth blaring in the background.

"You still looking at that stuff?" Titus said.

George glanced up. "You took these? All of them?"

Titus nodded. "Yeah."

"Did you take lessons?"

"No, why?"

"They're amazing. Even the early ones. The Polaroids. What made you stop?"

"My mom said I wasn't very good."

"Oh, I see," George said, and his nose wrinkled the way it did when he was displeased.

"What? My mom wouldn't lie to me," Titus said, somewhat agitated.

"I'm not suggesting that. Look, I don't want to speak ill of her, but from what Terry told me . . ."

"You talk to Terry about my mother? Do you talk to him about me too?"

"Sometimes," George admitted.

"Why? I didn't think you had the slightest interest in my life — except to disapprove."

"I don't disapprove. Not really. And if it seems like I'm not interested, it's only because I'm preoccupied."

"You mean, Waiting for GoDonald?" Titus said.

George appeared almost amused. "I'm not so far gone that I can't see the humor in that."

"So what did Terry say? About my mom?"

"He told me how frustrated she'd been by her lack of creative focus."

"It's not that she didn't try," Titus said, suddenly defensive. "She'd sit for hours working on one line of a poem, but she was never satisfied. She'd wind up tearing the whole thing up."

"It's a fairly common affliction," George noted. "Some people would rather produce nothing than anything that's less than brilliant. You can imagine what it must have been like to see a kid, her kid, produce this caliber of work so effortlessly. There must be 300 photos here, many of them professional grade. Must have been quite a blow to her."

"You're saying she was jealous? Get out. Even her boyfriend, who was an art dealer, said I had no real talent."

"I may not be an art dealer, but I'm an architect and I studied photography as well. And I respectfully disagree. If your mother thought they were rubbish, why did she go to all the trouble of organizing and storing them?"

"How am I supposed to know why she did what she did?" Titus said, annoyed.

George began to scramble through the photos. He held up the set Titus had taken of Monty when he and Terry were on vacation in Miami. "In this set here, it's clear you fancied Monty. They're like movie-star publicity shots." Then, he rifled through the photos for several other shots of Monty, taken at a later date. "But look here. Same subject. Only in these he looks chilly and menacing. As if you're trying to take him down a peg. Knowing a little about your history with Monty, I'd say these were shot around the time he and Terry had a falling out. It's amazing how, consciously or not, you captured his duality. Very revealing. Both of Monty and the photographer."

George's comments made him feel dizzy and angry. He threw himself onto the sofa and buried his face in his hands.

"I'm sorry. I didn't mean to upset you," George said. "I'll shut up now."

"No, it's okay," Titus said. "I mean, who doesn't want to hear they have talent? You really think they're good?"

"They're better than good. The whole series on Kyle and Lester blew me away. I had no idea they had an official chronicler."

"I'm sorry, who?"

George held up photos of the washerwomen, the church ladies, and others.

"For a kid to pick them out of the crowd and capture them so precisely, it requires more than talent. It requires instinct."

"You're the only person I know besides Shrimpy who's ever spoken to me about them, and even he didn't know who they were."

"That's odd. Terry knows Kyle and Lester quite well. I'm surprised you never met them. But in fairness, I wouldn't have known who they were except that they lived next door to Donald on Perry Street."

"Yeah, I know where they live. Kyle and Lester? That's their real names? Did you ever talk to them?"

"Only in passing, mostly to say hello if we ran into each other on the stairs."

"What are they like?"

"Quiet, unassuming. I think they're from down South originally. Donald said they were bookkeepers. They looked like bookkeepers. Anonymous. Like the drag they did."

"Not drag. My friend Shrimpy called it performance. Street theater."

"Yeah, I can see that," George said.

"I wonder if they still perform?" Titus asked. "I stopped looking for them after I . . ."

"I believe I saw them not long ago at church. Do you miss it? Photography?"

Titus pondered the question for a moment. "Sometimes."

"You could take it up again. You still have all the equipment."

"Why do you care?"

He shrugged. "Call it my latent paternalistic streak."

"Thanks, but I don't need a father," Titus railed.

"Then how about as a friend?" he suggested.

Titus seemed torn. "Even if I wanted to start up again, with two jobs where would I find the time? Plus, it's expensive."

"You'll find the time if you really want to. How about I waive your part of the rent for a few months? You can use it to buy supplies," George said.

"You'd do that?"

"Only if you're serious," he said. "By the way, do you still have all the negatives?"

"In the bottom of the box."

"Good. Because I have an idea. If you're open to it, we can put together a collection of the Kyle and Lester photos. The various characters. And maybe put together an exhibit. If not at a gallery, then maybe at the Reggio or the Borgia. I'm friendly with the owners."

"Whoa! I'm not ready for an exhibit," Titus laughed nervously.

"Think about it. In the meantime, if you don't mind, I'll cull through the negatives. I'm curious to see what shots you didn't develop. And some of these should be enlarged and others need to be printed on better stock."

"Why would you go to all that trouble?"

George shrugged his shoulders. "Because."

"Because?"

"Might be fun. Give me something to do instead of moping around here all the time."

"Well that would be a change," Titus teased. "Hey, I'm not feeling terribly sleepy. Want to go over to Julius's for a drink? My treat."

"You know I don't go to gay bars."

"Why not? They've stopped raiding them. You don't have to worry."

"It's not that," George said, squirming somewhat. "Someone might see me. Or get the wrong impression. About us."

"Afraid people will think you're sweet on me? I don't mind."

"You don't need attention from me. You can pretty much have the pick of any man you want."

"Including you?" he said, deliberately trying to provoke him.

George ignored the remark. He let out a giant yawn and stretched his arms over his head. "If you don't mind, I'm going to tidy up and hit the sack. I have a big meeting in the morning. But let's set aside some time this week to talk. I'm really impressed, Titus. I've learned more about you in the past few hours then in all this time we've been living together."

"Whose fault is that?"

"Mine. Both of ours, I guess," George countered. "But it doesn't have to stay that way." George extended his hand and Titus clasped it.

"Would you mind if I gave you a goodnight kiss?"

Bemused, George offered his cheek. But Titus went straight for his mouth.

"Kiss me back," Titus ordered.

"I don't think so," George said. "Besides, I'm used to being the aggressor."

"It's the seventies. Times have changed. Roles have changed," Titus said, placing his hands at the sides of George's temples and kissing him again.

"Goodnight, George," Titus said when their lips parted.

"Night," George said and sheepishly made his way to the bedroom. Unlike other nights, however, he left the door slightly ajar.

SORA AND DECLAN

Declan Kalimar's fascination with Sora Hayashi had been building for some time, if imperceptibly, like individual leaves of onion-skin paper one upon the other. Sora had a great deal to recommend. He was talented and bright and a dedicated friend. Yet it caught Declan up short when his regard for Sora shifted into full-on desire.

They'd met through Declan's late paramour Myrna Lyons and were now working together on the new musical *Day of Leisure*, an updating of a venerable French farce. Sora was designing the show's costumes, and Declan was assigned one of the leads, a comically hapless philanderer who receives a comeuppance from his patient wife.

He was seated in the almost-empty theater memorizing lines when Sora appeared from the wings. Declan followed his movements across the stage, sylphlike but also athletic. When Sora stopped partway to chat with the show's set designer, he stood with his legs wide apart, planted firmly, his small rump thrust outward. Declan experienced a clench of yearning.

How, until now, had Sora's sensuality not registered with him? True, he was no strutting peacock. His allure was subtler; it went tongue and groove with his unique aesthetic. Declan had long been an admirer of his understated yet regal presence. Myrna once mentioned that Sora was a descendent of "some kind of noble Japanese ancestry." He didn't make much of it. Myrna could be vague and provocative, and on occasion, both at the same time.

Even in a crowded room, the eye traveled to Sora. He projected a quiet confidence. In social situations, he tended to be taciturn, which made his unexpected flashes of wit all the more delightful. He engaged with Declan easily, without a trace of fawning. Since becoming a household name via a hit TV sitcom, Declan traveled under a permanent pin light, which even for an actor with a healthy ego could be tiresome.

Their friendship had deepened in the months leading up to Myrna's death. Sora had provided support and counsel without ever being obtrusive but was always available if needed and invisible in moments demanding privacy and reflection. Declan welcomed his calming influence amid the chaos that so often typifies the dying process — the sudden remissions followed by equally spontaneous reversals. Working together on the new musical with the bittersweet reminder of Myrna's passing still fresh in their minds brought them even closer, like two old army buddies reconnecting after having endured months in the trenches.

Could this shift in perspective on Declan's part be an accumulation of all these disparate factors? Strange, he thought, how someone standing in the wings of his life could, in an instant, move to center stage. As Declan continued to gaze at him enrapt, Sora turned and broke into a wide smile. "There you are," he said. "I've been looking all over for you. Would you be available this evening after rehearsal to try on some wardrobe?"

Declan struggled to fashion a reply. "Uh . . . uh . . . sure thing. Can it wait until I have dinner with my kid and put him to bed?"

Sora puffed out his lower lip. "Sure. If it doesn't get too late," he said.

"Benedick's usually tucked away by seven-thirty, eight at the latest. Does that work for you?"

"Think I have enough to keep me busy until then," he said, the genial smile crawling up his face again.

As Sora exited stage right, Declan's eyes followed him as if he had X-ray vision and could see the cool exertion of every muscle and sinew.

Strap-hanging his way down to 8th Street, Declan mulled over his newfound attraction and pondered the obstacles in his way. How might he approach Sora without jeopardizing his jewel box of a life? Not to mention that, in almost every way, he was Sora's antithesis: as vain as Sora was modest, as fretful and ill-at ease as Sora was focused and pacific.

Which only made him crave Sora's attentions all the more.

Declan's life had been marked by a series of obfuscations, accommodations, and subterfuge; virtually every decision informed by his desire for success. His acting career began with an open call, which landed the Jersey-born teenager a flashy supporting role in an off-Broadway comedy; and almost immediately thereafter, a replacement part in a long-running Broadway drama in which he came to the attention of prominent agent Sam Barton. Sam assured Declan that his all-American-boy good looks were a refreshing tonic in an era typified by "hippies and dippies and longhairs."

The conjugal favors Declan bestowed on Sam in return for taking him under his capable wing — and a nose job — led to his being cast in *Accidental Dad*, a sitcom about a rootless young man who inherits his late sister's two, precocious tots. The touching insecurity and heart he brought to the well-meaning but bumbling surrogate father bore strange parallels to his personal life.

At Sam's encouragement, he married Cynthia Sorel, a young actress he'd co-starred opposite in a production of *Much Ado About Nothing* on the L.A. stage during a hiatus. He was fond of Cynthia, fond enough to father a son, Benedick (named after his *Much Ado* character).

Though planned, the boy's arrival caught Declan off-guard, and he was not remotely chagrined to find himself playing out every cliché of a smitten, doting father. In his newborn son, he'd found a distraction from his alternating bouts of egotism, self-doubt and repression.

He and Cynthia were planning on a second child when she became embroiled in a new cult called Scientology, causing a strain in the marriage, especially when it became apparent that her recruitment was conceived as a conduit to her high-profile husband. They separated, and when the sitcom ended, divorced. Cynthia married a fellow traveler, who had no intention of raising another man's offspring, and Declan was granted full custody.

Otherwise, the marriage might have continued, if not indefinitely, then certainly for a few years longer. For the most part, Declan remained faithful. His agent had moved on to other young male hopefuls, and except for sub-rosa flings with one of the show's camera operators (also married) and a guest star, he took no chances. With the emergence of the gay rights movement in the early seventies, gossip that was once confined to scandal sheets now garnered mainstream attention. One misstep and his TVQ (and his career) would plummet.

After *Accidental Dad*, Declan turned down another sentimental comedy series and returned to New York in the hope of redefining his image. Though he looked no older than when he'd first starred in the sitcom, longevity would necessitate breaking free of the juvenile mold. Like many performers who enjoy a fluke mainstream success, he now wanted to be taken seriously as an actor. The stage, starting with notable supporting roles, became his avenue.

Declan's relationship with Myrna Lyons, thirty years his senior, began when they were introduced backstage after the opening night of the renowned pop-and-jazz singer's one-woman Broadway show. (It was also the first time he met Sora, who had designed her wardrobe and was one of Myrna's closest friends and confidants.) Declan had grown up listening to her records and was hardly the first man to be captivated by her combination of grit and aplomb. Neither the age difference nor his pent-up sexuality got in the way of their mutual attraction.

Soon he and Benedick were living on the lower floors of Myrna's brownstone on 10th Street just east of 6th Avenue. When they were out together, they poked fun at the media's obsession with their May-December romance by referring to each other as "Baby Boy" and "Mama Bear." The relationship, while genuine, also smacked of calculation. It dovetailed with Declan's desire to refashion his Goody Two-Shoes public reputation and reinforce his virility, and it flattered the older woman's fading sex appeal.

While infatuated with her young lover, Myrna had been around long enough to see through his facade. "You wouldn't be my first beau who enjoys an occasional boy on the side," she confessed one night when they were both sufficiently lubricated. "I don't have a problem with that, so long as you throw me a good fuck every now and then. Deal?"

Declan was relieved that, at least with Myrna, he didn't have to pretend, and she was willing to provide cover for his explorations — within limits, of course.

As he trudged up the subway steps, he wondered if Myrna and Sora had ever discussed his sexuality, specifically his dalliance with George, a similarly closeted, if more tortured, neighbor.

If Sora was aware, he didn't let on, but then he was not the type to betray confidences. In his profession, Sora didn't have to be quite as discreet. He had never denied his relationship with Errol Danowksi, a principal with the New York City Ballet, nor the dancer's self-destructiveness, which led to its dissolution. He and Errol had marched in pride parades and, over the years, Sora had become a visible public figure in New York's incipient gay lib movement.

In light of these profound differences, the possibility of an affair between them seemed remote, Declan concluded as he swung open the gate of the ground floor apartment and saw Benedick's beaming face peering at him from between the bars on the front window.

When Benedick leapt into his arms at the door every evening, the rigors of the day evanesced. But tonight was different. He would be returning to the theater later to confront his newfound desire. Sexual longing was not alien to him, but heretofore he'd been able to compartmentalize his urges. Instinctively, he sensed that Sora marked a turning point.

And, troublingly, that excited him.

"You're late," Sora said, looking up from his sketch pad, though it didn't sound like a reprimand.

"Benedick was a bit rambunctious tonight," Declan explained. "My sister Amy, who lives with us, bought him cupcakes at the school bake sale and, well, sugar and seven-year-olds . . ."

"Yes," Sora said, undoing the rubber band that held in place his rich, jet-black, shoulder-length mane in place.

Declan had a sudden impulse to reach out and stroke Sora's hair. How delicately it framed his unblemished smooth skin, made him appear pliant, accessible. Then with both hands, Sora pulled it all back tightly and rewrapped the rubber band around it twice. As he turned and glanced up at Declan, he betrayed a fierceness that punctured Declan's confidence, and only served to render him more attractive.

"You okay?" he asked.

"Yeah. Been a long day," Declan said with a nervous laugh.

"I'll try to make this as quick as possible. Take off your shirt," Sora commanded.

Clasping his chin in one hand, Sora studied Declan's bare torso. "You've been working out. Good," he remarked.

"The script has me walking around in my underpants in a couple of scenes. Guy's got to look his best," Declan said, struggling to maintain a jocular tone, all the while hoping that Sora didn't notice his rigid nipples.

"Chilly in here," he said, but Sora wasn't paying attention. He was sifting through a rack of dress shirts. Picking out a pale blue one, he held it against Declan's face, then tossed it aside. He reached for a slightly darker shade. "Here. Try this one."

The touch of Sora's long fingers as he buttoned the shirt and smoothed the cotton fabric and pulled it tight and pinned it on the side and back rippled through Declan's body. "Feels a little snug," Declan said.

"Yeah, but it's much sexier this way," he said, matter-of-factly, indicating with his hand that Declan should take off the shirt. "Provided you don't gain any weight before opening night."

Declan unbuttoned the shirt and handed it over; Sora opened a drawer and pulled out a jock strap. "Take off your pants. I need you to try on some undershorts."

Declan held up the jockstrap and eyed it quizzically. "We don't want any bulges or silhouettes. This is a family show," Sora explained. "Now go," he added, pointing to a changing screen.

It took all of Declan's willpower to retain his composure as he stripped and snuggled into the jockstrap. "Ready," he said, unsteadily.

A disembodied hand proffered a pair of striped underwear. "Boxers?" Declan grimaced.

"Well certainly not BVDs. They'll make your butt look big," Sora said.

"I have a big butt?" Declan said, stepping out from behind the screen.

"You have a man's rear end. Wide set," Sora said, walking around him. He tugged at the sides of the shorts and shook his head, displeased with the drape. He handed Declan another pair.

"Wide set," Declan said, as if troubled by the description.

"It's a good thing," Sora called to him from the other side of the screen. "Gives you gravitas. Myrna said she loved your butt."

"She said that?" he said, alarmed but also curious.

"We were discussing mutual interests," he replied. "Men's bottoms, not specifically yours."

"I wish you hadn't told me that," Declan said.

"Sorry. Can we put it behind us now?" Sora quipped, and it took Declan a moment to register the double entendre.

"These are kind of loose," Declan said, stepping out in the new shorts.

"But the color works," Sora said. He got down on his haunches and gathered the sides of the shorts and pinned them. Declan felt a stirring and closed his eyes tightly wishing it away —unsuccessfully.

When Sora was done, he twisted his head around to Declan's crotch. "Hmm," he said and sighed. "That's too bad. Hope we don't have to tape you."

The idea of being taped had the opposite effect on Declan, and he quickly retreated behind the screen. As he removed the shorts, a pin got loose and he cried out.

Sora popped his head behind the screen and noticed Declan's prominence emerging from the athletic supporter. "Oh," he said, and scooted away.

By the time he'd finished getting dressed, Declan was back to normal. "Involuntary response," he explained as he handed the pinned shorts to Sora, who didn't look up from his drawing table.

"Not the first time," Sora said, as if that would make Declan feel any better.

"Are you done?" he asked. Sora nodded without looking up.

While Declan was pulling on his coat, Sora added, "I don't think it would be a good idea."

"What?" Declan said with a nervous warble.

"We work together. We have a past history. We're friends."

"Gee, I hope you didn't get the wrong . . ."

"I have a great deal of experience with men. I can tell when someone is attracted to me. I'm familiar with the signals, even if they aren't."

"That was just nerves."

"I meant the hungry-wolf look you've been giving me all day."

"The what?" he said, and his stomach rumbled.

Sora turned up his chin and smiled at Declan. "Why, you're as red as a ripe peach. I'm flattered."

Declan shifted from foot to foot and shook his head but couldn't find the words to reinforce his denial.

"I also know about the neighbor."

Lowering his eyes, he asked, "Myrna told you about that?"

"She didn't have to. I saw the two of you leaving his apartment once."

"If I said he was just a friend . . .?"

Sora frowned. "Oh Declan, come on. Don't worry, your secret's safe with me, though I have to say, except for the fact that he seemed to be as deep in the closet as you are, I don't understand what you saw in him."

"George is very handsome," Declan argued, shattering his friendship argument.

"Yeah, but the two of you looked like bookends," Sora said with a chuckle. "Which I guess makes your attraction to me all the more surprising. I mean, we've known each other for several years, but until today, I never imagined that your intentions were anything but honorable."

Declan parked his wide rump on the edge of Sora's worktable. Impulsively, he reached for Sora's hand and toyed with his delicate, long fingers. "Does that mean you're not interested? Is that why you said it wouldn't be a good idea?"

"I will admit to undressing you on occasion," Sora said, and this time it was his turn to be discomfited.

"At least that part's no mystery anymore," Declan said with a smile. "Disappointed?"

"Myrna said you looked even better naked. I've never known her to lie. But as long as we're working together . . ."

"Which is only until opening night," Declan pointed out, rubbing Sora's hand between both of his.

"Perhaps we can pick up the discussion then," Sora said, as he fidgeted with the rubber band and shook his thick hair loose.

"I hope this doesn't make things between us awkward, but I think you're beautiful. Uh . . . handsome. Beautiful and handsome," Declan said, and boldly leaned in and kissed Sora, nibbling on his bottom lip before pulling away. "I apologize, but when you do that with your hair, it gets me going."

"Would you please go home?" Sora said, playfully.

"See you tomorrow," Declan said, beaming with confidence. But it was a bluff, like walking out of a successful audition with the lingering presentiment that you're not going to get the part.

Over the subsequent weeks, Declan and Sora didn't avoid each other exactly but kept their interchanges brief. Edie, the costumer's assistant, took over Declan's fittings. Sora begged off, claiming wardrobe crises with the show's leading lady, Dina Ford, who was as demanding as she was talented.

Whenever they were in each other's presence, however, a current of anticipation traveled between them. The casual observer could easily miss the signals: the way they leaned forward when speaking as if exchanging secrets, the discreet physical interactions, a double-cheek professional greeting that was more than perfunctory, a wardrobe adjustment in which Sora's hand lingered.

At the opening-night party, their eyes wandered across the room from whomever they were talking to until they'd located one another. Then a silent reassurance, a nod, a brief smile, a friendly wink.

Day of Leisure received mixed-to-upbeat notices; only a couple of churlish comments about the TV star who had the audacity to think he could carry a Broadway musical. Audiences, on the contrary, were enthusiastic and the already bullish presales soared after opening night. Declan's entrance in the first act and the curtain call prompted hearty applause, and his underwear scenes generated several wolf-whistles.

Declan had just finished showering and was sitting in front of the mirror removing the last stubborn traces of makeup after the Sunday matinee when Sora knocked at the dressing-room door. They exchanged pleasantries about the performance. Then Sora got to the point: "Since the show's dark tomorrow I was thinking of coming by your place so we can talk, that is if you're still interested," he said.

"You know I am," Declan said. "I'll be home all day. I'm on dad detail. My sister has a date."

"I'll be by around seven. But if it's okay with you, I'd like to fuck before we talk. I don't want our discussion to be clouded by sexual tension. Would you have time for that?"

"How about right now?" Declan said as he crossed the room and locked the door. Pulling Sora to him, Declan dropped his robe and carefully undressed Sora, unpinning his hair as they began to kiss, each one deeper and longer than the other. In one swift motion Declan lifted Sora in his arms and pinned him against the wall. He ran his lips and tongue over Sora's smooth face and neck and his even-smoother firm torso.

Sora wrapped his legs around him and his moans of expectation were soon superseded by louder expressions of pleasure. Watching as Sora tossed his luxuriant hair with abandon, Declan thought he would lose his mind.

When they were finished, Declan carried Sora to the sofa where they began kissing again and didn't stop until they were aroused anew, flipping around this time. His body flushed with heat and excitement, Declan bit into Sora's forearm like a half-ravenous animal.

For Declan, the afternoon was one of discovery, all the elation of the first time combined with the assurance and comfort of long-term lovers. The sex was marked by an absence of awkwardness and an implicit understanding of what Sora wanted and what he wanted from Sora. A running commentary, though neither spoke a word.

The silent communication continued as they dressed and went their separate ways. A nod became a compound sentence, and a tilt of the head a promise to continue the discussion. When he fell into bed naked that night, Declan rubbed the pillow over his unwashed body and inhaled Sora as he fell asleep.

The following evening, Sora arrived exactly at seven. The affectionate kiss in the doorway erred on the side of caution. Declan had spent the day reliving the Sunday matinee after-performance and trying to quell his renewed hunger. Don't get ahead of yourself, he thought. Let Sora have his say. That he cared so much about the outcome perplexed him. Usually his sexual desire could be transferred from one vessel to another. This was different.

"How was your day?" Sora asked as he moved toward the kitchen and sat at the round oak table.

"Benedick's been fighting a cold, so I let him stay home from school," Declan said. "Would you like some tea?"

"Yes, thanks," he said, and they smiled and held each other's gaze.

As he put on the kettle, Declan turned and said, "Tell me everything about yourself. Start in the womb and keep going."

But Sora didn't take the bait. "I hope yesterday wasn't a mistake," he said. "I was thinking that if we got that out of the way, we could have a serious talk about this thing that's happening between us."

"This thing? Do you mean mutual attraction?"

"At this point we can safely assume the attraction is mutual," Sora said.

"I'm glad to hear that, but are you as freaked out by it as I am?" Declan replied, holding his hand in midair to reveal a tremble. "Is this common between . . . ?"

"Two men? I guess as common as it is between a man and a woman or two women, which is to say, not all that common."

"Have you ever felt this way before? Because I haven't."

"I felt something similar with Edwin. But you've . . . never?"

Declan shook his head. "I've had my share of fixations. Nothing like this."

"Because you have no control over it, right?"

Declan thought about the question. "Uh-huh," he replied. "And I . . ."

Whatever he was about to say was interrupted by a plaintive call from the floor above. Declan walked to the foot of the stairs. "What is it, kiddo?"

"My tummy hurts again," Benedick said, standing at the top in his pajamas. Declan began climbing the stairs and the two of them met in the middle. He lifted his son and carried him to the kitchen.

"You remember Sora, don't you?" Declan asked.

Benedick bobbed his head. "I read all the books," he said, in Sora's direction.

"Did you enjoy them?" Sora said warmly.

"Yeah," he said and moaned slightly.

"Books?" Declan asked as he reached into a kitchen cabinet and removed a small vial of oil. Sitting down at the kitchen table, he lifted Benedick's shirt. After warming the oil between his palms, he rubbed it into the boy's stomach. "Old family remedy," he explained. "Don't ask me why, but it always seems to work. You were saying?"

"Oh, yeah. Once when I came to visit Myrna, Benedick and Amy stopped by and we talked about the Eloise novels, and I sent him the set," Sora related.

"Is that where they came from?" Declan asked. "I wondered. Thank you."

Sora's smile broadened and they all sat there quietly as Declan gently rocked Benedick. Before long, the boy was asleep. "Be right back," Declan whispered. "Don't go anywhere."

Declan carried Benedick up the stairs. When he returned, Sora said, "Sweet boy. How old is he now?"

"Almost eight. He's small for his age. Same as me. Then when I turned thirteen, I shot up light a bean sprout. I've lost my train of thought."

"I think you were trying to tell me that you're freaking out because you've fallen for me, if that doesn't sound presumptuous."

"You'd know better than I. It feels strange. Like I've lost my equilibrium. But in a good way."

"Oh," Sora said, his voice tinged with concern. "If that's the case, we'd better stop now. I can't see myself going backward."

"Meaning?" Declan said as he moved toward the living area and threw himself on the daybed, grabbing a cushion and pulling it to his chest. Sora got up and followed him.

"Let's be realistic. You have a career. An image. This is your first Broadway lead. You're not going to give that up to be with me."

"Who says I have to? My private life is my private life."

"If you were just working in the theater, you might have some flexibility. But not if you have other ambitions. I don't want to sneak around."

"But you've become so important to me," Declan declared.

"Normally, hearing that would make me very happy."

"So, what do we do now?"

"We don't do anything."

"I don't think that's possible after yesterday," Declan said.

"That was just sex," Sora argued.

"This time who's pretending?" Declan said.

"Look. I'm willing to be the bad guy in this," Sora said. "Even at the cost of our friendship. It'll sting for a while but believe me . . ."

Declan jumped up and grabbed Sora by the shoulders. "The only reason I'm not losing it right now is because we are friends, because I've always respected you and trusted you."

"Would it help if I said that until recently I thought of you mainly as a spoiled brat?"

"You weren't far wrong."

"But charming too," Sora said, softening, stroking Declan's arm. "If I thought I could handle a secret affair, I'd . . ."

Declan gritted his teeth. "That's not what I'm asking for. For me, the sex only confirmed what I've been feeling."

Sora shook his wild mane, angry. "No. I will not be the guy who screws up your life. It will only drag us both down."

The truth of Sora's statement stung, and Declan covered his face with his hands.

"I'm not asking you to choose. I'm making the choice for you, for both of us," Sora said, and got up to leave.

Declan jumped to his feet and grabbed him. "Don't give up just yet. Please."

"Why?"

"'Cause maybe there's a way for us to be together. There has to be," he said.

"We can be together, but not in the world. Tell me, other than Myrna, does anyone else even know that you're . . .?"

"Amy, since the first time I blew a guy after gym class in high school."

"And what does she think?"

"That I'm a brat, just like you do. But she loves me anyway."

"And we haven't even mentioned your son."

"Who seems to like you."

"The way you are with . . . it's definitely a point in your favor."

Declan laughed. "If you told me a few weeks ago I'd even consider upending my life, I would have had you committed."

"You probably consider that a compliment," Sora teased.

Declan pulled Sora's head to his chest. "I'm asking the world of you, I know. But . . . look, I'm going to be in this show for at least a year. Let's spend that time working on this."

"We'll only get ourselves in deeper," Sora said.

"If you're trying to scare me with that, it's not working," Declan smiled.

"You talk a good game," Sora said, allowing Declan to enfold him "I just don't . . ." Declan quieted him with a kiss. They fell onto the sofa and held each other until they drifted off.

In the middle of the night, Declan got up and quietly climbed the steps to check in on Benedick, who was sleeping soundly. Reassured, he went back downstairs, shut off all the lights and lay back down next to Sora. The sensation of Declan's body woke him up. He turned to face Declan and they kissed, which evolved into lovemaking, this time with less passion but greater tenderness and affection.

As he fell back to sleep, Declan considered the coming battles: How to convince Sora. How to convince himself. How to live with the decision if he succeeded. The reverberations on his professional life. His private life. His son.

Sora turned and now they were face-to-face. Even asleep, Sora projected a sense of strength and harmony that Declan envied. Whatever happened, Sora would emerge intact. He could not be sure the same applied to him.

SIMON

Standing in the doorway of Ty's, Simon considered hailing a taxi and heading home. The bar was crowded for a Monday: a ragtag assortment of solitary poseurs; men wearing plaid-flannel shirts over Wranglers tucked into their Tony Lama boots; a mustachioed denim-and-leather-clad bartender dispensing beer bottles with both hands while the cub-like, bare-chested barback refilled empty cases with discards and hauled them to the basement. Despite being cheek-by-jowl, the men seemed aloof, distracted, as if they'd wandered into the bar by mistake and were not sure what to do now.

The night air was raw with periods of rain; large intermittent drops that popped when they hit the sidewalk. Simon reconsidered. An instinct to get out of the cold overrode his hesitation. Pushing open the door, he deposited his brolly in a receptacle just inside. He removed his wool lined leather gloves and loosened his scarf and prepared to order a whiskey.

It was a whiskey kind of night.

Earlier, in an under-heated movie house on West 13th Street, Simon had shivered through a faded print of Altman's new film *The Long Goodbye*. His third viewing actually, the other two under more favorable circumstances back in Manchester while visiting the family. The film's determinedly syrupy theme was still stuck in his head, and he hummed it absentmindedly.

The foul weather reminded him of home, fondly so. During his harried internship at Bellevue, he'd had little time to scratch the nostalgia itch. With his days now more structured, he'd been plagued by visits from the homesickness hound baying outside his window. He missed the folks and also Dwight, the closeted man who'd brought him out and sworn to commit suicide if Simon emigrated to America. At Christmas, Dwight had sent a card and inserted a photo of himself beside an adoring young man, his after-life boyfriend, no doubt.

Spiteful bugger.

Though a few years earlier, the American Psychiatric Association had declassified homosexuality as a mental disorder, most of Dwight's Bellevue colleagues were still more comfortable treating certifiable lunatics than depressed queers. Consequently, gays and lesbians who'd tried to kill themselves (and not merely indulged in extortion like Dwight) were routed to

Simon. While not remotely out at work, he was regarded as "sympathetic."

Probably his accent. Brits. Queers. Same difference. An assumption that went hand in hand with the generalization that all Englishmen were whip smart and could quote Shakespeare and Keats on command. Only his fellow expats picked up on Simon's regional accent, which, despite his efforts at university to refine it, resurfaced, especially when he was fatigued. "You sound like John Lennon," one fellow medic mentioned. Liverpool. But close enough.

"Another?" the bartender asked, pointing to Simon's empty glass.

"For the road," Simon nodded. Since he had little experience in the etiquette of cruising — how to look, how to be looked at — he'd already grown restless and bored. "Going to the toilet. Be right back," he told the bartender, slapping down some bills.

As he relieved himself at the urinal, a blinding flash went off in the stall nearby. Then another. Simon rapped on the stall door. "Is everything all right in there?" he inquired.

"Yeah," said a voice from within. "Just trying to get a good shot of my stuff."

"Come again?" Simon said.

The door swung open. A young man was sitting on the toilet, a zoom lens bearing down on his crotch. The flash clicked several times. Then the man whipped the camera strap over his shoulder, rose to his feet and zipped up. He smiled at Simon, who thought him unnaturally beautiful though possibly deranged.

"Hi. I'm Titus. I notice that you're uncircumcised," he said, hovering over Simon who was now midstream. "Would you mind if I took a few shots while you have it out?"

"Yes, I think I would," he said, shuddering.

"Just so you know, I'm not a perv. I'm a professional photographer. I've had an exhibition."

"At the dirty bookstore on Hudson?" Simon scoffed.

"No. At a real gallery in Soho. Last year. Got good reviews too. Even sold a few prints," Titus said, digging into his jeans. He pulled out an embossed business card with an artful photo of two women folding laundry in one corner and flashed it at Simon. "What I'm working on now isn't porn. They're abstracts. I zoom in so close that they look like anything but genitals. It's freaky."

"I've no doubt. Just the same, thank you, no."

"Please," he said, tilting his adorable kinky-haired head to one side. "I don't have many uncut men. This is America. Foreskin is forbidden."

Simon couldn't help but be amused by Titus's affectless delivery, which only reinforced his angelic bad-boy aura.

"Very well, but let's be quick about it before someone comes in."

"No prob. I can get off a dozen shots in a flash," Titus said. "Now face me, and would you mind taking out your nuts too? I need the whole package."

Simon reached into his trousers and struggled to retrieve his testicles. *Why am I doing this?* he asked himself. *Me, the poster child for British propriety.*

"And I need for you to be totally flaccid," Titus said as he fiddled with the zoom lens.

"I am," Simon said, sternly.

"Oh. Well, congratulations," Titus said, as a series of blinding flashes went off in rapid succession.

"This is quite uncomfortable," Simon remarked, certain that he'd lost his mind.

"Almost done," Titus said, the shutter rapidly clicking. The door opened behind them, and Simon quickly packed up his equipment.

Titus jumped to his feet. "Thanks a heap, man. How about I buy you a drink?"

"I have one waiting for me, but I appreciate the offer," Simon said. As he opened the door, he added, "Perhaps you'd like to join me? I'm Simon, by the way."

"You're on, Simon," Titus said, bouncing on the balls of his feet ahead of him. Approaching the bar, he signaled to the bartender, "Hey, Billy. A Miller."

When Billy brought his drink, Titus said, "I just took a picture of his stuff. He's uncut."

"Must you?" Simon said, abashed.

"It's cool. I shot Billy last week. In the back room. Right?"

"Yup," Billy replied. "He showed me the pictures. Weird. Never in a million years would you think that's what you were looking at."

"I threw a blue wash over them. They have this Georgia O'Keefe vibe."

"The woman who painted flowers that looked like vaginas?"

"Well, aren't you the culture vulture?" Titus chortled. "By the way, I've also shot about a dozen vaginas. And a couple of them actually do look like flowers. Well, more like rose bushes. Did you know that pussies can look as different as dicks?"

"Can't say as I've had the pleasure," Simon said.

"Well, they do. I've done nipples too. But only on women. They're like moonscapes."

"How about buttholes?" Billy asked.

Titus shook his head. "Nah. I tried. Did mine and my roommate's, George, while he was asleep. They're just not that interesting."

"Ears," Simon interrupted. "What about ears? They can be quite diverse."

Titus brushed the hair away from Simon's right ear. "Hmm. It's a thought. Yours are nice, and so is your . . ."

Simon pushed his hair back into place, pretending to ignore the remark. Downing the last few drops in his glass, he turned up the collar on his mac. "Well, then. It's late. I should be in bed like a good boy."

"Thanks for doing that," Titus said. "I'm sure it wasn't easy for someone as uptight as you. You want to see the pictures when they're done?"

"Thanks just the same," Simon said, bridling at Titus's observation. The only reason he'd cooperated was to prove that he wasn't uptight. Wasn't it?

"Too bad. I was hoping to see it again. And not to photograph," he said casually, as if he'd asked Simon to tea.

"A tempting offer," Simon said. "I'm likely not the first person to say this, but you're quite fetching."

"No, you're not the first," Titus said. "Thanks, but I don't see it. I've done a few self-portraits. Except for my lips, my features are small and flat. There's no real character in my face."

"You'll get no pity from me," Simon said. "And I disagree. You've plenty of character."

"Now that's a compliment I'll take," Titus said.

"Tell me, this fellow you mentioned, the roommate whose bunghole you surreptitiously photographed, is he your . . .?"

"George? No, he belongs lock, stock and barrel to somebody who belongs to somebody else. But he lets me use his body from time to time."

"Is that another hobby of yours? Using men's bodies?"

"I told you already. Photography's not a hobby," Titus said, wrinkling his nose. "I plan to make a living at it someday. As for men's bodies, sometimes it takes the edge off being lonely."

"I shouldn't think that would be a problem for you. Whereas I . . ." he said with a shrug. "You know, stranger in a big city?"

Simon suddenly felt flummoxed. Displaying his privates seemed somehow less intimate than confessing to solitude. For the second time since meeting Titus, he'd done something completely out of character. Distressing. "Well, nice meeting you," he said, pulling on his gloves.

Titus leaned in and brushed his lips along Simon's cheek. "Take me with you?" he asked.

A simple request with no neediness. It would have been heartless for Simon to refuse.

They spent a cozy night together. The sex was tame. Felt somewhat like payment for the privilege of sharing his bed on a chilly night. In the morning, Titus offered to come by later in the week and show him the photos. Simon jotted down his number, though he didn't expect to hear from Titus again.

He was wrong. That weekend, Titus rang him up. He arrived at Simon's flat with a bottle of merlot. The photos, they concluded, resembled the tip of an elephant's trunk sinking into a swirling pool of quicksand. Titus then unzipped Simon and blew him.

"That was great, thanks," Titus said with a wink and kissed him for good measure. His directness and ease with sex seemed alien yet intoxicating. Simon was still coming to terms with his nature, which he continued to regard as somewhat aberrant despite years of psychiatric training. Studying Freud, Hirschfeld and Kinsey had done little to alleviate his internal struggle, and he pursued his yearnings only when resistance proved intolerable.

While Dwight had forced him out of denial, this capricious street urchin, who didn't seem to care a whit for social convention, threatened to drag him into the light of day. And he felt powerless to resist.

That Friday, they went out for a meal at a Polish restaurant on 2nd Avenue. Simon had argued against it. He was a boring eater, he said, strictly meat and potatoes. Titus assured him that the Poles served both. Simon ordered a goulash, which seemed safe, though he deemed the liberal use of paprika "exotic." Titus found it so funny he almost gagged. Simon was seized by the urge to throw him on the ground and bugger him right there in the restaurant.

Troubling, he thought, especially when it dawned on him that he desired more than Titus's body. He wanted to imbibe his antic spirit.

After dinner, they went to Titus's apartment and perused his portfolio. Simon was impressed, particularly by the photos from his first exhibit, a montage of Greenwich Village, where Titus was raised. Titus told him about his rootless upbringing. His white mother, a writer, and his black father, a jazz musician. To Simon's ears it sounded almost romantic, until Titus mentioned that his mother had murdered his father. Accidentally, but nonetheless.

How had Simon missed the dark undercurrent in Titus's sangfroid attitude and was only hearing it now when he discussed his childhood? Undoubtedly, infatuation had muddied his psychological faculties.

Since Titus's roommate, George, was in Atlanta visiting his children, Titus was free, as he put it, "to play music written in this century. Do you like Zeppelin?"

As the needle dropped on "When the Levee Breaks," Titus threw off his clothes and undid the buttons on Simon's shirt. He stretched out on the sofa, and Simon sat on the floor beside him and caressed and kissed him. He forcefully masturbated Titus and took immense pleasure in his rhythmic writhing and groans. Titus's release was so thrilling that Simon ejaculated without stimulation.

"How did you do that?" Titus marveled.

"Sorcery," Simon said. While his tone was playful, it was edged with truth. In Titus's presence, he felt possessed.

When the music ended, the silence was interrupted only by the occasional whir of a distant siren. Titus asked him about Dwight. Did Simon love him? No. Would he have known if he had? Probably not. Simon, in turn, was curious about George. "He's a great person. But tortured," Titus said. "He's been crazy in love with this guy, Donald. For years. And scared shitless about it the whole time. Then he ran away and by the time he came back, Donald had moved to Brooklyn to live with a cop who loved him as much as George did, except he didn't feel bad about it."

"Sad," Simon said. "How did you end up living with him?"

"Originally, I lived here with my mom's friend Terry, who got custody of me after she went to prison. Terry was walking past Donald's old apartment one day and found George sitting on a stoop across the street staring up at his window. Terry told George what had happened, and he completely fell apart. Terry felt bad for him and let him stay with us for a while. Then Terry moved in with his boyfriend, and George inherited the apartment. And me. He sleeps with me occasionally and other guys too, but he's still stuck on Donald."

"I'm sure there are dozens of men who are stuck on you," Simon assured him.

"I don't know of any. Not that I care. Why? Are you stuck on me?"

"I don't think that would be a good idea," Simon said.

"The transistor radio is a good idea," Titus snapped. "Frozen food is a good idea. Love is never a good idea. I've seen what it does to people. Nope. Not for me."

They saw each other sporadically over the next several months. They went to hear Alberta Hunter at the Cookery on 8th Street, saw Bob Fosse's astringent new musical *Chicago* (but only because their first choice, *A Chorus Line*, was completely sold out), and a couple of films, *Annie Hall* and *Star Wars*, which they enjoyed immensely if for different reasons. Simon was taken by the stories while Titus, true to form, was obsessed with the cinematography.

Then Simon's work schedule changed. His lease ended and he became preoccupied with finding a new apartment, finally settling on a doorman building on East 9th off University Place. Titus traveled to Berlin for a vernissage, which included several photos of the abstract genitalia series. They didn't communicate for two months and got together only once, for a drink, after Titus returned from Europe. He quickly ran off citing a prior commitment. Simon assumed that Titus's infatuation had run its course, and he had moved on. Now he needed to do likewise. A tall order.

With Dwight, he had felt safe. There'd been a line of demarcation which, by mutual agreement, they'd never breached. With Titus, emotional boundaries had been crossed from the onset, and Simon felt himself being drawn into dangerous territory. He rang Titus several times, and there was either no answer or George picked up and took a message. But Titus never returned his calls.

Perhaps a little heartache would do him good, he reasoned. Better now than later. Titus was impermanent by nature, carefree to the point of carelessness. His opposite in almost every way.

One good thing came of it, though. Titus had emboldened him. Given him confidence. He began dating a puckish young man named Darryl, whom he'd met — or rather made eye contact with — at John's Pizzeria on Bleecker and followed home hoping to be invited up. Which he was. He would never have dared such a bold move before he met Titus.

Darryl was a taciturn type, but frolicsome in bed. One Friday evening several weeks after they met, Darryl popped by with his next-door neighbor Patrick, with whom, he explained, he had an "on-and-off thing." Patrick, a sprightly, energetic bloke, was talkative and amusing. He had brought a spliff, and they passed it around. Simon only became aware that Patrick was to be included in the evening's entertainment when Darryl suggested Simon kiss him while he watched.

After a particularly trying day, which had included a grueling two-hour session with parents who were in deep denial about their daughter's sexuality and suicidal tendencies, Simon was at home finishing off two bangers (sorry, hot dogs) he'd bought at Gray's Papaya, when there was a knock at the door. Probably a neighbor he thought, since the doorman normally announced all visitors.

"Well this is a pleasant surprise," Simon said to Titus, who was standing in the doorway. "How did you get by the . . .?"

"He's probably on a cigarette break," Titus explained. "Can I come in?"

"Yes, yes, of course," Simon said, opening the door wide. It struck him that he hadn't given Titus his new address. "How did you find me?"

"I called information," Titus replied. "Nice place," he added, as he crossed into the dining area. "This wall needs something. You should come by sometime and pick out one of my photos and hang it here. I won't charge you for it."

"What a lovely offer. Perhaps I shall," Simon said, noting that Titus was uncharacteristically on edge. "Would you like something to drink?"

Titus turned sharply and looked directly at him. "I got your messages," he said. "I didn't call you back because, well, the thing is, I think you may have gotten the wrong idea. I was looking for a fuck buddy, someone to hang out with and maybe spend the night. You know, something casual."

"Oh, I see," Simon said, blindsided. "And I made it complicated?"

"Kind of. I still like you though and if it's okay with you, we could try again," Titus said. "But just so we're clear. Fuck buddies, right?"

"Fuck buddies," he repeated, though he hated the vulgar term. But if it meant seeing Titus again, he would have agreed to assassinate the Archbishop of Canterbury.

"Great. And since I'm here, do you want to have sex?"

Simon nodded meekly.

"Good. How about you get down on your knees?" Titus said, undoing his trousers.

When he had finished, Titus took Simon's hand and led him to the bedroom, where he straddled him, kissing him and gazing deeply into his eyes. Simon didn't want it to end. He resisted climaxing with all his might, but he was no match for the sorcerer.

"That was fun, wasn't it?" Titus said, resting his head on Simon's chest.

"I should think the answer is self-evident," Simon said.

"See. We can do this."

"I'm afraid you'll have to be patient. I don't have much experience at this sort of thing."

"So how many guys have you slept with? More or less."

"More than five, fewer than ten," Simon admitted.

Titus lifted his head and stared straight at him. "Really? God. I've been with more men than that in the past month."

Titus probably hadn't meant to sound disparaging. If Simon hadn't been awash on a post-coital high, he might have glossed over the comment. But at that moment he was feeling particularly vulnerable, and he was furious. He pushed Titus away and abruptly shifted to the other side of the bed. "You're a horrible boy. Put on your clothes and leave this instant."

Titus reacted as if he'd been struck. He dressed quickly and left without saying goodbye.

Simon regretted the words immediately. What did it matter how many men Titus was with so long as they could be together — even if only on a semi-regular basis? Surely that was preferable to losing him completely. He was rousted from his remorse by the screech of tires outside. He ran to the window and saw Titus standing in front of a taxi, which had missed hitting him by inches. He was pounding the hood of the yellow cab and swearing at the driver.

Simon opened the window and called out to him, "Are you all right?"

Titus glanced up four stories but didn't reply.

"I apologize for what I said," Simon blurted. "I can't help it that I'm in love with you."

"What?" Titus said as he walked away. Simon shut the window. What a damned fool thing to say. Hadn't he done enough damage for one evening?

Titus made no further attempts to reach him, and Simon suffered through it as best he could, distracting himself with a holiday visit to Manchester. On New Year's Eve, he even fell back into bed with Dwight. For auld lang syne.

On a bitter cold night in February, Darryl invited him to go dancing at a private club called Flamingo on lower Broadway. An open space crammed with sweaty, attractive, shirtless men. The walls and floors vibrated from the relentless beat. They split a quaalude and washed it down with chilled vodka, and Simon enjoyed the sensation of being lithe and lively on the dance floor. If he looked ridiculous, so what? He was enjoying himself thoroughly.

While Darryl was in the loo, Simon's eyes wandered until they fell on a familiar face, and it rendered him breathless. Titus was being pasted against the wall by a handsome young man, his neck and chest covered in kisses. Simon gazed open-mouthed, pain shooting through his numbness. When Darryl returned, they resumed dancing but, later, when he was unable to perform, he blamed it on the drugs.

That summer, Darryl invited him for the weekend to a house he was sharing on Fire Island. When Simon arrived, Darryl showed him to his room and explained that he would be away most of the time. He was "hot and heavy" with a boy who lived in a house on the bay. "I'd invite you along," he said, "But I'm not ready to share him just yet. Anyway, I think you and I are becoming more like friends, don't you?"

Simon was confounded by the fluidity of queer mating rituals. Hot and heavy, fuck buddies, friends, sisters. Arbitrary rules that changed as often as the players. Perhaps he should just head home on the last ferry. The Village was pleasantly sparse and quiet on summer weekends. The gays headed off to Fire Island and the straights to the Hamptons, with some crossover.

But first he'd spend the day at the beach and treat his pale, freckly skin to some sun. After a dip, he fell asleep on his towel. He woke from the nap, sat up and lit a cigarette. At that moment, Titus wandered past and stopped at a blanket about twenty feet away. He was naked as was the young man below him, who appeared to have swallowed barbells that went directly to his biceps and pectorals.

Their eyes met. Simon threw himself back down on the towel as if to wish him gone.

"What are you doing here?" Titus said, standing over him.

"I was invited out for the weekend," he replied, squeezing his eyes shut.

"By who?"

"I don't see how that's any of your concern," Simon said. He opened his eyes and tried to gauge Titus's reaction, but his face was in a shadow.

"Well goody for you," Titus said. Then he crouched down and pointed to the naked man on the blanket. "Hot, isn't he? He fucked me senseless last night. I don't think I've ever come so much in my life. Do you want to know why?"

"Not particularly," Simon said, angrily flicking his cigarette away.

"Because the only way I could get excited was by imagining that it was you," he said. "How screwed up is that?"

Without another word, Titus returned to the blanket. He bent down and kissed the man before running down to the water's edge and jumping in.

Simon hated Titus fiercely, in a way that only reinforced how much he still cared for him. *Oh physician, heal thyself.*

Simon boarded the next boat for the mainland.

When, in mid-September, Titus once again snuck past the doorman and pounded on his door, Simon guessed it was him.

"You busy?" he said, when Simon opened the door a crack.

"Yes, as a matter of fact. I'm entertaining," Simon replied, coldly.

"You are not. You came home alone. I know because I was taking pictures of you from the across the street," he said, pushing open the door. He ducked under Simon's arm and entered.

"You were photographing me? Why?"

"Part of a new series. I catch people going in and out of their buildings, like a private detective gathering incriminating shots of a criminal or an adulterer. The faces and bodies are blurry, which gives them this ghost-like quality. I think you'd like them."

"Yes. It does sound interesting," Simon conceded, noting that his heart was clocking at above average speed. *Control yourself, Simon.*

Without asking, Titus helped himself to a beer from the refrigerator. "Imported. Fancy," he said, scrounging through the drawers for a church key. He took two long swigs and peered out the window and sighed.

"This has got to stop," Titus mumbled. "It's getting boring."

"Whatever do you mean?" Simon asked.

"That night at Flamingo. The way you looked at the guy I was with, it was like you wanted to tear him apart. Where do you get off?"

"I can't say as I recall."

"You do so. You don't own me, Simon." Titus tossed himself into an armchair and propped his feet on the ottoman. "Did you know that the last time I cried was the day my mom went to prison? Oh wait, there was another time. After you told me I was horrible and kicked me out. Yeah, that was a rough night."

Simon was speechless.

Titus jumped up and began pacing the room as if he were encaged. "Look, are you still in love with me?"

"Whatever gave you that idea?"

"I heard you say it. From the window. After you told me to leave."

"Oh, I see," Simon said, hanging his head. "A momentary lapse. You needn't worry."

"Then why do you keep popping up wherever I go? You're spooking me, man."

"In the future, I shall endeavor to make myself invisible," Simon said with a sneer.

"Fuck you," Titus said.

"Titus, I've seen you exactly twice since the beginning of the year. That hardly qualifies as stalking. And you're the one who's been lurking outside my building and secretly photographing me. I wonder. Was it just tonight, or have you . . . ?

"Only once or twice," Titus said. "I wanted to have a wide choice of shots."

"Ah," Simon said. "But those other times you didn't make your presence known. Have you come up here just to upset me?"

"Oh, you're upset? Poor baby. Ask me if I give a shit."

"Do you? Do you give a shit?" Simon said defiantly.

"Not even a little."

"Then what are you doing here?"

"How do I know? You're the shrink. You figure it out."

Simon had figured it out. If he'd been a disinterested third party, he would have arrived at his diagnosis sooner. But as a participant, his objectivity had been compromised. The encounter on the beach had confirmed that they were both suffering from the same malady. Yet Simon had made no effort to contact Titus. It would have been useless. It had to be Titus's decision, or nothing would come of it.

"You know what, man? Forget you!" Titus said and bolted for the door. Simon blocked his exit. An impulsive move. As Titus reached past him for the doorknob, Simon burst out laughing.

"Sorry. I don't mean to make light. But this is oddly reminiscent of an old romantic melodrama I watched the other day with Bette Davis. Or was it Olivia de Havilland?"

"So what's wrong with that?" Titus said, resting his head against Simon's chest. "Are you so uptight that you can't put up with a little drama?"

Simon had the good sense not to irk Titus further. Instead, he enfolded him in his arms and held him tightly. Titus whimpered and, slowly, the tension left his body and he gave himself over to the embrace.

This time, the lovemaking was different, intense and absorbing but leavened with genuine affection, soft words, caring gestures, penetrating stares. When it was over, they fell into a deep, restful sleep still entwined, in the wake of what, if they'd been lovers — and not just fuck buddies — would have been classified as make-up sex.

THE LOST BROTHER

Kyle Brunner and Lester Gabler attended the Soho photo exhibit incognito. As themselves.

Except for George, the erstwhile beau of a former neighbor and Dee Andrea, their wig stylist-makeup consultant, they recognized only a smattering of the invited guests. Dee Andrea acknowledged them from across the room with a sly glance as if to say, "Don't worry. Your secret's safe with me."

They were surprised to receive the invitation. Any invitation, since they rarely socialized. They'd recognized the photo on the invite and guessed, correctly, that it had been taken by the young boy who had once tailed them with his camera, capturing them in their various personae. Still, they were unprepared for the impact of an entire exhibit devoted to their various alter egos. A fascinating if somewhat disorienting experience, though they were secretly proud to overhear that many of the attendees were also familiar with the characters.

"Ah, the laundry ladies," remarked the stunning redhead standing a few feet away. "Until tonight, I wasn't aware that they were also the frumpy women who always sit in the back pew at First Presbyterian."

"Frumpy, indeed," Lester whispered to Kyle. A great deal of attention and care had gone into transforming themselves into the proper churchgoing matrons. Reserved perhaps, but certainly not frumpy.

Perhaps the most gratifying comments came from two famous invited guests who arrived fashionably late — and were also traveling incognito as themselves. Cigarette holder poised in midair, the one man remarked, "Sometimes, when I saw them on the street or at the market, I could barely resist the urge to go up and speak to them."

"But that would have broken the illusion, wouldn't it?" his partner, also in disguise, replied.

Given the impressive range of characters the two men had embodied at the Ridiculous Theatrical Company over the years, Kyle and Lester were duly flattered. If anyone appreciated the almost-invisible line of demarcation between performer and craft, it was Mr. Ludlam and Mr. Quinton. As with Lester and Kyle, their characters defined them as a couple. Spoke to their spirit of collaboration. A shared sensibility that was the lifeblood of their relationship. As with their more celebrated counterparts, the quirky characters they brought to life became de facto family members.

Kyle and Lester had agreed beforehand to stay no longer than it took to satisfy their curiosity. But before they could make their getaway, George approached. "I don't know if you remember me," he said. "We were introduced through your neighbor across the hall, Donald. Several times."

They nodded. Indeed, they remembered George. His striking good looks, his erratic temperament. The passion between him and Donald had seeped through the walls, as had the tempests that sometimes ensued.

"The photographer, Titus, is a friend. He was wondering if he could finally meet you," George said. "He knows how much you value privacy, though, and doesn't want to presume."

"Perhaps another time," said Lester, the more reticent of the two, nervously tapping his foot.

Kyle whispered in his ear. "It would be rude not to at least say hello."

Lester nodded. He wasn't pleased but, as usual, deferred to his partner.

"Is it okay if we speak somewhere private?" Kyle asked.

"Sure thing," George said. He escorted Kyle and Lester to an empty office at the rear of the gallery. Titus appeared soon after, a brown-paper packet under his arm.

"Hi," he said extending his hand. "My name's Titus."

"We know who you are," Kyle said. "You've grown into quite the young man."

"Thanks. I'm so pleased you decided to come. It means a lot to me. You were my first real-life subjects, though maybe real life is not the proper term."

"Yes," Kyle said with a nod. "Well, we very much enjoyed the exhibit, though you can appreciate that it makes us feel a bit exposed."

Lester nodded and tried to force a smile, but his insides were churning. Why did Kyle have to say that? Wasn't it enough that he dragged him here almost against his will?

"I don't want to keep you," Titus continued, sensing their unease, "but on the off chance that you did attend, I made up some prints for you."

Kyle graciously accepted the package. "That's most kind. Isn't it, Lester?"

"Uh-huh," Lester said, studying his shoes. He recalled how he had wanted to discourage the then-incipient photographer's fascination with them. "We don't need anyone taking our picture," he'd complained. "The whole point is to be in plain sight but invisible. To be part of the flow."

But Kyle had seen no harm in it. "Let him be. He's just a boy. You do understand, don't you?"

"Yes, of course," Lester conceded.

"Whenever I see him lurking around a corner with that curious glint in his eye, it makes me wonder . . ." Kyle had said with a sigh.

"Now, now. You'll only upset yourself," Lester said.

Kyle had nodded, inhaled deeply, and straightened his back. But one or two stray tears had escaped and found their way down his cheeks.

They framed several of the photos and hung them in the living area at home. From time to time, Lester found himself staring at them, appreciating the precision with which they'd brought their various characters to life. "We were good, weren't we?" he said with a grin.

"We still are," Kyle reminded him, though they now ventured out less and less because, as Lester had remarked, "What we do isn't new anymore. Now it even has a name. Performance art."

Their most recent foray, their first-ever pride parade, marked the debut of two brand-new personae. Mike and Steve aka the Village clones: mustaches, backward baseball caps, frayed denim cut-offs and work boots. They pumped their fists in the air and hooted in unison with the others, brazenly kissed and held hands — behavior that would otherwise be strictly out-of-bounds if they attended as Kyle and Lester. But then, freedom of expression had been the whole point of their masquerades. To inhabit the spirit of characters different from themselves.

At the parade, no one remarked on them. No one noticed. At least not so far as they could tell. They were one and the same with hundreds of other young men, a perfect simulacrum of the real thing. As intended.

The re-creations, which had begun as homage and evolved into a form of street theater had now come full circle. Now they celebrated the celebrants, while at the same time delicately poking fun at the conformity of the non-conformists. Yet on a personal level they were moved that the Village-centered community, which had been in existence for decades, visible largely through coded signals, had now come out of hiding and begun to assert its collective voice.

One day, as Kyle was retrieving the mail, a letter slipped from his fingers. He stooped down to collect it and noticed the Arkansas postmark. He immediately tore it open and, inside, found a small newspaper clipping announcing the engagement of a Grace Lovelace to Rory Brunner. The article featured a studio-posed image of the bride-to-be, though none of her intended.

Kyle read the eight-line article over and over again hoping to unearth concealed clues. Was this Grace woman in love with Rory? Or had she accepted his proposal merely because it was time for her to marry? Would she make him happy? And Rory, what kind of man had he become? Was he . . . ?

A thousand questions. Not a single answer.

When he showed the clip to Lester, he said, "You see? You were worried for nothing. Rory's okay. He's grown up and has a life."

"Yes, but what kind of life?" Kyle mused.

"Stop it," Lester cautioned. "Just be happy that he's alive and well."

"Who do you suppose sent it?" Kyle said. The envelope contained no return address, and he seriously doubted whether it had been his parents. They hadn't spoken since he and Lester ran away together almost two decades earlier. He'd made several attempts to correspond with Rory, to apologize and tell his younger brother how much he missed him, but the letters were never answered.

Kyle Brunner had been awestruck the first time he saw his mother's "change-of-life baby" sleeping in the bassinette beside her bed at St. Luke's hospital. Georgia and Efrem Brunner had given birth to two other children, Kyle and his younger sister Patricia, who had contracted polio when she was three and died four years later. Since they didn't believe in contraception, Kyle's parents had slept in separate beds after Patricia was born. When Georgia began to experience hot flashes and the doctor informed her that she was going through menopause, they'd resumed shared sleeping arrangements.

Having already lost one child and worried that the later-in-life arrival might be somehow compromised, Rory was viewed less as a blessing from above than a burden. Kyle's parents had been more than happy when their elder son volunteered to help nurture the new arrival. When he wasn't at school, Kyle was busy feeding, changing and entertaining the fussy, colicky infant and, most nights, rocked him to sleep. Rory soon came to regard Kyle as his true parent and his mother and father as disinterested caretakers. And truly, the boy was the center of his older brother's life. Small and scrawny and introverted, Kyle's only friends at school were girls, most of whom lost interest in him when the other boys started to pay them mind.

His devotion to Rory took a sudden shift the day Kyle saw someone who appeared to be his doppelgänger through a cloud of dust across a rodeo arena at the Four States Fair in Texarkana.

On the excuse of getting himself a root beer, Kyle followed the boy behind a tent and they circled each other goggle-eyed and laughed until their buttons were ready to pop. Neither was much of a talker, but no explanation was necessary. They'd found one another. What more was there to say?

The attraction was not physical, at least not at first. He and the boy, whose name was Lester and who appeared even more withdrawn and awkward than Kyle, immediately grasped that they'd been traveling a parallel track. And on this day, it had miraculously converged. To turn one's back on this cosmic gift was unthinkable. Thereafter, Kyle and Lester were inseparable.

They lived two towns apart, a thirty-minute bike ride that one or the other made each day, regardless of the weather. Usually, it was Lester who visited Kyle, since he was the one laden with child-rearing responsibilities. Kyle escorted Rory to kindergarten each morning and picked him up in the afternoon. They played catch until dinnertime. After Rory started first grade, Kyle helped him with his homework in the evenings. Lester didn't mind being shoehorned into Kyle's life. He had no real home life to speak of as the only child of a single mother who blamed Lester for his bastard-hood and punished him anytime one of her short-lived beaus took a powder.

Kyle's parents and Lester's mother encouraged the friendship. They're like twin brothers, they said, glad that their socially graceless boys had found one another. During the summer months, Lester often stayed over at Kyle's in the bedroom he shared with Rory, who slept on a cot in the corner. After the boy fell asleep, they began to roam over each other's bodies, which provided them with an avenue of tacit communication. The arrangement might have continued indefinitely had Kyle's mother not discovered him sodomizing Lester in the barn one afternoon.

Subsequently, Lester was banished, and Kyle's movements carefully monitored, but not so carefully that the two boys weren't able to plot their escape.

Stuffing their belongings into pillowcases, they rendezvoused behind the same tent at the fair where they'd originally met — and absconded. They were never reported as missing. Like so many "fraternal-minded" youths, they were swallowed by the great American maw, unnoticed and unmourned. Deserving of whatever terrible fate awaited them.

Kyle and Lester were similar enough in appearance that they could pass for brothers or cousins, and they said nothing to contradict that assumption. It was safer that way. Settling in Little Rock, they took on menial jobs at a soda fountain and a hardware store and, at night, studied accounting. After becoming certified, Lester suggested they make their way east. But Kyle was hesitant about putting great distance between himself and Rory. "Suppose he needs me," Kyle said.

Lester suggested he make one last visit home to say goodbye. Kyle waited outside Rory's elementary school and, when he emerged, informed him that he was going away and they might not see each other for a while. Kyle promised to write and tell him where he was and hoped Rory would write back. His young brother accepted the news stoically, and they parted with several backward glances that Kyle had still not erased from his mind.

Anytime he heard of a child being abducted or being maimed or killed in an accident, Kyle couldn't sleep. And Lester would force himself to stay awake to comfort him.

On the journey eastward, whenever they ran short of money, they would stop and find work. Over time they lost interest in sex — with each other or anyone else. By then, they'd happened on a more satisfying means of shared intimacy.

One lazy summer afternoon, after swimming in Chickamauga Creek outside of Chattanooga, they noticed two sharecroppers carrying their dirty laundry toward the river. Peering through the bushes, Kyle and Lester watched as the two women solemnly went about their chores, communicating only with the occasional glance or nod. The sounds of splashing water and the beating of clothes against the rocks were accompanied by idle humming. And no sooner had one of the women trailed off than the other picked up the melody and continued.

The beauty and simplicity of the ritual impressed them. The idea to mimic the women began as a lark. But from the start, they were careful that it never be construed as mockery or disrespect. Lester had been taught to sew by his grandmother, and Kyle had a keen eye for fabrics, their weight and their drape. They scoured the shelves of the local dry goods store before settling on the appropriate cotton prints. Following a Simplicity pattern, Lester fashioned house dresses with complementary head scarves similar to the washerwomen's outfits.

Their first public appearance was at the local Laundromat in Chattanooga; not as Lester and Kyle, but as Arkansas sharecropper wives, whom they named Irma Jean Entwistle and Lula Braithwaite. They concocted a detailed history for each woman, assigning them relatives, friends and formative experiences. The women were so carefully etched that speech was unnecessary. They felt them in their bones. Every Saturday, rain or shine, Irma Jean and Lula left their apartment in their housedresses, support stockings rolled down around their ankles, feet sheathed in Scuffies, dragging a wire shopping cart behind them. During the wash cycle, they waited outside, sucking on cigarettes. Irma Jean and Lula, they'd determined, were secret smokers who indulged their vice behind the backs of their disapproving husbands, Artis and Jackson. They could have made better marriages, they reasoned, but they settled, and their contempt was evident in the haphazard way they folded their husbands' clothes.

It was only later, after they'd moved to the West Village, that Kyle and Lester began to regard these outings as performance; not drag exactly, since the women were human-scaled and not enhanced in any way. The approach hewed closer to pantomime, characters who expressed themselves through facial gestures and body language. For Kyle and Lester, silence was more than golden. It freed them to explore nuance as they continued to develop and refine their characters.

The rest of the week, Kyle and Lester were anonymous, walking the Village streets unnoticed on their way to and from work, Lester at an accounting firm on lower Broadway, Kyle as a bookkeeper in the garment district. Only as Irma Jean and Lula did they eventually attract eyeballs and comments, though no one connected them to the two unremarkable men living almost invisibly in their midst. At least not initially.

The urge to develop new characters evolved organically. Like Irma Jean and Lula, the church ladies, Miss Ida Jackson and Miss Louella Mae Carson, were familiar to them, how they carried themselves, what they thought, what they wore, and what they could and could not abide. Ida and Louella were two proper Christian women, who attended Sunday services at First Presbyterian on 12th Street and 5th Avenue. Both widowed young, they lived off the insurance policies their prescient husbands had taken out not long before their unexpected deaths. No shadow of suspicion fell over them, however, since it was inconceivable that two such upstanding, pious women would ever be involved in nefarious behavior.

Embodying Ida and Louella required more intricate disguises, and they decided to enlist the help of a professional. On his way uptown, Kyle one day happened upon Toujours Coiffures, located above Lady Flora's Flowers on West 16th Street, a few doors down from 5th. The proprietress, Dee Andrea Monet was a big-boned six-foot (even taller in heels) exotic, with skin the color of Mississippi silt. She featured only the finest coifs and was a whiz at maquillage, besides.

"May I suggest a soft perm look," Dee Andrea said, when Kyle and Lester explained their concept. She held up a honey-colored hairpiece, and they cooed in unison. The consultation took place in the back room of Dee Andrea's shop, where she instructed them in the care and maintenance of their wigs and provided useful makeup tips and accessory suggestions. "A proper churchgoing lady always carries a hard handbag," Dee Andrea insisted. "And wrist-length white gloves cover up a multitude of sins," she added, pointing to the ingrained ink stains on the backs of their hands from poring over ledgers.

Any worries that they might be unmasked were quickly put to rest when the other First Presbyterian congregants nodded at them, the men graciously tipping their hats. After the service, the pastor introduced himself and welcomed them to the church. They politely acknowledged him and went on their merry way.

Life in New York's melting pot inspired them to take on new and more urbane roles. Rachel and Deidre were two spoiled chorines, who secretly hated one another but were bound by a mutual affection for the ballet as well as a penchant for youthful rebellion. In their tunics, tights, and Capezio slippers, the bun-headed young ladies waddled bowlegged down the busy city streets. On Saturday evenings, Rachel and Deidre snuck away from their parents to sip espressos in Village coffeehouses and listen to poets or scruffy folk singers strumming their guitars. If the occasional patron made an advance, they politely demurred. Decidedly, neither Rachel nor Deidre was that kind of girl.

Gloria and Roselle, however, were each, exactly, that kind of girl. The new characters were inspired by the neighborhood ladies they encountered in Kew Gardens, where they first settled after decamping to New York, and were further informed by the office workers they came across in their daily lives.

Gloria and Roselle made their debut at the New York World's Fair in Flushing, cracking gum and sporting beehives and butterfly sunglasses, with tight skirts hitched up above the knees and low-heeled T-straps. When men approached to flirt, they would snort and skitter away, shaking their behinds provocatively. The attention was flattering but as Dee Andrea had warned them, until they developed a strong right hook, it was best to discourage admirers. Since they'd determined that Gloria and Roselle were risqué by nature, they conceived of Chick and Larry, two young men who inadvertently reinvigorated Kyle and Lester's sex lives.

Chick, his pompadour pomaded into place, sported a white T-shirt under a mustard-colored wool cardigan over blue jeans and black high-tops. He invited Roselle to the movies, where they necked — and sometimes misbehaved — in the back row. Other times, Larry, a true hellion, rented a car and drove Gloria to the Poconos, stopping in a secluded spot along the way where they hopped into the back seat for some hanky and panky.

Naomi and Harrison were products of the East Village. Free-love types — tie-dyed and long-haired — flashing peace signs, nibbling alfalfa sprouts and hanging out in head shops and record stores. When artist Joey Skaggs became fed up with tourist buses riding up and down St. Mark's Place ogling and taking photos of the counterculture denizens, he invited Naomi and Harrison aboard his Greyhound bus tour of Queens, where the hippies and other assorted oddballs treated the straitlaced residents to the same invasive scrutiny. The following year Naomi and Harrison followed the crowd to the Woodstock festival, where they ingested mushrooms and canoodled in the bushes.

"Did you forget your key again?" said Lester into the intercom, annoyed at having been interrupted from sewing a Give Peace a Chance decal onto Harrison's denim vest.

"Lester, is that you? This here's Rory," was the response.

Incredulous, Lester raced down the steps, his heart beating wildly, half certain he would find some practical jokester sent to devastate Kyle.

He recognized the woman first, from the wedding announcement. He studied the man standing beside her. It was indeed Rory. He could tell from the eyes — as big and trusting as he remembered.

"Hello, Lester," Rory said. "This here is Grace, my fiancée."

"Yes, I know," Lester said.

"Oh good," said Grace, "then you got the newspaper clipping."

"Was it you that sent it?" Lester asked, but before she could respond, Rory inquired "Is Kyle about? Can't wait to see him."

"At the moment, he's out on an errand," Lester said. "He'll be back soon though. Won't you come upstairs?"

After pouring them large glasses of lemonade (it was a hot, sticky July day and, even with the table fan turned up to high, the apartment was an oven), Lester excused himself. "I'll be right back. Make yourselves at home."

"Good to see you," Rory said, hoisting his glass, but Lester didn't hear him. He was out the door like a shot. His right foot thumping as it did when he was on edge, he waited for Kyle on the front stoop. When he saw him turn the corner, he ran down the steps. Kyle registered alarm as he approached. "Lester? What's wrong?"

"Give me the bag first," he said, noticing the carton of eggs at the top. "I got something to tell you." But Kyle somehow guessed. He handed Lester the groceries and rushed past him, taking the front steps in twos. The door to the apartment was wide open. He entered, excited and winded, to find Rory and Grace studying the photos on the living room wall.

Rory turned and offered up a toothy grin. "Well, Lordy," he said.

Rory explained that their mother had passed the previous year. Their father, also in poor health, was overwhelmed by the loss and Grace kindly offered to sort through his wife's things. While emptying a chiffonier, she found a pile of letters buried in the bottom drawer.

"Nearly jumped out of my skin when I read them," said Rory, whom Kyle noted had grown into a compact and somewhat stocky young man, though his face remained boyish and open. "You see, when I was about ten, Mama and Daddy sat me down and told me they got a call from the police in Kentucky sayin' you was killed in a accident. I thought it curious that they never sent the body home for a proper burial. A few years later, I asked Mama about it, and she said you didn't die straightaways, and you told a nurse you was to be cremated and your ashes scattered to the four winds."

Among the many possible explanations for why Rory had never responded to his letters, Kyle had neglected to factor in the cancellation of his existence. The news was harder to bear than even his parents' derision.

"After I finished reading your letters, I told Daddy what they'd done was wrong. He told me to go to hell," Rory said with a chortle.

"Yup. That's Daddy all right," Kyle said.

They spent the next hour catching up. Kyle mostly listened, intoxicated by the sound of his brother's voice and saddened by all the milestones he'd missed: the football scholarship to SMU, his courtship of Grace, who seemed sweet and clearly idolized Rory.

"Well, that's enough about me," Rory said finally. "I wanna know what you been up to. First off, can I ask you somethin'? Them pictures on the wall. They you and Lester?"

A sudden panic hit Kyle, but his pride of ownership overrode it. "Why, yes they are. They are indeed," he said.

"Well, I kinda guessed that you and Lester was ... good buddies ... but I gotta tell you that's a whole other kettle," he replied, sounding somewhat abashed.

"I don't expect you to understand," Kyle said. "And it don't matter. I'm just so gratified to see you. And to meet Grace."

"It's good to meet you too, Kyle," Grace chimed in. "One of the reasons we came east was to invite you to the wedding. Isn't that right, Rory?"

Rory acknowledged her request with a half-hearted nod.

"I don't gotta come if you don't really want me there," Kyle said. "It's okay. My feelings won't get hurt. All that's important is that you're sitting right here in front of me. All grown up and happy. You are happy, ain't you?" Kyle asked.

"I suppose I'm as happy as the next fella," Rory said. "Now about the wedding. Seeing as you're my brother and helped raise me, it wouldn't be a proper celebration without you."

"Then I'll be there. You can count on it," Kyle said, trying to maintain his composure. "And Lester?"

Rory sucked through his teeth. "I don't mean no disrespect, Lester. I always liked you. But the thing is, Daddy's going be upset enough as it is."

Lester, who had been sitting quietly in the background, said, "Don't you worry about a thing."

Kyle turned and eyed him quizzically but, from the tone of his voice, saw there was no point in arguing. Lester was not one to assert himself unless he felt something strongly. And once he was decided, he rarely changed his mind.

"I'm so pleased," Grace said. "Now, if y'all ain't too busy, would you mind showing us around the town a bit? I mean, both of you. See, we're only in New York for a couple of days and goodness knows if we'll ever get back here."

"We got nothing else planned, right Lester?" said Kyle, brightening. Again, he turned to gauge his partner's reaction. Lester bounced his head up and down. He would do it, but only because they could never deny one another a single thing. "Just give us a few minutes to put away the groceries and change into proper walking shoes."

When they were ready, they noticed Rory and Grace looking at the photos, bemused.

"I'll explain it to you someday if you're interested," Kyle said.

"Okay," said Rory, seeming doubtful.

Lester ushered Grace out the door and walked abreast of her down the steps. Kyle cocked his head at Rory. The younger brother stretched an arm across his shoulder and lay his head there for a moment as he had done so often as a boy. Then he recovered his composure and took a step forward. "Shall we, brother?"

CARMEN AND ALL THAT JAZZ

"**You been biting** your fingernails again, *querida*?" said Carmen's *abuela*, clucking her tongue in disapproval. "*Siéntate*," she commanded, laying her tools out on the kitchen table. She directed her granddaughter to soak her right hand. "These cuticles are a scandal," she complained. "Only a *delincuente* would kiss those fingers."

Carmen's *abuela*, a professional manicurist, had been employed by the beauty salon at Bonwit Teller for thirty-six years. As she boasted to anyone who would listen, she was hired because she passed: a complexion more Mediterranean than Caribbean, an accent leaning more heavily on *dems* and *dos* than rolled Rs, cedillas and tildes.

As Carmen endured the poking and filing and buffing, "The Latin Bird," played softly in the background. *L'abuela* had raised her on a nourishing diet of Afro-Cuban jazz: Machito, Chucho Valdés, Giovanni Hidalgo, and, of course, the essential collaborations with Parker and Gillespie and Puente. Carmen then graduated to other styles of jazz on her own and, to this day, listened exclusively to WRVR and haunted used record bins and sidewalk vendors. Jazz was dying, at least in the public mind, which meant she could scoop up LPs for a song.

She was conversant with pop music as well, but only because it was unavoidable — streaming out of windows, car radios, and blaring from those new boom-box contraptions hoisted on shoulders up and down the streets of Harlem. But jazz remained her lifeblood, an escape from the bewildering complications of human interaction. Her dream, one of them anyway, was to own a record store someday.

"You remember Arturo Colon, don't you?" her *abuela* asked.

"Uh, kinda," she replied, fingers tensing.

"What? I'm hurting you?" she asked.

"No, It's fine."

"Arturo Colon," her *abuela* repeated emphatically. "The *abogado* who did your mother's divorce? You remember. Not much to look at, but . . ." She rubbed her thumb and two fingers together, attesting to his solvency. "Well, eight months after his wife, Asunción, died," she said, pausing to make the sign of the cross, "he went out and married some *chica blanca*. All bones, little nose, small *tetas*."

Carmen abruptly pulled her hand away and shook it in the air. "Sorry, a cramp."

L'abuela grabbed the other hand and began digging into her cuticles like she was mining for coal. "So. A few weeks ago, *la blanca* announces 'I'm leaving you, Arturo.' And that's not all. She says, 'I'm leaving you for a woman.'" Her face twisted into incredulity. "I mean, two men I can see. But two women? What can they even do together?"

Carmen wondered whether her *abuela* suspected or was merely scratching her persistent gossip itch. If anyone could see into her heart it was the woman who, for all intents and purposes, had raised her. Who had instilled in her feelings of self-worth and optimism. And who, on more than one occasion, had remarked on her indifference to men — with relief. "Not like your mother, with a turnstile at her front door," she'd sneered.

Carmen was only nineteen when the affair began. She was on her way home from Lepke's Shoe Emporium on 125th Street, where she'd stocked shelves during high school and, after graduation, been promoted to salesgirl. Given her raven hair and full bosom and backside, men were her best customers, more than willing to spring for an extra pair of shoes just to have her cradle their feet again. Such queer creatures.

As she pushed through the gathering crowd in front of the Apollo, a sylphlike young woman stepped into her path, dangling a ticket in the air. "I have an extra ticket for Bob Marley tonight," she said. Carmen's brother would have jumped at the chance, she thought, but he was confined to the VA hospital, permanently curled up in a fetal position with a serious case of Vietnam-itis.

"I'm sorry. I can't afford it," Carmen said.

The pretty blonde shrugged and shifted from one foot to the other. "No charge. I'm just looking for someone to hang with. Interested?"

To thank her, Carmen treated the young woman, Allison, to a drink afterward. And another. And a third. She could ill afford such largesse but couldn't afford not to either. Allison was the kind of girl she'd seen only in fashion or cosmetic ads. They made out in an alley behind the bar and later, on the basement floor of Allison's building, where she lived with her husband, about whom she joked, "Artie's idea of sex, is rolling on top of me and flapping around like a seal for three minutes."

And though that pretty much summed up Carmen's experience with men, she felt a pang of guilt and vowed not to repeat the infraction. But when Allison bent over to brush her hair and tossed it back into place, her resolve crumpled. For the next several months, she regularly hopped the A train to rendezvous on the Upper West Side in an apartment Allison had once shared with a roommate. The woman was happy to oblige since Allison sometimes loaned her money when she couldn't come up with the rent. Lending the place for a tryst was the least she could do.

The idyll ended when Allison professed undying love and said she was leaving her husband so they could be together. Initially, Carmen had allowed herself to get caught up in the *telenovela* melodrama of it all. But she wasn't in love with Allison, not really. She didn't even much like her. For one thing, Allison referred to jazz as "traffic noise." For another, she was spoiled and autocratic, especially in bed. She managed to sidestep a messy break-up when the cuckolded Artie (whom Carmen only then learned was her mother's divorce attorney) stiffed Allison in the divorce, and she glommed onto the first well-heeled man willing to indulge her extravagances.

After eight years at Lepke's, Carmen gave notice for a dream job she almost didn't get. One of her mother's boyfriends arranged for an interview with Arvin Worthy, the manager of Sam Goody in Times Square. While impressed by her jazz savvy, Arvin felt that she lacked a sufficient grasp of popular music, which constituted the bulk of their sales. Rick and Dick, the two gangly longhairs who oversaw the pop music section, volunteered to bring Carmen up to speed. "C'mon, man, give her a chance," Rick pleaded.

"Yeah. She'll jazz up the place," added Dick. "No pun intended."

And truly, the store's mostly male sales staff consisted of misfits who knew a great deal about music and very little about anything else. While Rick and Dick's intentions were hardly selfless, they were too timorous to make a forward pass. As promised, they stayed on after closing some nights to help her bone up on popular music and invited her along to concerts and club dates to further broaden her horizons. The cred boost of being seen with Carmen on their arms was sufficient remuneration.

Carmen soon developed a loyal clientele who relied on her judgment and with whom she enjoyed swapping ephemera. Among them was the prominent critic and jazz historian Hannah Wolff. Tall and owlish with a frizzy salt-and-pepper nest atop her head, Hannah spoke with authority, yet never came off as pedantic or condescending. She hunted down rarities or out-of- print titles for Hannah, who in turn loaned Carmen classics from her vast collection — with the proviso "One scratch and I'll have you fired." Though uttered in jest, Carmen was not about to test her.

When Hannah failed to pick up some records she'd ordered, Carmen phoned to remind her. "Oh dear. I'm swamped. I've no idea when I'll get uptown," she moaned. "And I really need them for my research. Would it be too much trouble for you to bring them down here? I'd be more than happy to pay your cab fare."

"That won't be necessary," Carmen replied. "Give me your address and

I'll drop them off tomorrow after work."

Hannah greeted her at the door of her Mercer Street apartment in a yellow chenille bathrobe, a cigarette holder dangling from the side of her mouth. "Sorry for the mess," she apologized, ushering Carmen in, "but I've been overwhelmed."

And truly, the apartment was dusty and unkempt. It was also enormous. "How big is this place?" she asked.

"Seven rooms," Hannah said. "And in case you were wondering, it's rent-controlled. The lease is still in my grandmother's name. The landlord thinks she's living in a cabin upstate and I'm watching the place for her. Lucky for me he doesn't read the obituaries." She threw back her head and guffawed, and Carmen instantly fell in love. She didn't understand exactly why, nor did she bother to ask herself.

"Since you went out of your way, I suppose I should feed you. Afraid all I have on hand is tea and crackers," she sighed as she put on the kettle. "While we're waiting, would you like to see where the magic happens?" she asked, leading Carmen down a long hallway that ended in a smoky room crammed with LPs and an explosion of papers piled on every surface and scattered across the floor. Two typewriters, a manual and an electric, sat on facing desks, an old wooden swivel chair with rollers providing transportation from one to the other.

"How do you get anything done in here?" Carmen blurted, and again Hannah laughed uproariously.

"Good question, darling," she said, and Carmen realized that her heart could actually skip a beat. "I really should hire an organizer. And, come to think of it, someone to help me with research on the new book. The publisher is up my ass."

Over tea and Nilla Wafers ("my Proustian weakness," Hannah said, whatever that meant), she discussed the project, a study of the cross-pollination between jazz and Broadway. "Everyone from Berlin and Gershwin on the one hand to Ella, Satchmo and Coltrane on the other." Fertile ground, Carmen agreed as they swapped titles. When she spoke, Hannah stared at her intently, which was discomfiting. And special. "You know, I meant what I said earlier about needing an organizer and a researcher. I don't suppose I could entice you?"

Though the compensation was minimal, and it would take up every non-working moment, Carmen eagerly accepted. Her duties ultimately proved varied and fungible, but it was worth it to be around Hannah. Late one night, as Carmen was typing up notes from her research at the public library hunt-and-peck style, Hannah entered and stood over the desk. "You know, between your job at the record store and running all over town for me, the commute to Harlem at the end of the day must be a real drag. What do you think about camping out in the spare bedroom for the next few months?"

Again no carrot needed to be dangled, and the shift from the guest room to Hannah's bed followed like day into night. Even their lovemaking felt like jazz. Complex and improvisatory. Dense at times and at others, fluid. Alternately playful and intense.

Not one for sentiment, Hannah dismissed Carmen's endearments. "Skip the mushy-mush. I can intuit how you feel," she said, and Carmen believed her. In her mid-twenties, she was only now beginning to learn how the world worked. The different signals people send. And how to read them.

Hannah, she discovered, was an expert procrastinator, missing one deadline after another and, on several occasions, Carmen was called upon to finish reviews for her. Which wasn't difficult since Hannah wrote exactly like she spoke. Hannah would then edit Carmen's additions, changing a word here and there, and send it off to her editors, none of whom was the wiser.

The book, tentatively entitled *Favorite Things*, proved a thornier issue. The drafts were filled with inaccuracies and misspellings, and Carmen had to amend each chapter before forwarding it to Hannah's agent. The deadline was moved back four times, and by the time the final manuscript was delivered, Carmen had moved back into the spare room.

Disheartened and even a bit peeved, Carmen decided to return to her grandmother's apartment, which *l'abuela* insisted was "where unmarried women belong."

Hannah's reply was to put on Stan Getz's rendition of "I've Grown Accustomed to Her Face."

"I prefer Wes Montgomery's version," Carmen snapped.

"Why are you making such a big deal?" Hannah remarked. "So I suck at being a lover. Otherwise we get along great. And where else are you going to live rent-free in a giant apartment in the Village? Which now, thanks to you, is actually livable."

Another lesson in how the world worked: pragmatism. Carmen agreed to stay on, even at the risk of incurring her grandmother's displeasure. The one condition: Neither could bring anyone home. They hugged on it. Friends, lovers no more.

Another of Carmen's favored customers was a polished, to-the-manor-born gentleman named Monty. She knew nothing of his private life but fancied that in the evenings he contentedly smoked a pipe in front of a roaring fire surrounded by a devoted wife and adoring children. Monty stopped by one morning to exchange a defective Herbie Hancock LP, *Mr. Hands*. They were sold out, she said, but a new shipment was due any day now and she promised to set aside a copy for him. "I don't know if I've ever thanked you properly for your help," he said. "And I realize this may be short notice, but I was wondering if you'd like to be my guest tonight for the Miles Davis concert at Alice Tully. My friend Barbara was supposed to go but she's down with the flu, and I'd hate to see the ticket go to waste."

Carmen was touched but thought it wise to demur. "You're not really going to stand on ceremony and miss Miles Davis?" he said and, eventually, she capitulated. "Great. See you tonight, then," he said, handing her the ticket.

The undercurrent of excitement in the hall was palpable as an usher guided Carmen to her seat. She removed her coat and folded it. A bohemian middle-aged man with a ponytail was seated to her right. He leaned in. "Are you Carmen? Monty told me to keep an eye out for you. I'm Terry."

She tentatively shook his hand, surveilling him suspiciously. "Oh, hello. And how do you know Monty?"

Terry shook his head and chortled sardonically. "Well, I guess you could say I'm the love of his life."

And immediately, Carmen's vision of Monty in front of a fireplace with kith and kin crumbled to ash. "Well, it's nice to meet you," she said, politely.

"Oh, and by the way," he said, pointing forward. "I think someone's trying to get your attention."

She turned and saw Hannah waving to her from two rows down, a comely young woman in tow. Carmen nodded weakly in return. Hannah's date sat directly in front of Carmen and she wondered if this was Brenda, or Felicia or someone entirely new. They'd been strictly roommates long enough to feel comfortable discussing the various women in their lives. Yet for reasons she couldn't fathom, actually seeing Hannah with someone else unsettled her.

"Whoa," Terry said. "If you stare any harder, you're gonna burn a hole in the back of that poor girl's head."

A gasp escaped her. Was she being that obvious?

At that moment, Monty swept into the aisle. "Sorry I'm late. There was an electrical fire at the station on 59th Street. I had to hightail it up here on foot. Have you guys introduced yourselves?"

"Yes," Carmen said. "Terry here told me he's the love of your life."

"Oh, you did, did you?" Monty chuckled, and the two men's eyes locked, telling her all she needed to know.

Afterward, while sipping martinis at Café des Artistes, they were mostly silent, still in the thrall of Davis's performance. As they waited for their entrées, Monty reached into his briefcase. "I just picked this up at Brentano's," he said, holding up a copy of *Favorite Things*, "and who do I run into in the lobby tonight but Hannah Wolff herself. I told her I was blown away by her talk at the 92nd Street Y last week, and the tough old bird agreed to sign my copy." *Tough old bird*, Carmen thought, amused, stifling a laugh.

Monty opened the book to the flyleaf and flashed Hannah's messy script, then continued to thumb through to the table of contents. A few pages in, he stopped. "Huh. On the dedication page here, it says "To the invaluable Carmen. With all my gratitude."

"Lemme see," Terry said, grabbing the book. After reading the inscription, he flipped to Hannah's photo on the back flap. "Oh, I see now," he said.

With two sets of curious eyes bearing down on her, Carmen sought to minimize her contribution. Monty and Terry read between the lines but didn't push her for details. At the end of the evening, as she was getting out of the cab in front of her apartment, Terry said, "So good to meet ya, Carmen. Hey, listen. We're having a little powwow next Saturday. You up for it?"

"Oh yes, please come," Monty said. "It's very low-key, just some folks from the neighborhood. I think you'd enjoy it."

For the first half hour, she was stuck on the terrace with a Manhattan and Jonathan Frost, Monty's financial consultant. His comments were mostly directed at her chest, freeing Carmen to scope the living room, where she alighted on an attractive woman as svelte and stylish as Audrey Hepburn. "Excuse me," she interrupted, "who is that lady?"

"Barbara?" Jonathan said. "I thought everyone knew Barbara. She's practically a Village institution. Used to be quite beautiful."

"She still is," Carmen replied. Jonathan shrugged and continued his monologue. Finally, Monty came to her rescue. "Stop monopolizing my guests, Jonathan. My apologies, Carmen. Now go inside and mingle. I promise you, even the wallpaper is more interesting than his royal highness here."

Carmen refreshed her drink and chatted briefly with a tall, exotic-looking woman named Dee Andrea and two rather nondescript young men named Kyle and Lester, the latter of whom she assumed to be mute, all the while biding her time, waiting for an opportune moment to approach Barbara. She finally saw an opening when Barbara broke away from an Asian gentleman she was speaking to and wandered over to the far corner of the living room where she began to flip idly through Monty and Terry's record collection. "Hi," she said. "My name's Carmen, and I just wanted to thank you for letting me have your ticket for Miles Davis last week."

"You wouldn't have gotten it if I wasn't sick as a dog," Barbara laughed. "So, you're the famous dedicatee."

"I'm sorry?" Carmen said.

"Hannah Wolff's book." Barbara said. "Something about you being invaluable. Seems to be a popular sentiment. Monty says you're the one who got him hooked on Afro-Cuban jazz."

Carmen deftly sidestepped the compliment. "Oh yeah. Monty's one of our best customers. And so charming. Have you known him a long time?"

"Centuries," Barbara said, lifting a martini glass to her lips. Carmen noted the beautiful rings on her delicate fingers. She gave off a scent, tuberose if she wasn't mistaken, her *abuela's* favorite. "Yes, we grew up in the same neighborhood uptown. You've made quite an impression on him and Terry, though their description hardly does you justice. Your skin is positively luminescent."

Again, she ignored the praise. "Funny. I never would have taken them for a couple."

"Really? I can't imagine the one without the other. I guess it's true what they say. For every pot, a lid."

"And you? Do you have a lid?"

"I did, once," she said, lowering her chin and softly adding, "Years ago. Just yesterday."

"I'm so sorry," Carmen said.

"Thank you," Barbara replied with a slight wince.

"I hope you don't mind my being forward, but you're gorgeous."

"Not at all. I prefer women who are forward," Barbara giggled. Carmen sensed flirtation, though she might well be imagining it. Then Barbara glanced at her wristwatch. "Oh golly. Time to walk the dog. Lovely meeting you, Carmen. Hope to see you again."

"Mind if I join you?" Carmen said. "I could use the fresh air."

"Not at all. But I should warn you. My little girl doesn't like the ladies. Very possessive. Goes right for the ankles."

"I'll take my chances," she said.

They walked west to a run-down building on West 4th Street, chatting idly, though Carmen knew women well enough by now to ascertain that Barbara's seemingly off-hand queries were designed to take measure of her character. Family and community ties; her relative sanity or lack thereof.

"Be right back." Barbara smiled as she went inside, and Carmen was satisfied that she'd passed the test. When she emerged carrying a little pug, the dog immediately jumped from Barbara's arms into Carmen's and enthusiastically licked her face. "Extraordinary," Barbara remarked. "I guess your appeal isn't restricted to humans."

"And what is this little lamb chop's name?" she asked cooing and murmuring, as the dog's stumpy tail wagged wildly.

"I call her Pierogi."

Carmen's brow furrowed. "For any special reason?"

"Oh, I'd have to know you better before I told you that."

The coy reply gave Carmen hope, emboldened her and at the end of the fifteen-minute stroll, she said, "Tomorrow's my day off. Shall we walk her again?"

"If you like," Barbara said, kissing her goodbye on both cheeks, lingering for an encouraging moment on the second.

For the next several weeks, Barbara and Carmen walked Pierogi together several times a week. Barbara picked her brain for recommendations about contemporary jazz. Carmen asked her about the clubs on 52nd Street and in the Village that she'd frequented and some of the legendary performers — Parker, Tatum, Monk, Ellington — Carmen had only heard on disc.

Cautiously, they began to open up about their lives. Carmen's enduring bond with her *abuela*, despite the old woman's rigid, old-fashioned morality. Her middling relationship with her mother. Her absent father. Her unfortunate brother. Her complicated friendship with Hannah-turned-affair-turned-friendship again. Barbara spoke of her early marriage and the fraught relationship with JoAnn, her only daughter. It was now, thankfully, on the mend, she said. She was more circumspect about Adrian, her departed lover, the woman for whom she'd upended her life. Not much more than "No regrets," though that said a lot. *To have a love with no regrets*, Carmen thought. A genuine luxury.

Their goodbye kisses evolved from polite cheek pecks to full-fledged lip locks and, finally, one evening, Barbara invited her upstairs.

"Charming," Carmen said as she entered the studio apartment.

"You do know of course, that in real estate ads charming means tiny," Barbara giggled. "Which it is. Just think. Two of us used to live there. And Adrian wasn't what you'd call compact," she said, her gaze wandering to a framed photo mounted over her pull-out sofa bed. "Monty is always trying to get me to move to a bigger place. It's not that I can't afford it but . . . I don't know."

As she studied the photo, Carmen understood perfectly. "She was handsome," she remarked. "Chic."

"Adrian would have loved that," Barbara cooed, as she poured out two glasses of sauvignon blanc. "She always fancied herself a Dapper Dan."

"I can see why."

Barbara sat on one end of the sofa, Carmen on the other. She understood the slow-motion mating dance. The age difference was only part of it. Barbara was reticent about reopening the emotional vault that had remained tightly shut since Adrian's death. Carmen's hesitance was murkier. Her attraction to Barbara was genuine but confusing. It differed from her feelings for Hannah — admiration she'd mistaken for genuine affection — though she wasn't sure why and to what extent. And until she was certain, she would let Barbara take the lead.

"Do you know that I have never dated? Never in my whole life," Barbara said.

"Seriously?" Carmen said.

"In my youth, I was courted by men. But that wasn't really dating. More like a multiple-choice test. And with Adrian, well, that was a coup de foudre. After she was gone, I had drinks with a couple of women. But it never felt right."

"You're not lonely?" Carmen asked.

"Not particularly," Barbara said. "I'm very active in the community. I've lots of friends. And there's JoAnn and my grandchild. Pierogi here is excellent company."

"When we met, you said a lid for every pot. What happens if you lose the lid? Does the pot stay uncovered?"

"Never gave it much thought. Until now."

Carmen just let the comment sit there. "Are you going to help me out here?" Barbara asked, distressed.

"I've clearly been chasing you," Carmen said. "I'm just waiting for you to catch me."

"You've been very understanding," Barbara said, appreciatively.

Carmen got up. "Well, I have work in the morning. How's about a goodnight kiss?" she said and scooped Pierogi into her arms, covering the pup in smooches. She also kissed Barbara. But lightly. "Next time we walk the dog, maybe we could go out for ice cream after."

"Yes. Ice cream," she said. The simplicity of the decision seemed to please her.

The day had been a scorcher, and there was a long line at the ice-cream parlor on 8th Street. "I don't think I've gone out for ice cream since JoAnn was a little girl," Barbara said, as nervous and giggly as a teenager.

They walked across town to Cooper Union Square, where Barbara ran into friends on their way to a show at the Public. She recognized the actor, Declan Kalimar, from television and, later, Barbara explained that his companion, Sora Hayashi, was a noted Broadway costume designer. "I remember seeing him at the party. Where we met. They're a couple?" Carmen asked, and Barbara cocked her head in such a way that she understood they were indeed a couple, though not for public consumption.

When they got back to her place, Barbara suggested they take Pierogi out for a final evening walk. As soon as she saw Carmen, the pup sprang to life. "Sometimes I feel like the other woman," Barbara joshed.

"Don't be jealous," Carmen said, pecking her on the cheek. "I'm curious. Pierogi isn't your first dog, is she?"

"No, actually, she's my second."

"Let me guess. Also a pug named Pierogi? Who also didn't like other women?

"Very good," Barbara said, with a winsome smile.

"Pierogi. Because Adrian made unforgettable dumplings," Carmen said.

"My, but you're a clever girl," Barbara said.

"That first night, when Pierogi jumped into my arms, you pretty much decided then and there, didn't you?"

Barbara nodded but averted her eyes. "At your age, you can make a mistake and move on. I need to tread more carefully." She pulled Carmen into an embrace and a kiss that skittered on the edge of passion. Carmen felt gratified and more certain about her own feelings. The next steps would be easier.

As Barbara unlocked the front door she said, "Monty wants to show me an apartment on 6th Avenue tomorrow. Maybe we could look at it together? I would love to hear your opinion."

The next time Carmen visited her, the first thing her *abuela* noticed were her nails. "What? You spent money to go to a professional?" she gasped. "Hold them up. Let me see. Hmm. Nice work," she said, which for her was the highest of praise. "You're obviously trying to impress someone. Is it serious?"

"I think so," she said, resisting the impulse to bite her pristinely manicured forefinger.

"About time," her *abuela* snapped. "So, tell me, *querida*. Are we going to continue this little game, or are you going to introduce her to me?"

CURIOUS GEORGE

An inky night. An absent moon. A cold, fine mist in the air, tiny droplets clinging to George's Harris Tweed overcoat. He pinched the upturned lapels together and held them against his throat, walking at a clip from the IRT local stop at Sheridan Square, swallowing bile after an ill-conceived assignation at some rat trap in Hell's Kitchen with the best of a bad lot he'd encountered at a Broadway area bar. Mattress on the floor, no curtains. His skin crawled with imagined ants and, for the thousandth time, George pledged that never again would he place himself in such a demoralizing situation.

The traffic down 7th Avenue was sufficiently sparse, so ambient noise was audible. The clack of swaying overhead electrical wires. The creak of a rusty streetlamp. The muffled sound of fists hitting pliant flesh. A defeated moan. George picked up the pace as he turned the corner on West 10th. Only half a block to the apartment. Then he heard the swishing sound of feet running along the dampened pavement.

A faint light from the rear of a shop enabled George to discern a motionless clump in the alley. A twisted foot jutting out at an awkward angle was all that defined the mass as human. "Hello?" he called out. A question not a greeting.

The mound heaved slightly. "Are you okay?" George inquired. No response. No further movement. Getting involved was not George's style, yet he stepped cautiously into the alley. "Do you need help?" he called out as he neared the indistinct blob. An arm rose up from the shapeless form, fingers wriggling like strands of seaweed at the mercy of the tide.

George stood over the recumbent figure, tentative, nervous. He inhaled sharply, reached down and wrapped both hands around the crumpled mass, lifting it up and propping it against the rear wall of the shop. The contours of a person gradually emerged. A dark-complected youth attempted to raise his head but it kept falling forward as if weighed down by the bruises and blotches. George swung an arm across the man's back for support. "Come on. I'm taking you to the hospital."

The wiry youngster, only half George's height and weight, yanked himself away and tumbled back down. "No. No hospital. Go," he said with a defeated rasp.

George crouched down beside him. "You're hurt. If you don't get help you could die out here."

"Maybe it's good, then. Maybe it's what God wants," the lad mumbled, with a decidedly Hispanic intonation.

"If you won't come with me, I'm calling a cop," George said, though he didn't mean it as a threat.

The young man sprang up and tried to run. A few steps on, he collapsed. Standing over him, George saw that he'd passed out. From the pain, he guessed.

His name was Samuel. And he was an addict. George found identification in his pants pocket and tracks on his arms. The layering of a down vest and a woolen overcoat had offered some protection against the body blows that had been inflicted. His ribs were bruised but didn't seem fractured, though he couldn't be certain until the boy woke up. His face was swollen and even though he was unconscious, his body jerked whenever George applied warm compresses or attempted to wipe away blood or dirt from the abrasions. He dabbed alcohol along a forehead gash and secured it with a butterfly bandage. The wound needed stitches, but this would have to suffice. Either way he'd have a scar marring what, from the wallet photo, appeared to be a blemish-free, almost pretty face.

At his bedside, George dozed on and off and, in the morning, phoned his office. "I'm going to be out for a couple of days," George said. "A sick friend. I have the time coming to me." When he hung up, he chuckled at the curious notion of himself in the role of Good Samaritan.

Occasionally, Samuel's body quivered, minor electrical shocks, and George sensed that the worst was yet to come. The pain from the injuries would pale in comparison to the torture of full-on withdrawal. No wonder Samuel dismissed hospitals and the police. George had found a tin with "works" in his coat pocket. And a cock ring. A junkie and a hustler. Well, how else would a kid (couldn't be much older than 20, George reasoned), earn enough to maintain a heroin habit?

He wished he could call someone to prepare him for what to expect. His only references were melodramatic cold-turkey scenes from movies. He might ask Simon. Surely, some of his suicidal patients at Bellevue were also addicts. Of course, Simon would counsel him to get Samuel professional help. But for some reason, George couldn't bear the idea of this wisp of a boy going through so much torment while handcuffed to a metal bedpost.

Except for an occasional spasm, Samuel didn't open his eyes. George busied himself with rinsing out his underclothes and permanent-press shirt in the sink. Among his belongings, he'd found a second photo, probably Samuel's mother.

He remembered an old pair of pajamas his former roommate, Titus, had left behind. They'd fit Samuel. He imagined the boy would be sufficiently alarmed when he woke up shivering in agony, naked in a strange bed. One needn't be a cynic to imagine that an older man might have taken liberties while he was unconscious. As he fitted the pajamas over the boy, he considered the possibility that the beating might have been a godsend (though not in the way Samuel meant it). He was off the streets and, at least for now, the junk.

He might also be infected with HIV, though George didn't concern himself with that. It was already common knowledge that the virus was transmitted sexually or through needles, so he was in no danger.

George tried not to dwell on his motivation or try to link it to his own life, his own vulnerabilities. Several months ago, his ex-wife had discovered a stash of amphetamines in his son Jonathan's dresser. George had flown down to Atlanta and checked the boy into a private rehab facility. His son had cursed him. Called him a heartless, disgusting faggot, and George had endured the tirade stone-faced as he died inside.

Three days later, George had run out of clean sheets and, since he couldn't very well leave Samuel alone, decided to wash them in the tub. The entire apartment reeked of sweat and vomit. Samuel had veered between unconsciousness and convulsions and was so dehydrated George worried he might die. How would he explain that? *Oh, George. You can't even do a good deed right.*

On the fourth day, Samuel finally awoke, moaning in pain and recoiling at the slightest touch. "What's going on? Where am I?" he said, sucking on his fingers.

"I found you in an alley a few nights ago, and I need you to take some nourishment," George explained in a soft yet direct tone. "Think you can keep food down?"

Samuel nodded faintly, too far gone to offer more than token resistance.

"We'll start with soup," George said, and returned a few minutes later. Blowing on a steaming tablespoon of broth, he managed to jam it past Samuel's barely opened lips without scalding them.

Over the weekend, he phoned his friend Terry to discuss Samuel. Even Terry, the original do-gooder, upbraided him for taking in a street hustler, especially with an epidemic raging. George countered by accusing him of talking out of both sides of his mouth, since Terry had housed several dying men, even before he knew it was safe to do so. Chastened, Terry explained that he was only looking out for him. "Could you do me a big favor?" George asked. "I've been out of work for a few days, and I need to go in for at least a couple of hours on Monday for a big meeting," George said. "I can't very well leave him here alone."

Implicit was his concern that even in a weakened state, Samuel might bolt and grab anything of value on the way out. Less a judgment than a realistic assessment. Terry showed up at 8:30 Monday morning with a couple of homemade meatball subs under his arm. When George phoned later, Terry said that Samuel had wolfed down the sandwich and regurgitated half of it. George notched it up as a minor victory.

Another thing, Terry said. When he was done eating and upchucking, Samuel had asked Terry if he wanted his cock sucked. Terry politely declined. Then he asked if George would require servicing when he got home.

"I don't know what to make of that," George said, when he later confronted Samuel about his remarks.

"That *maricón*. He told you?" the boy said with a snarl.

George resented Samuel's sass and ingratitude. "I'd like you to know that I have a son who's almost your age."

"Is he a junkie too?"

The question took him aback, and George felt torn about having parallels drawn between this raggedy street urchin and his golden boy. "Uppers," he said. "He's in a rehab facility now. And getting counseling."

"Must be nice," Samuel said.

"Nothing nice about it," George said, raising his voice, and Samuel pulled back, anticipating a blow.

"I'm not going to hit you, and I don't want sex from you."

"Just so you know," Samuel said. "I only do it for the money. I'm not a fag."

"I'm not either. I just sleep with a lot of men," George scoffed.

"If you change your mind, it's okay," Samuel said. "You can fuck me, as long as you're careful about my ribs. But only 'cause I have no other way to pay you."

"How about you just get back on your feet and try to straighten out the mess you've made of your life? Would it help if I called your mother?"

"Dead," Samuel said.

"Anybody else?"

Samuel shook his head. "Only her *pendejo* brother. But for sure I'd have to let him fuck me."

"Is that why you left home?" George said.

Samuel flinched and quickly deflected. "I forgot your name. What was it again?"

"George. I'm not sure I ever told you."

"And by the way, it's Sam-well — not Samuel. I'll be out of your hair in a couple of days. I hate having to depend on anybody."

"Yeah. I'm the same way," George replied.

George marveled at Samuel's rapid rate of recovery. Ah, the resilience of youth. A few years on, though, he wouldn't bounce back so quickly, if at all.

Since Terry was busy with strays of his own, Titus agreed to play nursemaid. "Who'd ever have taken you for a softie?" Titus clucked as George laid out his duties.

"Hey, I resemble that," George replied in mock outrage. He'd long stopped taking offense at Titus's jabs. Titus was and always would be a handful — beautiful, creative, messy, outrageous, loving. Contradiction upon contradiction. Never a dull moment. George — and pretty much everyone else — adored him. When Titus had moved out of the apartment to move in with Simon, he'd pretended to be relieved. And when Titus had almost died after a bout of pneumonia, he'd chosen to get angry instead of devastated.

George had denial down pat.

That evening, Samuel made his first foray to the kitchen table. Takeout from Balducci's. "This shit is good," Samuel said. "You always eat fancy like this?"

George noted how his soft, good looks had begun to resurface from behind the bruises and his rusty coloring was reclaiming itself from his once-sickly olive pallor.

"So, this Titus . . ." Samuel began. "He's something else. How do you know him?"

"He's a friend of Terry's. This used to be Terry's apartment. Titus was living with him for a while, and I inherited him along with the apartment."

"You two lived together? Must have been hard to keep your hands off him."

George did not respond. It was none of Samuel's business whether George and Titus had been intimate. That's what it was. Intimacy, not really sex. The kind of consolation and warmth that only a friend can provide.

"Is that your type? Dinge?"

George bristled. "That's a horrible word. I wish you wouldn't use it. Titus is only half black, and he's so light most people can't tell."

"I grew up in Harlem. I can tell. And I'm much darker than he is. So why don't you want to fuck me? I'm not pretty enough?"

"First off, you're a kid. I prefer men to boys."

"Except Titus."

"What did he say to you?"

"Didn't have to. I'm not stupid," Samuel spit out. Then he fell silent and concentrated on sucking the bones of the roasted chicken piled on his plate. Afterward, as he cleared the dishes and put them into the sink, he stared out the window. "I don't want to go out there," he said.

"I understand. But you can't stay here. I need to go to work every day . . ."

"And you're afraid I'll rip you off," Samuel said as he ran the water and reached for a sponge. "I scoped out the place. The only thing I could sell is the TV, and it's part of an entertainment unit. Need three people to get it out of the building."

George was amused. His closet was packed with expensive suits, topcoats and shoes, cashmere sweaters, gold cuff links. Samuel had glossed right over them. Either that or he figured they'd be too difficult to fence. As he reached for a dishrag, George said, "I don't want the responsibility. You're a junkie and a hustler. How do I know that you won't start . . .?"

"You know what chicken-and-egg means?" Samuel countered, agitated. "It means, I sleep with a guy when I'm 17. He's into horse and to please him, I do it too. Then he ODs and I'm out on my ass, and I have to hustle to get more junk."

"Thought you said you weren't gay?"

"I'm not. Neither are you. We just like to sleep with men," Samuel said with a smirk.

"I don't want another roommate. I don't know you, and I can't say that I much like you."

"Fine," he said, throwing down the dishrag. "I'll leave in the morning, and I'll be dead in six months."

"I get enough emotional blackmail from my own son, thank you very much," George said, and headed for the living room, where he put on some Chopin to calm his nerves.

"You're a real piece of shit," Samuel said, following him. George turned and smacked him.

"I'm sorry. That was not what . . ." George said and protectively pulled the boy into his arms.

"C'mon. Let's go to bed. Let me make you feel good," Samuel said.

George pushed him away. "Stop it. I don't have much dignity left. At least leave me that."

"Why the fuck didn't you leave me to die?" Samuel railed.

George closed his eyes and tried to lose himself in the glissando of piano keys. "This is probably a mistake. But I'll let you stay for a while. No more talk about sex, though. I don't care who else you sleep with, young, old, but it won't be me. And if I find out you're using . . ."

"I only hustle to get drugs, and if I start that again just kick me down the stairs."

"You can count on it. I'm in the mood for frozen yogurt. Care to join me?" George said. "I washed your clothes. They're hanging in the hall closet."

As they consumed vanilla-chocolate swirls and promenaded along Christopher Street, George asked, "Did you really think it was God's will that those bastards should beat you half to death?"

"At least then all my problems would have been solved. Everybody feels that way sometimes."

George squeezed his eyes shut and bit his bottom lip. Hard.

The six-week deadline George initially proposed extended to nine months. Titus recommended Samuel for a stacking job at a bookstore where he'd once worked. "With your first paycheck, I expect you to buy groceries," George told Samuel.

In his spare time, Samuel subsisted on comic books and popsicles. He could be obstreperous, short-tempered but also ingratiating when he let down his defenses. To his credit, he stayed clean. Whenever he felt weak, he asked George to talk him through it. If Samuel seemed to be living out the adolescence he'd been deprived of, George was again playing out the role of surrogate father as he had with Titus, though without the emotional entanglement. The only time he'd slept with Samuel is when they both passed out on the sofa watching "Magnum P.I."

After Samuel came into his life, George stopped going out. He hadn't sworn off sex. He'd simply lost interest. Some guy had tried to jerk him off behind the lockers at the health club, but George didn't respond, and the guy gave up. Odd, he thought, because he certainly craved the attention. And the release. At the same time, he didn't.

"Do you have any leads on a place to live?" George asked as he went around the apartment shutting off lights, a skill Samuel had yet to master.

Samuel lifted his head from the pillow. "There's a guy at work whose roommate is moving out soon, and we've been talking."

"Good," George said, leaning over Samuel to turn off a lamp on the end table next to the sofa.

"Hey," Samuel said, sitting up. "What's that on your arm?"

George glanced at a large dark splotch. "A heat rash, I guess."

"It's November. Go get it checked out," Samuel said. There was no worry in his voice but he started to suck on his fingernails, which George had only seen him do when he was nervous.

A few weeks went by, and he finally went to the doctor who took one look and ended George's life as he knew it.

"You can't tell anyone," he said to Samuel, whose face drained at the news.

George lay awake all night, too numb to cry. Samuel knocked at his door. "I know you made me promise but . . ." He walked over to the side of the bed and slipped in.

"Are you crazy?" George said.

"Why? I can't get it from sleeping next to you. Besides, I probably have it too."

"I need you to move out soon. I need to be alone."

"That's too bad. You're going to have to change the locks to get rid of me."

"I will if I have to," George said.

Samuel placed an arm across his chest. "Let's get some sleep."

George allowed himself to be comforted. He held onto Samuel's hand and gazed at the ceiling as if it were a screen onto which he could project his attenuated future.

The splotches spread to every part of George's body, even his boldly handsome face. He contracted pneumonia, which he had just enough reserve strength to overcome. Samuel ran interference for him at the hospital whenever a nurse or orderly shirked his duties. A few of them were Latino, and Samuel strafed them with a merciless storm of Spanish deprecations they would not soon forget.

Samuel also argued with George over his insistence on keeping his condition a secret. Over the next several months, whenever friends called, even his daughter, DeeDee, he instructed Samuel to take a message.

Once he became seriously weakened, the doctors recommended he be moved to a hospital. George refused. Dying was bad enough. Being treated like a number in his final days was worse. Samuel quit his job and became George's full-time attendant. He still had good days but the pain medication often left him in a state of suspended animation.

"I wish it was over," George said to Samuel.

"Hey, that's my line," he replied.

"What are you going to do? I mean, after . . ." George asked. "I worry about you."

"If taking care of you doesn't kill me, I'll be fine," Samuel assured him. "The Strand said they'd take me back, but let's not . . ." His words went unheard. George had already fallen asleep.

When he awoke one morning, George could swear he was hallucinating and that his former lover, Donald, was sitting beside him.

"Hey, Georgie Porgie," Donald said.

"What are you doing here?" he said, startled.

"I came to see you."

"What are you talking about? How did you find me?" George started breathing irregularly and broke out into a cold sweat.

"I've always known where you were," Donald said. "Even saw you on the street a couple of times when I was in the city. From a safe distance, of course."

"Why didn't you come up and say hello?"

"You know why."

"I did terrible things to you."

"We did terrible things to each other. It was a different time. We were stupid," Donald said, rising and mopping George's brow with a washcloth.

George grabbed Donald's hand and held it with all his strength as if he were falling off a ledge.

"Yes. It's really me," Donald said, assuring him with the same open smile he had cast lovingly in George's direction a thousand times until George almost hated him for being so nakedly adoring.

"Where's Samuel?" George whispered through a throat choked with emotion.

"I gave the poor kid some R and R," Donald said. "It's just me and you."

"I hate that you have to see me this way," George said, turning away.

"What way?" Donald said.

"Don't do that," George said.

"You can't tell me what to do anymore. I've decided to move in. Samuel and I will take turns on the couch."

"What? But your boyfriend?" George said.

"Phil? He drove me here. I said I needed to be with you. And he said, 'Of course you do.'"

"He must make you happy," George said.

"He does. You made me happy too. Sometimes."

"I fuck up everything," George said.

"That's not what Samuel says. Or Titus. They think you walk on water."

"Who called you?" George asked, feeling a surge of energy. He had a million other questions behind that one.

"I don't want you to be mad, but Samuel decided to tell Terry. None of that matters now."

"If I fall asleep are you going to disappear?"

"No, George. You can't will me away. Not this time."

Over the next several days, Donald and Samuel alternated shifts. But when Samuel was around, George's eyes would scour the room for Donald. "He's taking a nap," Samuel said. "I never should have let that bitch come over. You pay no attention to me."

Samuel was teasing, kind of, but all George could say was, "Donald," as if running his name around on the tongue could summon him.

"It's funny. I always wondered who the guy was, the one whose picture is in your sock drawer."

"You went through my drawers?"

"You sound surprised."

"Yeah. No," George said, wryly, since this Samuel seemed like a completely different person from the near-catastrophe he'd dragged out of the alley a year earlier.

"I looked at it a few times and made up a story that he was your secret lover and imagined you kissing him and staring into his pretty blue eyes. But then I said, nah, no way. George is a cold fish."

"You little prick," George said, swatting at the open air. "I loved Donald."

"And you still do. I like how he calls you Georgie Porgie," he said, laughing heartily.

George continued to swat at him, feigning anger.

On one of George's better days, when he wasn't zonked out on painkillers and the lesions weren't bearing down on his lungs and compromising his breathing, Donald informed him that he'd be having visitors.

"I told you, I didn't want to see anyone. Why can't you respect that?"

"Because they have a right to see you. They care about you, George. I've never understood your peculiar aversion to being loved."

But George was having none of it. "Bad enough you have to see me looking like . . ."

"It's not as bad as you think," Donald said. "I bought some makeup this morning and I'm going to wash your hair."

"Why are you not listening to me?"

"Because when I do, I always regret it."

"Oh," George said, chastened.

"And you better be nice to them."

"I'll be who I always am."

"That should be fun," Donald sneered.

"You're really starting to get on my nerves, Donald."

"Poor baby," Donald said. He leaned in and kissed George on the lips. George gave himself over to the kiss at first, then pulled away. "Don't do that. You might . . ."

"Well, at least your lips still work. And from the looks of it . . . Donald's eyes traveled down to a rise under the sheets. "I guess I've still got it."

"And you always will. Bastard," George replied.

The visits from friends were trying. George couldn't tell from the looks on their faces whether they felt affection for him or pity. Titus, usually the hardest nut to crack, was so overcome, he had to leave the room.

Each visit served to strengthen George. And sap him. Then Donald sat on his bed and took another chance. "This time I'm asking your permission. I want to call your kids."

"I can't. I can't. And anyway, they don't want to see me. Jonathan hates me. And DeeDee, she's at best indifferent."

"Nonetheless, I want to extend the offer."

"I know what they'll think. I have this coming. They'll gloat."

"You're an idiot. Those kids were all you ever talked about. You were a terrific father."

"I left them," George said.

"You didn't leave them. Your wife kicked you out, and the court gave her full custody."

"Same difference."

"Maybe you're right, and they won't want to come. That's their choice. Not yours."

"Do what you want," George snarled. "But you have to promise me one thing."

"Which is?"

"Samuel. He's got nobody."

"Kid's a bit of a handful. But if you could put up with him, I'll do what I can."

"He's not so bad, really. Just needs someone to look out for him."

George's son declined, but DeeDee flew up the following weekend. George was glad he would soon be dead. He didn't know how long he could live with the image of her reaction when she came into the room. Or the tears she shed on his behalf.

"Jonathan's being stubborn because he's like you," she explained after she'd regained her composure. "Anyway, I don't think he could handle this."

"I get it," George said. "I need to rest now."

DeeDee tiptoed out, and Samuel came in and sat by the bed. "She's a pretty girl, isn't she?" George said as he drifted off.

"Her father's daughter," Samuel replied.

As Donald and DeeDee shared tea in the living room, she said. "You're not who I pictured. I figured that you'd be handsome, because Dad has really good taste. But I thought it was just sex between you."

"If only it had been that simple."

"Why are you here? I mean, Dad told me about the will. You're not in it."

Donald ignored her remark.

"And who's that guy, Samuel? He's weird,"

"We're all weird. Just in different ways," Donald said.

As George felt consciousness slip away, the moments when he was actually present grew fewer and were spaced further apart. The rest of the time he existed in some middle state. Not here. Not there. And even when fully awake, he rarely had much control over his thoughts and speech. But from to time, in short spurts, he could be lucid. "That night I found you in the alley, is this what you meant when you said maybe it's what God wants?" he asked Samuel.

"I don't remember saying that. But I probably believed it. Now I'm not sure what he wants."

"I never knew either," George said.

One of his last recollections was of Donald's lips pressed against his ear whispering tenderness, a balm that eased his pain, that gave him the strength to rest.

Donald was asleep on the couch, and Samuel had just entered the room with a glass of water when George took his last breath.

Samuel took his pulse and called out to Donald several times until he awoke. Looking down at George, all Donald could do was nod repeatedly. He phoned Phil to tell him the news and then called the ambulance service, which would provide verification. The final call was to the cremation facility.

The body was removed early that evening, taking more than George's physical presence with it. Samuel rode down in the elevator with the EMTs. He ran after the ambulance and after it turned a corner, he just kept running. On the way back home, he scored some heroin from a guy at the intersection of Gay Street and Bleecker. Since he had no works, he snorted it and dizzily wove his way back to the apartment. He made it up the first two steps before his legs buckled and he fell, smacking his head against the railing.

Donald went around the apartment, closing the windows. Glancing out, he saw Samuel splayed on the sidewalk. He and Phil went down, scooped Samuel up, put him in the back seat of their delivery van and drove out to Bay Ridge.

THE (UNLIKELY) BOOK OF SAMUEL

The odds against Samuel reaching thirty had not been in his favor. Yet here he was, on the brink of his fourth decade, alive, thriving and handcuffed to a kneeler in St. Patrick's Cathedral. An unlikely outcome facilitated by several unlikely allies.

Given Samuel's history as a street hustler and junkie, his ACT UP comrades assumed that, like many of them, he'd tested positive. And he let them assume. It was only a decade later, after he'd volunteered for a medical study, that Samuel would learn of the unlikely reason for his negative status. He was among the select few born with a natural immunity to the virus.

"Cops," screeched Sora Hayashi, looking over his shoulder as he lay prone in the center aisle. Sora, a noted Broadway costume designer, had agreed to commandeer the civil action even though he was still grieving the loss of his lover, TV sitcom star Declan Kalimar, who'd been one of the first celebrities to go public with his illness, helping give the epidemic a national face. "Go limp," Sora commanded as the NYPD officers closed in on him.

"Any news on the bathtub?" he asked Samuel, as he was being dragged down the cathedral's center aisle, and Samuel had to stifle a laugh.

"The manufacturer says six to eight weeks minimum," Samuel shouted after him.

"Motherfuckers," Sora growled, his voice echoing through the nave.

Becoming a plumber was merely the latest unexpected detour Samuel's life had taken. That rough-trodden road, which had included homelessness, hustling and heroin addiction, hardly pointed to a future as a tradesman.

The journey had begun when he came out to his mother at age 17, and she banished him from their East Harlem apartment, only to take him back when he contracted hepatitis. The respite was short-lived. Six months later, his mother suffered a fatal heart attack, and he was forced back onto the streets.

Permanently, he thought. At least until he overdosed or was murdered by a john. And but for the grace of George, the first of an improbable string of saviors, Samuel would have bled to death in the West Village alley from which he was rescued. Though his own health was rapidly failing, George took pity on Samuel, cauterized his wounds, and held his hand through a painful detox. He returned the favor, nursing George through the transition from this life into the next, a loss that sent Samuel into a drug-fueled tailspin.

He'd loved George in an unqualifiable way and was furious with God for taking him.

Enter another unlikely savior, Donald, George's ex, who'd promised to keep an eye on Samuel. Donald forced him into rehab and accompanied him to twelve-step meetings, where Samuel finally admitted that he was an addict and always would be, that a relapse was only one hit away. Donald's lover, Phil, hired him to do inventory and slice prosciutto in his Bay Ridge deli. Working behind the counter he met yet another unlikely patron, Mr. Cassini, an elderly plumber who offered to take him on as an apprentice. "You're a slip of a thing," Mr. Cassini said, "someone who can crawl into tight spaces, which comes in handy in my line of work. And I assume you speak Spanish."

Samuel discovered that he had been blessed with a strong stomach and a facility for working with his hands. When Mr. Cassini retired, Samuel asked Donald and Phil to float him a loan to set up his own business. He placed ads in the local Manhattan rags and, slowly, built up a steady clientele. He paid back the loan in under two years.

"Hang on, Sammy," said Barbara, who was chained to the cathedral's front door. "Carmen will be down to bail you out soon." As the cops dumped him into the paddy wagon, Samuel turned and blew her a kiss. Carmen and Barbara, his most-recent implausible allies. The former, a buxom no-nonsense Cubana, had grown up not ten blocks from him. They became fast friends after he took over the lease to her failing record store in the East Village. A sweet deal. Office in the front, living space in back. All Carmen asked for in return was a corner of the shop to hawk her remaining inventory. In lieu of rent, she agreed to answer the phone and schedule his appointments.

Barbara, Carmen's patrician and charismatic partner, was a tireless activist. It was she who persuaded Samuel to join ACT UP, which provided him with a much-needed sense of purpose, as well as the perfect excuse to be in her company. He'd developed a major platonic infatuation with Barbara, marveling at her tactical skills in handling the fractious members of the ragtag resistance. Quietly and with grace, she managed to mold chaos into consensus without ruffling egos.

Marking time in the midtown holding cell, Samuel reflected on the premonition he'd had that afternoon in the majestic cathedral. Perhaps it was the exalted setting or his mother watching out for him from above, but he sensed that his life would soon take another unforeseen turn. And though he wasn't religious, he prayed that he'd be ready for it.

After he was sprung, he returned home to find a package. The catalog from a recent photo exhibit, *The LTS: Soul Mirrors*. He'd meant to attend the show but, between work and civil disobedience, had never found the time. Titus, the photographer, whom he'd met through George, had tested positive several years earlier. Despite a couple of near-fatal bouts of pneumonia and a minuscule number of T-cells, he'd somehow managed to exceed the twelve-to-eighteen-month life expectancy diagnosis following the onset of a serious opportunistic infection.

Titus joined a long-term survivor group, and about a year ago, sought permission to photograph the other members. But only their eyes. He'd used a wide-angle lens, blown up each shot, floating the images on a white background. The results were compelling. The photos telegraphed a spectrum of emotions: sadness, coyness, vulnerability, cynicism, defiance. None of the stares were hollow, however. None defeated.

Halfway through the volume, Samuel came to rest on an intriguing pair of oversized orbs. The longer he gazed at them, the more he became convinced that they were staring back at him. He had to meet this person, he decided. But how? The participants had demanded anonymity. And, in the book's foreword, Titus mentioned that since the photo session, almost a third of the survivors had "run out of time."

"Yes, I know who he is," Titus told Samuel. "And I can confirm that he's still with us."

"I'd like to meet him, if that's okay," Samuel said. It was not okay, Titus replied. But after some wrangling and the promise of a free service call the next time his plumbing acted up, he agreed to at least ask. At first, the man said he had no interest in meeting Samuel. A week later, he changed his mind.

"The guy's name is Callaway Stevens," Titus said, "and I'm warning you in advance, he's a real odd duck."

Samuel reached Callaway's answering service and left a message: "Tell him I'd like to come by at ten o'clock next Sunday morning, if that's okay with him." The service called back two days later to confirm the appointment.

On Sunday, at ten on the dot, Samuel was standing on the front stoop of Callaway's Barrow Street apartment. He rang the bell. Once. Twice. Three times. Finally, he heard a scratchy, irritated voice through the intercom say, "I'm having a bad day. And the place is a mess. You can't come up."

"Then will you come down? Please. I really need to see you," Samuel said.

Ten minutes passed and he was about to leave when, through the glass panes of the inner door, he saw two giant bare feet punishing a flight of sagging wooden steps under their weight. An enormous man threw open the door and extended a pasty slab of beef masquerading as a hand. He gave Samuel the once over. "Well, you look harmless enough," he said. "I guess you can come up for a few minutes."

Callaway tossed himself into a rickety cane chair under the front window of the sparsely furnished studio. "So, what's this all about?"

"Didn't Titus tell you?"

"Yeah, but I want to hear it from you."

"I saw your eyes. In his book. And I felt that I had to meet you."

"Well, here I am," he said, rolling his thick, blond eyebrows. "Want some coffee?" Callaway dragged his feet across the floor to the kitchenette and poured some inky syrup into a mug. "Here you go, Samuel," he said.

"Actually, it's pronounced Sam-well," he replied.

"I see. So, tell me something about yourself, Sam-well."

"I'm a plumber," he said, flashing his business card.

"Huh. I don't think I've ever met a gay plumber before. Anything else?"

"Something I didn't realize until we met. We've slept together."

Callaway cocked his head to the side. "Really? You sure about that?"

Samuel nodded. "Positive. For one thing, you don't look like anyone else."

"No argument there. And when exactly did this happen?"

"Let's see. It had to be about seven or eight years ago. Back when I was turning tricks."

Callaway's already oversized eyes widened. "Yeah. That's sounds about right. Back then, I was strung out on coke and only did it with trade. My shrink says it's a familiar denial mechanism. Familiar to her, maybe."

"I'm not sure where you picked me up or where we went," Samuel continued. "The place was dark and the bed was on the floor."

Callaway snapped his fingers. "Chinatown. Real hellhole. I slept on a futon. Permanently screwed up my back," he said with a slight twinge.

"The thing I remember distinctly is this big, glowing moon face suspended over me and staring into those gigantic eyes the whole time."

"I guess the sex was memorable, then."

Samuel shrugged. "Actually, I don't remember the sex. Besides, smack was the only thing that got me off. I only hustled to pay for my next fix."

"Same with me and coke." Callaway pressed an index finger against one nostril and inhaled imaginary powder with the other. "Ooh. What a rush."

"I preferred heroin. I liked the way it swallowed you up and put you in its pocket." Samuel's sense memory was aroused, a danger signal, and he struggled to shake it off.

"Yeah, those were the days, huh?" Callaway said, his eyes glassy, unblinking. Then he leapt to his feet. "Well, nice meeting you. But I need for you to go now. I got stuff to do."

"Is it okay if I call you again?" Samuel said.

"Why?"

"Just to hang out," he replied.

"Nothing personal, but since I started living on borrowed time, I've sworn off making new friends."

"Then why'd you join a long-term survivor group?"

"Because my shrink threatened to have me committed. And by the way, if what you're looking for is a rematch, you should know, I'm celibate."

"That's fine. I just want to hang."

"Hey, kid. Take a hint," Callaway snapped, looming over Samuel.

"Does that usually work?"

"What?"

"Using your size to scare people away."

Callaway burst out laughing. "Feisty little pissant, aren't you?"

"Great. I'll be back next week. Same time."

When they were alone, Callaway could be fluid, congenial, even jaunty. Samuel enjoyed it when he laughed and his whole body jiggled. In public, however, he turned skittish and sensitive about his disproportionate size. Six-foot-three, 230 pounds. An enormous, perfectly rounded head, dotted with scattered wisps of hair and a fleshy baby face. When they walked down the street, he would slope his shoulders, draw in his arms and hide those giant mitts in his jacket pockets.

"I have to say, he's kind of ridiculous looking. And more than a little strange," Samuel told Carmen, "But I really like being around him."

"How is he in the sack?" Carmen inquired.

"Oh, we haven't slept together. After he was diagnosed, Callaway swore off sex. Besides, I don't think he's attracted to me."

"He was once," Carmen observed.

"Oh that? He was coked to the tits," Samuel argued. "And he was paying for it."

"Tell me again what's so special about this guy?"

How could he make Carmen understand, when he himself couldn't explain the attraction? Though they shared a past of drugs and dysfunction, the similarities ended there. Callaway had never held down a job. He lived off a trust fund. He'd prepped at Dalton and dropped out of Yale after only six months. "If those are the future leaders of the country, we are in serious trouble," he'd grimaced.

His father, an avid mountain climber, had been killed in a plane crash in the Rockies when Callaway was two. He rarely mentioned the person he referred to as "my surviving parent," except to note that his mother was "alive and kicking. Mostly kicking."

When he turned twenty-one, Callaway inherited a sprawling Fifth Avenue apartment near the Metropolitan Museum, which he maintained fully furnished and vacant. "I tried living there, but I was afraid that one day I'd open a window and next thing they'd be scraping me off the sidewalk." Over the past several years, he'd resided in a series of rat traps, mostly in Chinatown and Alphabet City. The place on Barrow Street was a palace by comparison, he said.

Talking about his poor-little-rich-boy upbringing never failed to sour his mood, and he would take it out on anyone within striking distance, which was usually Samuel. "Why are we talking about this?" he'd grouse, though it was Callaway who'd brought it up. "And why are you still here? You're like some yappy little Chihuahua, always nipping around my heels."

"Chihuahuas are Mexican. I'm Puerto Rican. Either way it's racist. So, next Sunday, ten a.m.? Meet you out front."

"Another thing. I hate getting up that early on a Sunday."

"Every day is Sunday for you. But okay. Ten-fifteen."

"We'll see," Callaway said, though he was always waiting for Samuel on the front stoop. And always pretending that he'd just come out for some air.

One Sunday, during an afternoon screening of *The Grifters*, Samuel reached for Callaway's hand and held it for the rest of the film. Later, over drinks at a bar in Chelsea, Samuel kissed him and he kissed back.

"Don't get the wrong idea," Callaway said. "I'm not into you in that way. All you're going to get from me is rejection."

"Why you making such a big deal, Cal? It was just a kiss."

"You know what? This is bullshit," Callaway fumed. He dropped some bills on the bar and departed without saying goodbye.

Samuel left messages on his service, but the calls were no longer returned. When he rang the doorbell the following Sunday, there was no reply. As he walked up Barrow toward 7th Avenue, he could feel those giant eyes peering at him from the upstairs window. But he refused to give Callaway the satisfaction of turning around.

He did not return the following Sunday, knowing that Callaway would be sitting in the window waiting for the chance to reject him again.

Then, on a crisp Wednesday afternoon in late November, he buzzed Callaway's intercom. "Who is it?"

"It's me. What are you doing right now?" Samuel said.

"Sleeping," Callaway replied, mid-yawn. "What time is it?"

"Two in the afternoon. Why are you still in bed?"

"None of your fucking business. Now go away."

"This is not a social call. I need a favor."

"What kind of favor?"

"I have to lug a bathtub up three flights of stairs. I need a big strong man to help me."

"Good luck finding one," Callaway said, clicking off the intercom.

Samuel walked across the street and glanced up. Sure enough, Callaway was standing at the window. He folded his arms, leaned back against a railing and waited. Twenty minutes later, Callaway came down.

"You're a real pain in my ass," Callaway sneered.

As they reached the third floor of Sora Hiyashi's Village brownstone, Callaway asked, "So where's this bathtub we're supposed to haul?"

"In the basement. We have to disconnect the old one first," Samuel replied.

"Oh, geez. This is going to take all day. Couldn't you just hire someone to help you?"

"And pay him with what? Not all of us live off trust funds, you know," Samuel said.

That seemed to shut him up. "Hey, isn't that . . .?" Callaway said, pointing to the framed photos of Declan Kalimar lining the walls.

"Yup," Samuel said.

"Didn't he . . .?"

"Yeah. I went to the memorial," Samuel said as he turned off the water and began to disconnect the old tub. "Let me help. It'll go faster so I can get the hell out of here," Callaway offered.

"And get back to your busy life?" Samuel said, handing him a chisel.

Callaway ran his tongue along his teeth and pretended to overlook the remark. "So, who lives here now?"

"His widower, Sora. Big-time costumer designer."

"He must be, to afford a place like this," he said.

"You could afford it too," Samuel said, "if you sold the Fifth Avenue apartment."

"Yeah. But what would be the point?"

"Did you ever think that the new drugs you're taking might keep you alive indefinitely?"

"If I thought that, I'd shoot myself. I'm just getting used to my days being numbered."

"Do you always have to behave like such an asshole?" Samuel fumed as he hoisted one side of the old tub.

"What?" Callaway said as he lifted the other end.

"Tell you what. Just help me lug this down to the basement, then you can go crawl back into your hole," Samuel said.

"How you gonna to bring up the new tub?"

"I'll figure it out."

"Look. You got me out of bed. I'm here now. So let's do it."

"Okay. But if you say one more stupid, hurtful thing, I swear to God, I'll . . ."

"Okay. Okay. I'm sorry. Why you being so touchy?"

Once the new tub was in place and secured, Samuel thanked Callaway and told him he was free to leave. "I should help you clean up," Callaway offered.

"Whatever. Stay, go, I don't care," Samuel said, and he meant it. Callaway's casual morbidity had sent him spiraling back. To George's last days and the helplessness he'd felt as he watched the first person who'd ever shown him true kindness slip away. How he'd gone out and scored enough smack to kill himself and almost succeeded.

Whenever he traveled back to that dark corner, he could almost smell the mixture of heroin and water heating in a spoon and alcohol-swabbed cotton balls to disinfect the syringe. "Once an addict, always an addict," he mumbled to himself.

"What'd ya say?"

"Nothing," Samuel replied. "We're done here."

"Hey, want to hear something crazy? I actually had a good time today. If you ever have anything like this again, I'd be glad to give you a hand."

Samuel eyed him skeptically. "I don't think so."

"How about if I keep my trap shut next time?" he said.

"Well, I am installing six new toilets in a walk-up on East 6th next week."

"Great. I'll be there," Callaway said.

Samuel should have been happy, but he was still in too deep a funk. Callaway's intimations on mortality were clouding his vision, weakening his will.

On the way out, they ran into Sora on the first-floor landing.

"All done," Samuel said. "But the caulking needs to dry for at least twenty-four hours."

"Oh well. I've waited this long," Sora said with a shrug. "So, who's this? You finally hire a helper?"

"Not really. I'm kind of his boyfriend," Callaway said.

"Well, well," Sora replied.

"What did you say that for?" Samuel said, when they reached the sidewalk.

"Isn't that what you wanted to hear?"

"Why would I want a boyfriend who goes out of his way to make me miserable?"

"You should have thought about that before you came knocking on my door." He lifted Samuel off the ground and kissed him. "Call me," he said before lumbering away.

While they were busy junking old toilets and installing the new ones, Callaway said, "You're really good at this. I'm impressed. I mean, it's kinda disgusting, but it's also satisfying. Maybe I should try my hand at a trade. Electrician. Carpenter."

"Carpenter? With those big mitts?" Samuel said, tickled that Callaway was entertaining the idea of doing something besides sitting around his underfurnished apartment waiting on the reaper.

"Or I could be your helper," Callaway said.

"I could sure use one. Only I can't afford it."

"Do I look like I need the money?"

"I couldn't let you work for free. Not to mention that it would mean we'd be together all day, six days a week."

"Got to take the good with the bad, right?" Callaway snapped. "Isn't that what being boyfriends is about?"

"I don't want a boyfriend," he said. "And if I did, it wouldn't be you."

"Now you're just trying to hurt my feelings," Callaway said, pouting like a wounded child, which Samuel found adorable. "I know I'm a mess. But you knew that from the get-go. Nobody forced you to fall in love me."

"Me in love with you? Where did that come from?"

"I figured it out," he said.

"Do I look like a masochist to you?"

"You'd have to be to put up with my shit. But you're right. I will make you miserable. But we can have fun too. What do you say, later, we head over to my place? You could shower there, and then we'll go grab a bite."

"Can I spend the night?" Samuel said.

"Now wait a minute," Callaway said, narrowing his large eyes. "I thought I made it clear that if that's what you want, you need to go elsewhere."

"Maybe I have."

"You're sleeping with somebody?" he said, sounding crestfallen.

"Why not? You're not attracted to me."

"Says who? Okay, maybe I wasn't at first, but if I was ever going to do it with someone again, it would be with you."

"Gee, thanks," Samuel said, wrinkling his nose. "I think I liked you better when you weren't attracted to me."

"Me too," Callaway said. "So, about tonight? What do you say?"

"Only if I can stay over."

"Oh, all right. I just hope you're not expecting too much from me," Callaway said.

Not expecting too much had gotten Samuel this far in life. The unlikelihood of him and Callaway succeeding as a couple gave him hope.

"Fine," he said. "Now make yourself useful. Hand me that wrench."

Opus 66

The rent on the apartment was a bit more than he'd hoped to pay, Douglas told Hillary, the real estate agent. She assured him that it was the going rate for a prewar building in the West Village and actually a bargain for a top-floor apartment. "Besides, you should always live slightly beyond your means," she replied through what sounded like a deviated septum. "It makes you work harder."

Hillary offered to show him a similar unit in Murray Hill that went for thirty percent less, and if he was willing to live up by Columbia, she had a place that was even cheaper, larger and with better amenities.

But Douglas hadn't moved to Manhattan to live in personality-free Murray Hill and certainly not to commute from Morningside Heights to Wall Street every day. Back in Muncie, he'd developed the romantic notion of one day getting a place in New York's famed bohemian enclave, tracing the footprints of the writers, artists and performers who had either lived or gotten their start in the Village; the cradle of gay liberation (at least officially), a safe haven where he could be himself and not have to button it up and deflect like he did every day at Lyman, Steers, the brokerage firm where he'd just been promoted to junior account executive.

He wasn't exactly in the closet at Lyman. And he wasn't the only one who chose to skip the after-work male bonding rituals in favor of going home and resting up for the next day's grueling trading session. Not that he would even consider discussing his personal life, especially not with cohorts who persistently sniffed around for frailties, actual or perceived.

While pricey, the apartment, located off Abingdon Square, was undeniably a find, a one-bedroom penthouse, both light and spacious. The main rooms were adorned with baroque moldings and the bathroom featured the original black-and-white-checkerboard tiles. The standout feature was a wraparound brick terrace with an on-a-clear-day-you-can-see-forever view of midtown on the north and a suggestion of the Hudson on the west. He would be sharing the floor with only one other tenant whose mirror apartment across the hall faced east and south. According to Hillary, the opposite apartment had not been on the market in more than thirty years, since the mid-fifties. The tenant, she said, was also a single man and "not a party type. Quiet. Keeps to himself."

Another plus: The freight elevator was ample enough to accommodate his prized Yamaha. The black-lacquer meticulously waxed piano had been bequeathed to him by his Uncle Fritz, a virtuoso, under whom Douglas had studied beginning at age six. While he did not possess his uncle's innate talent, he tried to make up for it with the kind of emotional investment he found so difficult to access in his daily life. On days when the tension of the sales floor rendered him as demon eyed as a speed freak, he would return home and toss off Rachmaninoff's *Prelude in G Minor* to restore his equilibrium. And whenever he was stymied in his search for personal intimacy a sojourn with Brahms's *6 Klavierstücke* soothed him and enabled him to sleep afterward.

The pricey flat proved to be money well spent, Douglas's sanctuary in the sky. For his summer vacation, instead of traveling abroad or trekking out to the Atlantic beaches, Douglas holed up for ten days, subsisting on takeout and viewing TV shows he'd recorded on his video recorder, playing piano and sunbathing nude on the terrace.

The cocooning led to a scolding from his best friend, Leila. "I don't understand," she said. "You move to the Village and instead of exploring the neighborhood you've always wanted to live in, you decide to float above it."

What could he say? Since childhood, he'd always been a little too Midwestern Methodist for his own good, taciturn and tending toward the solitary. Never had many friends, was hopeless at small talk and, unless a man propositioned him in graphic detail, was oblivious to even the most blatant come-ons. His idea of flirting was a gawky stare, which had the opposite of the desired effect.

In early fall, Douglas had a brief affair. Leila set him up with Andrew Solomon, a gynecologist she'd met in yoga class. When he refused to even meet Andrew, she arranged an "accidental" encounter at the Buffalo Roadhouse. The ruse was transparent, as was Leila's rushing off to an appointment she'd forgotten. Douglas didn't mind. Andrew was loquacious and self-confident. Not bad to look at either. When the doctor invited him to a concert the following Friday, he accepted, in part because it was an encore performance of the *Goldberg Variations,* which had been well reviewed in the *Times*. Andrew stroked his leg during the concert. They spent the night together and Andrew cooked him a hearty breakfast the next morning.

From the onset, Douglas prophesized the affair's eventual dissolution. An initial attraction to his ruddy Scandinavian features might keep Andrew on the hook for a while, but eventually he would grow weary of Douglas's asocial demeanor. He tried to offset his lack of social grace by being amenable in bed, content to fulfill his partner's fantasies while never proposing any of his own. Andrew came armed with an encyclopedic repertoire, including some borderline hilarious role playing. Apart from being physically in sync, they shared no real connection and eventually, Andrew did lose interest.

Though hardly enamored of his erstwhile beau, Douglas took the breakup hard. Despite Leila's reassurances that he would someday meet someone of a similar feather, he was so distracted by melancholy that he almost failed to notice the man in the elevator getting off at his floor. Only as he was unlocking the apartment door did Douglas think to turn and, on impulse, say, "Hi. I'm your new neighbor, Douglas."

"I know," the man replied with a smile and mimed playing the piano with both hands. "Mackenzie." With a terse nod, the man entered his apartment and shut the door. Slammed it, actually.

Douglas was intrigued and a bit abashed. Not only was this Mackenzie fellow striking, and in a completely original manner, but his droopy eyes and enigmatic grin seemed to harbor a precious secret. Then he quickly backtracked, chiding himself for making assumptions based on a fleeting sighting. In all likelihood, the next time he ran into Mackenzie and got a closer look, he would prove to be ordinary, even dull. But what exactly had he meant by "I know," when Douglas introduced himself? Was that a jab at Douglas's piano playing? If he had a complaint, he certainly hadn't voiced it. And the door? Did he slam it or merely shut it soundly?

Perhaps his curtness had to do with a more personal kind of disapproval. He might have espied Andrew's comings and goings. Then again, what of it? He'd been living in the apartment for the better part of a year, and this was the first time they'd crossed paths. He probably wouldn't see Mackenzie again until Christmas at the earliest.

Funny how that worked. On his way downtown, he saw many of the same people in the morning and sometimes coming home as well. The elderly woman who clung to the banister at the bottom of the stairwell until the train doors opened, obviously terrified that someone might push her onto the tracks; the schoolboy who counted backward from a hundred under his breath and, if the train had still not arrived, started all over again; the tall man who tapped his foot incessantly and sat on the edge of his seat as if to venture further back would wrinkle his suit; and several others who stared blankly into space like automatons whose battery packs were running low. Yet here he lived not fifty feet from someone he'd likely run into no more than once or twice a year.

Two Saturdays later, his doorbell rang. A UPS man held out a package and a clipboard for his signature. Glancing down at the carton, he noticed the name Mackenzie Frost. "No, this is for the apartment across the hall," he said. Douglas shut his door and immediately flipped open the peephole latch and watched as Mackenzie, clad only in gym shorts, signed for the package. Only after he'd slipped the copper cover back into place did he exhale.

Good work, Dougie, he chided himself. Spying on a partially clad straight guy was dodgy behavior at best. Nonetheless, the image lingered, and Douglas embellished it with details he couldn't possibly have discerned from his compromised vantage point. Beads of sweat on Mackenzie's chest, abdominal ridges, meaty thighs, large feet. He had a thing for men's big toes. Not a fetish. Just a thing, like other guys have for armpits. Then he mused about Mackenzie's armpits. Very hairy? Sparse?

Seeking refuge from his aimless ruminations, he sat down at the piano and decided it was time to finally risk Chopin's *Fantasie Impromptu*. Uncle Fritz had recorded the piece and given it to him as a birthday present the year before he died. Less a gift than a rebuke; as if to say that his nephew would never master the technical skills necessary to execute the initial movement of the *Opus 66,* which required equal parts dexterity and speed. He'd studied the sheet music and listened to Uncle Fritz's recording many times but hadn't yet drummed up the courage to tackle it.

The initial attempt was well-nigh disastrous. No more than four bars in, his fingers began to skim along the keys as if they'd been oiled. Punching the ivories in exasperation, he jumped up and threw on his coat.

Why did he imagine that in his befuddled state he could attempt such a complex work as if it were nothing more than an étude? When he saw the Out of Service sign on the elevator door, he took the stairs and ran smack into workmen loading a Steinway onto the service elevator. He ogled the piano, which was as beautiful and sleek as an African princess, then burst out onto the street, rounded the corner and headed straight for the White Horse Tavern to drink himself into a Dylan Thomas stupor. Like most of his foolhardy plans that day, it backfired. Douglas didn't have much of a palate or tolerance for undiluted spirits, and certainly not on an empty stomach. After downing a double whiskey, he stumbled to the men's room and surrendered it.

Determined to work up an at least passable *allegro agitato* over the next couple of weeks, he devoted all his spare time to cracking the *Opus 66* but made scant progress. What was it about this particular movement (not even the most difficult Chopin) he found so elusive? When he discussed his failure with Leila, she rolled her eyes. "You really need to go out and get your horns trimmed." When he recoiled, she added, "What? It always works for me. And Andrew says you're pretty good at it."

"He said that?" Douglas asked.

"Not directly. Something about 'It's always the quiet ones.' It's a compliment, Douglas. Take it."

"Then why did he break up with me?"

Leila let go an extended sigh. Douglas replied with one of his own.

Perhaps Leila was right. He should give it a go. Sadly, he was no more successful at finding a horn trimmer than he was at conquering the *Fantaisie-Impromptu*. He returned from the bars at one a.m. empty-handed and a little nauseated from drinking ginger ale. As he was checking his mailbox in the lobby, Mackenzie popped out of the elevator and waved at him. The best he could summon up in return was an uncomfortable grin.

"Don't let it get you down," Mackenzie said, stopping a moment.

Douglas's face contorted into a question mark.

"The Chopin. The first movement? It's a bitch," he said, then disappeared through the double doors.

Douglas pondered Mackenzie's remarks, and his mind reeled back to the previous week when he was out on the terrace and heard what sounded like a recording of *Moonlight Sonata*. He couldn't tell whether it was coming from across the way or an apartment below. Then he remembered the Steinway. But no, it had to be a recording. The playing was too proficient. Maybe Gould? No, not that good. Horowitz? Possibly. Curious, that. The Beethoven and the *Opus 66* shared thematic similarities. Almost as if the player was using the piece to mock his inability to get further than eight measures into the Chopin. Perhaps Uncle Fritz taunting him from the beyond.

Only in the elevator going up did he remember that he'd only been two feet from Mackenzie, close enough to notice the luminosity of his skin. His stare was dramatic, his eyes widened, large and brown-black. He was wearing a knit cap. And he looked great in it. Whenever Douglas tried on a woolen hat, he resembled a serial killer. Once, during a blizzard, Leila yanked it off his head. He complained that it was freezing out and snowing. "I don't care," she said. "I will not be seen walking next to a Most Wanted poster."

As he passed the Yamaha on the way to the bedroom, he decided to take Mackenzie's comment to heart. But when he sat down at the piano, his fingers fell onto the keys as if they were weighted down. He wanted to cry, but he didn't have much of a facility for that either.

Douglas crawled into bed and in the middle of the night fell into a dream in which he made it all the way through the first movement; a simple, competent performance that left him pleased and mollified. Even his unconscious was not foolish enough to conjure a performance that was beyond workmanlike, however. In the morning, he rose extra early and, before heading off to work, attempted to move his fingers as easily as he had in the dream. But only six measures in, they seized up.

The dream recurred over the next several nights, and each morning he managed to advance a measure or two. If only he could play the first movement through to the end, it would give him the confidence to attempt the key and tempo change of the piece's middle section, before it reverted back in the third movement. But if he conquered the first part, he could surely handle that as well.

Shortly after the closing bell, his boss, Barry Gray, called Douglas into his office and asked if he wouldn't mind mentoring an actor the following week. What his colleagues referred to as an unrefusable Don Corleone-type offer. Ethan Lack was researching his role as a trader for an upcoming movie about Wall Street. Douglas recognized the actor's name. He'd seen him in something on Broadway or maybe on TV.

Ethan was personable and unobtrusive and, though Douglas normally didn't relish being monitored, he begrudgingly adapted to the visitor's presence and constant notetaking. During lulls or at the end of a trading day, Ethan would ask him to explain bits of terminology he'd overheard. Douglas's responses were clear and succinct and, at times, even affable.

"I know this is a lot to ask," Ethan said on Friday afternoon, "but could I take you out for an early dinner tonight and pick your brain? If you don't want to give up your Friday evening, I'll understand."

"Tonight's no different than any other night, except I don't have to show up here first thing tomorrow morning," Douglas said, an unusually candid admission. He didn't mean it to sound pathetic, though it probably did.

"Great. You pick the restaurant. My treat."

They ate at Dino's, a hole-in-the-wall in Little Italy, and Ethan peppered him with questions. After a couple of glasses of wine and a hearty but not heavy plate of manicotti, Ethan leaned in and said, "I'm going to ask you something. I would never do this if I wasn't tipsy, and you don't have to answer. You're not out at work, are you?"

When Douglas's tongue tied, Ethan added, "I didn't mean closeted as much as you just don't share it with the others. I know because I'm the same way."

"I'm a private person. It's just who I am," Douglas said in his own defense.

"But you are, aren't you?"

Douglas nodded.

"Oh good. Because I hope to use it as subtext in my character."

Try as he might, Douglas could not fathom what that would entail.

"And just so you know," Ethan continued, "if I didn't have a boyfriend who is crazy jealous, I would so put the make on you right now."

Douglas turned beet red and was sufficiently well oiled to reply, "And I would probably take you up on the offer. I'm flattered."

They both laughed to ease the tension before reverting to stocks and bonds.

Standing on the sidewalk after dinner, Ethan hailed a cab. "I'm going uptown. Can I drop you off?"

"Abingdon Square," Douglas directed the driver, and when they pulled up, Ethan said, "Is this your building? You wouldn't happen to know if Mackenzie Frost still lives here?"

"Yeah, he's my neighbor across the hall. You know him?"

"Oh. This is more than a two-minute conversation," said Ethan. "Driver. I'm getting out here too." He pulled some bills from his wallet and stuffed them through the divider.

They retreated to the Elephant & Castle for coffee and a shared cobbler. Ethan did most of the talking and Douglas listened, rapt. Hard to tell who was more excited, Douglas to hear about Makenzie or Ethan to fill him in.

"We were at Performing Arts together," Ethan said. "He was wicked talented and peculiar like most near-genius guys are. Worked like a motherfucker. Could do anything. But other than school projects, he kept to himself. The only reason I know where he lives is because I grew up around the corner and would see him going in and out of the building. I think he was born there. His dad was Jonathan Frost, a big-shot financial guy."

"Anyway," Ethan continued, "Mackenzie got a scholarship to Juilliard and everybody was predicting big things for him. Then he dropped out during his first semester. They said he had a nervous breakdown, but I also heard that his father had taken sick and he quit school to play nurse. A few years back I read in the *Times* that the old man had passed away after a long illness. The obituary listed Mackenzie as a survivor and I think a sister, who lives in Boston. Haven't heard a word about him since. Tell me, does he still have that aura?"

"Aura?" Douglas repeated.

"Not handsome but really compelling," he clarified.

Douglas nodded. Yes, that was it, exactly. Compelling. "But I've only run into him once or twice, and I'm guessing he's probably straight."

"Well . . ." Ethan said with a shrug. "There were rumors of him fooling around in the school bathroom. There were rumors about me too. And those were true," he laughed. "But he never came on to me, and we did a couple of plays together. *Two Gentlemen of Verona* and *Guys and Dolls*. He had lead roles in both of course."

"Do you know if he played the piano?"

"Oh yeah. Guitar too and I think the trumpet. So talented. Poor bastard. Wonder what really happened? Anyway, next time you see him, say hello for me. I'm curious to see if he remembers me."

When they parted, Ethan kissed him on the lips at the subway steps. Douglas walked home, puzzling about Mackenzie the entire way. He got in after midnight and promptly fell asleep on the sofa, again falling into his recurrent dream. In the middle of his recital reverie, he rolled over and the sensation of falling woke him up.

But the Chopin continued to play. The first movement. Over and over. Not his Uncle Fritz's *Fantaisie-Impromptu*. This one was unembellished and dispassionate, stripped down, almost like a tutorial. He peered through the peephole and noticed Mackenzie's front door was ajar, confirming his suspicion.

Douglas threw open his door and sat down at the piano. The moment Mackenzie finished, he began to play, making it almost three-quarters of the way through before flubbing a note. Mackenzie immediately picked up the composition and took it to the end. Douglas began again. And again. On the fourth attempt, he played it all the way through. As he hit the final note, he became almost giddy. Sure, it was sloppy, more *agitato* than *allegro*. But what mattered is that he'd done it, which meant he could surely do it again. And better.

He looked up and across the hallway. Mackenzie's door was wide open now, and he was sitting at the piano in a pair of shorts and a floppy tee. He was looking directly at Douglas and smiling. Then he raised an index finger like a baton. They began to play in unison, and Douglas thought his heart would explode through his chest.

Afterward, Mackenzie rose and walked to the door. "Thank you," he called out to Douglas.

"Me? For what?" Douglas said.

"I'll explain at another time," he said. "But for now, just thank you. So, tomorrow night? Same time?"

"Really?" Douglas said.

"And have fun with it, Douglas. Don't try to be perfect. It'll mess you up," he said with a hint of sadness in his voice.

"It's not that. I don't want to let you down," Douglas said.

"I wouldn't worry about that. Just do it for yourself," he said. "Well, goodnight," he added softly as he slowly shut the door. The last thing Douglas saw were Mackenzie's dark eyes shooting through him.

THE HOUSE ON WEST 4TH

In 1995, Bee moved to New York. To study design, to be herself. Neither option was available in the farm town of Reid, Iowa.

She somehow lucked into a modest studio on West 4th in the Village, where the busy streets seemed to be teeming with women. Chatting, arguing, holding hands, collecting in bars and coffeehouses. She craved their acknowledgment. A nod would suffice. Any signal to crack her shell of diffidence. She knew who she was. Would anyone else?

The first person to take notice was Enrique, a classmate at design school with whom she'd been partnered on a project. Hand on chin, he opined, "You need an eye, girl. It's a sin to hide those baby blues."

"I don't like to wear makeup," Bee said, somewhat embarrassed, though she wasn't quite sure why.

"Ah. That explains the overalls and the Doc Martens," he replied, wrinkling his nose. "I mean, I get that you're from the boonies, and you want the other girls to know that you like them. But honey . . . *por favor*."

Curiously, Bee didn't feel dissed. Enrique had seen her. He'd classified her. The no-makeup, overalls, Doc Martens girl. From the boonies. With the baby blues. Who liked other girls. And wanted them to notice. She decided to own it.

Sue Lin, a tattooed, henna-dyed check-out girl at the local bodega, was the second person who saw her. Not initially, though. The first few times she rang up Bee, Sue Lin had her nose firmly planted in *The Village Voice*. Then one day she looked and chirped, "Cute outfit," and Bee's insides somersaulted. At Enrique's suggestion — "Would it hurt to add a splash of color up there?" he'd said, wriggling a hand in the air in the general area of her bosom — she'd sewn several appliqués across the bib of her overalls.

Sue Lin, she soon discovered, was a little out there, in stark contrast to her being barely out. She envied her eccentricities but was not always sure how to react. Spirited, wry and subtly jaded, Sue Lin flirted shamelessly with the clientele, particularly the straitlaced ladies, though that's as far as it went. She had a girlfriend, Meg. "You'd like her. She's from some little house on the prairie too. I want to say Missouri. You should come dancing with us sometime," she said.

The night she accompanied them to Club Catch, she was gobsmacked. So many women. Such variety. Such boundless energy. Sue and Meg dragged her onto the floor once or twice, though no one else asked her to dance. And she hadn't the nerve to make the first move. It hardly mattered. She returned home in a whirl, dizzy with possibility.

Too hyped up to sleep, as she sat in the front window watching the waning moon fade toward dawn, a horse-drawn Hansom cab pulled up to the boarded-up brownstone across the street. The driver opened the carriage door and out stepped a handsome woman in Edwardian dress topped by a large, plumed hat. As the carriage drove off, the woman mounted the steps to the building's parlor floor and was greeted at the door by a comely black maid, who ushered her inside.

Bee shook her head in disbelief. A trick of light and shadow, she reasoned. Or a waking dream. She had herself all but convinced that it was an illusion until the young servant threw open the shutters to a well-appointed second-floor bedroom directly opposite, and a flickering soft light streamed forth from within.

The maid removed her mistress's coat and hung it in a tall, polished oaken armoire. The lady doffed her hat and unpinned her shoulder-length hair. She sat at a vanity table from which the maid retrieved a gilded brush and gently stroked the flowing mane, posing her free hand on the lady's shoulder and eventually caressing the side of her neck. The woman closed her eyes and seemed to sigh. Then, abruptly, they both turned as if they sensed someone spying on them. The maid dashed to the window and closed the shutters.

Arguing against her eyes, Bee questioned what had sparked this perfervid fantasy. Sensory overload induced by the strobe lights and charged atmosphere of the club? A fractured mind meld from a British period drama she'd watched on PBS (mainly to study the meticulous production design)? Nonsense. She'd simply gone in and out of sleep while sitting up. Wouldn't be the first time.

Despite her adamant denial, the arcane images remained etched in her mind and, before retiring, she dashed off several sketches: The lady emerging from the carriage. The maid brushing her mistress's hair.

She awoke mid-morning bleary and coffee-deprived and jumped into her overalls. She distractedly crossed the street and stepped into a pile of flattened horse dung. No, it can't be, she told herself, concerned that she might be realizing her parents' worst fears about moving so far away from home: Hick goes haywire in the big city.

Like a blurry photo, the peculiar sighting gradually faded from memory, though it lingered in her mental storage bin. Not long after, she was jolted into the present by a more kinetic and roiling image: Her first sighting of Lacey Barnes at Sue Lin's Thanksgiving potluck. Lacey was what her mother would characterize as a "ball of fire," a vital energy force. Flames shooting in every direction, and she was, appropriately, red-haired. Lacey seemed to be on a first-name basis with every woman in the room, several of whom openly vied for her attention. But Lacey seemed bored, aimlessly scanning the horizon until she came to rest on the newcomer holding up the loft's far wall, nursing a by-now lukewarm Chardonnay.

"Hey, you," she called out, and Bee glanced over her shoulder certain that Lacey meant somebody else. "Yeah, you. Overalls girl. What's your name?" Lacey said, stabbing an index finger in her direction.

Bee had trouble getting her mouth to function and finally stuttered out of her name. "Buh-buh-Bee?" Lacey said, laughing and flapping her arms. "That's hilarious. C'mon. Buzz something for me." Bee's red face concealed a somewhat more primal reaction.

"How about you get me some food, Bee? I'm starved," Lacey commanded and, for some unknown reason, Bee headed straight for the buffet table.

"You didn't get yourself a plate?" Lacey said when she returned with a piled-high dish of turkey and trimmings. Bee shook her head. She was hungry, but felt she lacked the poise and coordination to eat standing up. Much less carry on a conversation at the same time.

"Well, this is way too much for me, anyway. How about we share?" she said.

Lacey delivered large forkfuls of turkey, dressing, and mashed potatoes to Bee, who thanked her after every bite, and was careful to chew as inconspicuously as possible. When they were finished Lacey said, "There. Feel better now?" and Bee grinned from ear to ear. Lacey put down the plate and moved her face toward Bee's. "What do you say we get out of here?" she said.

A whirlwind week followed during which Bee relinquished her free will in return for the privilege of satisfying long-held yearnings — and a few that had never even occurred to her. One evening, while they were lying together entangled in sweaty bedsheets, Lacey jumped up and threw on her clothes. "Think I'll hop over to John's and get us a pizza," she said.

"I'll go with you," Bee offered.

"That's okay, honey Bee," Lacey said, dropping a kiss on her forehead. "I won't be long."

Bee waited for the buzzer to ring, but it never did. Her phones calls went unreturned. Not that night, or the next, or the night after that.

"Did you bother to ask me about Lacey before you ran off with her?" Sue Lin said when Bee came to her mopey and dejected. "I would have warned you that she runs hot, and then she runs cold."

"I see," Bee said, though the information about Lacey's fickleness only served to make her feel more insignificant.

"All I'm saying is the girl's not a keeper," Sue Lin said. "Time to move on."

"I don't know how to do that," Bee confessed. Except for a couple of make-out sessions with Patti Hoffman in junior year and the time they borrowed her mother's vibrator, Bee hadn't actually had skin in the game before.

"Are you saying that the wide-eyed-little-farm-girl routine is for real?" Sue Lin asked. "I thought it was just your shtick."

Bee's lower lip jutted out, and she shook her head. "Aw, I'm sorry. Wait. I know something that'll make you feel better," Sue Lin said. "I get off early tonight. Drop by after class."

Sue Lin was right. Bee did feel better after getting her hair bobbed and purchasing a pearl-buttoned cowgirl blouse and a pair of 501s. And eyeliner. Just a hint and the baby blues popped, just like Enrique had sworn they would.

The respite was short-lived. The insomnia and melancholy returned. Her tossing and turning was interrupted by the blaring of a fire engine and yellow-and-red lights twirling a ballet across her bedroom wall. A basement fire was raging several doors down. Residents peeked out from upstairs windows or perched on their stoops, coats and scarves over their pajamas. The conflagration took on a communal air, and Bee's spirits lifted in spite of herself.

When she happened to glance across the way, through the spinning, colored lights, she could swear that she saw the mistress and her maid leaning out the bedroom window, also curious about the smoke and flames. Then they turned to one another and began to speak about things more private, more intimate. The lady smiled and caressed the maid's cheek. Their faces leaned into one another and just as they were about to kiss, the maid again closed the shutters — for modesty's sake.

Bee fought to steady her nervous hand as she penciled out this latest phantasmal episode. The intimacy between the two women struck her as a comment on her thwarted romance, but for some inexplicable reason also gave her hope. The drawing completed, she allowed herself one last good cry and, afterward, resolved to relegate Lacey to the dustbin.

She slept through the morning alarm and was late for class, applying her eyeliner on the subway. Enrique's face tightened when she approached him in the hallway. "Ooh, no, baby," he cried, and marched her into the boy's bathroom. He ordered her to wash off her lids and reached into her satchel for the eye pencil. "This is not a toy," he said, wagging it in front of her before he reapplied it. "You know, I'm liking this whole urban-cowgirl vibe you got going. It's definitely an improvement, and I wouldn't be surprised if the girls start hitting on you. But be careful. Never accept the first offer."

"Wish you'd told me that before," Bee said.

"Why, would you have listened?" he said.

Touché.

Bee didn't accept the first offer, or the second, but she did let a girl named Denny ask her out a couple of times. It was not a match. Too flighty. Laurette was the exact opposite. Serious, determined. She proposed on their second date. Bee gently turned her down, and Laurette stormed out mid-meal sticking her with the tab. Then she had a two-month fling with a girl named Cindy. Things were going well until she accused Bee of giving her chlamydia. (Bee went for a checkup. Clean.)

"She was just looking for a way out," Sue Lin explained.

"Why didn't she just say so?"

"You expected maybe honesty?"

"I don't know what I expected," Bee replied.

"It's just that, sometimes, when things start to get real, some gals freak," Sue Lin said.

"Why? What's wrong with real?" Bee asked.

Getting over Cindy proved to be easier. She had streaks put in her hair, bought a pair of high-tops, went to Club Catch by herself and actually screwed up the courage to ask a young woman named Sasha to dance. After a brief conversation, she couldn't tell whether Sasha's bubbliness was genuine or drug-induced. Either way, she didn't ask for her number. On the way home, she wondered whether she was merely making better choices or had already turned prematurely jaded.

Standing in front of the boarded-up brownstone, she pictured the lady and her maid and speculated on how they might have spent their evening. She found the musing a comfort and slept soundly that night.

April showers may engender May flowers, but that scented byproduct was of little consolation to Bee as she slogged through a downpour umbrellaless and laden with groceries. As she fumbled for the front-door key, a voice behind her called out, "Hello?" She twisted her head and could swear that someone was standing in the bedroom window of the abandoned brownstone.

But when she looked again and no one was there, Bee fretted that she was coming unglued. A moment later, however, a young lady under a large umbrella carefully descended the steps of the brownstone. "I have a bit of an emergency. Could I use your phone?" called out the flesh-and-blood woman who introduced herself as Jasmine.

The water had been turned on in the brownstone that morning and was gushing from a rusted bathroom pipe, she told Bee, as they climbed the stairs to her studio apartment.

"Thanks. The plumber will be here in an hour," Jasmine said, after hanging up. "In the meantime, he said to turn off the main valve. I have no idea where that is."

"I'll help you look," Bee volunteered. She was not about to pass up an opportunity to explore the mystery house. "Just let me change my shoes," she said, kicking off her soggy high-tops. With the money Grandma Mapleton had sent for her birthday, she'd purchased a pair of ankle boots, which Enrique deemed "a little rock and roll but still a little country."

Jasmine glanced at her schoolbooks. "You're studying design? Well, feel free to make suggestions. The place is in need of serious updating."

"Really?" Bee said, barely able to stifle her glee.

They located the valve in a closet behind the below-street-level kitchen. "Done. Mind if I look around now?" Bee asked.

"No. Go right ahead," Jasmine said with a smile.

Some of the décor on the first floor had been updated in the fifties, but the bedroom was essentially the same as in her (dream?). The oak armoire. The dressing table. The gold-plated hairbrush. Frightening. Fascinating.

"Who lived here?" she asked, after the plumber, Samuel, and his giant assistant got to work. Jasmine explained that the house had been bequeathed to her by Auntie Delia, who had inherited it from her employer, Louise Halberstram, in recognition of her years of service.

"My aunt was only seventeen when she started working here just before World War I," she said. "Over the years, she and Miss Louise became very close. After Mr. Halberstram died Auntie stayed on. The two of them lived here alone for almost forty years. Of course, Miss Louise's children tried to fight it, but the will was ironclad. After her own health declined, Auntie moved in with my family."

In addition to bequeathing her the house, Jasmine's aunt had paid for law school, which came in handy when the Halberstrams tried to reclaim the property after Delia passed away at the age of ninety-five. The house had been tied up in litigation for almost a decade but was finally released to Jasmine three months earlier. "I considered selling it," Jasmine said.

"Oh, you mustn't," Bee blurted. "There's so much history here."

"Exactly what I thought," she replied with a smile, and Bee tried hard not to be smitten.

When Samuel was finished, he mentioned that the house would probably need all new pipes, "and though I'm not an electrician, I'd say the wiring should be replaced," he added, indicating the flickering overhead light. "Yeah. The old cloth-covered wires could go up like that," his giant companion said, snapping his fingers.

Jasmine asked Samuel to send her an estimate on the plumbing redo and the name of a trustworthy electrician. "I'm about to apply for a home equity loan, and I want to make sure to borrow enough to cover all the big jobs."

"If it's any consolation, whatever you put into this place, it'll be worth it," Samuel assured her.

After he departed, Jasmine thanked Bee, adding, "I really like what you did with your apartment and since I have absolutely no design sense, I wonder if you have the time to help me. Of course, I'll pay you."

Bee said she'd be happy to help and Jasmine needn't worry about compensation, but Jasmine insisted, claiming she would be getting a bargain. "Who knows if I'll be able to afford you after you graduate and start a real business?"

They spent the next few weekends together devising a cohesive design scheme, one that would incorporate new pieces with some of the existing antiques, particularly the vanity and armoire in the bedroom. They shopped together and pored over paint swatches and fabric samples, sometimes working late into the evening, eating takeout and, eventually, sharing personal anecdotes. Such as how they'd both come from hardscrabble backgrounds and had their educations financed by unmarried aunts (Bee's by her father's sister, Irene). Or how growing up, their older brothers had received all the attention.

Bee skirted the details of her love life, saying she was still getting the hang of "the dating thing." She assumed that a savvy city girl like Jasmine had surmised her situation but was hesitant to fly her rainbow flag. If Jasmine had any reservations about their friendship, she kept them to herself.

For her part, Jasmine never mentioned a boyfriend, saying only that she worked crazy hours at the law firm, and between church, visiting her mother at the nursing home and now, refurbishing the house, was unable to squeeze in a social life.

Bee considered mentioning her visions, but since Jasmine had already told her about Mrs. Halberstram and Auntie Delia, she assumed she wouldn't be believed or, even worse, be thought disingenuous. Perhaps she could show Jasmine the sketches and gauge her reaction. But when she went looking for them, they were nowhere to be found, and Bee again questioned her sanity.

Bee volunteered to wait at the brownstone for the new living room furniture to arrive and again to supervise the painters. A few times she could swear that she heard whispered confidences and even laughter from the floor above. Once, Enrique offered to keep her company, and without prompting said, "This place feels haunted, but not necessarily in a spooky way, know what I'm saying?"

By late summer, Jasmine was finally ready to move in and asked if Bee wouldn't mind spending the night. "Sure thing," Bee said, and modestly offered to sleep on the living room sofa. "Would it be improper to ask you to sleep upstairs with me?" she said, tentatively. "The new bed's plenty big and very comfortable. And frankly, I'm nervous about being in this big house alone. I sometimes think I hear voices."

"Oh, so it isn't just me," Bee said. And rather than discuss it further, they just laughed.

They unpacked boxes for the rest of the day. Afterward, exhausted but also nervous and giddy, they put off going to sleep. They took turns putting on their PJs in the upstairs bathroom and lingered at the foot of the bed, neither wanting to be the first to climb in.

"It's warm in here," Jasmine complained, though the temperature was almost fall-crisp. "Maybe I should open the shutters and let in some air." Bee joined her at the window and they made small talk, mostly about decorating choices and the trouble they were having with the painters, who showed up whenever it suited their fancy. Eventually, they ran out of chatter and stood there watching passersby on their way home or going out for the evening.

Bee hadn't been this nervous since she went home with Lacey, though that encounter seemed like only a test run. Being here, inches away from Jasmine, was far more stressful. Her feelings were already rooted and, though there'd been hints that Jasmine shared similar stirrings, she was loath to presume that she would reciprocate.

"You know . . ." Jasmine said with a wrinkled grin before her voice trailed off and she turned silent.

Yes, I do, Bee thought.

A long stare, like two athletes waiting for the starting gun to fire. Jasmine reached up and gently stroked her cheek. Bee sighed and began to caress Jasmine's hair. As they embraced, she happened to glance over Jasmine's shoulder and was amazed to see the mistress and the maid sitting in the window of her apartment and could swear that they were poring over the sketches she'd done.

Jasmine's lips moved toward hers and she said, "Should we close the shutters?"

"No," Bee said. "Leave them open."

Jasmine and Bee spent the next fifteen minutes necking in the window to the appreciation of their audience across the way.

THE MAN IN WHITE

Mackenzie was awoken by a thunderous roar overhead, which caused a tremor that rattled the bedroom and upturned a water pitcher on the nightstand. Clad only in BVDs, he strode out onto the terrace to witness the tail of a low-flying jetliner whose smoky wake rippled through the air as it skimmed the tops of buildings in Soho and Tribeca. He waited for the plane to bank upward as it approached the towers. Instead, it continued on a low course and plowed directly into the belly of the north tower, which exploded outward. Smoke and dust and debris and flames.

Mackenzie felt a sudden chill, and in the next moment he was sweating. He heard a scream, perhaps his own, and turned toward the bedroom, half expecting to find himself safely asleep. A cacophony of auto horns filtered upward, and someone yelled, "Jesus, God!" He dashed inside and turned on the bedroom TV, which showed the "accident" from another angle. The news anchor speculated that, while it was too soon to tell, it was likely that the plane had lost altitude and its controls had frozen. He mentioned that, back in the Thirties, the fog-engulfed Empire State Building had also been struck by a wayward aircraft.

Perched on the edge of the bed, Mackenzie tried to steady his breathing and compose his thoughts. On what floor were the offices of Lyman, Steers and in which building? All these years and he'd never thought to ask. Had to be a high floor though, since Douglas said his office afforded him a view of the harbor. He threw on a pair of shorts and a tee and carried the phone handset with him onto the terrace – at the precise moment a second plane crashed into the south tower. The phone dropped from his grasp and cracked, the batteries rolling toward the roof gutter. Underneath him, the discordant roar of sirens — fire trucks, ambulances, police cars. All other traffic was at a standstill, and the streets were now thronged with people, staring skyward, slack-jawed, hands over their ears. One woman who'd fainted was being revived by a shopkeeper and her assistant.

By the time he returned to the TV, the newsman's narrative had altered. He now speculated that the crashes were deliberate. A coordinated attack. Not just the Twin Towers. The Pentagon as well. And a fourth plane disaster — perhaps unrelated? — in a field in Somerset County, Pennsylvania.

He grabbed the extension in the living room and checked to make sure he still had a dial tone. Douglas would call. To assure him. The offices had to have been evacuated by now. He returned to the terrace and staggered back as one of the towers collapsed on itself like a burning sheaf of papers. Particles of dirty white ash began to waft uptown, fatal snowflakes. Along with an acrid odor. He removed the tee and covered his nose and mouth.

Call, Douglas. Call. I don't care if you have trouble finding a functioning phone booth or have to endure long lines for one that works. Don't keep me hanging.

When, a half hour later, he still hadn't heard from Douglas, Mackenzie reconstructed the morning. Douglas had risen at five, his normal time on weekdays. His duck-like footfalls had registered with Mackenzie, always a light sleeper. He'd gone into the bathroom, peed, brushed his teeth. In his striped, button-down sleeping shirt, he'd then traipsed down the hall to his apartment and returned sometime later, showered, suited, toting a briefcase. He'd whispered affection into Mackenzie's ear. Deposited a kiss on the side of his forehead. But wait. No. That was the usual routine. This morning, he'd walked Douglas to the door. A full-mouth kiss. The crisp scent of Penhaligon's English Fern, "the best present ever," Douglas had said. Mackenzie had locked the door behind him and gone back to bed.

How long ago was that? Douglas was surely in his office, he thought, then tried to devise alternate scenarios in which he was delayed. He'd gotten stalled in the subway. There was a particularly long line at his favorite coffee place in the plaza underneath the towers. He was meeting with a client uptown and had forgotten to mention the appointment.

Another thought. A real longshot. He reached for his keys and ran down the hall, unlocked the door to Douglas's apartment and yelled his name. He didn't bother to check the bedroom since they always slept in his apartment. Douglas used his place only to shower and dress or to read or play piano whenever Mackenzie was composing or working with his lyricist or meeting with producers.

Douglas said he preferred the firmness of Mackenzie's mattress and the soft morning light that seeped in from the terrace. And the warmth and the opportunity to console Mackenzie when he was beset by midnight frights or fretting about the viability of the new show he was working on. Douglas would clasp his forearm and say "I'm here." Nothing else. Just "I'm here."

Keeping both apartments had been a wise move. A crucial buffer, particularly in the early days when Mackenzie was embroiled in therapy, before he was healthy enough to act on the developing attraction between Douglas and him. Douglas was a socially oafish but comfortingly stouthearted man with a propensity for syrupy avowals like, "I've been in love with you since day one." His mawkishness was offset by sincerity and humility.

Mackenzie, himself, was anything but artless. The ever-present smile, the twinkling eyes, the sexy rasp in his voice, adeptly masked the churn of inner turmoil. Self-hatred, anger, shame. Douglas, with his plodding-yet-open manner, was like a breath of resuscitation.

Initially however, Mackenzie had kept him at a distance. "I don't understand why you're doing this," Douglas said, and Mackenzie didn't dare tell him. It would surely break the spell. The glint of admiration would disappear from Douglas's eyes, and he'd retreat to his apartment and double-lock the door.

"Do you trust him enough?" his therapist, Simon, asked during one of their sessions. He'd been directed to Simon by his godfather and family friend, Monty Benson. After his father passed, Monty became alarmed when Mackenzie tried to starve himself to death. He hadn't a clue as to why Mackenzie would choose to express his grief in this manner. How could he? No one suspected, not even Simon, until session after torturous session, he managed to pry it out of Mackenzie. The first break in the yearslong cycle of humiliation and self-abnegation. The initial ray of light in the dark prison cell to which the sordid relationship had consigned him.

The decision to tell Douglas wasn't Simon's idea, who likely would have advised against it, at least until Mackenzie was further along in his therapy or had established a stronger bond between himself and his would-be beau. The decision arose from a dormant instinct which, like his creative impulses, Mackenzie thought he'd extinguished. Or maybe he did it to test Douglas, to prove that even the most devoted companion would find his abhorrent secret untenable.

"I have something to tell you, and I need you to just sit and listen. Don't interrupt," he told Douglas. "And if it becomes too much, feel free to get up and leave." A deep breath and Mackenzie laid it out, dispassionately, methodically. How, from the start, he had assumed all the responsibility for what had transpired based on the fact that from an early age he'd been attracted to men. How then could he refuse the one man he admired most, on whom he was most dependent, in whom he had total faith? A man who was bright, successful, strong. Flattered by the attention, he'd allowed his father's endearments to bleed over into intimacy (or what, to his unformed mind, constituted intimacy). At the time, he was certain that he'd encouraged the advances, and still thought so until Simon disabused him of that notion. It was only when he reached his teens and came into contact with other adolescents, at school, through friendships, that he began to understand his aberrancy. But by then the bond between father and son had already tangled itself into a tortured knot.

His subsequent rebellion had manifested itself through a burst of creativity, which he'd used as a means of separation. A way to limit his home exposure. To stay out of harm's way. Part of his defiance included clandestine encounters, the more inappropriate the better. Less youthful experimentation than confirmation of his ingrained depravity.

It all ended after his father suffered the first stroke. Mackenzie turned away from his ambitions, his promise, from all the encouragement and approbation he'd received, which only had the unforeseen effect of reinforcing his self-contempt. He dropped out of Juilliard and cut off contact with friends to care for his father full-time. What appeared, outwardly at least, to be altruism was the exact opposite. The decision to become his father's caretaker, to feed him, bathe him, read to him, change his bedpan, was actually a means of asserting control. For the first time in his life.

Mackenzie's omnipresence served as a daily reminder to his father of the grievous injury he'd perpetrated. His son took exquisite care of him. Did all he could to prolong his father's life. Mainly as punishment.

"I never lashed out at him," he told Douglas. "Neither did I ever utter a word of kindness. My father was a bright man. He knew exactly what I was doing. I can't say I took pleasure in watching him squirm helplessly. But it gave me enormous satisfaction."

When, after the third stroke, his father succumbed, Mackenzie was lost. "You can't imagine the pain that comes from loving the person that destroyed you. I stopped eating, bathing, sleeping."

Douglas listened quietly. "I am so sorry," he said. "And I thank you for telling me. Before you ask though, it doesn't change how I feel about you."

"I wasn't testing you or trying to scare you away," Mackenzie said, though they both knew that was a lie. "I'm still devastated by how I was preyed upon and by how I chose to take my revenge. I can't say that those feelings will ever go away. It will always be a part of me."

"But not all of you."

"Perhaps. But that'll take time. And a lot more therapy. I can't very well ask you to wait until I'm better."

"That's not your decision. I care about you, and that's not going to change. And if in the end you still can't love me back, I won't blame you. I can't explain why exactly, except to say that feelings have their own logic."

"That much I know," Mackenzie replied.

Douglas's doggedness, his even temper, and his devotion slowly paid off. After their first time together, Mackenzie locked himself in the bathroom and laughed. And cried. He'd been surprised by Douglas's adeptness at commingling playful affection with passion. The pleasure Douglas had given him made him hungry to return the favor. An effortless flow between them. So different from how his victimizer had behaved or the saturnine individuals Mackenzie had sought out to validate his warped self-image.

The phone rang. Mackenzie fumbled it in his hand. "Hello?" he said, his voice wire-taut.

"It's me," said the husky voice on the other end. Callaway, his oldest friend. They'd known each other since preschool but only recently reconnected after Mackenzie returned to the land of the living.

When Mackenzie did not reply, Callaway said. "You alone?"

"Yeah," he said, his tone answering the question Callaway had been afraid to ask.

"Me too. Sammy's on a job uptown. Seems that plumbing doesn't care about terrorism. Can I come over?"

"Yes, please." Mackenzie said without hesitation.

Callaway arrived with sandwiches and chips and cookies. A big enough bag that they couldn't manage a hug, which was fortunate. They might crack if they did.

Neither ate a bite. Or spoke. They just sat in front of the TV and watched the horror in repeat. The collisions. The collapse of the first tower. The second tower. The crater in the Pentagon. And the as-yet-unexplained, plane crash in an open field in Pennsylvania.

"It feels like the end of the world. Again," said Callaway, who'd survived an earlier cataclysm thanks to the introduction of life-sustaining medications.

Douglas's name hung in the air unmentioned, as if to speak it would bring down a curse.

The phone rang again. Callaway leaned forward when Mackenzie answered.

But it was only Simon, his therapist.

"No word," Mackenzie said. "My friend Callaway's here. We're thinking of heading down there," he said, though he hadn't yet broached the subject with him.

"I wouldn't recommend that. It's all cordoned off and the air is toxic," said Simon. "I just heard from Titus. He ran out with his cameras the moment the first plane hit. Somehow managed to wrangle his way past the barriers. And to find a phone that worked. It's too awful. Like the Blitz."

Titus had located a phone? Why hadn't Douglas?

"You can't possibly remember the Blitz," Mackenzie said. He estimated that Simon was, by now, in his early to mid-fifties.

"Collective memories are passed down," Simon said, his voice choking. "This one will be too. In ways we can't even foresee." The only other time Mackenzie had heard Simon lose his composure was when Titus was battling pneumonia for the third time. "It's too much," he'd said, his reserved facade crumpling.

"Would it be unprofessional if I came by?" Simon asked. "I'm going a little crazy here."

"If you're going crazy, then this is hardly the time to quibble over protocol," he said. Simon might be his therapist but as someone who'd helped him save his own life, counted as a friend.

After he hung up with Simon, he phoned Monty, who picked up on the first ring. "Today's my eightieth birthday," he said. "I'm so glad Terry didn't live to see this."

"Oh, my God, your birthday," Mackenzie said. He had written it down in his Filofax. He and Douglas had discussed taking Monty to dinner the following weekend to celebrate. Douglas adored Monty and when Mackenzie said he wished Monty had been his father, didn't disagree.

"Douglas went to work this morning?" Monty asked.

"Yes."

He could hear Monty inhale on the other end.

"Listen, Simon is on his way over. I'll ask him to pick you up. You shouldn't be alone on your birthday. Certainly not this one."

"I won't be alone. Barbara and Carmen came in from the Berkshires last night. We were supposed to go to Lutèce for lunch today but the universe had other plans. Ooh. There's my call waiting. Be right back."

"More birthday greetings?" Mackenzie said, when he returned.

"From Miami. Another friend from the war, Dee Andrea. Not WWII. The more recent one."

"Come by later, if you want," Mackenzie said.

"We'll see. Say hello to Simon. Please call me if you hear anything," he said before clicking off.

"Monty, my godfather. Today's his eightieth birthday," he explained to Callaway.

"Today? Shit," Callaway said.

Simon brought a bottle of Scotch, though neither Mackenzie nor Callaway had touched alcohol in years and had no intention of falling off the wagon today.

"Would it be rude if I indulged?" Simon asked. Always so British. So proper.

"Rude, how? If I could, I would bathe in it," Mackenzie said, looking up from the bedroom TV around which they were all gathered. "Though it isn't even noon."

Call, Douglas. Call now.

Without taking his eyes off the continuous replays of the plane crashes and falling towers, Simon disagreed. "You're wrong. It's the middle of the night. The part when, try as you might, you can't shake yourself awake. I wonder if this is the end of it, or just the beginning."

Mackenzie was amazed. Simon was usually so level-headed, the one person who could be counted on to refrain from uttering the awful thoughts everyone else was thinking.

"Sorry. The scotch talking."

"Your glass is still full," said Mackenzie.

Simon examined his glass. "Right you are."

"Fuck me," Callaway said as photos and footage of bodies plunging from the towers flashed across the TV screen. Mackenzie covered his eyes. The last thing he wanted to see.

Simon drained the glass in one gulp. "Oh God. Come home, Titus." As soon as he said it, he realized his faux pas. "I don't know what's wrong with me today."

"Don't worry. Titus hast nine lives," Mackenzie said, which underlined the fact that Douglas had only one.

"Titus? You're that Simon?" Callaway said, and Simon looked at him quizzically.

"Titus and I were in a long-term survivor group together. He's the one who introduced me to Samuel. They'd met through some guy named George."

"But of course. Goodness me. How is Samuel?" Simon asked, pouring himself another scotch.

"Spunky as ever," Callaway said. "Wouldn't want him any other way."

"Here's to six degrees," Simon said, hoisting his glass.

Mackenzie lifted his eyebrows. "More like two degrees. We're all gay. We all live within twenty blocks of each other."

"Yeah, the Village idiots," Callaway said as he began sniffing the air. "What's that stench?"

"From outside," Mackenzie said. "It's the smell of . . ." He stopped short of saying the word "death."

"No," Callaway said, leaning into Mackenzie. "It's you."

Mackenzie realized he hadn't brushed his teeth or showered, and his already bracing natural body odor worsened when he was anxious.

"Skunk," is how Douglas endearingly referred to it. "Fuck you," Mackenzie would say, feigning umbrage. "Not until you wash off that stank," Douglas would reply.

Call, Douglas. Call.

At around two, they shut off the television and ambled out onto the terrace. The clashing sound of car horns and sirens had intensified. A crowd had gathered in Abingdon Square and they would have joined them, if Mackenzie hadn't wanted to be near the phone and since both Callaway and Simon had left messages telling Samuel and Titus how to reach them.

Simon was worried that Titus, in his photo-taking frenzy, might have been hit by a falling body or debris. Callaway fretted that anarchy had broken out in other parts of the city and Samuel would get caught in the crossfire. He was relieved when the buzzer rang and he heard Samuel's voice on the intercom. Simon, by now well lubricated, embraced Samuel. "Look at you," he said, pointing to his monogrammed plumber's outfit. "I don't believe I've seen you since George's funeral."

"I don't remember that. I was on smack," Samuel said. "But you're wrong. We ran into each other at Sora's memorial."

"Ah yes," Simon said with a sigh. "God bless them all."

"What's it like out there?" Callaway asked.

"No subways. The streets are a parking lot. Cops everywhere. People walking around in a daze," Samuel said. "Crying. Talking to themselves. Cursing. Like the whole city's gone crazy."

"I have to do something," said Mackenzie. "If you guys would stay by the phone, I could check the hospitals."

Simon offered to accompany him. As they were making plans, the buzzer rang again. Titus walked in, covered in soot, eyes unblinking and wide as saucers. He made a beeline for Simon. "Jesus-fucking-Christ," he said and collapsed in Simon's arms.

"Let's get you cleaned up," Simon said. "Let me take the cameras."

"No. I'll keep them."

Mackenzie directed them to the bathroom and handed Simon fresh towels. They were all shaken by Titus's unfettered display of emotion.

"He's taking a bath. I hope you don't mind," Simon said. "I won't even repeat what he told me. And the photos." Simon shook his head, vacantly.

Mackenzie's legs gave out from under him. Callaway lifted him into his bulky arms and carried him to the bedroom. "I have some Xanax in my pocket. But you need them more than I do." Mackenzie had an aversion to sedatives but dutifully swallowed two tablets.

"Rest. We're here," Callaway said, patting his arm, and Mackenzie heard Douglas's voice. "I'm here," he was saying.

Only he wasn't.

Mackenzie eased into a thankfully dream-free sleep, awakening at dusk. He found Samuel and Titus nestled together on the sofa. Callaway and Simon were in the kitchen, cobbling together ingredients from the fridge and cupboards for a makeshift meal.

"We took the liberty," Simon said.

"Knock yourselves out," he said.

"Oh, while you were asleep, two lovely young ladies, Bee and Jasmine dropped by," Simon added. "To check up on you."

"That was nice of them. Bee redid my apartment," he explained, though he didn't add, "to obliterate every trace of my father."

"I said you'd phone with any news. They brought some homemade soda bread. Not much left, I'm afraid."

"That's okay. I have no appetite," Mackenzie said.

"You'll eat nonetheless," Callaway said, making it sound like an order.

"I should get dressed now and check out the hospitals."

"I don't know that you'll get any satisfaction. Titus said it's probably chaos. I doubt they're even asking names."

"I don't care. I have to do something."

"Right. I'll go with you," Simon said. "I'm fluent in hospital-ese."

"Go ahead, guys," Callaway said. "I'll hold down the fort. Call me when you get the chance. To see if I've heard anything."

"I love you," Mackenzie said, planting a kiss on Callaway's cheek.

"Back at ya," Callaway said.

Mackenzie wandered through the living room and into the bedroom where he dressed, gargled mouthwash, de-skunked himself with a few spritzes of cologne and tucked his mop into a baseball cap. Simon was chatting with Titus and Samuel when he returned, and they were almost out the door when the buzzer rang.

"Hello?" Mackenzie spoke into the intercom. But there was no reply. "Hello?" he said again.

"We're headed downstairs anyway," said Simon. He pressed the elevator button. "With what's going on outside, we shouldn't be letting anyone in unannounced."

The buzzer rang again, and Mackenzie was unnerved.

"Where you going?" Simon asked, as Mackenzie threw open the fire door and raced down the steps.

Through the double-glass entry doors, from across the way, Mackenzie saw a stooped figure covered in a thick white powder. From head to toe, obliterating his features, his shape, his garb. Granules flaked off him like expired skin cells, though the man barely moved. Slowly, with great effort, he lifted his head and gazed at Mackenzie, who froze as if caught in a trance. "He's here," he thought, praying he wasn't mistaken, hoping he wasn't still asleep upstairs in bed.

Hoping.

About the Author

Richard Natale is a Los Angeles-based journalist and writer whose stories have appeared in such publications as *Mollyhouse*, *Otherwise Engaged*, *Confetti*, *Chelsea Station*, the *MCB Quarterly*, and the anthologies *Image/Out*, *Love is Love*, and *Off the Rocks*. His novels include *Mystery Dance*, *Pigeon*, *The Rushes*, *Love on the Jersey Shore*, *Cafe Eisenhower*, the novella *Junior Willis*, and the YA fantasy novel *The Golden City of Dubloon*.

Natale won the National Playwright's Competition for his two-act comedy-drama *Shuffle Off This Mortal Buffalo*, which was subsequently staged in Kansas City and Los Angeles. He also wrote and directed the feature film *Green Plaid Shirt*, which was the closing night selection at the Palm Springs Film Festival and was screened at more than a dozen film festivals worldwide.